"It would be a serious mistake to dismiss *Hide Me Among the Graves* as something less than art. It's literary fiction in two senses of the word. First, it's a fascinating fictionalized look at some of England's most interesting authors—not just Polidori and the Rossettis, but also the long-underappreciated Trelawny. Second, it's written impeccably. Powers is a master of suspenseful plotting, and his descriptions of the gaslighted streets and underground tunnels of 19th-century London are awesomely creepy. . . . Above all, though, *Hide Me Among the Graves* is just pure fun. Powers knows how to temper terror with humor, and he knows something that a lot of adventure writers never learn: Without well-rounded, fully realized characters, it doesn't matter how good your concept is. It's a smart, exciting and perfectly constructed novel, and it's hard as hell to put down. Let the kids have their overwrought, sullen romances—*Hide Me Among the Graves* is a vampire novel for readers who still believe in the power, and the joy, of great literature."

—NPR.org

"[A] fine example of the work of a much-beloved author, and a spooky ride through Victorian London to boot. . . . Powers's work engages with something prerational that is buried deep, deep in our brains, and that won't be bullied into submission by mere reason."

—Cory Doctorow, boingboing.com, on *Hide Me Among the Graves*

"[*Three Days to Never*] contains so many genuine pleasures . . . plenty of action, humor and unexpectedly touching human drama. . . . [A] welcoming entry point to [Powers's] singular fictional universe."

—*San Francisco Chronicle*

"Endlessly inventive. . . . You might finish this overstuffed novel still unsure about the connection between Einstein and astral projection, but if you give in to Powers's imaginative leaps and relentless pacing you may find that a mere quibble."

—*New York Times Book Review,* on *Three Days to Never*

"Tim Powers has long been one of my absolutely favorite writers, those whose new books I snatch up as soon as they appear, and *Three Days to Never* puts on display all the qualities I most admire in him: intelligence, narrative sparkle, great dialogue, speculative imagination, and emotional power. This is a wonderful novel."

—Peter Straub

"Powers has forged a style of narrative uniquely his own, one filled with sharply drawn characters, fully imagined settings, elaborate underpinnings that pull all rugs out from under us and let us glimpse terrible, ragged floors beneath."

—*Los Angeles Times Book Review,* on *Last Call*

"[Powers] orchestrates reality and fantasy so artfully that the reader is not allowed a moment's doubt throughout this tall tale."

—*The New Yorker,* on *Declare*

"Dazzling . . . a tour de force, a brilliant blend of John le Carré spy fiction with the otherworldly." —Dean Koontz, on *Declare*

THREE
DAYS
TO
NEVER

THREE
DAYS
TO
NEVER

TIM POWERS

𝓌𝓂
WILLIAM MORROW
An Imprint of HarperCollinsPublishers

P.S.™ is a trademark of HarperCollins Publishers.

A hardcover edition of this book was published in 2006 by William Morrow, an imprint of HarperCollins Publishers.

FIRST HARPER PAPERBACK EDITION PUBLISHED DECEMBER 2007.
FIRST WILLIAM MORROW PAPERBACK EDITION PUBLISHED 2013.

Library of Congress Cataloging-in-Publication Data has been applied for.

ISBN 978-0-06-222139-1

13 14 15 16 17   OV/RRD   10 9 8 7 6 5 4 3 2 1

For Chris and Teresa Arena

*And with thanks to Assaf Asheri,
Mike Backes, John Bierer, Jim Blaylock,
Chris Branch, Didi Chanoch, Russell Galen,
Patricia Geary, Tom Gilchrist, Rani Graff,
Julia Halperin, John Hertz, Jon Hodge,
Varnum Honey, Pat Hough, Barry Levin,
Brian and Cathy McCaleb, Karen Meisner,
Denny Meyer, Eric Nylund, Serena Powers,
Aya Shacham, Dave Sandoval, Bill Schafer,
Sunila Sen Gupta, David Silberstein,
Kristine Sobrero, Ed Thomas,
Vered Tochterman, Guy Wiener,
Hagit Wiener, Naomi Wiener,
Par Winzell, and Mike Yanovich.*

THREE
DAYS
TO
NEVER

Prologue

Sitting on a bank,
Weeping again the King my father's wrack,
This music crept by me upon the waters.

—WILLIAM SHAKESPEARE, *THE TEMPEST*

The ambulance came bobbing out of the Mercy Medical Center parking lot and swung south on Pine Street, its blue and red lights just winking dots in the bright noon sunshine and the siren echoing away into the cloudless blue vault of the sky. At East Lake Street the ambulance turned left, avoiding most of the traffic farther south, where reports of a miraculous angel appearing on somebody's TV set had attracted hundreds of the spiritual pilgrims who had come to town for this weekend.

At the Everett Memorial Highway the ambulance turned north, and accelerated; in five minutes it had left the city behind and was ascending the narrow blacktop strip through cool pine forests, and when the highway curved east the white peaks of Shasta and Shastina stood up high above the timberline.

Traffic was heavier as the highway switchbacked up the mountain slope—Volkswagen vans, campers, buses—and the shoulder was dotted with hitchhikers in jeans and robes and knapsacks.

The red-and-white ambulance weaved between the vehicles on the highway, and it was able to speed up again when the highway straightened out past the Bunny Flats campgrounds. Three miles farther on, the parking lot at Panther Meadows was clogged with cars and vans, but the hospital had radioed ahead and Forest Service officers had cleared a path to the north end of the lot, where trails led away among the trees.

In the clearings around the trailhead, people were strolling aimlessly or staring up into the sky or sitting in meditation circles, and the woods were noisy with ringing bells and the yells of children; two white-clad paramedics got out of the ambulance and carried a stretcher through a sea of beards and gray ponytails and pastel robes, with the tang of patchouli oil spicing the scent of Douglas fir on the chilly breeze—but they didn't have to hike far, because six people had already made a stretcher of flannel shirts and cherry branches and had carried the limp body most of the way back from the high glades of Squaw Meadow; the body was wrapped in an old brown army blanket and wreathed with Shasta daisies and the white flowers of wild strawberry.

The paramedics lifted the old woman's body onto their aluminum-and-nylon stretcher, and within minutes the ambulance was accelerating back down the mountain, but with no siren now.

Back in the clearing up on Squaw Meadow, the people who had not carried the stretcher were dismembering a swastika-shaped framework of gold wire, having to bend it repeatedly to break it, since none of them was carrying a pocketknife.

ACT ONE

I'll Drown My Book

I have done nothing but in care of thee,
Of thee my dear one, thee my daughter,
   who
Art ignorant of what thou art, not knowing
Of whence I am . . .

—WILLIAM SHAKESPEARE, *THE TEMPEST*

One

I t doesn't look burned."

"No," said her father, squinting and shading his eyes with his hand. They had paused halfway across the weedy backyard.

"Are you sure she said 'shed'?"

"Yes—'I've burned down the Kaleidoscope Shed,' she told me."

Daphne Marrity sat down on a patch of grass and straightened her skirt, peering at the crooked old gray structure that was visible now under the shadow of the shaggy avocado tree. It would probably burn up pretty fast, if anybody was to try to burn it.

The shingled roof was patchy, sagging in the middle, and the two dusty wood-framed windows on either side of the closed door seemed to be falling out of the clapboard wall; it probably leaked badly in the rain.

Daphne had heard that her father and aunt had some-times sneaked out here to play in the shed when they were children, though they weren't allowed to. The door was so low that Daphne herself might have to stoop to get through, and she was not a particularly tall twelve-year-old.

It was probably when they were too young to go to school, she thought. Or else it's because I was born in 1975, and kids are taller now than they were back then.

"The tree would have burned up too," she noted.

"You're going to get red ants all over you. She might have dreamed it. I don't think it was a, a joke." Her father glanced around, frowning, clearly irritated. He was sweating, even with his jacket folded over his arm.

"Gold under the bricks," Daphne reminded him.

"And she dreamed that too. I wonder where she is." There had been no answer to his knock on the front door of the house, but when they had walked around the corner and pushed open the backyard gate they had seen that the old green Rambler station wagon was in the carport, in the yellow shade of the corrugated fiberglass roof.

Daphne crossed her legs on the grass and squinted up at him against the sun's glare. "Why did she call it the Kaleidoscope Shed?"

"It—" He laughed. "We all called it that. I don't know."

He had stepped on what he'd been about to say. She sighed and looked toward the shed again. "Let's go in it and pull up some bricks. I can watch out for spiders," she added.

Her father shook his head. "I can see from here that it's padlocked. We shouldn't even be hanging around back here when Grammar's not home." Grammar was the family name for the old lady, and it had not made Daphne like her any better.

"We had to, to see if she really did burn it down like she said. Now we should see if"—she thought quickly—"if she passed out in there from gasoline fumes. Maybe she meant, 'I'm *about* to burn it down.' "

"How could she have padlocked it from the outside?"

"Maybe she's passed out behind the shed. She *did* call you about the shed, and she doesn't answer the door, and her car *is* here."

"Oh . . ." He squinted and began to shake his head, so she went on quickly.

" 'Screw your courage to the sticking place,' " she said. "Maybe there really is gold under the bricks. Didn't she have a lot of money?"

He smiled distractedly. " 'And we'll not fail.' She did get some money in '55, I've heard."

"How old was she then?" Daphne got to her feet, brushing down the back of her skirt.

"About fifty-five, I guess. She's probably about eighty-seven now. Any money she's got is in the bank."

"Not in the bank—she's a hippie, isn't she?" Even now, at twelve, Daphne was still somewhat afraid of her chain-smoking great-grandmother, with her white hair, her grinding German accent, and her wrinkly old cheeks always wet with the artificial tears she bought in little bottles at Thrifty. Daphne had never been allowed in the old woman's backyard, and this was the first time she'd ever been farther out than the back porch. "Or a witch," she added.

Daphne took her father's hand as a tentative prelude to starting toward the shed.

"She isn't a witch," he said, laughing. "And she isn't a hippie either. She's too old to have been a hippie."

"She went to Woodstock. You never went to Woodstock."

"She probably just went to sell her necklaces."

"As weapons, I bet," Daphne said, recalling the clunky talismans. The old woman had given Daphne one on her seventh birthday, a stone thing on a necklace chain, and before the day was out, Daphne had nearly given herself a concussion with it, swinging it around; when her favorite cat had died six months later, she had buried the object with the cat.

She tried to project the thought to him: *Let's check out the shed.*

"Hippies didn't have weapons. Okay, I'll look around in back of the shed."

He began walking forward, leading the way and holding her hand, stepping carefully through the dry grass and high green weeds. His brown leather Top-Siders ground creosote smells out of the bristly green stalks.

"Watch where you put your feet," he said over his shoulder, "she's got all kinds of old crap out here."

"Old crap," Daphne echoed.

"Car-engine parts, broken air conditioners, suits of medieval armor I wouldn't be surprised. I should carry you, your legs are going to get all scratched."

"Even skinny I'm too heavy now. You'd get apoplexy."

"I could carry two girls your size, one under each arm."

They had stepped in under the shade of the tree limbs, and her father handed her his brown corduroy jacket.

He shook his head as if at the silliness of all this, then waded through the rank greenery to the corner of the shed and disappeared around it. She could hear him brushing against the shed's far wall, and cussing, and knocking boards over.

Daphne had folded his jacket and tucked it under her left arm, and now she walked up to the shed door and reached out with her right hand, took hold of the brown padlock, and pulled. The whole rusted hasp and lock came away from the wood in one stiff piece.

A few moments later her father appeared from around the far corner, red faced and sweating. His white shirt was streaked with dust and cobwebs.

"Well, she's not back there," he said, brushing dead leaves out of his hair. "I don't think she's been out here in months. Years. Let's get out of here."

Daphne held out the rusted hasp and padlock for him to see, then dropped it and brushed her fingers on her pink blouse.

"I didn't tear the wood," she said. "The screws were just sitting in the holes."

"Good lord, Daph," said her father, "nobody's going to mind."

"I know, but I mean the thing was just hung there, in the holes—somebody else pulled it out, and then hung it back up." She wrinkled her nose. "And I smell gasoline."

"You do not."

"Honest, I do." They both knew her sense of smell was better than his.

"You just want to look in there for gold."

But he sighed and tugged on the purple glass doorknob, and the door creaked open, sliding easily over the dead grass.

"Probably she keeps whisky out here," Daphne said, a little nervously. "Sneaks out at night to drink it." Her father said her uncle Bennett kept a bottle of whisky in his garage, and that's why he kept all his business files out there.

"She doesn't drink whisky," her father said absently, crouching to peer inside. "I wish we had a flashlight— somebody's pulled up half the floor." He leaned back and exhaled. "And I smell gasoline too."

Daphne bent down and looked past her father's elbow into the dimness. A roughly four-foot-square cement slab was leaned up against the shelves on the left-side wall, and seemed to be responsible for that wall's outward tilt; and a square patch of bare black dirt at the foot of the slab seemed to indicate where it had been pried up. The rest of the floor was pale bricks.

The floor was clear except for a scattering of cigarette butts and a pair of tire-soled sandals lying on the bricks.

The gasoline reek was strong enough to mask whatever moldy smells the place might ordinarily have; and Daphne could see a red-and-yellow metal gasoline can on a wooden shelf against the back wall.

Her father ducked inside and took hold of the handle on top of the can and lifted it. She could hear swishing inside the can as he stepped past her, and it seemed to be heavy as he carried it outside. She noticed that there was no cap on it. No wonder the place reeks, she thought.

There was a nearly opaque window in the back wall, and Daphne stepped in across the bricks and stood on tiptoe to twist the latch on its frame; the latch snapped off, but when she pushed on the window the entire thing fell outside, frame and all, thumping in the thick weeds. Dry summer air puffed in through the ragged square hole, fluttering her brown bangs. She inhaled it gratefully.

"I've got ventilation," she called over her shoulder. "And some light too."

A television sat on a metal cart to the left of the door, with a VCR on top of it. The VCR was flashing 12:00, though it must be past one by now.

"The time's wrong," she said to her father, pointing at the VCR as he ducked his head to step inside again.

"What?"

"On her VCR. Weird to have electricity out here."

"Oh! It's always had electrical outlets. God knows why. This is the first time I've seen anything plugged in, out here. Lucky there was no spark." He glanced past her and smiled. "I'm glad you got that window open."

Daphne thought he was relieved to learn that her "time's wrong" remark had been about the VCR. But before she could think of a way to ask him about it, he had stepped to the shelf and picked up a green metal box that had been hidden behind the gasoline can.

"What's that?" she asked.

"An ammunition box. I don't think she's ever had a gun, though." He swung the lid up, then tipped it sideways so Daphne could see that it was full of old yellowed papers. He righted it and began flipping through them.

Daphne glanced at the nearly upright cement slab—and then looked at it more closely. It was lumpy with damp mud, but somebody had cleaned four patches of it—two hand-prints and two shoe prints, clearly pressed into the cement when it had still been wet. And behind the undisturbed clumps of mud she could see looping grooves in the face of the block; somebody had scrawled something in it too.

She put her father's jacket on the shelf beside the ammu-nition box and then stepped down onto the patch of sunken dirt next to the block. She pressed her open right hand into the right-hand print in the block—and then quickly pulled her hand away. The cement there was as smooth and warm as flesh, and damp.

With the side of her shoe, she scuffed mud off the bottom

of the slab, and then stepped back. *Jan 12—1928,* she read. The writing seemed to have been done with a stick.

"Bunch of old letters," her father said behind her. "New Jersey postmarks, 1933, '39, '55 . . ."

"To her?"

Daphne pried off some more mud with her fingers. There was a long, smooth groove next to the shoe prints, as if a rod too had been pressed into the wet cement. She noticed that the shoe prints were awfully long and narrow, and set at a duck-foot angle.

"Lisa Marrity, yup," said her father.

Above the rod indentation was a crude caricature of a man with a bowler hat and a Hitler mustache.

"The letters are all in German," her father said. She could hear him rifling through the stack. "Well, no, some in English. Ugh, they're sticky, the envelopes! Was she *licking* them?"

Daphne could puzzle out the words at the top of the block, since the grooves of the writing were neatly filled in with black mud. *To Sid—Best of Luck.* And the last clump of dirt fell off all at once when she tugged at it. Exposed now was the carefully incised name, *Charlie Chaplin.*

Daphne looked over her shoulder at her father, who was holding the metal box and peering into it. "Hey," she said.

"Hmm?"

"Check this out."

Marrity looked at her, then past her at the cement slab; his face went blank. He put the box down on the shelf. "Is that *real*?" he said softly.

She tried to think of a funny answer, then just shrugged. "I don't know."

He was staring at the slab. "I mean, isn't the real one at the Chinese Theater?"

"I don't know."

He glanced at her and smiled. "Sorry. But this *might* be real. Maybe they made two. She says she knew Chaplin. She flew to Switzerland after he died."

"Where did he die?"

"In Switzerland, goof. I wonder if these letters—" He paused, for Daphne had got down on her hands and knees and begun prying up the bricks along the edge of the exposed patch of wet dirt. "What?" he said. "Gold?"

"She *almost* burned up the shed," Daphne said without looking up. "Got the cap off the gas can, at least."

"Well—true." Her father knelt beside her, on the bricks instead of the mud—which Daphne was pleased to see, as she didn't want to wash a fresh pair of pants for him to wear to work tomorrow—and pulled up a couple of bricks himself. His dark hair was falling into his eyes, and he streaked a big smudge of grime onto his forehead when he pushed it back. Great, Daphne thought; he looks—probably we both look—as if we just tunneled out of a jail.

Daphne saw a glint of brightness in the flat mud where one brick had been, and she rubbed at it; it was a piece of wire about as thick as a pencil. It was looped, and she hooked a finger through it to pull it up, but the rest of the loop was stuck fast under the other bricks.

"Is this gold?" she asked her father.

He grunted and rubbed more dirt off the wire. "I can't say it's not," he said. "Right color, at least, and it's pliable."

"She said you should get the gold up from under the bricks, right? So let's—"

From outside, on the street, a car horn honked three times, and then a man's voice called, "Frank?"

"It's your uncle Bennett," said her father, quickly slamming back into place the bricks he had moved. Daphne fit hers back in too, suppressing a giggle at the idea of hiding the treasure from her dumb uncle.

The bricks replaced, her father leaped up and grabbed all the papers in the ammunition box into one fist and shoved them deep into an inside pocket of his jacket on the shelf. He wiped his hand on his shirt, and Daphne remembered that he had said the envelopes were sticky.

"Stand back," he said, and Daphne stepped back beside the television set.

Then he cautiously put one foot on the square of black dirt and gripped the cement slab by the top edges and pulled it toward himself. It swayed forward, and then he hopped backward out of the way as it overbalanced and thudded heavily to the floor, breaking one row of bricks. The whole shed shook, and black dust sifted down onto the two of them from the rotted ceiling.

The block's near edge was visibly canted up, resting on the row of broken bricks.

"Both of us," said Daphne, sitting down on the bricks to set her heels against the raised edge. Her father knelt on the bricks and braced his hands on the slab.

"On three," he said. "One, two, *three.*"

Daphne and her father both pushed, and then pushed harder, and at last the slab shifted, slid to its original position and thumped down flush with the bricks. Its top face was dry and blank.

Daphne heard the click of the backyard gate, and she scrambled up and ran two steps to the VCR and hit the eject button. The machine whirred as her uncle's footsteps thrashed through the weeds, and then the tape had popped out and Daphne snatched it and dropped it into her purse as her father hastily grabbed his jacket from the shelf, slid his arms into the sleeves and shrugged it onto his shoulders.

"Frank!" came Bennett's shout again, this time from just outside the open door. "I saw your car! Where are you?"

"In here, Bennett!" Daphne's father called.

Her uncle's red face peered in under the sagging door lintel, and for once his expression was simply wide-eyed dismay. His mustache was already spiky with sweat, though he would have had the air conditioner on in his car.

"What the fuck's going on?" he yelled shrilly. "Why the— bloody hell does it smell like gasoline in here?" Daphne guessed that he was embarrassed at having said *fuck,* and so hurried to cover it with his habitual *bloody*—though he wasn't British. "You've got Daphne with you!"

"Grammar left the top off a gas can," her father said. "We were trying to get some ventilation in here."

"What was that almighty crash?"

Her father jerked his thumb over his shoulder. "The window fell out when I tried to open it."

"Sash weights," put in Daphne.

"Why are you even here?" Bennett demanded. He ducked in under the lintel and stood up inside; the shed was very crowded with three people in it.

"My grandmother called me this morning," said Marrity evenly, "and asked me to come over and look at the shed. She said she was afraid it was going to burn down, and with that uncapped gasoline can in here, it might have."

Daphne noted the details of her father's half lie; and she noted his emphasis on *my grandmother*—Bennett had only married into the family.

"It's a little academic at this point," snapped Bennett, "and there's nothing valuable out here." He looked more closely at Daphne and her father, presumably only now noticing the dust in their hair and the mud on their hands, and suddenly his eyes widened. "Or *is* there?"

His hand darted out and pulled the videocassette from Daphne's purse. "What's this?"

Daphne could read the label on it: *Pee-wee's Big Adventure*. It was a movie she'd seen in a theater two years ago. "That's mine," she said. "It's about bad people stealing Pee-wee's bicycle."

"My daughter's not a thief, Bennett," her father said mildly. Daphne reflected that right now she *was* a thief, actually.

"I know, sorry." Bennett tossed the cassette, and Daphne caught it. "But you shouldn't be here," he said to her father as he bent down to step out of the shed, "now that she's dead." From outside he called, "Not unless Moira and I are here too."

Marrity followed him outside, and Daphne was right behind him.

"Who's dead?" asked her father.

Bennett frowned. "Your grandmother. You don't know this? She died an hour and a half ago, at Mount Shasta. The hospital just called me—Moira and I are to fly up this afternoon and take care of the funeral arrangements." He peered at his brother-in-law. "You really didn't know?"

"Mount Shasta, at like"—Marrity glanced at his watch—"noon? That's not possible. Why would she be at Mount Shasta?"

"She was communing with angels or something—well, that turned out to be right. She was there for the Harmonic Convergence."

Behind the grime and the tangles of dark hair, Frank Marrity's face was pale. "Where's Moira?"

"She's at home, packing. Now if we want to avoid things like restraining orders, I think we should all agree—"

"I'm going to call her." He started toward the house, and Daphne trotted along behind him, clutching her Pee-wee videocassette.

"It'll be locked," Bennett called after him.

Daphne's father didn't answer, but pulled his key ring out of his pants pocket.

"You've got a key? You shouldn't have a key!"

Grammar's house was a white Spanish adobe with a red-tile roof, and the back patio had a trellis shading it, tangled with roses and grapevines. Over the back door was a wooden sign, with hand-carved letters: *Everyone Who Dwells Here Is Safe.* Daphne had wondered about it ever since she had been able to read, and only last summer she had found the sentence in a Grimm Brothers fairy tale, "The Maiden Without Hands." The sentence had been on a sign in front of the house of a good fairy who had taken in a fugitive queen and her baby son.

The air was cooler under the trellis, and Daphne could smell roses on the breeze. She wondered how her father was taking the news of his grandmother's death. He and his sister had been toddlers when they lost their parents—their father ran away and their mother died in a car crash soon after—and they had been raised here, by Grammar.

Her father stopped on the step up to the back door, and Daphne saw that one of the vertical windows beside the door was broken; and when her father walked to the door and twisted the knob, the door swung inward. None of the locks here are any good, she thought.

"You've erased fingerprints!" panted Bennett, who was right behind Daphne now. "It was probably a burglar that broke the window."

"A burglar would have reached through and turned the knob inside," Daphne told him. "My dad isn't going to touch that one."

"Daph," said her father. "Wait out here with Bennett."

Her father stepped into the kitchen, and her uncle at least waited with her.

"Probably broke it herself," muttered Bennett. *"Marritys."*

"'Divil a man can say a word agin them,'" said Daphne. She and her father had recently watched *Yankee Doodle Dandy,* and her head was full of George M. Cohan lyrics.

Bennett glanced away from the door to give her an irritable look. "All that Shakespeare won't help you get a job. Except—" He shook his head and resumed staring at the kitchen door.

"It'll help me get a job as a literature professor," she said blandly, knowing that that was what his *except* had referred to. Her father was a literature professor at the University of Redlands. "Best job there is." Her uncle Bennett was a location manager for TV commercials, and apparently made way more money than her father did.

Her uncle opened his mouth and then after a second snapped it shut again, clearly not wanting to get into an argument with a girl. "You absolutely *reek* of gasoline," he said instead.

She heard footsteps on linoleum in the house, and then her father pulled the kitchen door wide open. "If there was a thief, he's gone," he said. "Let's see if she has any beers in her 'frigerator."

"We shouldn't touch anything," said Bennett, but he stepped in ahead of Daphne. The house was cool, and the kitchen smelled faintly of bacon and onions and cigarettes, as usual.

Daphne couldn't see that anything in the room was different from the way it had looked at Easter—the spotless sink and counter, the garlic-and-dried-rosemary centerpiece on the kitchen table; the broom was upside down in the corner, but the old lady always kept it that way—to scare off nightmares, according to her father.

Bennett picked up a business card from the kitchen counter. "See?" he said. "Bell Cabs. She must have taken a taxi to the airport." He set it back down again.

Her father had lifted the receiver from the yellow telephone on the wall and was using the forefinger of the same hand to spin the dial. With his other hand he pointed at the refrigerator. "Daph, could you see if there's a beer in there?"

Daphne pulled open the door of the big green refrigerator—it was older than her father, who had once said that it looked like a 1950 Buick stood on its nose—and found two cans of Budweiser among the jars of nasty black concoctions.

She put one into her father's hand and waved the other at her uncle.

"Not *Budweiser,* thank you," he said stiffly.

Daphne put the other can on the counter by her father, and looked at the cork bulletin board on the wall. "Her keys are gone," she noted.

"Probably in her purse," her father said. "Moira?" he said into the telephone. "Did Grammar die? What? This is a lousy connection. Bennett told me—we're at her house. What? *At her house,* I said." He popped open the beer one-handed. "I don't know. Listen, are you sure?" He took a long sip of the beer. "I mean, could it have been a prank call?" For several seconds he just listened, and he put the beer can down on the tile counter to touch Grammar's electric coffee grinder; he flipped the switch on it, and the little upright cylinder chattered as it ground up some beans that must still have been in it. He switched it off again. "When did the hospital call you? Talk slower. Uh-huh. And when you called them back, what was the number?"

He lifted a pencil from a vase full of pens and pencils and wrote the number on the back of the Bell Cabs card.

"What were the last two numbers? Okay, got it." He put the card in his shirt pocket. "Yeah, me too kid. Okay, thanks." He held the receiver out to Bennett. "She wants to talk to you. Bad connection—it keeps getting screechy or silent."

Bennett nodded impatiently and took the phone, and he was saying, "I just wanted to see if—are you there?—if there was anything here we'd need to bring along, birth certificate . . ." as Frank Marrity led Daphne into the dark living room.

Grammar's violin and bow were hanging in their usual place between two framed parchments with Jewish writing on them, and in spite of having been scared of the old woman, Daphne suddenly felt like crying at the thought that Grammar would never play it anymore. Daphne remembered her bow skating over the strings in the first four notes of one of her favorite Mozart violin concertos.

A moment later her father softly whistled the next six notes.

Daphne blinked. "And!" she whispered, "you're sad about Grammar, and mad at her too—and you're very freaked about her coffee grinder! I . . . can't see why."

After a pause, he nodded. "That's right." He looked at her with one eyebrow raised. "This is the first time you and I have both had it at the same time."

"Like turn blinkers on a couple of cars," she said quietly. "It was bound to match up eventually." She looked up at him. "What's so weird about her coffee grinder?"

"I'll tell you later." In a normal tone he said, over her shoulder, "I don't think my grandmother ever had a birth certificate."

Daphne turned and saw that Bennett had entered the living room and was frowning at the drawn curtains.

"I suppose they don't give birth certificates in Oz," he said. "We should fix that window."

"I can use her Makita to screw a piece of plywood over it from the inside. You think we should call the police?" Her father waved at the violin on the wall. "If there was a thief, he didn't take her Stradivarius."

Bennett blinked and started forward. "Is that a Stradivarius?"

"I was kidding. No. I don't think anything's been taken."

"Very funny. I don't think we need to call the police. But fix the window now—we should all leave together, and only come here all together." He rubbed his mustache. "I wonder if she left a will."

"Moira and I are on the deed already. I can't imagine there's much besides the house."

"Her car, her books. Some of this . . . artwork might be valuable to some people."

To some weirdos, you mean, thought Daphne. She was suddenly defensive about the old woman's crystals and copper bells and paintings of unicorns and eyes in pyramids and sleepy-looking bearded guys wearing robes.

"We'll want to inventory it all, get an appraiser," Bennett went on. "She was a collector, and she might have happened to pick up some valuable items, amid all the crap. Even a broken clock is right twice a day."

Daphne could feel that the mention of broken clocks, in this house, jarred her father. There were a lot of things she wanted to remember to ask him about, once they were in their truck again.

Two

Outside the vibrating windowpane, the narrow trunks of palm trees swayed in the hard sun glare over the glittering traffic on La Brea Avenue. This was south of Olympic, south of the dressy stores around Melrose with black or green awnings out front, and way south of Charlie Chaplin's old studio up at Sunset where you could see the individual houses on the green Hollywood hills; down here it was car washes and Chinese fast food and one-hour photo booths and old apartment buildings, like this one, with fenced-in front lawns. The apartment was stuffy, and reeked of coffee and cigarette smoke.

Oren Lepidopt had crushed out his latest cigarette in the coffee cup on the blocky living room table, and he held the telephone receiver tight to his ear. *Answer the page,* he thought. It's a land line, obviously it's something I don't want broadcast.

The only sound in the apartment aside from the faint

music at the window was the soft rattle of keystrokes on an electronic keyboard in the kitchen.

At last Malk's voice came on the line—"Hello?"—and Lepidopt leaned back against the couch cushions.

"Bert," he said. "It's daylight here."

There was a pause, then Malk said, "I thought it was daylight here too."

"Well I think it's . . . brighter, here. Now. We got another installment from the ether. I think more is going on here than where you were going."

"I probably can't get a refund on the ticket."

"Screw the ticket. You need to hear Sam's new tape."

"Ala bab Allah," sighed Malk.

Lepidopt laughed at the ironic use of the Arabic phrase— it meant, more or less, "What will be will be." "So get back here now. Full APAM dry-cleaning while you're driving too—stops and double backs, watch for multiple cars, and if you can even *see* a helicopter, drive on by and lose the car."

"Okay. Don't start the John Wayne stuff till I get there."

Lepidopt's elbows jerked in against his ribs in a sudden shudder.

The line went dead, and Lepidopt's face was cold as he replaced the receiver in its cradle.

Don't start the John Wayne stuff till I get there. Bert, Bert, he thought, so carelessly and unknowingly you shorten my life! Or show me a new, even closer boundary of it, anyway.

He made himself take a deep breath and then let it out.

The faint clicking of the keyboard had stopped. "You were laughing," said young Ernie Bozzaris from the table in the kitchen, "and then you look as if you saw a demon. What did he say?"

Lepidopt waved his left hand in a dismissive gesture. "I shouldn't have borscht for lunch," he said gruffly. "He's coming back here, not getting on the plane. Should be here in half an hour or less." Suddenly self-conscious, he slid his maimed right hand into his pocket.

Bozzaris stared at him for another moment, then

shrugged and returned his attention to his computer monitor. He was in his late twenties, fresh from the Midrasha academy; there was no gray in *his* black hair yet, and though he shaved several times a day, his lean jaw always seemed to be dark. "It's not the borscht," he said absently, "it's the Tabasco you pour into it."

With his left hand Lepidopt shook out another Camel from the pack, then used the same hand to snap his lighter at it. He inhaled deeply—it seemed even less likely now that he would have time to die of cancer. He had always heard the saying, *You're scared until the first shot.* And that had proved true twenty years ago, in Jerusalem. For a little while, at least.

He sighed. "Any activity?" he asked as he stood up and carried his coffee cup to the kitchen. His shoes were as silent on the kitchen's linoleum floor as they had been on the carpet in the living room.

Bozzaris had hung his gray linen sport coat over the back of the plastic chair and rolled up his sleeves.

"No unusual activity," he said, not looking away from the dark green monitor screen and the bright green lines of type scrolling upward, "But we don't know who else is out there. The one in New Jersey who tried to get into the mainframe Honeywell in Tel Aviv an hour ago uses the Unix disk-operating system on a Vax machine, and, like everybody else, he doesn't know about the three built-in accounts the machines always come with. I got into his machine by logging on to the 'Field' account, default password 'Service.'"

He paused to knot his long, thin fingers over the monitor and stretch. "Their e-mails," he went on, "show nothing but the usual cover-business stuff, assuming it *is* a cover business—the real guys might be covertly routed through real businesses, like we are. And there's been no notable increase or decrease in the traffic during this last hour and a half."

Bozzaris had insisted that the Institute pay for a new IBM model 80 computer with a 32-bit processor, and a Hayes Smartmodem 1200 that could operate at either 300 or

1200 baud. Lepidopt was used to the shoe-type modems that a telephone receiver had to be fitted into.

"Are any of the travel messages suspicious?"

"How should I know? It's a travel agency. A number of flights here to L.A., which I've copied, but that seems to be usual for them. And of course any of them could be codes. But there hasn't been any 'Johnny, this is your mother, take the casserole out of the oven.'"

"Any of them could be codes," Lepidopt agreed.

"I doubt they've got anything more than the Harmonic Convergence static; a hundred thousand New Agers standing on mountaintops, holding hands and blanking their minds all at once to realign the earth's soul."

Static? thought Lepidopt. They're making a blasphemous *Tzimtzum,* is what they're doing. In the beginning *En-Sof,* the unknowable Infinite Light, contracted itself to make space for the creation of the finite worlds, since without that contraction there would have been no room for anything besides Itself.

And now these wretched hippies and mystics have all contracted their minds at the same time! What sort of things will spring into existence in *this* vacuum?

Bozzaris seemed to answer his thought. "Every sort of critter is likely to be poking its head through from the other side," the younger man said, "with that kind of door open."

"The New Jersey crowd tried to hack Tel Aviv *after* the noon event."

Bozzaris shrugged. "It's unlikely that they'd have been listening on that, uh, wavelength," he said. "But I suppose the event might have registered with other media. Of course people *do* try to hack Tel Aviv, for lots of reasons."

"Assume it's not a coincidence," said Lepidopt.

He stepped to the kitchen counter and poured hot coffee into his cup, then stared at the cigarette butt floating in it.

With his left hand he fished the cigarette butt out of the cup and tossed it into the sink, shaking his fingers afterward. Then he sighed and took a sip of the coffee.

Bozzaris typed *H->* to hang up the phone line, then

immediately typed in *DT* and a new telephone number. The modem's LED lights flickered.

Lepidopt sipped his coffee and looked nervously toward the front window while Bozzaris clicked his way through now familiar passwords and directories. This telephone line was routed through a number of locations, and if Bozzaris's intrusions were fingered by the National Security Agency, there would probably be a warning soon enough for them to abandon this safe house.

And Bozzaris, for all his youth, was meticulous about security, always checking his computers for unsuspected "back doors" and intrusions. Only Bozzaris touched the machine, but he had told Lepidopt about all sorts of computer perils, such as programs that would mimic the IBM opening screen and ask for the user's password, and when the password had been entered would store it, and then flash "INVALID PASSWORD. TRY AGAIN," so that the user would assume he had typed the password wrong, and enter it again, at which point the real log-in sequence would start, and the user would never know that the intruder had copied his password. Bozzaris watched for intrusive programs and changed his passwords all the time. He even made allowances for the possibility of microphones in the room, and made sure to hit each key of his passwords in a measured pace, not hitting a double letter with two fast clicks; and, just to make any inquisitive listeners think his passwords included more characters than they actually did, he always hit a couple of random keys after pressing carriage-return.

Now Bozzaris sat back. "I see no unusual activity among the 'special Arabic' crowd at the NSA." This was the NSA euphemism for their Hebrew linguists monitoring Israel. Lepidopt was relieved to see him hit *H->* again, terminating the phone connection.

A moment later Bozzaris began typing again, and Lepidopt sat down on the pebbled gray-steel safe that sat against the wall next to the stove.

He got up when the daisy-wheel printer on the counter beside him started chattering.

Bozzaris pushed his chair back and stood up, yawning cavernously. He waved at the printer. "The billing addresses the New Jersey guys have booked to or from LAX so far today. Not likely to be anything, and probably not worth checking out now—but we can keep them in the safe and see if they show up in anything that develops."

"Compare them against all Los Angeles lists we've got, of anything. And send a copy to Tel Aviv."

"To *who,* in Tel Aviv? Who are we working for? Who are *we,* anymore?"

"To Admoni, as usual."

Lepidopt wished it were still Isser Harel instead of Nahum Admoni, though Harel had resigned as director general of the Mossad in 1963, four years before Lepidopt had been recruited into the Israeli secret service. It had been Harel who had instituted this off-paper "Halomot" division, the agents of which used target-country passports—American, in this case—and didn't work through the Israeli embassies. The Halomot was even more insulated from the rest of the Mossad than the *Kidon,* the assassin division.

Young Bozzaris had a point, though, when he had asked, *Who are we, anymore?* Since 1960 the Halomot had been concealed as a succession of anonymous committees in the LAKAM, the Israeli Bureau of Scientific Liaison; but the LAKAM had been shut down amid international scandal a year and a half ago after the FBI arrested Jonathan Pollard, the LAKAM's paid spy in the U. S. Naval Investigations Service. The LAKAM had not been part of the Mossad, but its chief had once been a Mossad agent, and any Mossad activity in the United States was now potential diplomatic catastrophe.

The Halomot was left with no cover identity at all, and Lepidopt was afraid that Nahum Admoni didn't share Isser Harel's conviction that the Halomot function was necessary, or even real.

Lepidopt held up a loop of the continuous sheet that was ratcheting out of the printer, another inch appearing every time the spinning printhead reversed its direction across the paper. The billing addresses were in Glendale, Santa Ana, Palm Springs . . .

Lepidopt walked back into the living room and crossed to the wide front window. He put his cup down on the sill and stared down at the afternoon traffic on La Brea.

You're scared until the first shot.

Lepidopt had been twenty years old in early 1967, working for a plumbing-supply company in Tel Aviv, and the idea of war had been almost inconceivable. Throughout May he had followed the news—U Thant had capitulated to Nasser's demand that the UN peacekeepers be pulled out of the Sinai desert, which was the buffer zone between Egypt and Israel, and Egyptian forces had taken control of the Gulf of Aqaba—but everybody knew that Egyptian troops were too busy fighting in Yemen to attack Israel.

Buses in Tel Aviv had been running irregularly because many of the drivers had been called into military service; late in May Prime Minister Eshkol had broadcast to the nation his famous "stammering speech," in which he had sounded uncertain and scared; and every Arab radio station from Cairo to Damascus had been joyfully predicting that all the Jews would shortly be driven into the sea; but it wasn't until his own reserve unit was called up that the young Lepidopt had believed there might actually be a war.

He had been making a delivery to a kibbutz outside Tel Aviv, he recalled, unloading lengths of copper pipe from a truck, sweating in the morning sunlight and watching a group of young men under the corrugated steel awning of a grocery store across the street. They were huddled around a little transistor radio with its volume turned all the way up; the station was Kol Ysrael, and the voice from the radio was reading out call signs—"Open Window . . . Ham and Eggs . . . Top Hat" —and every few minutes one of the young men would jerk, and then step into the sunlight and hurry away. The voice was echoing from other radios too, and up and down the street Lepidopt saw men and women stepping out of shops, taking off aprons and locking doors; and then he heard his own call sign, and he dropped the

last armload of pipe onto the street so that he could drive
the truck to the army base at Peta Tiqwa. What he remembered later was how quiet it had all been—no weeping or
cheering, just the voice on the radio and the footsteps
receding away on the pavement.

Forty years old now, he stared at the Marlboro billboard
over the muffler-and-tune-up shop across La Brea, and he
pressed the four fingers of his scarred right hand against the
sun-warmed glass.

He had been trained in parachuting, and he had found
himself abruptly reassigned to the "red berets," the 55th
Parachute Brigade under Colonel Mordecai Gur. For three
days he lived in one of a row of military tents outside the
Lod Airport, halfway between Tel Aviv and Jerusalem, and
then on Sunday the third of June the brigade had boarded
air-conditioned tourist buses and been driven to the Tel Nov
military jet field near Rehovoth.

The next morning he saw six of the French-built Mirage
jet fighters take off to the west, the blue Star of David insignia
gleaming on the silvery fuselages, and then somehow everyone knew that the war had actually begun. Egypt and Syria
were certainly the enemy, and probably Jordan as well, and
France and Britain and the United States would not help.

Most of the paratroopers of the 55th were to be dropped
into the desert at the southern tip of the Sinai, near the Egyptian air base at Sharm el-Sheikh; but Lepidopt had been in
the hastily assembled Fourth Battalion, and they had been
briefed separately from the other three battalions.

Standing on the tarmac away from the cargo planes and
the buses, Lepidopt and his companions had been told that
the Fourth Battalion was to be dropped later, over the town
of E-Tur on the east shore of the Gulf of Suez, there to link
up with a unit of General Yoffe's tank division, which would
by then have come down the shoreline from the north; from
there they were to proceed inland to a site near the ancient
Saint Catherine's Monastery. They were told that their destination was to be a peculiar stone formation in that dry
wasteland of granite and sand—the briefing officer referred

to it as the Rephidim, which Lepidopt had known was the place where Moses had struck a dry rock with his staff to produce a spring for the mutinous Israelites.

Every man in the Fourth Battalion had been given a cellophane-laminated map and a green plastic film badge, which several of the men recognized as being devices to measure the wearer's exposure to radiation; the badges were heavier than they looked, and bore only the initials ORNL. They were apparently from the Oak Ridge National Laboratory in Tennessee, in the United States. Lepidopt pinned his onto his khaki shirt, under his camouflage jacket.

But at a little past noon, the orders were changed. No flying would be involved after all—Sharm el-Sheikh had already been taken, and the 55th was to proceed by bus to the Old City of Jerusalem instead, thirty-five miles away to the southeast.

That meant Jordan had entered the war against Israel too, and Lepidopt and his companions would be fighting the elite British-trained Arab Legion. Equipped with new maps and having shed their parachutes, they boarded the buses at 6:00 P.M.

Only after his bus was under way did Lepidopt learn that an officer had collected the film badges from the rest of the men who had been designated as the Fourth Battalion— Lepidopt still had his pinned to his shirt.

Rocking in his bus seat as dusk fell over the ancient Judaean hills, Lepidopt had discovered that fear felt very much like grief—his father had died two years before, and now he found himself once again unable to hold on to or even complete a thought, and he clung to the view of trees moving past outside the window because staying in one place would be intolerable, and he was yawning frequently though he wasn't sleepy at all.

And in the streets of Mount Scopus that night, still a day's march north of Jerusalem's walls, he had found a cold Hieronymus Bosch landscape of domes and towers lit in silhouette by mortar explosions close behind them, and skeletons of jeeps and trucks white as bone in the glare of the Israeli searchlights—he was stunned by the ceaseless hammering of .50-caliber machine guns and tank-turret guns that concussed the night air; and the crescent moon riding above the veils of smoke seemed to be an omen for Islam.

The ringing night had been enormous, and he had been grateful for the men huddled around him in a courtyard of the abandoned Hebrew University.

But still he wasn't at the front. When the bell in the YMCA tower struck one, the paratroopers began to advance south through the crashing darkness toward the walls of the Old City. The dawn came soon, and at midmorning they regrouped in the wrecked lobby of the Ambassador Hotel. By now they could see Jerusalem's walls, and Herod's Gate, but it wasn't until late in the afternoon that they passed the Rivoli Hotel and saw, past the burned-out shell of a Jordanian bus, the tall stone crenellations over the Lion's Gate. The paratroopers cautiously advanced toward it.

Visible through the gate was a corner of the gold Dome of the Rock, where Mohammed was supposed to have ascended to Heaven—and from just inside the gate a .30-caliber machine gun began firing into the column of paratroopers. Their captain appeared to be blown out of the jeep he'd been riding in, and all around Lepidopt, men were spinning and falling as the bullets tore and punched at them.

Lepidopt had dived into the gutter, and then he had his Uzi up and was firing at the flutter of glare that was the machine-gun muzzle, and seconds later he and a dozen of his fellows were up and running through the gate.

They soon fell back, to wait for reinforcements and enter the city the following day; but that night, wrapped in a blanket on the lobby floor of the Rivoli Hotel, Lepidopt had realized that it was true—*You're scared until the first shot.* After that first machine gun had begun firing in the Lion's Gate, he had simply been dealing with each moment as if it were a ball pitched at him, not looking ahead at all. Fear was the future, and all his attention had been fixed on grappling with each new piece of *now*.

The next day he had learned that the future could chop you down too; and that there was no way of getting around the fear of that.

"The door light's on," said Bozzaris now from the kitchen. "That'll be Malk, or the FBI."

Lepidopt turned away from the window and hurried across the tan carpet to the kitchen, where he pulled up the long accordioned sheet from behind the printer and tore it off; the touch of a cigarette would flash the paper to ash in a second, and he glanced at the pin in the side of the computer, which only had to be yanked out to ignite a thermite charge over the hard drive. As he quickly lit a cigarette, he mentally rehearsed how he would do both actions, if he should have to.

A muffled knock sounded from the door in the living room.

It was today's two-and-two recognition knock, but Lepidopt stepped behind the kitchen wall, reinforced now with white-painted sheet steel, and he glanced at the bowl of dry macaroni on the shelf by his left hand; but when Bozzaris had got the door unbolted, it was Bert Malk who stepped in, his jacket wrapped around his fist, his tie loosened over his unbuttoned collar, and his sandy hair visibly damp.

"*Matzáv mesukán?*" he asked quietly. It meant *Dangerous situation?*

"No," Lepidopt said, leaning out from behind the wall. "Just new information."

Malk slid a small automatic pistol out of his bundled jacket and tucked it into a holster behind his hip. "It's worse in here than on the street," he complained. "I'll take a cut in pay if you'll get an air conditioner."

When Bozzaris had closed and rebolted the door, Lepidopt tossed the stack of printout onto the counter and stepped out from behind the kitchen wall. "It's not the cost, it's the constant evaporation."

"Sam's gotta learn to screen out phase changes," Malk said irritably. "Why don't cigarettes bother him?"

Malk already knew the answer—*smaller scale, and the*

fire hides it—and Lepidopt just said, "Come listen to this new tape he made."

He led Malk to the closed door off the kitchen, and knocked.

A scratchy voice from the other side of the door said, "Gimme a minute to get dressed."

"Sorry, Sam," said Lepidopt around his cigarette as he opened the door, "time untied waits for no man." He led Malk into the cluttered room.

Skinny old Sam Glatzer was sitting up on the bed, strands of his gray hair plastered to his gleaming forehead, and in the glare from the unshaded bulb on the ceiling, his face seemed particularly haggard. The window in here was covered with aluminum foil, though Lepidopt could hear the speaker behind it—violins and an orchestra; Lepidopt hadn't been a fan of classical music since 1970, but Sam always brought along Deutsche Grammophon tapes in preference to whatever the radio might provide, though there was a strict rule against bringing any Rimsky-Korsakov. The stale air smelled of gun oil and Mennen aftershave.

Sam was wearing only boxer shorts and an undershirt, and he hooked his glasses onto his nose, scowled at Lepidopt and then levered himself up off the bed and began to pull on his baggy wool trousers. A whirring fan turned slowly back and forth on one of the cluttered desks, fluttering the fringe of one of Lepidopt's toupees that sat on a Styrofoam head on another desk.

"Bert needs to hear the tape," Lepidopt said.

"Right, right," the old man said, turning away to zip up his trousers and fasten his belt. "I haven't got anything since that one burst. I'll wait in the living room, I don't like to hear myself talk." The old man caught the "holograph" medallion that was swinging on a string around his neck—required equipment for every Halomot remote viewer—and tucked it into his shirt before buttoning it up.

When he had left and closed the door, Lepidopt sat on the bed to rewind the little tape recorder. Malk leaned against the nearest desk and cocked his head, attentive now.

The tape stopped rewinding, and Lepidopt pushed the play button.

"—on, right," came Sam's reedy old voice, "turn off the light, I don't want afterimages." There was a pause of perhaps half a minute. Lepidopt tapped ash onto the carpet.

"Okay," came Sam's voice again, "probable AOL gives me the Swiss Family Robinson tree house in Disneyland, I don't think that's right, just AOL, analytical overlay—let me get back to the signal line—voices, a man is speaking—'And we'll not fail.' Following somebody saying, 'Screw your courage to the sticking place,' that's Shakespeare, Lady Macbeth, this may be off track too—the man says, 'She's probably about eighty-seven now.' The house is on the ground, not up in the tree, little house, it's a shed. Very crapped-out old shed . . . 'She doesn't drink whisky,' says the man. They're inside the little house now, a man and a little girl, and there's a gasoline smell—I see a window, then it's gone, just empty air there—and a TV set—'An ammunition box,' says the man, 'I don't think she's ever had a gun, though.'"

Sam's voice broke up in a coughing fit at this point, and Lepidopt's recorded voice said, "Can you see any locating details? Where *are* they?"

After a few seconds Sam's voice stopped coughing and went on. "No locating details. I see a headstone, a tombstone. Bas-relief stuff and writing on it, but I won't even try to read it. There's mud on it, fresh wet mud. The man says, 'Bunch of old letters, New Jersey postmarks, 1933, '39, '55—Lisa Marrity, yup.' Uh—and then he says, 'Is that real? . . . I mean, isn't the real one at the Chinese Theater? But this might be real . . . She says she knew Chaplin. She flew to Switzerland after he died.' Now there's someone else, 'It's your uncle Bennett . . .' Uh—'One, two, three,' and . . . a big crash, he pulled the tombstone down . . . and sunlight again—three people walking toward a house, the back door, with a trellis over it—a broken window—something about fingerprints, and a burglar—'Marritys,' says the new man, and the little girl says, '"Divil a man can say a word agin them"'—the first man is at the back door, saying, 'If there was a thief, he's gone.'"

Lepidopt reached out now and switched off the recorder. "Sam loses the link at that point," he said mournfully.

"Wow," said Bert Malk, who had perched himself on the corner of a desk in line with one of the fans. "He said Marity. And Lisa, which is close enough. Did Sam know that name?"

"No."

"We could call the coroner in Shasta, now that we've got a name, see if a Lisa Marity died there today."

"For now we can assume she did. We can get Ernie's detective to call later to confirm it."

"It wasn't a tombstone," Malk went on thoughtfully.

"No, pretty clearly it was Chaplin's footprint square at Grauman's Chinese Theater, and in fact that square *isn't* in the theater forecourt anymore, it was removed in the 1950s when everybody was saying Chaplin was a communist, and then it got lost. We've already got a couple of *sayanim* trying to trace where it went."

Malk sighed heavily. "She'd be eighty-*five* this year, actually. Born in '02." He pulled his sweaty shirt away from his chest to let the fan cool the fabric. "Why wouldn't Sam try to read the writing on the stone?"

"It's like trying to read in dreams, apparently—if you engage the part of the brain that knows how to read, you fall out of the projected state. Ideally we'd have totally illiterate remote viewers, who could just *draw* the letters and numbers they see, with no inclination to try to read them. But I think it obviously said something like *'To Sid Grauman, from Charlie Chaplin.'*"

"I think *this* is in L.A., not Shasta," Malk said. "The guy didn't say 'the Chinese Theater in Hollywood,' he just said the Chinese Theater, like you'd mention a restaurant in your area."

"Maybe." Lepidopt looked at his watch. "This here tape is only . . . fifty-five minutes old. Scoot right now to the Chinese Theater and see if there's a man and a little girl there, looking for the Chaplin footprints or asking about them."

"Should I yell 'Marity,' and see who looks?"

Lepidopt paused for a moment with his cigarette lifted

halfway to his mouth. "Uh—no. There may be other people around who are aware of the name. And don't be followed yourself! Go! Now!" He stood up and opened the bedroom door.

Malk hurried past him to the apartment's front door and unbolted it; and when he had left, pulling it closed behind him, Lepidopt walked over and twisted the dead-bolt knobs back into the locked positions.

"One minute," he said to Glatzer and Bozzaris, and he strode past them into the spare bedroom and closed the door. The faint music still vibrated in the aluminum foil over the window.

Lepidopt crouched by the bedside table, ejected the new tape and then slotted the cassette they had made at noon—the session that had made him send Malk off on his aborted trip to Mount Shasta—and pushed the play button.

"—goddamn machine," said Glatzer's voice. "I'm seeing an old woman in a long tan skirt, white hair, barefoot, she's just appeared on a Navajo-looking blanket on green grass, beside a tree, lying on her back, eyes closed; it's cold, she's way up high on a mountain. There are people around her—hippies, they're wearing robes, some of them, and face paint—beards, beads—very mystical scene. They're all surprised, asking her questions; she just *appeared* in the meadow, she didn't walk in. They're asking her if she fell out of the tree. She's—lying on a swastika!—made out of gold wire; it was under the blanket, but they've moved her, and they've seen the swastika. Now one of the hippies is taking a cellular telephone from his backpack—some hippie—and he's making a call, probably 911. Uh—'unconscious,' he's saying; 'In Squaw Meadow, on Mount Shasta . . . ambulance'—now she's speaking—two words? *'Voyo, voyo,'* she said, without opening her eyes. Ach! Her heart is stopping—she's dead, and I'm out, it's gone."

Lepidopt pushed the stop button, and slowly stood up. Yes, he thought, it was her. We found her at last, just as she died.

He walked back into the living room.

"Can I go too?" asked old Sam Glatzer, getting up from the couch. "I never did get any lunch."

Lepidopt paused and looked over his shoulder at him. Glatzer reminded him of the tired old man in the joke, whose friends arrange for a dazzling prostitute to come to his room on his birthday—*I'm here to give you super sex!* she exclaims when he opens the door; and he says, querulously, *I'll take the soup.*

But he was a good remote viewer, and one of the most reliable of the *sayanim,* the civilian Jews who would efficiently and discreetly provide their skills to aid Mossad operations, for the sake of Israel. Sam was a retired researcher from the CIA-sponsored think tank at Stanford Research Institute in Menlo Park, up near San Francisco, and he was a widower with no children; and Lepidopt told himself that the old man must enjoy using again the clairvoyant techniques he had pioneered back in '72. And over the last several years, Glatzer and Lepidopt had played many games of chess while sitting in safe houses like this, and Lepidopt believed the old man had found them as welcome a break from tension or boredom as he had.

"I'm sorry, Sam," said Lepidopt, spreading his hands, "but I really think we should monitor the 'holograph' line until it's been twenty-four hours. Till noon tomorrow. I'll send Ernie out for any food you'd like." *I'll take the soup,* he thought.

"Good idea," said Bozzaris, getting up from his keyboard. "Pizza?" Bozzaris did not observe the dietary laws, and ate all sorts of *trefe* food.

"Whatever he wants," Lepidopt told Bozzaris. "Get enough for three—Bert might be back pretty quick." Bert Malk didn't bother about kosher food either.

After Bozzaris left, tacos and enchiladas having been decided on, Glatzer went to sleep on the couch, and Lepidopt sat down in a chair against the door-side wall, for the afternoon sun was slanting in through the front window, and he stared almost enviously at Glatzer.

A widower with no children. It occurred to him that Glatzer could expire there on the couch, and—though Lepidopt would lose a friend and chess opponent—nobody's life would be devastated. Two lines from an Ivor Winters poem flitted through his head—*By a moment's calm beguiled, / I have got a wife and child.*

Lepidopt had a wife and an eleven-year-old son in Tel Aviv. His son, Louis, would be envious if he knew his father was working in Hollywood. And Deborah would worry that he'd be seduced by a starlet.

All *katsas,* Mossad gathering officers, were married men with wives back in Israel; the theory was that married men would be immune to sex traps abroad. Broad traps a-sex, he thought. *To preserve you from the evil woman, from the smooth tongue of the adventuress,* as the Psalmist said.

Don't start the John Wayne stuff till I get there, he thought, then shuddered.

In that war twenty years ago, Lepidopt's battalion had stormed the Lion's Gate again at 8:30 the following morning. Israeli artillery and jet fighters had pounded the Jordanian defense forces within the city, but Lepidopt and his fellow soldiers had had to fight for every narrow street, and the morning was an eternity of dust exploding from ancient walls, hot shell casings flying in brassy ribbons from the Uzi in his aching hands, blood spattering on jeep windshields and pooling between paving stones, and the shaky effort of changing magazines while crouched in one or another of the drainage ditches.

I see a headstone, a tombstone.

Lepidopt recalled noticing that the bridges propped over the narrow ditches had been Jewish gravestones, and he had learned later that they had been scavenged from the cemetery on Mount Zion; and now he wondered if, in the subsequent gathering and burial of hundreds of dead Israeli and Jordanian soldiers, anyone had thought to restore the stones to those older graves.

By midmorning the city had fallen to the Israeli forces; sniper fire still echoed among the ancient buildings, but Jordanians were lined up by the gate with their hands in the air while Israeli soldiers scrutinized their identity papers to see if any were soldiers who had changed into civilian clothing;

dead bodies were already being carried out on stretchers, with handkerchiefs over the faces so that medics would not mistake them for the many wounded.

Lepidopt had fought his way through the Moghrabi Quarter, and he was one of the first to reach the Kotel ha-Ma-aravi, the Western Wall of the Temple Mount.

At first he didn't realize what it was—just a very high ancient wall along the left side of an alley; clumps of weeds, far too high to be pulled out, patched its rows of weathered stones. It wasn't until he noticed other Israeli soldiers hesitantly touching the uneven old masonry that it dawned on him what it must be.

This wall was all that remained of the Second Temple, built on the site of Solomon's Temple, its construction completed by Herod at around the time of Jesus and then destroyed by the Romans in 70 A.D. This was the place of the *Shekinah*, the presence of God, to which Jewish pilgrims had come for nearly two thousand years until Jordan's borders had enclosed it and excluded them in 1948.

Soldiers were on their knees, weeping, oblivious to the sniper fire; and Lepidopt shuffled up to the craggy, eroded white masonry, absently unstrapping his helmet and feeling the breeze in his wet hair as he pulled it off. He wiped one shaky hand down the front of his camouflage jacket and then reached out and touched the wall.

He pulled his hand back—and powerfully in his mind had come the conviction that he would never touch the wall again.

He had stepped back in confusion at this sudden, intrusive certainty; and then, defiantly, had reached his hand out toward the wall again—and a blow that seemed to come from nowhere punched his hand away and spun him around to kneel on the street, staring at blood jetting from the ragged edge of his right hand where his little finger and knuckle had been.

Several of the other soldiers were firing short bursts at the source of the shot, and a couple more of them dragged Lepidopt away. His wound was a minor one on that day, but within an hour he had been taken to the Hadassah Hospital, and for him the Six-Day War was over.

Four days later it was over for Israel too—Israel had beaten the hostile nations to the north, east, and south, and had taken the Golan Heights, the West Bank of the Jordan River, and the Sinai desert.

And eleven times—twelve times now, thank you, Bert!—in the twenty years since then, Lepidopt had again experienced that certainty about something he had just done: *You will never do this again.* In 1970, three years after he had touched the Western Wall for the first and last time, he had attended a performance of Rimsky-Korsakov's *Scheherazade* at the Mann Auditorium in Tel Aviv, and as the last notes of the Allegro Molto echoed away, he had suddenly been positive that he would not ever hear *Scheherazade* again.

Two years after that he had visited Paris for the last time; not long afterward he had discovered that he would never again swim in the ocean. After having part of his hand shot off in testing the premonition about the Western Wall, he was reluctant to test any of these subsequent ones.

Just during this last year he had, for the last time, changed a tire, eaten a tuna sandwich, petted a cat, and seen a movie in a theater—and now he knew that he would never again hear the name John Wayne spoken. How soon, he wondered bleakly, until I've started a car for the last time, closed a door, brushed my teeth, coughed?

Lepidopt had gone to the Anshe Emet Synagogue on Robertson at dawn today for recitation of the *Sh'ma* and the *Shachrit* prayer, as usual, but clearly he was not going to be able to get there for the afternoon prayers, nor probably the evening ones either. He might as well say the afternoon *Mincha* prayer alone, here; he stood up to go into the other bedroom, where he kept the velvet bag that contained his *tallit* shawl and the little leather *tefillin* boxes. Every day he shaved the top of his head so that a toupee could be his head covering, and the one he wore to pray was in the bedroom too. He never kept his yarmulke-toupee in the bathroom.

Rabbi Hiyya bar Ashi had written that a man whose mind is conflicted should not pray; Lepidopt hoped God would forgive him for that too.

Three

The truck cab smelled like book paper and tobacco.

"When we *do* go," Daphne said, cheerfully enough, "we can go to Grammar's house again too, and pull up the bricks. A-*zoo*-sa," she added derisively, seeing the Azusa exit through the windshield. And Claremont and Montclair were coming up.

She used to think Azusa was an interesting name for a city, but recently she had heard that it meant "A-to-Z USA," and now she classed it with other ridiculous words, like *brouhaha* and *patty melt*.

She also disapproved of a city called Claremont being right next to one named Montclair. She thought there should be a third one, Mairn-Clot.

Traffic was heavy on the eastbound 10, and an hour after they had left Pasadena their six-year-old Ford pickup truck was still west of the 15, with San Bernardino and their house still twenty miles ahead. The afternoon sunlight glittered fiercely on the chrome all around them; brake lights glowed like coals. Daphne knew the traffic justified her father's decision not to go look at the Chinese Theater today, and she had stopped sulking about it.

"We'd have to split it with Bennett and Moira," her father said absently, his right foot gunning the accelerator while his left foot let the clutch out every few seconds in little surges. The gearshift lever was on the steering column, and it didn't seem likely that he'd be reaching up to shift out of first gear anytime soon. "If there's really gold under the bricks," he added.

Daphne nodded. "That's right. *If* you don't want to do what Grammar wanted you to do with it."

"As in, she told *me* about it, and didn't tell *them*. Why is everybody going east out of L.A. on a Sunday afternoon?"

Daphne nodded. "She knew they've got plenty of money already, and that's why she told you. Her—last wishes." *Last wishes* was a good phrase.

"I'll think about it. It might not *be* gold. Though—wow, look at that," he said, his finger tapping the windshield. An old Lockheed Neptune bomber was flying north over the freeway ahead of them, its piston engines roaring. Its shadow flickered over a patch of cars a mile ahead.

"There must be fires in the mountains," Daphne said.

"It's the season for it. We'll probably—" He paused, and glanced at her. "You're worrying about me," he said. "And it's not to do with money. I—can't quite *get* the reason, just a sort of image of me, and worry like some kind of steady background music." He peered at her again. "What about?"

Daphne shrugged and looked away, embarrassed that he had caught her thoughts. "Just—everybody leaves you. Your dad ran off and then your mom died in a car crash, and Mom died two years ago, and now Grammar." She looked at him, but he was watching the traffic again. "I'm not going to leave you."

"Thanks, Daph. I won't—" He stopped. "*Now* you're shocked. What did *you* see?"

"You think your mother killed herself!"

"Oh." He exhaled, and she sensed that he was finally

near tears, so she looked out the side window at a railway bridge over a shallow arroyo. "Well, yes," he said, with evident control, "I—now you mention it—I think she did. I'm sorry, I shouldn't have—I guess she just couldn't handle it, foreclosure on the house, got arrested for being drunk in public—after my father—"

Daphne had to stop him or she'd start crying herself. "Why were you on your guard," she interrupted, "when Uncle Bennett and I mentioned broken clocks?" Her own voice was quavering, but she went on, "I said the time wasn't right on her VCR in the shed, and he said something about a broken clock, and both times you thought for a second that we meant something else."

Her father took a deep breath, and managed a laugh. "It's hard to explain. Ask your aunt Moira sometime, she grew up there too."

Daphne knew he'd say more if she didn't say anything, so she stared out through the windshield, looking past the cars surrounding them. This far east of Los Angeles there weren't housing tracts around the freeway, just two rows of tall eucalyptus trees. A railway line paralleled the freeway to the south, and occasional farmhouse-looking buildings were scattered across the foothills to the north; the mountains beyond the foothills were brown outlines in the summer smog.

"Okay," her father went on at last. "Grammar—what, had no respect for time. You know the way she carried on sometimes, as if she was still a teenager, like going to Woodstock; and she'd plant primroses in midsummer, and they'd thrive; food got cold real quick sometimes even though she just took it out of the pan, and other times it stayed hot for hours; well, a long time. It never surprised *her*. Maybe she was just pulling tricks on us, but time didn't seem to work right, around her."

A big blue charter bus swerved into their lane ahead of them without signaling, and her father hit the brake and tapped the horn irritably. He didn't mind if people cut him off, even rudely, as long as they used their blinkers. "Dipshit," he said.

"Dipshit," Daphne agreed.

"I know all this sounds weird," her father said. "Maybe us kids imagined it."

"You remember it. Most grown-ups forget all that kind of stuff."

"Anyway," he went on, "the Kaleidoscope Shed—one time Moira and I, when we were about eight and ten, found our initials carved in one of the boards of it, though we hadn't done it; and then a year or so later we noticed that they were gone—the board didn't even show a scratch—and we'd got so used to them being there that we carved 'em in again. And when we stood back and looked at it—I swear—what we had carved was *exactly* what had been there before. Not copied, see, but the same exact cuts, around the same bumps of wood grain. And then a year or so later they were gone again."

"Were they there today?"

"I honestly forgot to look. I might have, after your 'time's wrong' remark, but then Bennett showed up."

Daphne was watching the back of the blue bus ahead of them; it was speeding up and then slowing down. Under the back window, in a blocky typeface, was lettered HELIX. "Why did you call it the Kaleidoscope Shed?" she asked.

"I should get away from Felix here, he's probably drunk," her father said. "Okay, sometimes the edges of the shed, the boundaries from wherever you were looking—rippled. And the shed made a noise too at those times, like a lot of wooden wind chimes or somebody shaking maracas. And sometimes it just looked less decrepit, for a while."

He pressed the brake and signaled for a lane change to the right, shaking his head. "She couldn't stand it when my dad left—the police said she was drunk when her car went off the highway, and I don't blame her for that, I don't blame her for killing herself—my dad drove her to it, by abandoning her with two little kids and no money."

Daphne had known his thoughts were still on his mother even before he abruptly switched topics. She tried to blank her mind, but her father picked up her reflexive thought anyway.

"True," he said, "she abandoned us too. But she sent a note to Grammar, asking her to take Moira and me in, raise us, if anything ever happened to her. A couple of weeks later was the car crash. See, she entrusted us to her mother-in-law, she at least made some provision for us, not—not like *him*."

Daphne couldn't help asking—her father so seldom talked about all this. "What became of him?"

"I think he sent Grammar some money, the year he left. 1955. She got some, anyway. So he must have known where we were—but aside from that money, nothing. He'd be nearly sixty now." Her father's voice was hoarse and level. "He—I'd like to meet him someday."

Daphne was dizzy with the vicarious emotion, and she consciously unclenched her jaw. It was anger as bitter as vinegar, but Daphne knew that vinegar was what wine turned into if it was left to lie too long, and she knew, though her father might not, that his anger was baffled and humiliated love, longing for a fair hearing.

"I always—" he began. "Grammar never seemed to wonder what had become of him, so I always figured she knew. He was her son, and—and she did treat me and Moira as her own children, loved us, after my mom dumped us on her." He thumped the clutch down and shifted up to second, though a moment later he had to pull it back down to first again.

"It is hard to understand why people kill themselves," he went on quietly, as if to himself. "You look at the ways they do it—jump off buildings, shoot themselves in the mouth, pipe carbon monoxide into an idling car in the garage— what terrible last moments! I'd just eat a bunch of sleeping pills and drink a bottle of bourbon, myself—which probably shows I'm not a candidate."

"Portia ate hot coals," Daphne said, relieved that the cramp of aching anger had passed. "Caesar's wife. That's pretty dumb—I always wondered why they named a car after such a dumb person."

Her father laughed, and she was pleased that he had known she was joking.

"You're looking at it like killing *yourself,* though," she said. "The way they do it, real suicides, is like they're just killing a person. Throwing somebody off a building is a rotten way to kill *yourself,* but it's a fine way to kill a person."

For a few seconds her father didn't answer. Since Daphne's mother had died two years ago, he had talked to Daphne as he would talk to an adult, and often she felt helplessly out of her depth; she hoped her last remark hadn't been stupid, or thoughtless. She had pretty much been talking about his mother, after all.

But, "That's pretty good, Daph," he said finally, and she could tell that he meant it.

"What's so weird about Grammar's coffee grinder?" she asked.

"Don't I get a turn? Who's the boy with the glasses and dark hair? I've been seeing him ever since we left Pasadena."

"I don't—" Daphne could feel her face heating up. "He's just a boy in school. What about the coffee grinder?"

Her father glanced sideways at her, and it was clear that he was considering not telling her. She didn't lower her eyebrows or look away.

"Okay," he said at last, returning his attention to the lane ahead. "Damn, that crazy bus has changed lanes too, look— maybe I could pass him now."

Daphne peered over the dashboard and the rust-specked white hood beyond the windshield. Though there were two cars between their truck and the bus, she thought she could see a face in the bus's tinted high back window—but the face seemed to have silver patches on its forehead, cheeks and chin.

She pushed herself back in the seat.

"Don't pass it, Dad," she said quickly. "Slow down, get off the freeway if you have to."

He might not have seen the face, but he slowed down. "No harm getting off at Haven," he said quietly. The Haven Avenue exit was almost upon them, and he swung the car through the lane on their right and directly onto the exit ramp, making the engine roar in first gear.

"Her coffee grinder," he said when they had got off the freeway and turned left onto Haven. It was empty country around here, and sprawling grapevines made still-orderly lines across the untended fields, leftovers from the days when this had all been wine country.

"Well, somebody's got part of the story confused," he went on. "See, when Grammar called me today—what was it, eleven-thirty?"

"About that, yeah."

"Well, when she called me she was using her coffee grinder. I ran it for a second in her kitchen back there, and the acoustics are unmistakable. She was still in her kitchen at—well, at the earliest!—eleven o'clock this morning."

"And the hospital at Mount Shasta called Aunt Moira when?"

"About twelve-thirty."

"How far away is Mount Shasta?"

"Five hundred miles, easy. Almost up at the Oregon border." He shook his head. "Moira must have misunderstood the time somehow. Or I guess Grammar could have raced to LAX right after she called me, got straight onto a plane, direct flight, no layover, and then died just as she got off the plane . . ."

Daphne simply understood that there was no way her great-grandmother could have got to Shasta, but that the old lady had done it anyway. And she was sure her father realized this too.

"Did she build the Kaleidoscope Shed?" Daphne asked.

"Hah. Yes. I don't think she even hired anybody to help. But her father drew the plans, she said. I never met him— she called him Prospero, but as a nickname."

"Prospero from *The Tempest*? What did he do?—like for a job?"

"I got the impression he was a violinist."

"What's the bit, in *The Tempest*? About the creepy music?"

Her father sighed. "'Sitting on a bank,'" he recited, "'Weeping again the King my father's wrack, this music crept by me upon the waters.'"

Daphne knew she'd be scared tonight in her bed, but that would be then—right now, among familiar fields and roads, and the hour no later than 3:30, she was just tense, as if she'd had several fast Cokes in a row. "I said she was a witch."

"She was a good mother to us," he said. "But!" he added, holding up his hand to stop her reflexive apology, "it looks like she may have been something like a witch." He turned right onto Foothill, the highway that used to be Route 66, still dotted with 1950s-era motels; travel time was predictable on surface streets, and Daphne knew they should be home by 4:30 at the latest. Her father added, "I think Grammar killed herself too."

Daphne didn't answer; she knew he could tell she thought so too.

Another World War II-era bomber roared overhead. There must be fires in the mountains here as well.

Her father was teaching a summer school class in Twain to Modern at Cal State San Bernardino tomorrow, and he had a stack of papers to correct, so when he opened a beer and shuffled up the hall to his office, Daphne took a Coke from the refrigerator and walked into the living room. Two or three cats ran away in front of her, as usual acting as if they'd never seen her before.

The kitchen and living room were the oldest parts of the house, built in 1929, when San Bernardino had been mostly orange groves. The house was built on a slope, and the newer sections were uphill—two bedrooms and two bathrooms that had been added on in the '50s, and at the top end of the hall was a big second living room and her father's office, built in the '70s. The walls of the downhill end of the house were stone behind the drywall, and this living room by the kitchen was always the coolest part of the house.

She fitted the *Pee-wee's Big Adventure* cassette into the

VCR slot and sat down on the couch across from the TV set. If her father wanted to watch the movie, she'd see it again with him, but usually he fretted till bedtime over his lecture notes.

Remembered circus music spun behind the credits on the TV screen, and then the movie opened with a view of the Eiffel Tower painted on a billboard. This was Pee-wee's dream, she recalled; he was about to be awakened by his alarm clock. In the dream a cluster of bicyclists streaked past the billboard, and Pee-wee was winning the Tour de France on his crazy red bike, yapping like a parrot in his too tight gray suit; then he had ridden past the finish line, breaking the yellow tape, and all the spectators lifted him off his bike and carried him to a bandstand in a green field—and after some woman had put a crown on his head, she and all the other people hurried away, leaving Pee-wee alone on the platform in the middle of the field—

—and then it was a different movie.

This was black and white, and it started abruptly, with no credits. There was jazzy atonal piano music, but shots of the ocean were accompanied by no surf sounds, and Daphne knew even before the first dialogue card appeared that this was a silent movie.

It was about two sisters, Joan and Magdalen, living in a house on the California coast. One of the sisters was engaged to a simpleminded fisherman named Peter, and the other wasn't; but the actresses seemed to switch roles from scene to scene, so that Daphne could only guess that the engaged sister was the one who met a glossy-haired "playboy novelist" and ran off with him to some glamorous big city, maybe San Francisco. Peter seemed upset by it, anyway. Everybody's facial expressions were exaggerated, even for a silent movie—grotesque, almost imbecilic—and they all seemed to walk awkwardly.

Daphne had never heard the sound-track music before, and it didn't have any recognizable melody, but she kept being jarred by the absence of certain notes that the music had seemed to call for, as if she had tried to step up onto a curb that wasn't there. She had no sooner wondered if the implied notes formed a concealed melody than she was sure that they did—she thought she could remember it and hum it, if she wanted to, but she didn't want to.

She was sweating, and she was glad she was sitting down. The couch, the whole living room, seemed to be spinning. Once when her mother and father had had a party, she had sneaked into the kitchen and poured a splash of each kind of liquor into an empty Skippy peanut butter jar—brandy, gin, bourbon, vodka—and taken it back to her room. When she had finished the "cocktail" and lain down on her bed, the bed had seemed to spin like this. Really, though, this was now more like *teetering*—as if the whole house were balanced on a pole over a pit without walls or a bottom.

She was aware of her father's hands—one hand holding a sheet of paper and the other holding a pencil and scribbling something in the margin; and the writing hand paused, for he was aware of her intrusion. In the bones of her head, over the jagged piano music, she heard him say, *What's up, Daph?*

She had to keep flexing her right hand to dispel the impression that another hand was holding it—a warm, damp hand, not her father's. Someone standing behind her . . .

Maybe it hadn't been Peter's fianceé who'd run away, because now in the movie he was marrying the sister who had stayed. But the wedding was taking place in some sort of elegant Victorian hotel—a white-draped table appeared to be an altar, and a man in black robes was standing behind it with his arms raised; he was wearing a crownless white hat that exposed his bald white scalp, and the brim of the hat had been cut into triangular points, like a child's cutout of a star. He leaned down to press his forehead against the tablecloth, so that his bald head with the ring of triangles seemed to be a symbol of the sun, and then the bride was stepping up to the altar with a knife—there was a quick cut to the other sister, on the seashore, plunging a knife into the center of a starfish—

—and suddenly Daphne realized that it had been only one woman all along, somehow split in two so that one of her could go away while the other stayed home—the woman was in two places at once, and so was Daphne—Daphne was standing up very tall from her father's desk, tossing the paper to the floor and saying in her father's voice, "Daph, *who's in the house?*"

And then the house lost its balance and began to tip over into the pit—for a moment Daphne couldn't feel the couch under her, she was falling—and in a panic she *grabbed* with her whole mind.

The house lurched violently back to level solidity again, though the curtains in the front window didn't even sway; and black smoke was jetting out of the vent slots in the VCR.

Daphne was sobbing, and her ears were ringing, but she could hear her father in the hall shout, "Daph, the fire extinguisher, quick!"

She got dizzily to her feet and blundered to the kitchen, and she muscled the heavy red cylinder up from beside the tool chest. Then her father was there, yanking it from her arms with a brief "Thanks!" and turning away—but instead of going straight across into the living room, he ran left, up the hall.

Daphne peered around the corner after him, and saw smoke billowing out across the hall ceiling from the far-right-hand doorway—her bedroom.

Her father could handle that. Daphne hurried back into the living room, coughing and blinking in the fumes of burning plastic, and she tugged the VCR's cord from the wall and then yanked the still smoking thing down off the TV set; she gave it a few more jerks, and when it lay smoking on the rug, free of all connecting cables, she dragged it through the kitchen and out the door, onto the grass. She took a couple of deep breaths of the fresh air before hurrying back inside.

She ran back through the kitchen and up the hall, and she stepped wide around the doorway to her room in case her father might come out fast; smoke made a hazy layer under the hall ceiling and the air smelled of burning cloth.

Her father was shooting her blackened bed with quick

bursts of white fog from the extinguisher, but the fire seemed to be out. Her pillow was charred, and the blue wall behind the bed was streaked with soot.

She was wringing her hands. "What burned?"

"Rumbold," her father panted. Rumbold was a teddy bear Daphne's mother had given her years and years ago. "Was there somebody in the house, at the door?"

"Oh, I didn't mean to *burn* Rumbold! No, that was in Grammar's movie. It wasn't Pee-wee, it was a scary movie. I'm sorry, Daddy!"

"Your mattress might be okay. But we'd better drag your sheets and blankets and pillow outside. And Rumbold, what's left of him."

The teddy bear had melted as much as burned, and Daphne carried him outside on a cushion because he was still very hot.

"The VCR too?" her father asked in the fresh air as he stepped over the charred machine on his way to the trash cans.

Trotting along after him, Daphne called, "Yes, it too. Dad, it was a *really* scary movie!" Tears blurred her vision—she was crying as much about Rumbold as about all the rest of it. The late afternoon breeze was chilly in her sweaty hair.

Stepping around the truck, her father dumped the still smoking bedding into one of the cans.

"I want to bury Rumbold," Daphne said.

Her father crouched beside her, wiping his hands on his shirt. "Okay. What happened?"

"It was the movie—it wasn't Pee-wee except for the first couple of minutes, then it was a black and white, a silent. And I felt myself falling—the whole house felt like it was falling!—and I grabbed on—I guess I grabbed the VCR and Rumbold, both." She blinked at him through her tears. "I've never been that scared before. But how could I set stuff on fire?"

He put his arms around her. "Maybe you didn't. Anyway, the movie's gone now."

His kindness, when she had expected to be yelled at, set her sobbing again. "She was a *witch!*" she choked.

"She's dead and gone. Don't—"

She felt her father shiver through his shirt, and when she looked up she saw that he was looking past her, down the driveway.

Daphne turned around and saw Grammar's old green Rambler station wagon rocking to a halt on the dirt driveway, thirty feet away, under the overhanging boughs of the Paraiso tree.

Daphne had begun moaning and thrashing in her father's arms before she heard him saying, "It's not her! Daph! It's some old guy, it's *not her*! She's dead and gone and her movie's burned up! Look, it's just some *guy!*"

Daphne clutched her father's shoulders and blinked fearfully at the car.

There was only one person visible in it, a gray-haired man with a pouchy, frowning face; perhaps he had only now noticed the child and the crouching man beside the Ford truck. As she watched, the car quickly reversed out of the driveway back into the street, and then sped away east. She lost sight of it behind the fence and the trunks of the neighbor's eucalyptus trees.

"That was Grammar's car!" Daphne wailed.

"Yes it was," her father said grimly, straightening up. "Probably that guy was the burglar who broke into Grammar's house. Casing our place now, I bet."

"Her keys were gone," said Daphne, shivering and sniffling now. "He must have waited till we were all gone, then took her car." And followed us, she thought.

"I'll call the police. We're dealing with thieves here, Daph, not witches."

And a girl who can set things on fire in rooms she's not even in, Daphne thought unhappily. Even things she doesn't want to burn up. What if I have nightmares about that movie? Could I set fires in my sleep?

A shrill screeching from behind her made her jump and grab her father's leg.

He ruffled her hair. "It's the smoke alarm, goof. It just now noticed that there was a fire."

Four blocks away, the green Rambler had pulled over to the dirt shoulder of Highland Avenue, and a couple of children on bicycles laughed to see the gray-haired old driver open the door and lean out to vomit on the pavement.

Four

When Lepidopt unbolted the door and pulled it open, Malk was startled by how exhausted the man looked—Malk knew Lepidopt was forty, but at this moment, with the lines in his hollow cheeks and the wrinkles around his eyes, and with the stray curls of his prayer-toupee stuck to his forehead, he looked twenty years older. In his hand was a piece of white paper that he had clearly written out as a report, in the strict Mossad format with the addressee and subject line underlined.

Malk knew there was no superior officer for Lepidopt to give it to—it could only be a copy-to-file letter; a bit of *kastach,* covering one's ass.

"What did I miss?" Malk asked cautiously after he had stepped inside and Lepidopt had closed and rebolted the door. The curtains were drawn, and a lamp by the window had been switched on. "There was no particular man and girl at the Chinese Theater."

Young Bozzaris was standing in the kitchen doorway

by the bowl of macaroni this time, silhouetted by the fluorescent ceiling light, and Sam Glatzer was sitting on the couch, asleep. The room smelled of salsa and corn tortillas.

Lepidopt nodded. "No, they went straight home. Glatzer received another transmission."

Malk noticed the tape recorder on the coffee table, among a litter of greasy waxed paper and cardboard cups; apparently the transmission had arrived so suddenly that it had been easier to bring the recorder to Glatzer than to bring Glatzer to the recorder.

"Any locators this time?"

Lepidopt leaned his back against the curtained window and rubbed his eyes. "No, still no locators." He lowered his hands. "Glatzer's *gamúr.*"

Malk looked again at the old man on the couch. Glatzer's chin was on his chest, and he wasn't moving at all. The holograph talisman lay on his belt buckle, its cord curled slackly across his shirt.

"Oh weh," Malk said softly. "Was it . . . stressful?"

"I'll play it back for you. After dark we can drive him to Pershing Square, sit him at one of those chess tables, and then call the police to report a body there. Perishing Square. Poor Sam. Sit down."

Malk sat down in the chair next to the door, across from the couch.

Lepidopt had apparently rewound the tape to the right place, for when he pushed the play button there was only a moment of silence and then the abrupt beginning of a recording.

Lepidopt's voice began it, a few syllables ending with "—go!" Then Malk heard Glatzer's frail voice: "The girl, in a house, with cats. Now the Eiffel Tower—no, it's just a picture of it—a bicycle race, in France—some crazy giggling guy in a gray suit is riding in it, passing everybody—he's riding a red bicycle, not any kind of racing bike—he won, he broke the tape—"

Lepidopt now reached down and switched off the recorder. "And then he died."

And we lost our remote viewer, Lepidopt thought. Our psychic eyes are gone. We killed this old man—and what did we get for it? Not even any locators.

Through the curtain he could hear the faint music from the speaker taped to the living room window: Madonna's "Who's That Girl?"

Lepidopt didn't think he had ever been this tired. Malk and Bozzaris had better not need help walking the dead body from the car to one of those cement tables in Pershing Square with a chessboard on it in mosaic tile. They'd have to remember to take the talisman off the body.

He thought of the old man sitting there abandoned in the night, with no player on the other side of the table; and he almost asked, *Who played Rooster Cogburn in* True Grit?

Instead he pushed away from the window and said to Bozzaris, "What have we got right now?"

"From the noon tape," said Malk, "we've got an old woman who died on Mount Shasta, and she was probably the Marity woman: Sam said she just *appeared* there, and of course Sam saw her via the holograph talisman, which would indicate *her*. What was it she said, just before she died?"

"It sounded like '*voyo, voyo,*'" said Bozzaris. "*Voyou* is French for hoodlum, if that's worth anything. And then an hour and a half later," he went on, sitting down in his white plastic chair by the computer, "we have a man and a little girl who quote Shakespeare. And they apparently know the Marity woman fairly well—he said she doesn't drink, or own a gun."

"And the guy knew her age, within two years," put in Malk. "And he says she went to Switzerland after Chaplin died in '77, and she's got the Chaplin footprints from the Chinese Theater in this shed."

Lepidopt was pleased that they were thinking, and let them go on with it.

Bozzaris's recorded voice interjected, *"Pee-wee's 1 Adventure* is what that is."

"—crowd is carrying him to a lawn—"

"What?" said Lepidopt's voice.

"It's a movie," Bozzaris had explained then, "somebody's watching it."

"It's a movie, on a TV set," said Glatzer's voice. "Now it's a different movie, one woman playing two roles—no no, two women playing one role—" For several seconds the old man was as silent on the tape as he was now on the couch. Malk wished he'd asked for a cigarette before the tape started; he couldn't shake the thought that the tape voice was Glatzer talking live from wherever dead people go.

A hoarse cry shook out of the machine, and then Glatzer's voice went on breathlessly, "I *can't* follow her, she's falling out of here and now. I almost fell out with her— Wait, she's back—everything's on fire, up the hall and the TV set—running through smoke—I'm fine, let me get this!—a man's voice says, 'Was there somebody in the house, at the door?' "

Malk kept looking at Glatzer's dead body in its shirt and tie, half expecting gestures to accompany these terse, fragmentary impressions.

From the recorder Glatzer's voice said, " 'I didn't mean to burn Rumbold,' says the little girl."

The tape recorder was quiet again for a while, though Malk could hear recorded panting. He made himself look away from the body.

Glatzer's voice went on finally, " 'I want to bury Rumbold,' says the girl. 'It was the movie—it wasn't Pee-wee except for the first couple of minutes, then it was a black and white, a silent'—uh—'She was a witch!' Now—now a car is pulling into the driveway, an old guy in it, in a, a green station wagon—he's—the girl is holding on to her father—I can see the old guy, he's—"

Then there was the sound of a sharply indrawn breath, and blurred exclamations from Lepidopt and Bozzaris.

"I still think they're locals, the man and the girl," Malk went on. "This seems like L.A. to me."

"But the old woman got mail as Lisa Marity," Bozzaris reminded him, "and we've checked L.A., past and present, for any Marity."

Malk nodded. "And there's no indication that this man and girl *know* anything," he said. "They were surprised by the Chinese Theater slab, and the guy said 'a bunch of old letters' with no evident informed guessing, and they assumed it was a plain thief who broke into the house, not a reconnaissance team. Obviously they don't—"

"Hah!" interrupted Bozzaris, springing lithely from his chair. He grabbed a hefty telephone book from the kitchen shelf and began flipping through it.

"What?" asked Lepidopt.

"The little girl said, 'Divil a man can say a word agin them,'" Bozzaris said excitedly, "it's a Cohan song. It's Harrigan in the song, but with Marity it'd be 'M-A-double R-I,' see? We've been"—he was tossing his way through the white pages—"looking for either the Serbian *Maric* or the Hungarianized *Marity,* with one *r,* but what if the old lady added an extra *r* to make it look Irish? Nothing in L.A.—Bert, give me Long Beach, and you get busy on Pomona or something."

Lepidopt shambled past Malk and Bozzaris into the stuffy kitchen and took a telephone book from the shelf. He thumbed through the pages to the *Marriage–Martinez* page, and squinted down the columns.

"Here's a *Marrity, L,*" he said, "with two *r*s." He flipped to the cover. "Pasadena."

There proved to be no more Marritys at all in the Los Angeles area.

"I bet that's her," Malk said. "I knew this was local."

Lepidopt stared at the telephone book in his hands. "We should have found this . . . years ago," he said sadly.

"Natural oversight, though," said Bozzaris with a shrug. "If you were looking for M-A-R-I, you'd never see that solitary Marrity way over there. There's a whole nation of

Marquezes in between—and Marriots. And you wouldn't expect to find her *listed* anyway."

"Still," said Lepidopt, "there it was, all this time."

"Hey," Bozzaris said, "nobody's human." It was an old Mossad line, a mixture of *"nobody's perfect"* and *"I'm only human."*

Lepidopt nodded tiredly. "Get on the phone," he told Bozzaris, "and tell your *sayan* to look up Lisa Marrity with two *r*s. Your San Diego detective. Have him check L.A. and Shasta."

He sat down on the couch facing Sam, and when Malk stepped toward him, he waved him off.

When he had returned to Tel Aviv in mid-June of 1967, unable to work because his hand was still bandaged, he had brooded, and checked out various books on Hebrew mysticism from the library, and finally he had visited a friend who was an amateur photographer.

Lepidopt had wondered if it had been the *Shekinah,* the presence of God, that had given him the prediction that he would never again touch the Western Wall—the prediction that he had foolishly tested, at the cost of his finger and a good bit of his hand—and he remembered how the Lord had warned Moses to keep everyone back from Mount Sinai, in the book of Exodus: *"You shall set bounds for the people round about, saying, 'Beware of going up the mountain or touching the border of it. Whosoever touches the mountain shall be put to death: no hand shall touch him, but he shall be either stoned or shot; beast or man, he shall not live.' "*

To Lepidopt this had sounded like precautions, in terms a primitive people could follow, against exposure to radiation; especially the order that anyone who got too close to the mountain should be killed from a distance. So he gave his photographer friend the film badge he had been issued when the Fourth Battalion's mission had been to find the Rephidim stone in the southern wastes of the Sinai desert. Lepidopt wanted to know if the film showed that he had been exposed to divine radiation.

The photographer broke open the film badge in his darkroom and developed the patch of film it contained, but while it wasn't transparent and unexposed, neither did it show the graduated fogged bands of radiation exposure—instead the negative showed, in white lines against a black background, a Star of David inside two concentric rings, with a lot of Hebrew words in all the spaces and four Hebrew words evenly spaced around the outer circle. The words in the corners proved to be the names of the four rivers of Paradise—Pishon, Gihon, Prath, and Hiddekel—and the script inside the star read, "Your life story be sacrosanct, and all who are in your train." Between the rings had been various names such as Adam and Eve and Lilith, and word fragments in all the diamond-shaped spaces had been rearrangements of the letters of the Hebrew word for "unchanged" or "unedited."

To his own surprise, Lepidopt had *not* taken this as evidence of divine intervention; his belief, he discovered, was that the diagram had been exposed onto the film and inserted into the ORNL badge before it was issued to him.

Perhaps the photographer had mentioned the odd "photograph" to friends; or perhaps all the men who had so briefly been assigned to the Fourth Battalion were monitored; in any case, Lepidopt received postwar orders to report to the army base in Shalishut, outside Tel Aviv. There, in a garage that was empty except for himself and half a dozen white-coated technicians, he was given a series of peculiar tests—he was asked to describe photographs in sealed cardboard envelopes, to identify playing cards just by looking at the backs of them, and to heat up coffee in a cup inside a glass box. To this day he had no idea if his guesses about the photos and the cards had been accurate, or if the coffee had heated up at all.

For the next several months he was called back for more tests, but these were more mundane—he was given a number of thorough physical examinations, and his reflexes were tested; the medical staff gave him strict dietary instructions, steering him away from preservatives, hard liquor, and most meats.

After three months the program had become more instruction than testing. If he hadn't been amply paid for the time all this took, he might have refused to go on, even though he understood this was part of his army reserve service. Certainly it was *pazam* in both senses of the word: service time, and a long time too. Luckily he had still been single in those days.

The instruction was mostly done in a windowless trailer that was driven from place to place throughout the day, perhaps at random; five other students, all males of about his own age, sat with him at a bolted-down trestle table that ran the length of the trailer, and the twenty-one-year-old Lepidopt was soon able to take readable notes with his left hand, even when the truck braked or turned unexpectedly. The students seldom had the same instructor twice, but Lepidopt was surprised that each instructor was a tanned, fit-looking man of obviously military bearing, in spite of the anonymous suits and ties they all wore.

He would have expected bent old scholars, or disheveled fanatics—for the texts the students analyzed were spiral-bound photocopies of old Hebrew mystical books. Some had titles—*Sepher Yezirah, Raza Rabba*—but others just bore headings like *British Museum Ms. 784* or *Ashesegnen xvii* or *Leipzig Ms. 40d.*

Often when the texts were in Hebrew they had to be copied out in the student's handwriting before they could be read aloud, and in those cases the students had also had to fast for twenty-four hours before beginning, and make sure to write each letter of the text so that it touched no other letter; and often the lectures were delivered in whispers—though surely there could have been no risk of being overheard.

The texts had largely been antique natural histories with interesting but outlandish theories, such as Zeno's paradoxes that appeared to show that physical motion was impossible; but Lepidopt had been surprised to see that the fourteenth-century Kabbalist Moses Cordovero, in his book *Pardes Rimmonim,* had defined lasers while describing God and the amplified light that connects Him with His ten emanations;

and that the succession of these emanations, or *sephirot*, seemed to be a stylized but clear presentation of the Big Bang theory; and that these medieval mystics apparently knew that matter was a condensed form of energy.

It had seemed to young Lepidopt that the instructors emphasized these things a bit defensively, in order to lend some frail plausibility to the wilder things in the texts.

Those wilder things began to have a stark, firsthand plausibility on the day when the students were taken in several jeeps out to some ruins in the desert north of Ramle—and that night in his own room, having pulled the curtains closed to block the view of the night sky, Lepidopt had wondered what sort of action the Fourth Battalion would have been faced with in the Sinai desert, at the Rephidim stone, if the orders had not been changed.

The instructor that day had been a deeply tanned, gray-haired old fellow with eyes as pale as spit; he had taken them into the wilderness to show them a thing that he claimed was "one of the Aeons"—specifically the Babylonian air devil Pazuzu.

Far out in the desert, half an hour's steep hike from where they had had to park the jeeps, the students and the instructor had finally stood at noon in a shadeless, yards-wide summit ring of carved, weathered stones under an empty sky, and the old instructor had meditated for a while and then pressed his right hand on to an indentation in one of the stones—and then they were reeling with vertigo in the center of a clanging whirlwind, but it had palpably been a living, sentient whirlwind; and young Lepidopt had known in his spine and his viscera that it was the world that was spinning, and the alien creature, the Aeon Pazuzu, that was holding still. In comparison to it, nothing he had ever encountered had been motionless.

Nothing else in the training had been as dramatic as that, but some things had been more upsetting—as when the students had been trained in astral projection. On the several occasions when Lepidopt's consciousness had hung in the air, looking down at his own slack body on a couch, he had always been afraid that he would be spun away into the whirling honeycomb of the world and never find his way back to his physical body. Every time he had pulled himself back into his body, sliding into it as if he were inching into a tight sleeping bag, it had been with a profound sense of relief and a resolution never to leave it again.

There had always been afternoon prayers in the truck, and evening ones if the lessons went on that long, but the Psalms all seemed to Lepidopt to have been chosen for their apologetic or resentful tone.

Lepidopt realized he'd been staring across the table at Glatzer's collapsed body. He stood up and crossed to the wide front window, and leaned his forehead against the curtained glass, idly listening to the faint music audible from the speaker taped against the windowpane—it was the new U2 song, "I Still Haven't Found What I'm Looking For."

Neither have I, Lepidopt thought. We seem to be very close now, but I wonder if I'll live to find the . . . the technique, the technology, the breakthrough that Isser Harel has been searching for ever since learning of a nameless little boy who appeared in England in 1935 long enough to leave impossible fingerprints on a water glass.

It had opened up a whole new direction of scientific inquiry. Isser Harel had kept it very secret, but perhaps not everyone else involved had been as discreet.

The Iraqis had been pursuing research in the same direction in the late 1970s; and Lepidopt, working with a Halomot team on a war-surplus destroyer in the Persian Gulf in '79, had detected the Iraqi research station at Al-Tuweitha, a few miles southwest of Baghdad. The world thought it was simply an Iraqi nuclear reactor that Israeli F-16s bombed to rubble in June 1981; only Menachem Begin and a few agents in the Halomot—and Saddam Hussein and his top advisors—had known what sort of device the Iraqis had been trying to build behind the cover of installing the French-built Tammuz reactor.

How odd, he thought, that Moslems could even get close! Had *they* studied the Hebrew Kabbalah?

The intelligence services of several countries seemed to be aware of the new possibility, just as they had vaguely known of "the uranium bomb" in the early '40s; in 1975 the Soviet premier Brezhnev had asked for an international ban on weapons "more terrible" than any the world had yet seen.

But it had been a Jew who discovered this thing, twenty years before the establishment of the state of Israel in 1948; and in the text of the second-century *Zohar* was the passage, *At the present time this door remains unknown because Israel is in exile; and therefore all the other doors are removed from them, so that they cannot know or commune; but when Israel will return from exile, all the supernal grades are destined to rest harmoniously upon this one. Then men will obtain a knowledge of the precious supernal wisdom of which hitherto they knew not.*

And Israel wasn't in exile anymore.

It's all been one war for me, Lepidopt thought—and he made a narrow fist with the thumb and three fingers of his misshapen right hand.

Bozzaris had said something to him. Lepidopt looked up. "What?"

"I said the dead woman on Mount Shasta was definitely the woman known as Lisa Marrity. I got my *sayan* on the phone, and I had him call police departments in L.A. and Shasta and ask about a Lisa Marrity, with two *r*s. The guy just called back—a hospital in Shasta pronounced her dead at 12:20 this afternoon. Driver's license says she was born in 1902 and lived at 204 Batsford Street in Pasadena. The Siskiyou County sheriff wants to look into it—it may have been suicide, since she had hardly anything but a note on her with next-of-kin phone numbers—which my man got and passed on to us, yes!—and witnesses say there was a big gold swastika on the grass under her body, made out of gold wire, just like Sam saw at noon. Real gold, they claim, though it was all gone by the time the cops got there."

"Some hippies," said Lepidopt, echoing what poor old Sam had said. He got to his feet. "Airline tickets, gas receipts?"

"None, and no keys at all, and no cash or credit cards at all. And she was barefoot, like Sam said, no shoes anywhere near her. Way up a hiking trail, and no cuts on her feet."

"Huh. So who are these next of kin?"

"A Frank Marrity—two *r*s—and a Moira Bradley. Frank's in the 909 area code, that's an hour east of Pasadena, and Moira's 818, which is Pasadena."

Bozzaris was in the kitchen with the Pasadena telephone directory. "Bradley," he read, *"Bennett* and Moira, as in 'Uncle Bennett,' note. 106 Almaraz Street. We haven't got any 909 directories here."

"Yes, that's got to be the 'Uncle Bennett' that Sam caught a reference to," said Lepidopt. "Right before 'pulled the tombstone down.' Get your *sayan* to look up Frank Marrity. And then you can take Sam to Pershing Square. *Don't* forget to take off the holograph talisman."

"I won't. But you'd better get Tel Aviv to send us another remote viewer to hang it on."

"Yes. Won't be as good as poor old Sam, I'm sure. I'll send Admoni an e-mail tonight." He wasn't looking forward to sending the report—the Mossad strongly disapproved of letting *sayanim* get hurt, much less killed; still, Glatzer had been in his seventies, and a heart attack had never been unlikely. "What's our safe-house situation like in the 909 area?"

"The two apartments are still stocked and paid up, in San Bernardino and Riverside," said Malk. "But for this kind of work your best bet is—"

"I know," said Lepidopt. "The tepee place."

"The Wigwam Motel on Route 66, right."

"Book us a room. A tepee. A wigwam."

I'll start with Frank Marrity, Lepidopt thought. He's almost certainly the guy Glatzer was reading this afternoon, the guy with the little girl.

Five

"Huck Finn is told by Huck Finn himself, from his point of view."

Suddenly unwilling to read whatever sentence might follow that first one, Frank Marrity let the Blue Book test pamphlet fall into his lap. The stack of similar Blue Books stood on the table beside him, but he had just this moment decided to call in sick tomorrow, so they didn't depress him nearly as much as they had when he had sat down.

He was in the uphill living room, in a chair by the cold fireplace, and Daphne was asleep on the couch in front of the uphill TV set. She had drifted off during *Mary Poppins,* and he had turned the set off. She seemed to be sleeping peacefully, and he was reluctant to wake her.

He tamped his pipe and puffed a cloud of smoke toward the set of Dickens on the mantel. His hands weren't trembling now, but he still felt sick to his stomach.

Poltergeist? he thought, allowing the morbid, impossible thought to surface again. It must—actually—have been a poltergeist! A girl in her teens—well, close enough—and sudden breakages or fires in the house when she was emotionally stressed. *Are* there child psychologists who specialize in . . . poltergeistery? Maybe it was a one-shot thing, maybe it will have worn off by morning. We'll be able to forget about the whole thing.

One of the cats, a tailless black-and-gray male, was clawing the back of the couch, which was already hanging in tatters from the previous attentions of the cats. "No no, Chaz," said Marrity absently, saying what Daphne always told the cats, "we don't do that. We've talked about it, remember?"

What the hell kind of movie did Grammar leave lying around, anyway, driving little kids nuts? But apparently Grammar *did* mean to burn it. She would never knowingly hurt a child. Would never have.

Marrity didn't want to use the word *poltergeist* in Daphne's hearing, since she had seen the Steven Spielberg movie with that title. The little girl in that movie had been contacted by some kind of ghosts through a television screen, and he didn't want Daphne to develop a phobia about TV sets.

His Encyclopedia Britannica—admittedly a set published in 1951—seemed to take poltergeist phenomena seriously. In the article on psychical research he had also read the section on telepathy and clairvoyance, but though the writer of the article seemed credulous of these things too, there was no mention of the sort of psychic link he and Daphne had.

Their link had shown up in the two years since Lucy's death, but until today it had alternated between them—for a week or so he would be able to catch occasional thoughts of Daphne's, and then the ability would fade out, and a month later Daphne would be able to see some of his thoughts for six to ten days. Maybe the no-telepathy periods had been getting longer, the alternating telepathic periods getting closer together, until now they had actually overlapped. Would they stop, now, after having finally occurred together? He hoped so, even though he was glad he and Daphne had been linked this afternoon, when the fires had started.

At dinner Daphne hadn't eaten much of her chili con carne. Twice she had choked, as if she was having difficulty swallowing; but he had caught an image from her thoughts— a brief glimpse of somebody spooning out brains from a broken bald head with a splayed crown on it, seen in black and white and therefore obviously from the damned movie she had watched—and he had not asked her to say what was wrong. Maybe he should have.

More strongly than he had in a long time, he wished that Lucy had not died, leaving Daphne and him adrift. Even two parents were hardly enough to raise a child. He remembered a passage from Chesterton: "Although this child is much better than I, yet I must teach it. Although this being has much purer passions than I, yet I must control it."

Daphne's fingernails were always bitten down to the quick; for these last two years, anyway.

I do my best, he thought, trying the phrase on; and then he wondered how often he really did do his best, and for how long at a time.

Since he wouldn't be setting the alarm clock for tomorrow, he poured more Scotch into his glass, though the ice had long since melted. He wouldn't be paid for tomorrow either.

But there's gold under the bricks in Grammar's shed, he thought. Possibly.

Gold, which Grammar could have expected to survive the shed burning down; and some kind of movie, and some letters, which would reliably have been destroyed. Well, the movie was now burned up.

There had been a message on the telephone answering machine from Mercy Medical Center in Shasta when he and Daphne had got home; he had called them back, and they had confirmed that Grammar had died on Mount Shasta at about noon.

He took a sip of the lukewarm whisky, grateful for the full-orchestra burn of it in his throat, and then reached into his inside jacket pocket and carefully drew out the sheaf of letters that he had taken from the ammunition box in Grammar's shed. Some flecks of broken old brown paper fell onto the Blue Book on his lap, and he brushed them and the booklet off onto the rug. The letters smelled of gasoline, and he laid his pipe carefully in the ashtray.

The first envelope he looked into was postmarked June 10, 1933, from Oxford, but the letter inside was handwritten in German, and Marrity was only able to puzzle out the salutation—*Meine liebe Tochter,* which clearly meant "my dear daughter," and the signature, *Peccavit,* which he believed was Latin for "I have sinned."

He flipped through the stack, poking his fingers into the envelopes to find one of the English-language letters he recalled seeing in the shed, and pulled free the first one he found.

The postmark was Princeton, New Jersey, August 2, 1939; the printed return address on the envelope was Fuld Hall, Princeton Institute for Advanced Study; and under it, in pencil, someone had scrawled *Einstein Rm. 215.*

Marrity paused. Had Albert Einstein written Grammar a letter? That would be worth something!

Hoping it might be from Einstein, and hoping that a couple of others in the batch might be too, he carefully unfolded the yellowed letter. It was typed, and addressed to "Miranda," though the addressee on the envelope was Lisa Marrity.

My dear Miranda, Marrity read, *I have sent today a Letter to the King of Naples, advising him of the ominous Behavior of Antonio, and advising him to busy himself in acquiring pre-emptively for Naples the Power toward which Antonio is looking.*

Marrity recognized these names—Miranda was the daughter of the magician Prospero in Shakespeare's play *The Tempest,* and Antonio was Prospero's treacherous brother who had usurped the dukedom of Milan and driven Prospero and his daughter into exile.

Grammar had called her father Prospero.

I did not mention the other Power, the letter went on, *and did not the Caliban who is now your chaste Incubus. (And whose Fault?) I can assist Naples with the First, but I will work only to conceal and obliterate all Records of the Other. I'll break my Staff, and bury it certain Fathoms in the Earth, and deeper than did ever Plummet sound I'll drown my Book.*

Caliban was an inhuman monster in the Shakespeare play, and the *break my Staff* sentence was a verbatim quote from the Prospero character.

The letter ended with, *And you should do the Same also. Forgive yourself about 1933, and then forget even what it was you did. Starve Caliban with Inattention. I should never have given him Shelter—I've learned my lesson, not to interfere with Suicides! Twice the Interfering has made Disasters, and so I must somehow have the Palm Springs Singularity to be destroyed. And you must burn the* verdammter *Kaleidoscope Shed!*

Marrity actually lowered the age-yellowed letter and looked around the dim corners of the room, as if this were a trick being played on him.

Then he looked back at the sheet of old paper. The letter was signed *Peccavit,* in the same hand as the first letter he'd looked at.

Was this *Peccavit* Grammar's father? And was he Albert Einstein? Were all these letters from him?

Marrity realized glumly that he couldn't believe it. It was inconceivable that Albert Einstein could know about the shed he and Moira had played in as children. There were any number of plausible reasons why someone might write *Einstein* on an envelope.

But hadn't Einstein taught at Princeton?

Marrity flipped through the stack again, peeking into the envelopes, and saw another in English. He carefully drew the letter out of the envelope—which was plain, postmarked Princeton, New Jersey, April 15, 1955. The letter was handwritten, in the same difficult scrawl as the *Peccavit* signatures.

My dear Daughter, Marrity managed to puzzle out, *Derek was here—did you know?*

And Marrity stopped reading again, his face suddenly cold. Derek, he thought. That's my father's name. He ditched us in '55—sometime before May, since my mother killed herself in May. Was he just off visiting his grandfather? If so, why didn't he ever come back? Did he die? If he died, why wouldn't Grammar have told Moira and me?

Quickly he worked his way through the rest of the letter.

I hope you have not told him too much! I said to him to go Home, I am always watched, can tell him Nothing. And Derek not knows his own Origin, that he has no lineal Status. I have spoken to NB when he was here in October, just enough to assure he has no Inkling of the Maschinchen. And he has not. I am in Hospital, with a ruptured Aortic Aneurism, and I know I do not survive. I wish to have seen you one more Time! We are such Stuff as Dreams are made on, and our little Life is rounded with a Sleep.

It was signed simply, *Your Father.*

That last sentence was of course from *The Tempest.*

With a shaking hand Marrity laid the letters aside, and stood up and tiptoed into the hall, where the Britannica volumes stood on a shelf above head height. He pulled down the EDWA to EXTRACT volume, blew dust off the top page edges, and flipped to the article on Einstein.

It listed his birth year as 1879, but there was no death date in this 1951 edition. Marrity only skimmed the accounts of Einstein's discoveries, but noted that Einstein had become professor of mathematics at the Institute for Advanced Study at Princeton, New Jersey, in 1933.

An image more vivid than a daydream unfocused his view of the page—Daphne was dreaming. In her dream a young man with long hair was tied up and gagged, lying on his back in some kind of recessed space in a metal floor between padded, bolted-down seats, and a hand with a knife hovered over his throat; then it was Daphne lying on her back on a red-and-black linoleum floor, and Marrity was crouched over her with an opened pocketknife in one hand, pushing her chin up with the other—

"Daph!" he called, stepping quickly back into the living room. He was anxious to wake her before the dream could go any further. "Daph, hey, your movie's over! Up up up! You can sleep with me tonight, since your bed's all smoked. Right right?"

She was sitting up, blinking. "Okay," she said, apparently mystified by his liveliness. The dream was clearly forgotten.

"And I don't have time to correct those papers tonight," he went on, "so I'm going to call in sick tomorrow. We can have lunch at Alfredo's."

"Okay. Did you clean up my bedroom?"

"Yes. Come on, up."

"How does it look?"

"Halbfooshin'." It was a family word that meant *pretty bad, but not near as bad as a little while ago.*

She smiled. "Tomorrow we can flip the mattress and put the bed different?"

"Right. You've been east-west—we'll put you north-south for a while. The cats will still land on you when they come in the window."

She nodded contentedly and followed him down the hall.

Viewed by the other drivers on the westbound 10 freeway this evening, the bus generally looked black—its bright blue showed up only when it sped past under one of the high-arching streetlights—and a driver passing it had to squint to make out the word HELIX along its side.

The windows along the side of the bus were gleamingly dark in the back, but the two or three right behind the driver's seat glowed yellow, and a driver passing the bus in the fast lane was able to glimpse a white-haired man sitting as if at a table.

In the lounge area behind the bus's driver, Denis Rascasse sat back in one of the two captain's chairs and with his open hand rolled his Bic pen across the flat newspaper in front of him.

"Lieserl Marity came out of hiding in order to die," he said formally, as if he were dictating a newspaper photo caption.

"In effect," agreed Paul Golze. He sighed and audibly shifted his bulk in the other captain's chair, probably passing from one ear to the other the telephone that was connected to the modified CCS scrambler. "A Moira Bradley called the hospital at twelve forty-five—she's one of the next of kin. And at six-ten a cop from San Diego called too, a detective, asking about Lisa Marrity. Nobody else, no press."

By the interior lights glowing over the seats and fold-out tables at the front of the bus, Rascasse was working on the *Los Angeles Times* crossword puzzle. Without looking up, he said, "I think we should get that cop." His French accent made the last word into something like *coop* or *cope*.

The Vespers radar dish at Pyramid Peak near the Nevada border covertly monitored all telephone communications that the NSA bounced off the moon, and *swastika* and *Marity* were two of the hundred high-specificity words the Vespers computer was programmed to flag. Tonight these two had occurred in the same conversation, and one of the technicians at the compound outside Amboy, all of whom had been on full alert since shortly after noon, had telephoned the New Jersey headquarters as soon as the correlation was noted and transcribed, and the New Jersey people had called Rascasse.

Paul Golze spoke into the telephone: "Read me the entire conversation, slowly." He began scribbling on a yellow legal pad.

Stretched out on a couch by the dark galley in the back of the bus, Charlotte Sinclair paid wary attention to the two men at the tables ten rows forward.

Charlotte had lost both eyes in an accident, but she could see through the eyes of anyone near her.

She was tensely amused whenever one of the two men looked at the other; they were such opposites, physically—Rascasse tall and straight with close-cropped white hair, Golze slouchy and fat and bearded, and always pushing his stringy black hair away from his glasses.

Charlotte wondered if she would be able to sleep.

She had lit a cigarette to kill the spicy smell of the thing they called the Baphomet head, but the smoke irritated her eyelids, and she crushed it out in the armrest ashtray.

Instead she reached under the seat and lifted out of her bag the bottle of Wild Turkey bourbon, still reassuringly heavy, and twisted out the cork cap. A mouthful of the warm liquor dispelled the incense-and-myrrh smell perfectly, so she had another to work on dispelling the memory of the thing as well, and then corked the bottle and tucked it beside her under her coat.

It had been three years now since Rascasse had picked her up in a poker club in Los Angeles and she had begun working for the Vespers, but she still didn't know much about the organization or its history.

The thing they were looking for now was apparently invented in 1928, but the Vespers had supposedly been pursuing it under other forms for centuries. Before the advances in physics during the twentieth century, it had been categorized as magic—but so had hypnotism, and transmutation of elements, and ESP.

Rascasse had told her once that the Vespers were a secret survival of the true Albigenses, the twelfth-century natural philosophers of Languedoc whose discoveries in the areas of time and so-called reincarnation had so alarmed the Catholic Church that Pope Innocent III had ordered the entire group to be wiped out. "The pope knew that we had rediscovered the real Holy Grail," Rascasse had said, nodding toward the chalice-shaped copper handles on the black wood cabinet behind the driver's seat. "We lost it during the Church's Albigensian Crusade, when Arnold of Citeaux destroyed all of our possessions at Carcassonne." When Charlotte had dutifully made some derogatory remark about the

Catholic Church, Rascasse had shrugged. "Einstein suppressed it too, after rediscovering it in 1928."

Another time Rascasse had told her that in the 1920s the Vespers—called the Ahnenerbe then—had worked with Adolf Hitler, and had even provided him with the swastika as an emblem; though Rascasse had added that the group's core had never been interested in the screwy Nazi racial philosophies, but had only hoped to use Hitler's government to fund their researches. The association had apparently not worked out, and long before the Ahnenerbe had been incorporated into the SS, the core members had stolen the archives and left Germany and taken on, or possibly reassumed, the name Vespers. Golze said *Vespers* was a corruption of *Wespen,* the German word for wasps, though Charlotte liked to think it referred to the French term for evening prayers. Rascasse himself was French, and probably old enough to have been active during the war, but she had never been able to figure out when he had joined the Vespers.

Their researches had to do with the nature of time, and her payment for working with them was going to be derived from that.

But "researches" probably wasn't the right word, except in a historical-detective sense—they weren't hoping to discover how to manipulate time, but to rediscover work that had already been done toward that, work that had subsequently been lost or hidden or suppressed.

In these three years Charlotte had seen them pursue a number of leads—clues that took them to private European libraries, and odd old temples in India and Nepal, and remote ruins in Middle Eastern deserts—all of which had proved to be dead ends. Rumored scrolls or inscriptions were gone or had been misleadingly described, alchemical procedures proved to be too obscure to follow or did nothing, and disembodied Masters turned out to be disembodied imbeciles, if not complete fabrications.

It had been Charlotte herself who had obtained the one solid lead for them: She had got access to a secret archive in New Jersey, and had stolen several files of papers that contained information about a woman who had been living under a false name in Southern California as recently as 1955, a woman who had at one time had possession of some sort of potent artifact. Charlotte hadn't been told all the details, but it had been this discovery that had led Rascasse and his team here to Los Angeles to work with the California branch of the Vespers.

A mouthful of bourbon heated her throat now as she banished the memory of what she had done to get access to that archive.

Charlotte didn't think Rascasse and Golze had truly believed the old woman's device still existed; certainly they had assumed she must have died years ago. But at noon all the Vespers electronic Ouija boards had shaken into activity, with ghosts anxious to know if they still had identities—this and a careful study of the day's seismological charts convinced Rascasse that the device had been activated and used.

He had immediately got the Vespers remote viewers busy trying to triangulate its location; and after an hour they had narrowed it down to somewhere in the Los Angeles area.

Then the old woman's gadget had reportedly moved east, at about 1:30—the viewers couldn't be precise, since the device had not been activated at the time—and so Rascasse had rounded up Golze and Charlotte and set out in the bus toward Palm Springs.

At one point on that long drive a gong had sounded from the cabinet behind the driver's seat, and the cursor on the electronic Ouija board above the cabinet had been bouncing like the virtual ball on a Pong game, lighting up random letters and numbers. Charlotte had faintly heard the thing in the cabinet moaning.

After a quick, whispered argument with Rascasse, Golze had opened the cabinet doors with evident reluctance.

Charlotte had had to fight down sudden nausea. It seemed to her that the head always smelled worse—like hot rum spiced with "blood and honey and the scrapings of old church bells," as Thurber had once written—when it was agitated. And even though it had no eyes, she always imagined that it was looking at her.

Golze had gingerly lifted the tarry-black head and its wooden base out of the cabinet and shuffled around to the windows with it held out at arm's length, to let the thing, as he said, "scope the traffic," but though the head seemed to quiver with more excitement when he carried it back to the galley and held it up to the back window, none of the vehicles nor anything in the sky had seemed unusual.

Rascasse had curtly told Charlotte to scan the nearby perspectives, but she got nothing more significant than a view of the dashboard of a car or truck, and a rust-flecked white hood. Nothing that looked like opposition.

Charlotte had tried to avoid seeing the awful black head, but at one point while she was using Rascasse's eyes he had looked straight at it.

Polished black skin clung tightly to the eyeless skull, and paisley-shaped panels of silver filigree had been glued or tacked onto the forehead, cheeks, nose and chin, like metal Maori tattoos—probably to cover worm holes, Charlotte thought nervously—and a slack ribbon around its neck swung back and forth underneath the wooden stand. "Charlie Chaplin's hat," Golze and Rascasse called the ribbon. According to Golze it was the liner ribbon from a hat that had once belonged to Chaplin, cut now and fitted with a button and loop.

Charlotte had hastily switched to the driver's point of view.

Golze had eventually put the head back in its cabinet and closed the doors, wiping his hands afterward. Only then had Charlotte taken a deep breath.

At 4:10 P.M., though, the head had begun moaning again behind its closed doors, and again the electronic Ouija board had rapidly indicated meaningless numbers and letters; but, luckily before they could open the cabinet again, Rascasse had got a frantic call from the Amboy compound, reporting that the old woman's gadget had disappeared—dropped right out of the perceptions of all the remote viewers.

Rascasse had immediately made another call to the seismology lab at Cal Tech, but there had been no earthquakes within the last half hour. Apparently the gadget had been briefly activated again—too briefly to hope to triangulate it—but had disappeared without having been used.

They were headed back to the L.A. office now, and Charlotte had long since calmed her nerves with the bourbon. Rascasse would surely get the device soon, whatever it was, and there was nothing she could do to help right now.

She knew that she could look at the highway ahead, and see the lights of windows in the darkness—distant kitchens and bedrooms and living rooms—but she didn't exert herself to look. Right now she didn't want that *heimweh,* that homesick longing for strangers' lives. She was too distressingly close now to getting a life for herself.

Golze had said he could never sleep on the bus, but usually Charlotte could—the noise and the rocking took Charlotte back to her childhood.

From the age of eight until the age of nineteen, when she had been honorably discharged because of disability, Charlotte Sinclair had been one of several children working for the United States Air Force in a remote string of Minuteman ICBM missile silos in the Mojave Desert south of Panamint Springs. She and the other children had spent most of their days and nights in the underground Launch Control Centers, each of which was a compact three-story house suspended inside a concrete sphere on "shock isolators," four huge compressed-air shock absorbers, and the floor had constantly tilted one way and then the other as the Boeing air compressors tried to compensate for pressure loss in one or another of the shock isolators. Sometimes the floor would stay tilted for hours before the compressor came on, and she and the crew would get used to it—and then it was always disorienting to notice that the stationary blast door appeared to be rotated to one side or the other.

Golze had hung up the telephone in the slot in its carrying case and was reading the notes he had made on the legal pad. "Her next of kin are the Moira Bradley who called the hospital, and one Frank Marrity, spelled with two *r*s. Pasadena and San Bernardino area codes. We could visit Marrity in San Bernardino tonight. He's east, and the thing moved east."

"We won't call on him," said Rascasse, "especialy not at night. Don't want to scare anybody, we don't. We will call Marrity tomorrow, offer to buy it, if he's got it. Fifty thousand dollars should be . . . effective. And in case there's a *hitch,* it should be Charlotte that does the visiting."

In the darkness at the back of the bus, Charlotte nodded. Visiting I can do, she thought; and I'm good at looking. I don't mind if you ask me to do those things.

Back in the early '60s, someone in Army Intelligence at Fort Meade had been worried that Soviet psychics might identify American missile silos, and so he had designed this secret cluster of silos to confuse any such remote viewers. The tar-and-gravel runway was concealed behind a row of gaudy carnival tents and booths and rides, and the gray walls of the underground Launch Control Centers were all hung with pictures of Bozo the Clown and Engineer Bill and Gumby, and the Launch Control consoles were painted in such garish stripes and circles that the functional lights and buttons could hardly be distinguished; and the commander's launch key had a little clown's head epoxied to the top of it. Charlotte and the other children had been required to play with Tinkertoys and Lincoln Logs in the LCCs, and to accompany maintenance men into the tunnels and silos, which had been decorated with enormous Dr. Seuss murals. Any Soviet psychic who managed to view the missile launch site would, it was hoped, assume that he was seeing some sort of amusement park or progressive elementary school instead, and would write off the session as a miss.

Charlotte had been the queen of the Silo Rascals, since she had been able to sense the intrusion when a distant psychic was using her eyes to look out through; and it had happened two or three times every year. At those moments she was trained to begin singing "Bye Bye Blackbird" as loudly as she could, at which signal all the air force personnel would drop their official work and begin dancing or putting on hand puppets or blowing through cheap tin trumpets. There had been times—when a favorite officer was being yelled at, or when she had been assigned to accompany the Corrosion Control crew below Level 7 at dawn in the middle of winter, or even when she had simply been bored—when she had begun singing the song without having sensed any outside monitoring. Even at the time she had been sure that the crew commanders sometimes suspected her of raising a false alarm, but they had apparently been under strict orders not to question her alerts.

Eventually she had become able to fix on a remote viewer who was looking through her eyes, and follow the link back, and get a glimpse of *his* surroundings—generally just some featureless dark room, though on a couple of occasions she had found herself staring at the dashboard of a moving car.

She had never mentioned this emergent homing ability to her control officers at Fort Meade, though, because even as a child she had known that they would immediately reassign her to a site that was reliably watched by foreign psychics, just so that she could spy on the psychics. She didn't want to leave the secret underground kingdom of the Silo Rascals.

The Launch Control Centers were her home, along with the stairs and corridors between the entrapment doors, and the two-hundred-foot cableway with its infinity of hiding places between the support girders, and the vast silo itself, ten stories deep with the shiny bulk of the Minuteman missile filling the infinite volume.

An exploding battery in the charger bay had blinded her in 1978, when she was nineteen.

In the nightmare months that followed—after the hospitals and the therapy, and after her extensive debriefing and eventual honorable discharge—she had discovered two things that had made her blindness and exile bearable. She learned that she could see through the eyes of anyone who was within about a hundred feet of her—the distance varied a bit, depending on the seasons—and she discovered alcohol.

Golze got up from his table now and descended the tight stairs to the tiny restroom just behind the front door of the bus; idly Charlotte monitored him, and she smiled at the way he was careful to do his business at the urinal by touch alone, staring up at the close plastic ceiling. He wasn't what anyone would call a gentleman, so it must be shyness. Men who knew about her ability always, when they went into a restroom, made a point of either modestly looking up or arrogantly looking down. Rascasse always looked down, but with Rascasse somehow it always seemed to be in surprise.

She shifted her attention to Rascasse, and she saw that he was staring at one of the crossword-puzzle clues: a four-letter word that meant "underground fence."

"Haha," she called toward the front of the rocking bus.

"What's funny back there?" he called.

"An underground fence is called a haha," she told him.

In the newspaper margin he wrote, *Y dont U finish the bottle and sleep. Bzy day morrow.*

"Haha," she said, and then set about taking his advice.

Six

When Frank Marrity walked down the gravel driveway at eight the next morning to pick up the *Los Angeles Times,* the green Rambler was parked just outside the chain-link gate.

He had awakened before Daphne, and slid out from under the covers without disturbing her, and in his pajamas and slippers he padded out to the kitchen to call the college and then make breakfast.

After he'd explained to the English Department secretary that he would not be coming in today, he boiled milk on the stove and poured it into two bowls of Quaker instant oatmeal, then stirred into each bowl a tablespoon of Cool Whip and a teaspoon of Southern Comfort liqueur. Daphne appeared just as he was carrying the bowls to the kitchen table.

"I looked in my room just now," she said as she pulled out a chair.

"We'll fix it up today," Marrity told her.

"Crazy day, yesterday," was all she said before digging into the oatmeal.

"The craziest," he agreed.

He was glad that she didn't comment on being served what was usually her "sick girl" breakfast instead of the routine cereal or bacon and eggs; but after the choking she'd experienced last night at dinner, he wanted to put off giving her anything that required chewing.

The telephone rang, and he decided to stay where he was and let the answering machine get it.

"You're reached the Marritys," said his voice from the machine, *"and we're not able to come to the phone right now, but leave a message and your number and we'll get back to you."* The beep followed, and two seconds of silence, and then the dial tone, which soon shut off.

He glanced at Daphne. She was frowning, but for a moment it seemed to him that it was his voice coming from the other side of the room, and not the hang-up, that had disturbed her.

A black-and-white cat jumped up onto the table, sliding on yesterday's newspaper, and Daphne nudged him off and then absently stared at the headlines. "Yesterday was the tenth anniversary of Elvis's death," she said. "I wonder if ghosts come back on their anniversaries."

"I'll get dressed and go fetch today's paper," Marrity said, pushing his chair back.

T he sun in the east was throwing shadows across the gravel driveway from the lemon and peach trees, and the sky to the south was a deep, cold blue. Tiny white flakes of ash glittered as they fell silently through the sunlit air, for the northern sky over the mountains was a white haze of smoke.

The newspaper was lying on the gravel just inside the gate, but Marrity had seen the green Rambler now and he slowly walked past the newspaper and unhooked the padlock from the chain, not taking his eyes off the car. Behind the wheel, staring back at him, was the same gray-haired man who had driven the car into their driveway yesterday afternoon, and had then reversed out and driven away.

Marrity pulled the gate back enough to step through, and then walked out into the street to approach the driver's-side window. It was rolled down.

Before Marrity could speak, the man in the car said, "She called me yesterday, early. She said I could have her car."

Marrity stared at the lined, slack face under the combed gray hair, wondering where he'd seen it before. "So you broke her kitchen window to get the keys," he said. "Who are you? Why are you here?"

"I'm here because—" The old man appeared to try the door handle, and then give up on getting out. He leaned back in the seat. "There's no easy way to say this." His voice was rough, as if from decades of cigarettes and liquor. "I'm Derek Marrity."

Marrity was dizzy, and his stomach was suddenly cold. He took a step back to catch his balance, but he made his voice steady when he said, "You're my father?"

"That's right. Your grandmother—my mother—listen, youngster—she said I should—she said it would be best for everybody if I just went away. Back in '55. Now that she's dead she can't blackmail me anymore. I could have killed her, and stayed—maybe I should have—but how can you kill your own mother?"

"You killed *my* mother."

The man exhaled through clenched teeth. "Goddammit, boy, I didn't know that. I sent money to your grandmother, to give to Veronica. And letters too. I guess your grandmother just kept the money and trashed the letters. Typical."

"You left your children with her."

"Would you rather have been in a foster home? Was Grammar a bad parent to you? Remember, she didn't know Veronica would *kill* herself."

Marrity wanted to tell the old man about Veronica's drunken, hopeless last days, before the car-crash suicide— and he wanted to hear, very much wanted to hear the old man's replies— but he didn't want to do it out here on the street.

"Who was Grammar's father?" he asked instead. "What was Prospero's actual name?"

The gray-haired man shook his head. "No concern of yours, boy. Prosper O. will do fine."

"Albert Einstein," said Daphne from the shadows behind the half-opened gate.

"*Daph*—" snapped Marrity in alarm, stepping toward her, "you shouldn't be out here. This man is—"

"Your father," Daphne finished for him. She was still in her pajamas, and barefoot on the gravel. "That *was* Albert Einstein you were picturing, wasn't it, Dad? The crazy-haired old scientist?" She stepped through the gate into the chilly, slanting sunlight and walked up to Marrity and took hold of his hand. "Why was Grammar blackmailing you?" she asked the man in the car.

"Daph," said Marrity desperately, "we don't know who this man is. Go wait for me inside."

"Okay. But he must be your father—he looks just like you." Daphne let go of his hand and scampered back through the gate and up the driveway.

Marrity couldn't help glancing at the man in the car, though the glance must clearly have shown that he had found Daphne's statement unflattering.

But his father's eyes were tightly shut, and he was frowning, as if with sudden indigestion.

"Are you okay?" asked Marrity.

The old man opened his eyes and blotted them on the sleeve of his nylon jacket. He took a deep breath and let it out. "I hope to be, I hope to be. What did she say?"

"She said you look like me."

"The Marrity jaw," said his father, smiling now, a little sourly. "And I think there's something about the eyes and the bridge of the nose. Look at some photos of Einstein, back when he was in his thirties."

"I thought—we were Irish."

"My father might have been, whoever was Ferdinand to my mother's Miranda. His name wasn't Marrity, though—that was your grandmother's maiden name, with an extra

R added to make it look Irish. It's Serbian, originally, by way of Hungary. I guess fathers tend to be delinquent, in our family. Though I had—I really believe I had—no choice." He opened his mouth and closed it, then said, "But I'm sorry—sorrier than I can say."

Marrity gave him a brittle smile. "Maybe you are. No help at this point, of course."

After a pause, his father shook his head. "I suppose it isn't. Can I come in?"

Marrity blinked at him. "Of course not! We can meet sometime—give me your phone number—in fact, when you leave here, you, you'd better walk—I've got the license number of that car now, and I'm going to report it as stolen."

"Can I come in?" the man repeated. "My mother—your grandmother—died yesterday."

Marrity frowned. He wouldn't be able to ask his father about unpleasant things around Daphne; but maybe they shouldn't start with the unpleasant things anyway. And if he sent the old man away right now, he might never reappear, and that would be intolerable, again.

Marrity sighed heavily. "Of course you can come in. But—you have to promise to leave with no scene as soon as I say it's time for you to go."

"Fair enough."

Bert Malk was leaning in under the open hood of a rented Ford LTD on the opposite side of the street half a block away, and he didn't dare straighten up to peer after Marrity and the old man who had been sitting in the station wagon, though he noticed that the old man limped; but it was a fair guess that they were going into Marrity's house. Malk had seen the little girl come out in pajamas and say something to them before going back in.

Malk had laid an open toolbox on the radiator and was pretending to assemble or disassemble the clamp on the positive battery terminal. He had been standing here for ten minutes now, alternately bending over the engine and sitting behind the wheel as if trying to start the car, and he would have to leave soon.

This neighborhood was in an unincorporated area outside the San Bernardino city limits, and there were no streetlights or sidewalks; Malk was standing on a patch of grass flattened and rutted by tires. The house he was parked in front of had plywood bolted over the windows and doors, and a brown steel Dumpster nearly as big as the house sat in the driveway.

At the east end of the street a blue BMW appeared, and drove slowly toward him. He bent over the battery, as if looking very closely for any corrosion on the terminal.

The BMW passed him, and the brake lights flashed briefly as it passed the Marrity house, and then it had gone on past, its rear window a featureless block of sun glare. It paused at the stop sign at the west end of the block, then made a right turn.

Malk's face was cold, and he began tossing the tools back into the box. Get out now, he thought.

The woman sitting beside the driver had also been in the passenger seat of a Honda Prelude that had passed him here four minutes ago, also driving slowly east to west. He made mental notes: shoulder-length dark hair, slim, thirty-ish, with sunglasses; blue short-sleeve blouse. A real *pzaza,* he thought, a dark-haired beauty. In both passes she had appeared to be looking straight ahead, not toward the Marrity house, and she might just be a local resident; but she had passed the house twice in different cars, and the cars had had different drivers.

He snapped the toolbox closed and unhooked the support rod from the hood. It was time to get out of here.

I remember the fires," Marrity's father said, looking over the top of the house at the white northern sky.

" 'Tenderly the haughty day fills his blue urn with fire,' " said Marrity, randomly quoting Emerson as he strode up the driveway. He was impatient to get inside now, and it irked him to wait for his limping father to catch up.

As Marrity pushed open the kitchen door, his father nodded toward the blistered VCR that still lay on the grass.

"That's an unfamiliar sight," he said.

"The machine burned up," said Marrity shortly. "Bad wiring, I guess." He pulled the door closed behind him when the old man had limped unsteadily inside. "Daph! We've—got company."

When Daphne appeared in the kitchen doorway she had changed out of her pajamas and was wearing green corduroy overalls over a white T-shirt; clearly she had expected her father to ask the old man in. "I was just explaining," Marrity went on, "that a short circuit in the VCR burned it up yesterday. Did you shut your bedroom door to keep the cats out?"

She nodded, and then told her grandfather, "Burnt up the movie in it too."

"Really?" said Marrity's father. "What movie?" He unzipped his olive green Members Only jacket, and Marrity noticed that it was still stiffly pressed, and the long-sleeved red-and-white-striped shirt under it was stiff too, and creased where it had been folded. Marrity wondered if Grammar had had any cash lying around at her house.

"*Pee-wee's Big Adventure*," Daphne said.

Marrity's father seemed to have some trouble draping his jacket over the back of a chair. "I—" he began hoarsely; then he cleared his throat and went on, "I hope it wasn't a rental."

"No, one of ours," Marrity told him. "Can I get you some coffee?"

"Coffee," echoed his father absently. "Coffee." He blinked at his son. "No, I've been up for so long it's near lunchtime for me. A glass of that Southern Comfort on the rocks would be bracing."

It occurred to Marrity that the man's odd smell was a mix of Juicy Fruit gum, cigarette smoke, and vodka. Vodka before eight, he thought, and Southern Comfort as a chaser? If a cop pulls him over and gives him a 502 when he drives away from here, am I liable, for having served him the alcohol? Marrity discovered that he didn't care, and poured a generous slug of the amber liquor into a water glass.

"Ice in the freezer," he said as he handed it to him. "Help yourself."

"Can I have a bracing drink?" asked Daphne.

"No!" said the old man.

Marrity smiled at her. "No. Sit down and be seen and not heard."

"Aye aye."

Daphne had sat down at the table, so Marrity did too; and as soon as his father had fumbled a couple of ice cubes into his glass, he settled into the chair with his new jacket on it.

The old man was leaning back and looking around the kitchen, and Marrity found himself resenting his father looking at the things he and Lucy and Daphne had assembled over the years—the Kliban coffee cups and dish towels, the cat calendar on the pantry door, the collection of cartoony salt-and-pepper shakers on the high shelves. But maybe the old man was envious of a settled home—certainly he seemed rootless.

Finally the old man looked at Marrity. "It's a very bad idea to give children alcohol," he said earnestly.

"How did you hurt your leg?" Daphne asked him.

"A car ran over me," the old man said. He seemed angry at Daphne for asking.

"Grammar called you yesterday?" Marrity said. "How did you know she's dead?"

The old man shifted his gaze to Marrity. "I got worried and called the police in Shasta," he said. "When she called me from there, she was talking as if she thought she would die soon, giving me the car and all. Even calling me."

Marrity realized that he didn't believe him. Maybe, he thought, he *did* kill her! Well no, he couldn't have got back from Shasta in time to break Grammar's window and take her keys.

"You asked," the old man said, apparently to Daphne, though he was staring into his drink, "why she was blackmailing me. A man died, and some money was *absconded* with, and she knew of evidence that would *implicate* me in it. She might even have believed I was the guilty party. But she didn't blackmail me for money, she only wanted me to go away and not contact any of you again. I'd have gone to prison, almost certainly—it was a very good circumstantial case. I even wondered if *she*—" He stopped, and groped clumsily for his glass; after closing his hand on empty air a few inches short of it, he managed to get hold of it and take a deep sip of the liquor.

Marrity could see that Daphne was anxious to ask a question, so he asked it for her. "Why did she want you to go away, to disappear?"

"It's not—really a subject for a little girl to hear," said Marrity's father haltingly. "Uh—I married your mother, to some extent, just a little bit, to prove to myself that I—could love a woman. In the 1950s there was no other option, really. It—wasn't entirely a success." The old man's face was red, and he gulped some more of the liquor and exhaled through his teeth in a near whistle.

"So was your grandfather Albert Einstein?" asked Marrity quickly. "My great-grandfather?"

"You seem to know it already," old Marrity said cautiously.

"Why is it such a secret? I never got a hint of it till yesterday. The Britannica doesn't mention Grammar, and she never said a word about it."

"Grammar was born in 1902, before Einstein and her mother were married. Uh—too much of a scandal. He wanted to be a professor, and this was really still nineteenth-century Switzerland. After a while the lie, and the little girl's new identity, were too established to change."

"Huh. Why did you visit him in '55, right after leaving my mother?"

His father stared at him with no expression. "I don't think you have the story entirely correct," he said. "We can go over all the old history later."

"Were you going to blackmail Einstein?" asked Marrity. "About his daughter?"

"Can I smoke?" his father asked, reaching behind him to fumble in the pocket of his jacket.

"Sure. Daph, would you get an ashtray?" Daphne nodded and pushed her chair back.

"You don't know me at all," the old man went on, "so I can't take any offense at that remark. But no, I didn't try to blackmail him. My mother may have."

"To get what?" asked Marrity.

Daphne laid a glass ashtray on the table at the man's elbow, but he didn't look at her as he tugged out of his pocket an opened pack of Marlboros and shook one out. "The same thing she extorted from me, maybe. Absence. He never came back to California after '33." He looked at Daphne at last. "I bet your movie wasn't wrecked. Did you pull it out?"

"It sure smoked," she said cautiously. "And it's been outside all night. Snails probably ate it."

The old man tore off two matches and lost hold of both of them, then with evident care tore off another and managed to strike it alight and hold it to the end of his cigarette. "I've got," he said as he puffed on the cigarette and blew out the match, "a friend who restores all kinds of electromagnetic hardware—computer disks, cassette tapes. You give it to me and I'll show it to him."

"No," said Marrity. "I'm going to—fix it myself."

"Right," said Daphne.

His father stared at Marrity. "You know about that stuff, do you?"

"For all you know, that's what I do for a living," Marrity said.

The old man frowned in evident puzzlement. "I suppose that's true. I've got some errands to run, but I'd like to take the two of you to lunch." He dropped the burnt match into the ashtray. "On me!" he added.

"We've got a lunch date already," Marrity said.

His father nodded, as if he'd expected the answer. "Uh— tomorrow?"

"I'll be working," said Marrity. Reluctantly he added, "Maybe dinner tomorrow?"

"Dinner's good. Seven?"

"'Kay. Have you got a phone number?"

"Not, not right at the moment. You're listed—I'll call you at six, to make sure we're still on. Let's make it Italian—so don't have Italian today, okay?"

"Okay."

"Promise?" The old man seemed anxious.

"Yes, I promise." Marrity stood up. "Well, it's been—distressing." He didn't hold out his hand.

"Bound to be, just at first," the old man said, pushing back his chair. "Probably we'll get more friendly. I truly hope so. Daphne, a—pleasure to meet you. I wish you well."

"Thanks," said Daphne, staring down at the table.

"No Italian today, remember," said Marrity's father as he got laboriously to his feet. "Tomorrow night we'll do it all—lasagna, pizza—antipasto—"

As Marrity and his father walked out the kitchen door, Marrity stood between the old man and the wrecked VCR, and when his father had hobbled away down the driveway, he bent down to pick it up.

"Daph," he called into the kitchen, "would you get the gas can for the lawn mower? I'm going to just plain inciner-ate this thing."

And, he thought, I believe I'll keep those letters of Gram-mar's with me, in my briefcase.

The old guy's walking out," said Golze as he drove by the Marrity house for the fourth time, in a white Toyota now; "limping, to be more precise. The guy who was fixing his car on the other side of the street is gone."

"Our man didn't answer his phone," said Rascasse's voice from the radio clipped to the dashboard. "He let the ma-chine take it. Charlotte, did you get anything? You never give me your money," he added.

Golze reached out and clicked the radio's channel selector to the next frequency in their agreed-on sequence—they were using titles from the Beatles' *Abbey Road* album as cues.

"That house is set awful far back from the road," Charlotte said. "I was able to see through a child, a bit—must have been the little girl. Two men at a kitchen table, one clearly her father: thirty-five, dark haired, six foot, thin; the other was this old guy who just got into the—oh! darling." After Golze had switched channels again, she went on, "just got into the green Rambler. They're clearly related, the two men, strong resemblance. Old guy was smoking a cigarette, and drinking whiskey or brandy, brown stuff. That's all."

Golze made a slow right turn, eyeing his mirrors. The yards around here all seemed to be scattered with wrecked trucks or live goats.

"No help with the floor plan?" asked Rascasse's voice from the radio.

"Not much. The kitchen is about ten by twenty, narrow ends at north and south; doorway at the north end of the east wall, a step up to a landing, I don't know what's past it."

"Okay. You didn't see—mean Mr. Mustard." Again Golze reached out and clicked the channel selector. "—see a videocassette, or some round, flat film cans—"

"No, but aside from the kitchen, all I saw was the bottom half of the driveway." So, thought Charlotte, the dead old woman's magical device was a *movie*?

She suppressed a nervous smile—she'd been imagining something more like a candelabra made from a mummified hand, at least.

"Charlotte," said the voice from the speaker, "I may want you to approach the girl's father, Maxwell's silver hammer." Click. "—assuming we get a chance to get into his house and work up a profile. Preliminary, just establish a relationship, no questions yet. Come together." Click. "Very accidental meeting, you know, the sort of thing that even in retrospect he won't think could have been planned. Be charming. Right?"

"Right," she said.

Since first hearing of him last night, the Vespers had found out that Francis Thomas Marrity was a widower with one twelve-year-old daughter, Daphne; his wife, Lucy, had died in '85 of pancreatic cancer, when the child was ten. Marrity was a college literature professor, with a thirty-thousand-dollar mortgage, life insurance through the Automobile Club, and no criminal record at all.

She wasn't going to mention it to Rascasse or Golze, but while she'd briefly been looking through the little girl's eyes, she had momentarily got a flicker image of the little girl herself, though there hadn't been a mirror nearby—it was as if the girl had for an instant been sharing the perspective of one of the men on the other side of the table. She was a pretty little thing, apparently, with big eyes and brown bangs.

Charlotte had decided way back in her missile-silo days that there was no gain in mentioning details that might complicate settled arrangements. Do what's best for little Charlotte, she thought.

Through Golze's eyes now Charlotte saw a woman pause from hanging T-shirts and jeans in a fenced-in yard to glance at the white Toyota, and for a moment Charlotte shifted her viewpoint to the woman; and she eyed her own silhouette critically as the car drove past. Still cheerleader pretty, as always, she thought. And ideally I won't need it much longer.

Opus is always looking for his mother," said Daphne, sitting at the kitchen table. She was belatedly reading the comics, and clearly had got to the *Bloom County* strip. "I suppose she's a penguin too."

"I suppose," agreed Marrity, standing at the sink.

Daphne pushed the newspaper away. "It must be weird," she said, "to suddenly have a real father, sitting in your kitchen smoking a cigarette."

"It is," said Marrity. He was washing his hands with dishwashing detergent. "He's got a good explanation, hasn't he?"

He dried his hands on a paper towel and smelled them—the gasoline reek was hardly detectable. My life stinks of gasoline lately, he thought.

"Did he mean he's gay?" asked Daphne.

"Um, yes."

"He's not gay," she said.

Marrity walked back to the table and sat down. "How do you know?" he asked her.

"Paul and Webster, at your college, they're gay. And some of Uncle Bennett's friends. They're—it's not like they're always joking, or always sad, but—they're not like your father."

"Well, that's a small sample, and this father guy wasn't anything like relaxed."

She shrugged, clearly not conceding the point. "We can't go to Alfredo's?"

"Sure we can."

"You promised not to."

"Actually I'd—" Marrity paused, then laughed uncertainly. "I think I'd like a chance to break a promise to him. He deserves a lot of broken promises." He shrugged. "We can tell him we had Mexican."

"Okay. And can we fix up my room this morning? Can I paint the walls?"

"Sure, if you don't mind that Swiss Coffee color we used in the hall. In fact, I should paint over the smoke marks on the hall ceiling." Marrity picked up the glass his father had used and swirled the diminished ice cubes in it. "What do you think of him? Short acquaintance, I admit."

"He wants something. From us."

"That video?"

"I think so! But even with it gone, something." She pushed her cold bowl of oatmeal away. "What do *you* think of him?"

"I'm embarrassed by him. I feel sorry for him. I think he's an alcoholic. And just telling me *why* he abandoned Moira and me and our mother doesn't change the math." He shook his head. "I don't think he'll . . . ever be more than a stranger to me."

Tears stood in Daphne's eyes. "This is worse than before, isn't it?"

Marrity took a breath to answer, paused, and then let it out. "I guess it is," he said finally. "No more hundreds of possibilities, just this one old drunk cranking around in Grammar's car."

Seven

As Marrity held open the tinted glass door of Alfredo's for her, Daphne asked him, "What are you going to have *besides* beer?"

The air was cooler inside the dark restaurant, and smelled of fennel and garlic.

"Two for lunch, please, smoking or nonsmoking doesn't matter," Marrity said to the hostess behind the cash-register counter. They had missed the lunch crowd because of having painted Daphne's room and the hall ceiling, and he could see several empty booths with fresh silverware and red-and-white paper place mats on the tables.

"It's a hot day," he told Daphne as they followed a waitress to a booth against the west wall. "I'm thinking about a beer because that's what I want first. I don't know why sausage and bell peppers looks so good to you on a day like this."

"I haven't absolutely made up my mind."

"It's all I see in there," he said as he sat down across from her. "The young lady will have a—" Marrity said to the waitress, "—don't tell me—a lemon in it, that's an iced tea. And could I have a Coors, please."

"You were picturing two," Daphne said after the waitress had walked away.

"And I'm going to have two," Marrity told her, "but not both at once."

"You should get the chicken and broccoli. You don't eat enough vegetables."

"Onions and potatoes are vegetables."

"They're not green. You don't eat right. Your guts are probably all creepy looking."

"You've got paint in your hair."

She looked dismayed, and glanced back toward the cashier's counter as she patted her bangs. "A lot?"

"No. Here." He reached across the table, pinched a strand of her brown hair and drew the fleck of paint down to the ends, where it slid off. "Only somebody sitting right across from you under this light could have seen it."

"Thank God for that."

C harlotte Sinclair strolled from the back of the parking lot toward the entrance to Alfredo's, trailing the fingers of her right hand along the brick wall for balance. She had changed into black jeans and a burgundy short-sleeved blouse, and her dark brown hair was now pulled back in a ponytail, though her sunglasses were the same. She carried a purse in her left hand, letting the strap swing free.

She lingered at one section of the wall for a full thirty seconds, then moved on, rounding the building's northwest corner and shuffling carefully right past the entry door. By the coolness of the air, she knew she was in shadow now. At the northeast corner she turned right again and made her way along the restaurant's eastern wall, again trailing her fingers along the brick surface.

She turned around and walked back to the curb, and when she heard a car squeak to a stop in front of her, she looked out of the driver's eyes and saw herself standing in the sunlight beyond the open passenger-side window; with that view to guide her, she was able to put her hand on the door handle and lean down to speak to the driver.

"Mirror," she said.

"I always forget." The man bent sideways to look at himself in the rearview mirror, and Charlotte recognized the lean, white-mustached face of Roger Canino, the Vespers security chief at the Amboy compound. Charlotte opened the door and got into the passenger seat.

"How's my favorite girl?"

"Fine, Roger."

As the car began moving, she groped in her purse—no sense in asking old Canino to look in there for her—and by touch found the radio and switched it on. In a moment she heard Rascasse's voice say, "Prime here." He pronounced it *preem*.

Leaning down over the purse and pressing the send button, she said, "Seconde here. The old guy from the green Rambler, octopus's garden"—she switched the frequency up one notch—"is sitting way in the back on the east side, by the restrooms; it's the smoking section, there are ashtrays on the tables. He's got a couple of empty beer bottles and the remains of spaghetti in a white sauce in front of him, but he's done eating and it looks cold to me, polythene Pam." Again she clicked the dial. "Our man and his daughter are in a booth against the west wall, toward the front, north, on the other side of the kitchen. They're just ordering now."

"Got it, thanks," came Rascasse's voice.

"Can I be one of the parties?" she said. "I'm hungry." Actually she wanted to monitor Marrity and his daughter from a closer vantage point, without the restaurant wall between her and them; for a moment there, as she had been looking at Daphne through Marrity's eyes, she had found herself seeing Marrity's face, and she remembered the same skipping-across phenomenon happening this morning when she had been monitoring Daphne from the car.

I've never slipped from one viewpoint to another accidentally before today, she thought. Am I losing my grip? Will I start seeing everybody's viewpoint at once?

"No, Charlotte," came the voice from the speaker, "because."

The radio was silent. "That was a cue, sweetie," said Canino without looking away from the traffic.

"What," said Charlotte, " 'Because'? Shit." She switched the frequency dial again.

"—bumper-beeper on his Ford—" Rascasse was saying.

"Again, from the bridge," said Charlotte.

"Oh," came Rascasse's voice. "Okay, You can't go in because you're going to *cute-meet* him later, remember? If we don't find the artifact in his house or truck. We're doing research in the house right now, to prep you for it. And we've got a bumper-beeper on his Ford pickup—if we need you, we should be able to make an opportunity before sundown."

"Right."

"Any clues about who the old fellow *is*? She came in through the bathroom window."

"That one I get," Charlotte muttered, switching the frequency again. "No," she said. "Strong family resemblance with our man, as you've seen. His father, maybe."

"Probably in town for the funeral," said Rascasse. "Obviously he is supposed to meet them in the restaurant."

Charlotte didn't correct him, but it seemed to her that neither Marrity nor the old man expected the other to be there.

W ho *are* these guys?" whispered Bert Malk to himself as he drove past Alfredo's in the opposite direction. He had just seen the dark-haired girl in the sunglasses climb into a car that then sped away with her; she had probably been a lookout—probably another one had stepped up. And she was pretty definitely the same girl he had seen this morning cruising twice past Marrity's house.

Bozzaris would probably already be in the restaurant. Malk had stopped at a 7-Eleven parking lot pay phone to call the relay *sayan,* and had got a message from Lepidopt: *Crew of three entered M's house as soon as father and daughter drove away. You two prevent any kidnap. Daylight.*

"Daylight" meant "highest state of alert."

This was a full-scale operation by somebody.

Malk was aware of the angular shape of the Beretta Model 70S against his hip. It held nine .22 long-rifle rounds—a small caliber, but it was the Mossad standard, and the theory was that it didn't need a silencer since the report of a .22 round, though loud, didn't exactly sound like a gunshot. It was more a loud *snap* than the deafening *pop* of bigger calibers. And the long-rifle .22s were plenty deadly if they were put in the right places.

He steered left onto E Street to check for alternate exits from the parking lot and any back doors of the restaurant.

W hen Malk had finally parked and walked into the restaurant, Bozzaris was already inside, waiting on a vinyl couch by the west-side nonsmoking dining room, and he stood up and jerked his head in that direction.

"Yo, Steve," he said. "Table's waiting."

Any name that began with "S" meant *I haven't had time to do a route, to be sure I'm not being followed.*

Swell, thought Malk as he followed the younger man to a table only a couple of yards away from a booth occupied by a preteen girl and a dark-haired man of about his own age, mid-thirties. That's our quarry, he thought, not letting himself look directly at Frank and Daphne Marrity. He noticed that Frank had lasagna, and Daphne was eating some kind of pasta with sausage and bell peppers on it.

Malk and Bozzaris sat at adjoining sides of the square table, more or less between the Marritys and everyone else. Malk was mentally rehearsing the old training on how to throw himself backward in his chair and shoot under the table.

When he had sat down, he pulled his Chap Stick out of his pocket and nervously twisted off the cap; then, reflecting that it was probably bad manners to use it in a restaurant, he snapped the cap back on. He looked more closely at it.

"Shit," he said absently to Bozzaris, "this isn't Chap Stick—it's . . . 'Nose Soother'! There's a picture of a red nose on it. I've been putting it on my mouth!"

"Oh boy," said Bozzaris. "They test those things in the factory, you know. Guys that test 'em, they can't get any other jobs."

"Shut up," said Malk, shoving the tube back into his pocket.

"Some big old retard had that up his nose." Bozzaris looked at his watch and then toward the door, as if they were expecting a third person, and then he looked around at the tables and booths. "Bailey did say one o'clock, didn't he?"

"That's what the message on my machine said," Malk agreed, looking around himself. Waiting impatiently for an imaginary third person was a good excuse to check out the surrounding people; he memorized the other diners—a man and a woman in the booth south of the Marritys, three older women toward the north end, and three college-looking boys in T-shirts against the inner wall, under a shelf full of pasta boxes and Italian cookie cans. At least one party, he told himself, must be operatives of the other force, whatever it is, and they'll be speculatively noting Bozzaris and me. At least we're talking spontaneously, what with the Nose Soother and all.

"What are you going to have?" Malk asked.

"I don't know. A beer, a sandwich."

Because he was listening for it, Malk could hear Bozzaris suppressing his Israeli accent, pronouncing the *r* at the front of his mouth and flattening the emphases; somehow the cadence of American English wasn't as sociable as the Israeli cadence.

"Me too, I guess," said Malk.

"I'm gonna hit the head first," said Bozzaris, pushing his chair back. "A Budweiser, if the lady comes by."

Malk nodded, and when Bozzaris strode away he took a ball point pen from his pocket and began doodling on the paper place mat so that he could keep his eyes in an unfocused stare that took in the periphery—absently he drew a dog wearing a bowler hat and a snail with a mustache and pince-nez glasses.

"No," Marrity was saying six feet away, "I imagine the funeral will be down here. I guess Bennett and Moira will arrange to have the body flown down from Shasta. I should have called them this morning."

Malk noted that Marrity was apparently not aware of any need for secrecy. As he'd told Bozzaris last night, Marrity didn't seem to know anything about his grandmother's history.

From the corner of his eye, he saw the girl nod.

Bozzaris came back and sat down. "You should go to the head too," he said, very quietly. "Check out an old party sitting in the last booth by the east wall."

Malk nodded, guessing that he meant the old man who had visited the Marritys five hours ago. What the hell did that mean? "Bailey can do it or not," he said in a normal tone, "doesn't matter to us." He pushed back his chair.

"Daph?" said Marrity urgently, and Malk looked over at them.

The girl was holding her throat with one hand, and her face was blank.

"Daph, can you talk?"

She shook her head, her eyes showing alarm now; and Marrity slid out of the booth and stood up, pulling her to her feet. He grabbed her by the shoulders and turned her around, then he crouched and linked his fists over her abdomen from behind.

"Relax, Daph," he said. "Heimlich."

He jerked his fists back and up, ramming the inner one into her stomach just below the ribs; her hands gripped her thighs, but apparently no food was dislodged.

"Hang on," Marrity said hoarsely, "one more time, harder."

Again he drove his fist upward into her abdomen, but again there was no result.

Malk had tensed, and his hands were tingling, but he was sure he couldn't do any better than the girl's father was.

"Somebody call 911," Marrity shouted, and then yanked his fist powerfully into Daphne one more time. His shirt was already dark with sweat.

A gray-haired man in a green Members Only jacket had shuffled in from the other dining room, and now stood by Malk's table, looking on in evident horror; and he was indeed the man who had driven the green Rambler and spoken to Marrity this morning.

Malk looked back at the girl and her father, and gripped the edge of his table. He realized that he was praying.

The couple in the booth behind Marrity had got to their feet, but were only staring at the man holding the girl, and the three old women had all put down their forks and were blinking in evident confusion. Malk's training overrode his horrified fascination, and it occurred to him that this conspicuous emergency would probably wreck any kidnap plans.

Daphne opened her mouth and Malk could see her abdomen tighten as she tried uselessly to expel the blockage.

One of the college boys had a cellular phone out, and the cashier was anxiously looking their way and speaking into a telephone at the counter.

"And another, Daph," said Marrity in a voice that was nearly a sob. This time her knees folded after the forceful upward thrust, and Marrity sat down hard on the linoleum, holding her in his lap now.

He looked up desperately, and clearly noticed the old man in the green jacket. Marrity opened his mouth as if to say something to him, then just closed his eyes and jerked his fists up again. Malk heard the girl's teeth snap shut as the thrust rocked her head back.

Four minutes until brain damage, Malk thought. How quickly can the paramedics get here?

He noted that everyone in the restaurant seemed to have

crowded in the doorway to watch. A distraction not to be wasted, he thought. Choose your moment.

Marrity could only think of how humiliated Daphne must be by this public spectacle. He would not permit himself to imagine that she might die here.

He loosened his cramped hands and reached forward to roll her head back; she was unconscious now, her face white, her lips and half-closed eyelids shadowed with a bluish tint. Of course she was not breathing.

The Heimlich maneuver was not working, would not work; it dawned on him finally that very soon he would be uselessly pummeling a limp corpse. "Dammit, Daphne," he whispered, "why couldn't you *chew*?"

He looked up at his father. The old man was nodding in evident sympathy.

Marrity lifted Daphne's limp body off his lap and laid her face-up on the black-and-red linoleum.

"A sharp knife," he said, holding out his right hand. "Quick!"

The older of the two men who had been at the nearest table flicked open a flat stainless-steel pocketknife and slapped the grip into Marrity's hand.

Marrity's father stepped forward. "No, Frank!" he shouted. "You'll kill her! Somebody stop him!"

The man who had given Marrity the knife stood up and threw an arm across the old man's chest, and one of the college boys from the farther booth gripped his upper arm.

"It's all he can do," the boy said.

"Hold him," said the man who had provided the knife, and then he pushed his way through the crowd in the doorway.

One of the old women in the north-wall booth shouted something in German, and was shushed by her companions; and peripherally Marrity was aware that his father was struggling very hard with the college boys, who were holding him back; but Marrity's attention was fixed on Daphne.

He pushed her chin up and back, then felt her throat. The

larynx muscles were convulsing weakly under his hand, and he felt for the rings of cartilage in her throat.

The younger man from the nearest table had crouched beside him and was holding something in Marrity's field of vision—it was the clear barrel of a Bic pen, with the ink tube pulled out. Marrity nodded, sweat dripping from his face onto Daphne's blouse.

His heart was pounding so hard that he was twitching with it.

Gripping the knife by the blade like a pencil so that only three-quarters of an inch of steel protruded below his thumb, Marrity pushed the point of it into Daphne's throat below the thyroid cartilage, denting the skin and then, as he despairingly pushed harder, puncturing it.

A bloody spray followed the knife blade when he pulled it out, and he snatched the Bic pen barrel from the outstretched hand and pushed it into the makeshift incision.

Air whistled out through the clear plastic tube that now stood up out of Daphne's throat like a dart, and Marrity held the tube in place with his trembling thumb and forefinger.

"Goddammit, stop him!" roared his father.

"Shut up, man," said somebody else. "It's working."

Now air was being sucked into the tube, and a moment later Daphne's legs shifted on the floor and her hands flexed.

The man crouched beside Marrity gave one bark of tense laughter. "You've saved her," he said.

Daphne's eyes fluttered open.

"Don't move, Daph," Marrity said, feeling the smile tugging at his face. "You're fine, just lie still." He sat down more comfortably next to her on the floor.

She managed a slight nod. Her hands floated up toward her throat, but Marrity pushed them back with his free hand. "Don't move, kid, just lie still. Trust me."

She nodded again, and even managed a flickering, uncertain smile, and relaxed. As Marrity watched, the healthy pink color was returning to her face like sunlight filling in shadow.

Marrity glanced at the man beside him; he looked to be in his late twenties, with a dark brush cut, and he needed a shave; he wore a gray linen sport coat with no tie.

"Th-thank you," Marrity said. His hands were trembling and his ears were ringing. He leaned back carefully against a table leg.

"My pleasure," the young man said. "Keep the pen."

Marrity nodded, then tried with one hand to wipe the blade of the knife off on his shirt. The man gently took the knife from Marrity's shaking hands.

"Give that back to your friend," Marrity said.

"Right."

Marrity looked up at his father, who was still gaping down at Daphne in dismay. "She's *breathing*," Marrity told him. He nodded toward the tube he was still holding in Daphne's throat. "That's a—a tracheotomy."

"I know," the old man said. "I've done one. The results were bad." He blinked a couple of times. "I told you not to have Italian, didn't I?"

"Yes." I think he's more upset by this than Daphne is, Marrity thought. "We should have listened to you."

Three men in white paramedics' uniforms shouldered through the front door and into the dining room now, one of them rolling a folded gurney and the other two carrying aluminum cases and a green oxygen cylinder; they visibly relaxed when they took in the scene, but one of them crouched by Daphne, murmuring reassurances as he shined a penlight into one of her eyes and then the other, while another man was unstringing an IV bag and line from one of the cases. The third man was talking into a radio.

The man who was crouched on the floor gently opened Daphne's mouth and peered down her throat with his light, then shook his head. "They better get it out in ER." He looked over at Marrity. "You okay?"

"Sure," Marrity said. He took a deep breath and let it out. "Tired."

"How long was she unconscious?"

"Not more than a minute," Marrity said.

"How old is she?"

"Twelve."

"Is she on any medications, or allergic to any?"

"No, and no."

"Okay, we'll get an IV going, mainly to get some glucose into her, and we'll run her to St. Bernardine's to get the blockage out and suture her throat. Probably they'll keep her overnight, observation and antibiotics. But this looks good. Who did the tracheotomy?"

"I did," said Marrity.

"You do good work."

"That's what they told me too," muttered Marrity's father.

"I think dinner's off, tomorrow," Marrity told him.

S tanding on the shaded sidewalk outside the restaurant, old Derek Marrity watched the paramedics slide the folding stainless-steel gurney with Daphne on it into the back of their white-and-red van, and then Frank Marrity climbed in the back too. A moment later the doors had been slammed shut and the ambulance van had steered out into the sunlight and sped away down Base Line Street to the east, its lights flashing.

The old man was still dizzy, and his ears were still ringing. He had been staring at Frank Marrity's haggard face so intently that now he could still see the afterimage of the straight jaw, the squinting eyes, the compressed mouth.

He looks just like you, Daphne had said.

"What was that you gave him, when he cut her throat?" said an overweight old woman standing behind him; he turned, but saw that she was speaking to the younger man who had been sitting at the table nearest Marrity's booth. He had been with another man, who had disappeared while Daphne was choking.

"A Bic pen," the man said, "with the ink cartridge taken out of it."

"Not very sterile," said Derek Marrity.

"Least of the worries, at that point," the man said shortly. "He's her father?"

"Yes." Yes, Derek Marrity thought, *he's* her father. I'm a stranger in this picture, soon to disappear. An ineffective, useless stranger, as it turns out.

The young man didn't say anything, just kept looking at Derek Marrity; but Marrity wouldn't fall for that old cop trick of prompting a fuller answer by appearing to expect it. This guy's tipped his hand right here, the old man thought with nervous defiance; he and the guy he was with are from one of the secret outfits, the Mossad, the NSA, whoever, whoever. But what could I tell any of them now? I have no idea at all.

They'll probably follow me. They've probably already bugged the Rambler, with some clunky "state-of-the-art" devices.

His smile was brief and twitchy as he imagined big metal boxes with lights on them, and antennae like sections of polished rebar. *Man from U.N.C.L.E.* stuff.

He found that he was limping rapidly east down the sunny Base Line Street sidewalk, past the grand yellow stucco arch of a car-repair garage and then a couple of faded bungalow-style houses looking shackled behind chain-link fencing and black iron window bars, and he couldn't remember how he had left the young spy and the fat old woman. The Rambler was parked on a side street up ahead; he had stashed a fifth of vodka under the seat, and he would need a bit of its vitamin supplement before he considered what to do now, today having gone so badly wrong. Frank and Daphne must think I'm crazy now, he thought.

Soon to disappear, he thought again.

When he had stepped barefoot out of the Kaleidoscope Shed yesterday, a good hour before Frank and Daphne had arrived, he had seen naked infants lying among the tall weeds, their waving pink limbs stark against the black dirt and the green stalks; the dozen?—half dozen?—tiny wailing forms had flickered out of existence when he had blinked at them in astonishment.

Delirium tremens, he thought; still mild, really. But in fact we're all just sparks arcing across the vacuum left by God when He withdrew, none of us any more substantial than those alcohol-conjured infants. What's one wasted life?

He's her father. Yes. Not me, damn my soul, not me. I had a daughter once, but she died. She will not come back to life. She will *not,* and I mustn't imagine anymore that she could.

I have . . . *another* daughter. *She'll* grow up, God help her, and God help me.

Through his mind flickered the quickly dismissed image of a dark-haired little girl frowning in concentration over a book; and then, just as quickly dismissed, another image: of a drunken woman resolutely climbing into the driver's seat of a Ford LTD and slamming the door.

He turned right at the next street, his bad leg aching now, and he could see the green Rambler parked in the shade of a pepper tree at the curb ahead of him—but he saw it blurrily, through tears.

By the rivers of Babylon, he thought, *I sat down, yea, weeping again the King my father's wrack.*

But he knew he was weeping for Daphne.

Bozzaris watched the old man hobble away, reflecting that he hadn't seemed quite sane. But Lepidopt had *sayanim* to follow him; any of the people on the street now might be one of them.

He turned to the old woman. "You said something in German, inside. Are you German?"

The question seemed to nettle her. "My mother was German," she said. "That was part of a prayer she used to say."

Bozzaris was about to ask her what it meant, but her two companions came bustling and chattering out of the restaurant then, and a moment later a boxy white Dial-A-Ride bus pulled up at the curb, and when the doors had hissed open the three of them clambered aboard.

Bozzaris waved cheerfully at the bus's opaque tinted glass, then turned to go back into the restaurant; but Malk stepped out onto the pavement and told him, "Lunch hour's over. To hell with Bailey."

"Right," said Bozzaris, falling into step beside the older man as he walked around the west corner to the parking lot. They both squinted in the direct sunlight.

Quietly, Malk told him, "Grab the bag by the Dumpster outside the back door; you'll probably have to jump a fence, but *do* it. I took the beer bottles from the old guy's table, re-placed them with a couple of bottles from another table. Fingerprints."

"Got you."

Paul Golze was driving the Dial-A-Ride bus, and Char-lotte Sinclair was sitting on the corrugated rubber floor in the back.

"That guy met up with the one he was with before," she said as the van speeded up, "and they're walking out to the parking lot, talking—and I'm out of range."

"Okay," Golze said. "We'll play the tapes soon," he went on, scowling into the rearview mirror, "but Tina, why did you speak German?"

Tina Iyana-Kurtycz closed her eyes and shook her head. "How should I know? I don't even know German."

"Schneid mal die Kehle auf," repeated the gaunt woman in the seat next to her, staring out the window.

"What you said means 'Cut open her throat,'" Golze said. "It was involuntary, yes?"

"Yes. I wouldn't *voluntarily* interfere in a, an area of measurement."

Golze seemed almost pleased. He looked down and clenched one fist in front of his chest, where only Charlotte could see, if she happened to be paying attention to him.

Eight

While Daphne was in surgery, Marrity blundered outside for a much needed cigarette. The glow of self-satisfaction at having saved her life was beginning to fade into shadows of worry. *What if she does this* again? he asked himself as he plodded across the glossy brown-tile floor of the hospital lobby to the electric-eye doors.

Should I start making sure I've always got a knife and a Bic pen on me? Give the sitter instructions on how to do a tracheotomy?

He was only aware of how chilly the hospital air was when the doors swung open and he stepped out into the the dry, sage-scented breeze. *I wonder if I can go back to work tomorrow*, he thought. *Tomorrow is Modern Novel, and I should prepare a lecture tonight. My briefcase is in the truck at the Alfredo's parking lot—I'll take a cab there, drive the truck back, and then put the lecture together in the lobby here.*

A slim, dark-haired woman in sunglasses was standing by the planter to the left of the door, and as he fumbled a pack of Dunhill cigarettes out of his coat pocket, she dropped a smoking cigarette butt onto the pavement and stepped on it and then took a pack of Dunhills out of her black leather purse.

"If they're going to kill us, we may as well smoke the best, right?" he said, holding up his pack.

She frowned at him, then tucked her own pack back into her purse and hurried past him into the lobby.

"Good, Frank, good," he muttered to himself, feeling his face heat up. "Always break the ice with a remark about dying. Especially to somebody standing in front of a hospital." But maybe she didn't speak English. He noticed half a dozen identical flattened cigarette butts on the pavement where she'd been standing.

He lit a cigarette and took a deep drag on it, then exhaled and leaned back against the pebbled-stone planter. Passing cars glinted in the afternoon sun on Twenty-first Street just beyond the iron fence at the edge of the hospital lawn, and he envied the drivers whatever concerns were theirs.

She's just got to be meticulous about chewing everything very thoroughly, he thought. Every swallow should be a careful, conscious action. Probably after this she won't even need reminding. I'm glad we painted her bedroom today. I wonder what that damned movie was, and why my father seemed to be interested in it.

And why was he at Alfredo's today? He must have followed us. That's unpleasant. I think we'd be better off having no further contact with him; to hell with why he visited Einstein in '55. Maybe the letters will give me a clue, before I sell them.

"I'm sorry," said a woman's voice behind him; he turned and saw that it was the woman in the sunglasses.

I was distracted," said Charlotte Sinclair. "You were talking about the cigarettes. You're right, we may as well kill ourselves with the best."

So far so good, she thought, and she checked herself out

through Francis Marrity's eyes: black jeans, loose burgundy short-sleeved blouse, and dark brown hair pulled back in a ponytail; she noted a strand of stray hair dangling above one eyebrow and smoothed it back.

They were alone on this breezy strip of shaded sidewalk, and she wished she could see Marrity's face.

"That was my last, in fact," she added, assessing her rueful smile.

"Would you like one of mine?" he said, and he held his pack out in front of himself.

"Thanks," she said, watching her own fingers to guide them as she reached out and picked a cigarette from the pack. "I owe you."

Denis Rascasse's Vespers research gang had reported that Marrity smoked Dunhills, so they had found a liquor store that carried the British cigarettes; on the drive here one of the Vespers men had broken several of the cigarettes and lit them and instantly ground them out, so that Charlotte could scatter the butts around where she'd stand.

Marrity's field of vision shifted from her to the lawn, so she said, "Are you visiting somebody?"

Again she saw herself in his vision. "Yes, my daughter's having her throat stitched up. Uh—tracheotomy." He paused, and then his left hand was holding out his wallet, tilted toward her. "Daphne," he said. "She's twelve."

Apparently he was showing Charlotte a photograph of his daughter. She took off her sunglasses and lowered her eyes until she seemed to be staring at the wallet. "Very pretty girl," Charlotte said.

"Yes." Marrity glanced at the picture himself before putting the wallet away.

She looks like I used to, Charlotte thought, and then thrust the thought away.

After a pause in which he might have smiled, Marrity went on, "You too? I mean, not a daughter with a tracheotomy—"

"A neighbor of mine. They won't let me see her yet, but—'We also serve who only stand and wait.'"

"'When I consider how my light is spent,'" Marrity said,

quoting the beginning of the poem, "'ere half my days in this dark world and wide—"

This one she hadn't been prompted with on the drive over here; it was Milton's sonnet "On His Blindness," and years ago she had got someone to read it onto a tape and had memorized it. "'And that one Talent which is death to hide, lodged with me useless,'" she said, keeping the usual bitterness out of her voice. "You don't meet a lot of Milton fans in San Bernardino."

"My excuse is that I teach literature at Redlands."

"Ah. I was a career English major. I quote poetry the way Christians quote the Bible." Time for one of the Housman bits she'd been primed with: "'And starry darkness paces the land from sea to sea, and blots the foolish faces of my poor friends and me.'" That was adequately placed, she thought, and Rascasse said it was underlined in Marrity's copy.

"Housman!" she heard him exclaim. "My favorite! My name's Frank Marrity. And you are . . . ?"

"Libra Nosamalo Morrison." She held out her right hand. "My parents were Catholic, with an odd sense of humor."

"*Libera nos a malo,* deliver us from evil." She watched him reach out and take her hand. "Well, it's unforgettable."

She smiled, admiring her white teeth.

"I've got to say I'll be ready for a drink," she said, "not too long after the sun goes down." She leaned back against the planter and closed her eyelids to check the eyeshadow through Marrity's gaze. It looked fine, and she raised her eyelids and swiveled the plastic eyes until Marrity saw the carbon pupils seeming to look straight at him. "A scotch on the rocks—Laphroaig, ideally."

He let go of her hand, and his voice was cautious when he said, "Yes, that's good scotch. I'd love to join you, but I can't."

Charlotte wished someone would walk by so that she could see Marrity's face—were his eyebrows up in surprise? lowered in a suspicious frown?—for she was suddenly sure that she had pushed it too far. You were doing fine without the Laphroaig, she told herself furiously; just because Rascasse's crew found several bottles of it in Marrity's cupboard didn't mean you had to go and mention it right away. What must Rascasse be thinking, listening to the transmission of this conversation?

She found that she was reflexively thinking of the song "Bye Bye Blackbird" —*no one here can love or understand me*— and she recalled that it had been her old eavesdropper-warning signal in the missile-silo days of her childhood. But of course Marrity doesn't even know that the song was a code, she thought; and why should I want to *warn* Marrity, anyway?

She put her sunglasses back on.

"Another time?" she asked, watching her face to be sure she kept the expression cheerful. "I'd trust my phone number to anybody who knows Milton and Housman."

"Yes, thanks. I just can't really think about anything but my daughter right now."

"Of course." By touch she found a card in her purse, and held it out to him. She read it through his eyes: *Libra Nosamalo Morrison, Veterinary Medicine, (909) JKL-HYDE.*

"A Stevenson fan too," she heard him say.

The hastily printed card seemed idiotically clumsy now. "Well," she stammered, "like Heckle and Jeckle—those crows, in the cartoons—and hide—"

"And I bet you specialize in cats." The card disappeared from his view, and she hoped he had put it in his pocket and not just dropped it. "I'd better go back and see if she's out of surgery yet," he said. "It's been nice meeting you, uh, Libra!"

"You too, Frank! Give me a call!"

His view was of the opening doors now, and the reception desk and gift-shop counter in the lobby; she turned away, so that when he looked back at her he wouldn't hesitate to stare; but he looked only straight ahead, at the corridor leading to the elevators.

When he had rounded the corner and pushed one of the elevator buttons, she raised her right hand, wide open, and heard a car accelerating toward the curb where she stood.

"I'm a viewer, not a spy," she muttered into the microphone at her throat.

The driver of the car that had now stopped in front of her

craned his neck to peer into the rearview mirror, and she saw it was Rascasse himself.

She groped till she felt the door, then found the handle and opened it.

"You knew his birth date too," said Rascasse. "Why did you not tell him you had the same birthday? You could have shouted it after him, as he was leaving." His French accent was more pronounced when he was angry, and higher in pitch. Charlotte could imagine it was a woman speaking.

"So what do we do now," she asked dully as she pulled the door closed.

"If this . . . debacle just now was enough to let him know somebody's trying to approach him covertly, probably we will have to kill him, and then get somebody less clumsy to approach Moira and Bennett Bradley, and the daughter."

She looks like I used to, thought Charlotte again.

She settled back in the seat and fastened the shoulder strap. It was good meeting you, Frank, she thought as Rascasse steered the car out of the hospital driveway and clicked the turn-signal lever for a right turn onto Waterman. You seem like a good man, a widower doing his best with a young daughter—you even saved her life today!—and you're the first guy I've met who's known what the Milton line was from. But I'm afraid I've killed you by mentioning your favorite scotch.

And I won't try to stop it. *I'm* not a good person, you see. I used to be, and soon—if Rascasse succeeds in this and keeps his promises—I'll get another chance to be one, starting over again.

I'll get a better life then; or she will, anyway—the girl I used to be, my "little daughter," who looks so much like your Daphne. *I have done nothing but in care of thee.* And she won't know about any of this terrible stuff I do to get it for her. And she won't be blind. She won't be blind.

Oren Lepidopt stood on the carpet in Frank Marrity's now dark living room, looking around at the shapes that were the table and the television and the rows of shelved books whose titles he couldn't read now. He had studied them when there had still been light, though—lots of Stevenson and the Brontës and Trollope in this room, while poetry and drama and encyclopedias lined the shelves that hung above head height up the hall, and history and philosophy and modern novels filled the shelves in the uphill living room. Poetry, history, and philosophy were in chronological order, novels alphabetical.

The girl's room had been painted today—the bed had been moved to the center of the linoleum floor, and a little desk and a couple of bookcases had been shoved up against it, with a rolled-up rug and a couple of wicker baskets stacked right on the bed, everything covered by a brown paper drop cloth. When he had peered under it, Lepidopt had seen *The Wind in the Willows* and *Watership Down* among the books in one of the bookcases; the baskets contained recent rock tapes and albums, with a lot of Queen. A black shellac jewelry box with blue-velvet-covered dividers and slits for rings held two gold bracelets, some earrings, and a wedding ring— presumably her mother's.

Lepidopt thought of his son's disorderly room, in their apartment on Dizengoff Street in Tel Aviv. Louis was only a year younger than Daphne, and he liked Queen too. Lepidopt's wife, Deborah, had been uneasy about the fact that the group's lead singer appeared to be a homosexual, but young Louis already liked girls. Lepidopt wondered if the two children would be friends, if they could impossibly meet; surely they would be; surely Daphne would like the curly-haired Jewish boy with his father's intense brown eyes.

Standing in the dark living room now, Lepidopt wondered if the house was at all psychically flexed by his presence, his inappropriateness. Certainly he was aware of it, standing here with latex gloves on his hands, a Polaroid camera around his neck and a Beretta automatic tucked into the back of his pants.

Twice before in his career he had broken into people's

houses when they were absent, and again he felt the sense that the house was poised, like a tennis player who has just sent the ball flying back over the net and is catching his balance to see how it will return; Lepidopt imagined he could hear echoes of the last conversations that had taken place here, and could nearly hear the tones of the next to come.

Being alone in a stranger's house didn't so much convey an acquaintance with the absent owner as give a wide-angle snapshot. Marrity smoked Balkan Sobranie number 759 pipe tobacco, which wasn't the usual sweet-smelling stuff, but Lepidopt didn't know if he was one of those pipe smokers who always had the thing in his mouth and talked around the stem, or one of the ones who was always fiddling with it in his hands, tamping it and relighting it and shoving a pipe cleaner down it; they were different sorts of men. Marrity apparently drank single-malt scotch and Southern Comfort, but Lepidopt couldn't guess, within a very wide range, what sort of drinker he was.

Who are you, Frank Marrity? he thought. Who are you, Daphne Marrity?

The snapshot impression was of a happy father and daughter, comfortable with each other. Books everywhere, a disorder of clothes on the washing machine, cats scuffling in the hall. Marrity kept the house at about 20 degrees Celsius or 70 degrees Fahrenheit; twice Lepidopt had heard the rooftop air conditioner whisper into activity. He probed his mind for the familiar envy of normal lives, and found that it was there as usual.

He was glad the cat or cats were shy of him, for a year ago he had petted one, and a moment later had experienced the certainty that he would never again touch a cat.

Lepidopt had taken Polaroid photographs of the Marrity wastebaskets and then picked through their contents—without much optimism, since the previous intruders had certainly done it too—afterward consulting the photographs to replace the trash exactly as it had been. He had found Marrity's box of paid bills and photographed the telephone bills, again sure that he was the second person in six hours to do it.

If the movie and the machine had been findable, the other crowd had found them. But maybe they had not been findable. Assume the ball is still in play, thought Lepidopt.

Lepidopt had been careful to move quietly throughout the house, assuming that the preceding crew, whoever they were, had left microphones; and he had left some too.

He had stayed away from the telephones—one in Marrity's bedroom, one in the downhill living room and one in Marrity's uphill office—because of the likelihood that the other crowd would already have attached infinity transmitters or keep-alive circuits to the wiring, effectively making microphones out of the telephone receivers even when they were resting in the cradles, apparently hung up.

Lepidopt had left three electret microphones disguised as empty Bic cigarette lighters—one on a high kitchen shelf, one in a gap between two books in the living room, and one inside a dusty spiderweb on the office windowsill. They were tuned from 100 to 120 megahertz, which spanned the high end of the commercial FM band and the low end of the aircraft voice-communication band, but the range of their transmission was no more than five hundred yards, and Lepidopt had rented a house at the west end of the block and set up receivers and tape recorders. The alkali AA batteries in the transmitters should be good for a week or two, at least.

He had also left, in the back of a kitchen drawer full of dusty chopsticks and parts to an old coffee percolator, two little *teraphim* statues made of fired tan clay, each with the names of the four rivers of Paradise carefully inscribed into their bases; and on top of the refrigerator he had tucked a postage-stamp-size scrap of leather with a Star of David inked on one side, and on the other a Hebrew inscription that said "and it dwindled"—the phrase was from Numbers 11:2, when a fire had broken out among the tents of the Israelites, and had then subsided when Moses prayed.

And now, before leaving, he was trying to guess what the other gang might have missed.

Here in the dark living room there was a faint reek of burnt plastic under the smells of tobacco and book paper and cat box; up the hall the air was just heavy with the cake-frosting smell of fresh paint.

Yesterday's newspapers are still on the kitchen table, he thought. Somebody had oatmeal and Southern Comfort for breakfast. There must be at least one cat, but I don't see him right now, thank God. There are two TV sets, one in the north living room and one in here, and neither one seems to have burned. But, *everything's on fire,* Sam Glatzer had said, moments before he died, *up the hall and the TV set . . .*

The girl's bedroom was up the hall, and Marrity had painted it today.

Lepidopt stepped toward the TV set, though it meant approaching the unshaded window, and he took the penlight from his pocket. He clicked it on, and then crouched to play its narrow beam over the top surface of the television set. It showed no particle of dust, though earlier he had noted that the table and all the bookshelves were faintly frosted with it. He clicked the light off again and tucked it back into his pocket.

He pulled a white handkerchief out of his pocket and wrapped it around his latex-gloved forefinger and drew it across the top of the television set—he would look at it later in a bright light, but he sniffed it now, and smelled burnt plastic.

He backed away from the window. If my amulets had been in place yesterday, he thought, the little *teraphim* statues and the fire-extinguishing Star of David, I bet there would be a working VCR sitting on top of this television set now. And they might very well provide protection in the future.

But he knew the thought was sophistry. It was wrong to use magic, wrong to try to compel God's will.

Next month would be Selichot, beginning on the first Saturday night before Rosh Hashanah, and Lepidopt—if he were still alive—would pray for God's forgiveness through the following two weeks and would finally be restored to holiness on October third, Yom Kippur. As, often in the past, the duties of his job would be prominent among the things he would ask forgiveness for.

It was time to leave. Marrity might come home at any time. Admoni's brief radio message had said that a senior *katsa* from Prague was being dispatched and would arrive at LAX tomorrow afternoon to take over the operation; Lepidopt was to leave the Marritys and the Bradleys alone until then, and never mind the rival team, whoever they might be.

But Lepidopt paused, and for the second time he laid three pennies at the edges of the paperback book that lay open and facedown on the living room table, and then he carefully lifted the book. When he had picked it up an hour and a half ago there had still been enough light in the living room to read by, but now he took it to the lighted hall.

The paperback was Shakespeare's *The Tempest,* and when he'd first looked at it he had noted that it was a mess of inked underlining and margin notations, as would be expected from a literature professor. Lepidopt had photographed the two facing pages that the book was opened to, but he hadn't bothered to photograph every marked-up page. He doubted that the other crowd had either.

Now, up the landing and standing under the hall light, he flipped through the pages. It had been opened to the last page of the play, and one sentence from the Caliban character had been deeply underlined: *What a thrice-double ass / Was I to take this drunkard for a god / And worship this dull fool!* Now Lepidopt turned back through the text, looking at every page.

Marrity's inked notes were all clearly written: obviously not just hasty thoughts of a moment, but points that he would want to be reminded of every time he taught the play in a class.

And so Lepidopt paused when he came to a couple of nearly illegible words scribbled vertically in the margin of page 110, next to a doubly underlined speech in which the Prospero character said, *I'll break my staff / Bury it certain fathoms in the earth, and deeper than did ever plummet sound / I'll drown my book.*

The inked phrase in the margin was scrawled in such evident haste that the pen had not at any point lifted from the paper, but when Lepidopt squinted at it he saw that it was probably, and then certainly, *Peccavit to LM.*

Peccavit. Lepidopt's heart had begun thumping in his chest.

Break my staff, drown my book—Peccavit—Marrity must know who his great-grandfather was, and must know something of the man's work too. Not the public work, relativity and the photoelectric effect and the 1939 letter to Roosevelt about the atomic bomb, but the secret work, the weapon Einstein had *not* told Roosevelt about.

The *LM* must be Lisa Marrity, or Lieserl Marity. Frank Marrity must know something about it all.

Quickly Lepidopt flipped through the rest of the pages, but found only one more hasty scrawl of *Peccavit to LM,* on page 104, next to another twice-underlined sentence: *We are such stuff / As dreams are made on, and our little life / Is rounded with a sleep.*

Lepidopt was sweating as he hurried back to the living room to put the book back exactly the way it had been and retrieve his pennies. He didn't have enough film or time to photograph every page of the book now, and he prayed that Marrity wouldn't move it too far before somebody could come back and photograph the entire text.

And—in spite of Admoni's order—Lepidopt clearly *had* to keep the rival group away from Marrity.

He was padding back up the hall toward the laundry-room door, which fortunately faced trees and an empty yard next door, when the telephone rang in Marrity's bedroom, loud in the silent house. He paused; the phone rang three times and then stopped, not enough rings to trigger the answering machine.

And a moment later Lepidopt had to force his legs to go on supporting him, and not let him collapse against the wall; for in the instant that the phone had stopped ringing, he had been forcibly convinced that he would never again hear a telephone bell ring.

And surely I will never see Deborah again, he thought; and surely I will never see Louis again.

He clenched his narrow, maimed right hand and thumped the misshapen fist once, very softly, against the wall.

Bennett Bradley pulled open his desk drawer and lifted out the bottle of Christian Brothers brandy, and he was glaring at the white plastic telephone-answering machine.

His office was in what had been the garage, but he had put in a hardwood floor and pale paneling, and fluorescent tubes glowed behind frosted sheets of plastic set into the ceiling. Gray metal filing cabinets full of contracts and photographs stood against the west wall, and a long blond-wood table ran down the middle of the room. Right now there were dozens of four-by-six-inch color photographs laid out on the table, taped together into long strips, but he would have to be putting them away now, with no recompense.

Now they were just on-spec samples, to be folded into a file and labeled "Hollywood Hills, Panoramic View w. Hollywood Sign & Easy Access," and tucked away with all the others: "Laguna Cliff & Sea, w. Easy Parking," and "Eaglerock Typical Middle-class 1960s House," and "15,000 sf French Chateau in Brentwood, Shooting-Friendly." And a thousand others, and probably a quarter of them were obsolete by now: torn down or renovated, or owned by uncooperative people, or with inappropriate freeways visible behind them.

Bennett unscrewed the bottle's cap and took a drink right from the neck of it, grimacing at the sting of the lukewarm brandy; and then he set it on the desk and stood up to put away the photographs.

The Subaru agent had originally said they wanted the thirty-second commercial to have an "old Hollywood" feel.

Bennett had driven up to his proposed site half a dozen times last week, starting north on Beachwood from Franklin, just a block up from modern Hollywood Boulevard but

fifty years backward in architecture and atmosphere, with
neoclassical apartment buildings shaded by shaggy carob
trees along cracked and canted sidewalks; farther up the hill
he had stopped to take pictures of the Beachwood Gates,
two towering stonework pillars on either side of the street,
and he had taken a picture of the brass plaque on the eastern
pillar, with its raised letters that spelled HOLLYWOODLAND
1923.

He had followed Beachwood up to the left, and the street
wound up Beachwood Canyon between old Spanish houses
with red-tile roofs and brown-painted wooden balconies and
old double-doored garages that were crowded right up to the
street. There was no level ground—the roof of one house
blocked the view of the foundations of another, and stairs
and arched windows could be seen anywhere among the
trees.

Beachwood Drive was too narrow for trucks to pass easily, and at the top of the hill the road curled sharply to the
right into Hollyridge Drive, which was so narrow that one
car would have to pull to the curb for an oncoming car to get
by—but right at the top, a pair of iron gates opened to the
left onto a wide dirt lot.

That was Griffith Park land, with an unobstructed view
down the north slopes to Forest Lawn Memorial Park and
the Ventura Freeway, with Burbank and Glendale beyond,
and the Mulholland Highway could provide access for any
sort of trucks from that direction. He had drawn a map of
the unpaved hilltop lot, showing where the trucks could be
parked and lunch tables set up.

And on Hollyridge Drive he had found a vacant house
with a wide balcony overlooking Beachwood Canyon and—
at the same height as the balcony and so close that the cross
girders were clearly visible—the nine huge white letters of
the Hollywood sign standing on the hill right across the
canyon. Quickly he had contacted the Los Angeles Department of Recreation and Parks and the owner of the vacant
house, and he had already begun the work of arranging all
the permissions and insurance coverage.

He tipped the stack of pictures vertical now, and rapped them on the polished tabletop to get the edges straight.

And with his new Nikon RF he had taken these photographs of the site. From the house's balcony he had taken two panoramic series of shots, of the skyline and of the road below, and he had stood at the top of Beachwood Drive and slowly turned on his heel and taken fourteen level shots— a full 180 degrees—to show the Subaru people that there would be no billboards or other inappropriate structures behind the camera to be reflected in the polished bodywork of the car as it drove past; there was a big mirror mounted on the canyon wall where Beachwood looped into Hollyridge, but they could hang a camouflage cloth over it. He had even got down on his hands and knees and photographed the street surface, to indicate what sort of dolly moves would be possible for the cameraman.

And then sometime this afternoon, while Bennett had been on the plane back from Shasta, the Subaru agent had called and left a message—they had decided to film the car on the Antelope Valley Highway east of Agua Dulce, way out north in the desert, and to hell with the "old Hollywood" idea. They'd pay Bennett for the days he had put into the project, but he would have no further part in it.

All the on-site emergencies, the unforseen shadow patches or glare spots, the traffic and parking screwups, the crises with the available voltage and amperage, would be dealt with by another location manager. And that guy would get all the on-location pay too.

Several thousand dollars that Bennett had been counting on—gone. Before the end of the month, he thought, we'll be hurtin' for certain.

The telephone rang, and he hurried to the desk to answer it, thinking the Subaru people might have reconsidered.

"Bradley Locations," he said.

A man's voice said, "I'd like to speak to Bennett or Moira Bradley, please." It wasn't the Subaru agent.

"This is Bennett Bradley."

"Mr. Bradley, I represent a company that's always actively

trying to expand its database, and we're now in negotiation with a Francis Marrity for some items that belonged to his grandmother, a Ms. Lisa Marrity. There will probably be a substantial amount of money involved, and our research department has just established that Mr. Marrity is not the sole heir of Ms. Marrity."

"That's true, my wife is coheir." Son of a bitch! thought Bennett. "What items? Uh, in particular?"

"I'm not involved in acquisitions, I'm afraid. But it's probably papers, floppy disks, or films; even electrical machinery or precious metals, possibly."

Bennett had seized a pen and begun scrawling meaningless spirals on a legal pad. "What is your company?"

"The remuneration would be greater if I didn't say. Anonymity is our policy."

"How did—Mr. Marrity—approach you?—and when?"

"We've been in negotiation with Lisa Marrity for some time. Yesterday we learned that she had died, and the only contact she had provided us with was Francis Marrity. We called him, and he expressed interest in consummating the sale we had arranged with Lisa Marrity."

"Well you definitely need to talk to my wife too. She's coheir. As I said. As you know." Bennett was breathing hard. "Now."

"Are you aware of the nature of the items to be sold?"

"Of course I am," Bennett said. What on earth could they be? he wondered—what papers, what precious metals? What *electrical machinery*? "My wife and I were in Shasta yesterday afternoon and today, making funeral arrangements—for, uh, Ms. Marrity—and we just got back from the airport half an hour ago. I'm sure Frank meant to get in touch with my wife before concluding any deal," he said. "With my wife and I. Because no sale could be finalized without our cooperation."

"Who currently has physical possession of the items in question?"

"Well, they're—divvied up. Some here, some there. I'd need to see a list of which particular—items—are being discussed. The—" Bennett considered, and then dismissed, the idea of sneaking another drink from the bottle. "The old lady had a lot of valuable things. What's your phone number?"

"We'll get in touch with you, probably tomorrow. Good night."

Bennett heard a click, and then the dial tone.

He hung up the telephone, had another mouthful of the brandy, and then banged out through the door that led to the kitchen of his house, yelling, "Moira! Your bloody damned brother—!"

Nine

"He doesn't know what I was talking about," said Rascasse, pushing his chair back from the telephone on the folding desk and standing up, gripping an overhead rail to steady himself as the bus rocked around a sharp housing-tract corner in the evening darkness. To the young man driving the bus he said, "But pull up in front of his house anyway, so Charlotte can take a look."

"He *was* just up in Shasta," said Golze hopefully.

Through Rascasse's eyes Charlotte Sinclair looked down at herself and the chubby figure of Golze sitting on the first bus seat aft of the cleared rubber-tiled floor, both of them leaning forward to hear the radio speaker. She lifted her chin and pushed a wing of dark hair back from her face.

From the speaker they could now dimly hear Bennett Bradley shouting at his wife.

"Lousy signal," said Rascasse.

"I think they're in the hall," said Golze. "I didn't put a mike in the hall."

"Yes," said Charlotte, leaning back in her seat with her eyes closed, "they're in a hall."

The bus was close enough to the Bradley house now for her to be able to see through the eyes of the people inside—and she saw a tanned blond woman in jeans, standing in a lighted hallway, with suitcases visible beside a door behind her; Charlotte switched to the woman's view, and found herself looking at a man shouting; he had styled reddish hair, and a bristling mustache, and he was wearing a white shirt with the sleeves rolled back on his forearms.

Charlotte felt the bus jolt to a stop, presumably at the curb in front of the Bradley house, but she kept her attention on Moira Bradley's field of vision.

The man was walking backward into a brightly lit kitchen, and the woman's viewpoint followed, and all at once the sound from the speaker in the bus became clearer, and Charlotte had words to go with the man's moving lips.

"—that he doesn't like *you*, it's that he doesn't like *me*," Bennett Bradley was saying. "He's always been jealous of me."

"Jealous? He likes teaching," said the woman Charlotte was monitoring; Charlotte's field of vision bobbed slightly at the syllables.

"Out in the middle of nowhere?" said Bennett. Charlotte saw him wave a hand in the air. "With a dead wife and a bratty kid? And a million cats? He knows he's rotting out there—he'd move west to L.A. or south to Orange County in a second, if he could, but that house of his is probably worth about a hundred dollars. Look at that joke truck he drives! And I drive a Mercedes and I'm on a first-name basis with Richard Dreyfuss!"

"Frank wouldn't try to gyp us out of any money," said Moira. "I'm sure he—"

"There were no messages on the machine from him, just from that damned Subaru agent. You think your brother wouldn't try to keep this for himself? 'Substantial amount of money,' this guy said—"

Charlotte's view rocked as Moira's voice from the speaker

said, "For—what was it? Machinery? That doesn't make any—"

"Or papers, or gold. She knew Charlie Chaplin! Your grandmother—" Bennett backed into some decorative glass candleholders on the counter by the sink, and clattering sounded from the speaker. "What *is* all this trash?" He shoved the jars that hadn't fallen into the sink back against the wall, breaking at least one more.

Bennett shifted out of Charlotte's line of sight as Moira looked into the sink instead of at her husband; but his voice on the speaker said, "Your grandmother might have letters, manuscripts, even lost Chaplin films."

"Well, they're trash now," said Moira's voice as Charlotte saw Bennett swing into view again. "The candles, I mean. So now you believe she knew Chaplin."

"Well obviously she had *something.* Maybe her violin *is* a Stradivarius."

"Frank will tell us. He'll tell me, anyway. Unless this was a crank phone call. 'Anonymity policy'! It's certainly made trouble."

"Call him. Ask him. Or I will."

Charlotte's field of vision swung away from Bennett to a calendar above a telephone on the wall, and then back. "We'll see him Thursday."

Bennett shook his head. "This money guy wants to meet me tomorrow. And Frank won't want to talk at his grand-mother's funeral, with Daffy underfoot. Call him."

"*Okay.*"

Charlotte watched the telephone bob closer, and then she saw one of Moira's hands lift the receiver while the other spun the dial. Charlotte read the number out loud as she watched Moira dial it—while from the speaker she heard the clicking of the dial being turned, and the hiss of it spin-ning back—and she felt Golze shift beside her on the bus seat. "That's Marrity's number, all right," Golze said.

Charlotte could smell tobacco smoke; evidently Golze had lit a cigarette.

Charlotte watched the telephone receiver swing closer

and then disappear beyond her right-side peripheral vision; of course she couldn't hear anything from the phone. Then after about twenty seconds it appeared again, receding, and Moira's hand hung it back in the cradle with a loud clatter from the speaker. The microphone must be very near the phone, Charlotte thought.

" 'You've reached the Marritys,' " quoted Moira's voice, " 'and we're not able to come to the phone right now.' "

"You should have left a message," grumbled Bennett. " 'We're onto your filthy tricks.' "

Bennett's frowning face swung back into Charlotte's sight, and Moira laughed. "Or, 'You're not fooling anyone.' "

Bennett laughed too, though he was still frowning. "Do it in a disguised voice," he said. Then, growling in a Bronx accent, " 'I know what you been doin', an' you better stop it.' "

"He'd lock the gate," said Moira, "and never answer the phone again."

"Right, and then we'd find out this *was* a joke call, and your crazy grandmother didn't own anything but old Creedence records. But—he'd never dare go to another X-rated movie."

"Frank doesn't go to X-rated movies. You go to X-rated movies."

"I have to, sometimes, it's business. Anyway, that's why he's jealous of me."

"Drive on," said Rascasse to the young man in the driver's seat. "No use having the bus get noticed for this."

Moira was saying something back, but Golze said, "He mentioned lost Charlie Chaplin films."

The bus surged forward with no more noise than a car would have made; the Vespers had replaced its diesel engine with a Chevrolet 454 V-8, and put disk brakes on instead of noisy air brakes.

"He was just choosing random examples," said Rascasse. "It was an obvious thing to say, after I mentioned films in my call to him. He doesn't know anything about it. Neither does she, probably."

Bennett Bradley's voice was coming out of the speaker

now, talking about the Subaru deal that Rascasse had managed to get taken away from him, but already the bus was too far away from the house for Charlotte to see any more. She shifted her attention to Rascasse, who was still standing and looking down at her and Golze. Charlotte took the opportunity to check her lipstick, but it was still fine.

"The artifact moved east, yesterday," Rascasse went on, "and Francis Marrity and his daughter are in a, a *crisis*. It's got to be Marrity who took it. We should have been at that hospital, not wasting our time here."

But I've soured the appoach to Francis Marrity, Charlotte thought, bracing herself for reminders of it; but then the soft gong sounded from the cabinet behind the driver's seat, and in sudden fright Charlotte's vision bounced several times between the driver and Golze and Rascasse, so that in rapid succession she was seeing the empty curbside cars and pools of streetlight ahead of them and two views of her own face—lips pinched and brown eyes wide—one in profile and one head-on.

"See—what it wants," said Rascasse to Golze.

Charlotte thought she could already hear the filigreed-silver jaw hinges snapping inside the cabinet.

"Right," said Golze.

He stood up from beside Charlotte and swayed forward toward the cabinet, and Rascasse stared after him, so Charlotte fixed her attention on the driver, a humorless physics student from UC Berkeley, and watched the cars ahead of the bus through his eyes. They had left the housing tract and were on East Orange Grove Boulevard, passing a Pizza Hut and a Shell station.

She heard the cabinet lock snap, and then she really could hear the Baphomet's jaws clicking; and though she was staring at the dashboard and the taillights beyond the windshield, she could smell the head now, the spicy shellac reek.

She heard several voices whispering—and she had never heard the thing form words before. Reluctantly she let herself share Rascasse's perspective.

The cabinet doors were swung open and the shiny head inside was gleaming in the yellow overhead light; its black jaw, with the chin capped in silver like the toe of a cowboy boot, was wagging up and down rapidly, but it was not synchronized with the whispering.

Golze had switched on the Ouija-board monitor over the cabinet: The cursor on the screen was motionless, but there were several breathy voices huffing out between the Baphomet head's crooked ivory teeth.

"Call *me* flies in summer," hissed one.

"Eighty cents," whispered another. "Can I bum one of your smokes, at least?"

Charlotte swallowed. "What—who the hell are they?" she managed to ask in a level voice.

"Ghosts," said Rascasse in disgust. "The Harmonic Convergence has brought them out like . . . flies in summer, and the head attracts them when it's not properly occupied. I think it's worse when we're moving—the head is a psychic charge moving through the Harmonic Convergence field. If we weren't smoking cigarettes right now, we'd draw hundreds of them—probably condensed enough for us to *see* them."

Charlotte shuddered and reached into her purse for the pack of Dunhills.

The feathery-frail ghost voices were coming faster now, overlapping one another:

"Why will you do it?"

"One, nineteen, twenty-four, twenty-seven, thirty-eight, nineteen."

"Will you show me your tits if I can guess how much money you've got in your pocket?"

"Two whole days."

"Why don't you try a real man?"

"Hello, pretty lady! I can tell you what lottery numbers are gonna win!"

Charlotte cleared her throat. "Should I say hello back? It seems rude to snub a ghost." She was still holding her unlit cigarette—neither Golze nor Rascasse had looked at her, and she didn't want to light it just by touch with her shaking fingers.

Golze answered, "You already snubbed him. They run backward in time. But you could say, 'Hello, ghost!' and then his remark would be a reply to that, not an unprompted salutation."

"Hello, ghost!" she said.

Golze glanced at her, and Charlotte saw her nervous smile through his eyes. Quickly she used his perspective to snap her lighter below the tip of her cigarette. "Is he going to tell us the winning lottery numbers?" she said, exhaling smoke.

"He did already," said Golze. "And he guessed you've got eighty cents in your pocket. No use showing him your tits now, it would be before he asked. I don't think they can actually see anyway."

"Nineteen . . . twenty-four," said Charlotte quickly. "You should have written down the numbers!"

"They're lying," Golze said. "They don't know which lottery numbers are going to win."

"If they're moving backward in time," said Charlotte, "how come they talk forward? They don't sound like records played backward."

"Very good!" said Golze. "They're mostly on the freeway, just dabbling their toes in here for a few seconds at a time. While they're down here with us, they're carried along with the stream in the same direction we are. So each sentence is beginning-first, end-last, but the next remark for us is the *previous* remark to them."

"Lock it up," Rascasse said to Golze. "But leave the monitor on."

"Two days," whispered one last ghost, "I sat beside my body, staring at the holes in my chest."

Charlotte kept her attention on Golze, and watched his pudgy hands close the cabinet. The copper handles were miniature reproductions of the Vespers emblem: the Grail cup—two plain, smooth cones joined at the tips, one cone opening upward, the other downward, like a double-jigger measure in a Bauhaus bar.

Charlotte used Golze's brief glance to focus hungrily on the little copper chalices. Then he had straightened up and was looking at her.

"How does the Harmonic Converence bring out ghosts?" she asked, and Golze helpfully looked toward Rascasse.

"It's like Gargamelle," said Rascasse.

"What, Gargantua's mother?—in Rabelais?"

"No—or maybe they named it after that, what you said— Gigantor's mother—no, it's the name of a big bubble chamber at the CERN laboratory in Switzerland. Ten tons of liquid is kept very near its boiling temperature, but under high pressure; then they suddenly release the pressure, and any invisible particles shooting through the liquid form lines of bubbles. They become actual, manifest, rather than unseen potential."

Rascasse waved out at the night. "All these mystics on the mountaintops, emptying their minds all at once, have suddenly dropped the pressure in the common psychic water-table, and things are becoming actual that should only be low-probability potentials."

Charlotte dug coins out of the pocket of her jeans and held them out on her palm. Golze looked, and so she was able to see that it was three quarters and a nickel.

"I do have eighty cents," she said.

"If it was five coins they'd have been stumped," Golze said. "They're like some primitive culture, with five numbers: one, two, three, four, and countless."

Rascasse was leaning on the folded-down desk to look outside through one of the starboard bus windows. Charlotte shifted to his perspective, and was able to see the dots of orange light on the mountains.

"Fires all the way up from here to Humboldt and Trinity and Siskiyou," Rascasse said softly. "All started from lightning strikes at about noon yesterday."

"Well," said Golze, "A .50-caliber bullet will rip up dust under it as it goes by. And Lieserl Marity was moving a whole hell of a lot faster."

A lot of rest you'll be getting in here," said Marrity.

He had pushed the heavy door nearly closed, but the voices and squeaking wheeled carts outside the room were still just as audible. The hospital hallways had a scent like the chlorophyll wood shavings at the bottom of a hamster's cage, but this room still smelled of lemon custard and beef gravy, even though a nurse had taken away Daphne's tray of pureed brown and white and yellow stuff half an hour ago. On the wall behind Daphne's bed was taped a page of typescript headed "Swallowing Instructions." There seemed to be a dozen crucial points. Daphne couldn't see it from where she lay.

A gauze pad was taped across her throat. Two of her ribs had been cracked during the useless Heimlich maneuver, but they hadn't required any tape or bandage.

Daphne picked up the pencil on the wheeled table beside her bed and wrote *sleep pill probly* on the top page of the pocket notebook he had fetched from the truck. *Ask fr you too.* The clear plastic bag on the IV pole swayed when she wrote; fortunately the tube was taped to her arm above her wrist where the needle was inserted, so it wasn't likely to be pulled out.

Marrity glanced at the blue canvas cot the nurse had brought in for him to sleep on after he had turned down the offer of a "cardiac chair," which had seemed to be a half-size hospital bed, complete with an electric motor bolted to the underside of it.

"I'll be fine," he told Daphne. He was sitting in one of the two plain wooden chairs in this half of the room; the other chair had a cotton square like a diaper laid across its seat, and he hadn't wanted to ask why.

St. Bernardine's Hospital had transferred Daphne here to the Arrowhead Pediatric Hospital after her emergency throat surgery, and Marrity was pleased that his frantic knife cut of this afternoon had only required four stitches in the skin of her throat. The surgeon had done "undermining," put in a row of sutures under the skin, to leave a negligible scar while still keeping the wound securely closed.

Marrity had called Cal State San Bernardino to cancel his Modern Novels class for tomorrow, and he was planning to sleep in his own bed as soon as Daphne was released in the morning. Sleep all day.

There was another bed in this room, farther from the door, but it was empty at the moment and Marrity hoped it would stay that way. The emergency room at St. Bernardine's had seemed to be full of hoboes who just wanted painkillers, and he didn't want another stranger imposed on his daughter when she was so helpless—she looked very frail in this up-tilted hospital bed, with the thin sheets and threadbare blankets tumbled around her. He would have fetched Rumbold for her, if Rumbold had not been burned up and buried.

She was idly drawing spirals on the pad, and his spirits fell further at the familiar sight of her bitten-down fingernails—then he saw that she had written more words.

Yr father was at Alfredo's?

"Yes," Marrity said. He didn't want to make her write more, so he added, "I guess he probably followed us."

She drew two dots with a V between them: frowning eyes.

"I agree." Marrity shifted in his chair. "He did seem to be very upset by . . . it all."

Daphne wrote some more: *You saved my life.* She didn't look up from the paper.

"Um—yes. I was glad to be able to."

must have been hard to do—cut me

He nodded, though her head was still lowered and her face was hidden behind her brown bangs.

"Yes," he said. "Yes, it was very hard to do."

A spot appeared on the paper; and then another. *I love you*

"I love you too, Daph," he said. He wanted to get up out of the chair and try to hug her, but he knew it would embarrass her; they never talked this way ordinarily. Marrity had always assumed that their avoidance of sentiment was an Irish thing, but today he had learned that they were not Irish. A Serbian thing, then.

"I'm—proud of you," she whispered, still looking down. *"I hope it leaves a scar—excuse to brag about you."*

"Don't stretch your voice box. They say it won't leave much of a scar at all. But—thanks."

She nodded and sat back against the sloping mattress and smiled at him, and when she closed her eyes she didn't open them again; and after a few moments Marrity took from his coat pocket a beat-up paperback copy of *Tristram Shandy* that he always kept in the truck. His briefcase was in the truck too, but he wasn't in the mood to read student papers and he didn't want to look at Grammar's old Peccavit letters in here.

He stood up to switch off the fluorescent tube over her bed, noting the spotty horizontal line of chips in the wall plaster at the height of the bed frame—what did they do, play bumper cars with the things?—and then he pulled the bed curtain closed on the hall side and resumed his seat, reading by the light from the hallway.

The book's chapters were short, and when he came to the black page at the end of Chapter Seven he found himself staring into the blackness, and exhaustion gave the page a faint green border. Vaguely he wondered if there might be words hidden in the black field.

He only realized that he had gone to sleep in the chair when he began to drift back into wakefulness. He could hear voices from a television—he knew it was television because he recognized the show that was playing. It was . . . some cartoon that used to come on very late at night when he and Moira had been in early grade school; irritatingly 1950s-style animation, blocky characters with huge square heads and barrel bodies and tiny pointed feet. Both eyes on the same side of their nose, like in dumb old Picasso pictures.

One character was named Matt, and was always coming home drunk, with his hair spiky and his shirt untucked, and he'd bang on his own locked front door and yell, "Can I come in? Say I can come in!"

Grammar had caught them watching it one night, long after bedtime, and told them that they couldn't watch it anymore. Marrity had assumed it was the late hour, rather than the show iself, that had prompted the ban.

Matt was saying it now: "Can I come in? Say I can come in, Daphne!"

That made Marrity open his eyes. Had Matt's wife been named Daphne?

Daphne was awake in her hospital bed; Marrity could see the gleam of her eyes staring at the far end of the dark room, where the glowing television was mounted high on the wall. Marrity blinked at it himself—it was showing the same program he remembered, the sketchy black-and-white figures who moved only in precisely repetitive gestures. Probably to save animation work.

Marrity noticed that the curtain around Daphne's bed had been pulled all the way open, though he hadn't heard the rollers move in the track on the ceiling.

Then, "Daphne, don't say it!" came a man's voice from behind him, and Marrity came fully awake with a start.

A man was silhouetted against the now open door, with one hand gripping the door frame and the other hand pulling something out of his ear.

Marrity scrambled to his feet, and the paperback book smacked on the linoleum floor.

"Why not?" said Daphne in a hoarse voice, and Marrity realized that she was only half awake. He couldn't see her expression in the dim light from the TV.

"Say I can come in, Daphne!" repeated the cartoon voice from the television. "The mountains are burning!"

"Why shouldn't she let him in?" Daphne asked the figure in the doorway. She turned back to the television, and by the gleam of her teeth Marrity knew that she had opened her mouth.

"No, Daph," said Marrity loudly. He was suddenly sure that it had not been the late hour that had made Grammar forbid them to watch this show; and, irrationally, he suspected now that it had not appeared on any TV set except for Grammar's. "Don't say anything. Don't—strain your voice box."

Daphne stared at her father, and didn't speak.

"Daphne!" called the voice from the television. "Just nod, if I can come in! When the fires are out it will be too late."

"Daph, don't move," said Marrity, stepping toward the television set. He wasn't at all sure he believed that this animated cartoon was actually talking to his daughter, but he could feel the hairs standing up on his forearms.

"You can't turn it off," said the man in the doorway, speaking quickly, "it's not turned on. Tell Matt to go away."

Marrity swayed with sudden vertigo, but he clung to the urgency in the stranger's disorienting words.

"Go away—Matt," he said hoarsely to the blunt outlines of the face on the screen.

For a moment the eyes that were just black circles on the featureless white face seemed to stare at him from the screen, and Marrity felt sweat chilling his forehead as he helplessly stared back. Then the pen slash of a mouth began opening and closing, and the unsynchronized voice said, "When thou cam'st first, thou strok'st me and made much of me."

It was a line from *The Tempest—The Tempest* again!— and Marrity automatically responded with Prospero's reply to Caliban: " 'Hence, hagseed!' " The jagged outlines of the figure shifted, so Marrity went on dizzily, " 'Shrugg'st thou, malice? So, slave; hence!' "

"Schneid mal die Kehle auf," the thing said, and then its already minimal face sprang apart into random lines.

The screen went dark—and Marrity backed away from it fast. He suspected that if he could stand on something and feel the top of the television set, it would be cold.

Or maybe very hot.

"Exit Caliban," he said in a whispery exhalation. Then he turned to face the man in the doorway. "What was that?"

His voice shook. "And who are you?" He crossed to Daphne's bed and switched on the fluorescent light over her.

The man stepped into the room. He was wearing a dark suit and tie, and gray leather gloves, and he appeared to be in his forties. "My name is Eugene Jackson," he said. "I'm with the National Security Agency." He was shifting his weight from one foot to the other, apparently impatient.

Marrity squinted at him. "And what was that cartoon? It was—it was talking to my daughter! What did it mean about the fires? How could it talk to her?" He forced himself to gather his routed thoughts. "National . . . Do you have some identification?"

Daphne was clearly wide awake now, clutching the bleach-paled blankets around her shoulders and blinking unhappily at the stranger.

Y es, it was talking to your daughter."
Lepidopt reached into his inner jacket pocket and pulled out a badge wallet and showed Marrity his plastic NSA card; it was the current configuration—not that Marrity would know—with the blue band at the top edge that indicated a field agent, and the pattern of computer punch holes along the left side that would provide a scanner with the name "Eugene Jackson," and a null identification number.

He was far, far beyond the bounds of ordinary caution here. This was not how or where he would have preferred to approach Marrity—but when he'd seen the figure on the television screen, he'd had to pull out his earplugs and jump in. He gripped the little rubber plugs in his narrow right fist, aching to screw them back into his ear canals, but he was paying very close attention to the man and the girl.

Clearly Marrity had not expected the dybbuk on the television, nor anything like it. That was good and bad—it meant Marrity wasn't committed, but it also meant he didn't know very much about what he was playing with.

"What . . . *was* it?" asked Marrity.

Lepidopt pushed the heavy door almost closed, and stood next to it so as not to be seen from the hall. He wished he could close it all the way, and make it impossible for the sounds of the nearest nursing station to reach him. What would happen, in the moment before a ringing telephone would be audible here? Would he simply drop dead of a massive stroke?

"We're hoping," he said, "that you'll be able to help us figure out what that was. We know it has to do with Peccavit."

"Einstein," said Marrity blankly.

"Yes, Einstein. And your grandmother, and Charlie Chaplin."

Marrity took a deep breath and let it out. "How is it—you're a government agency, right? Like the FBI? How is this something you'd be involved with?"

Get what you can here and now, thought Lepidopt. And quick. Marrity won't leave the girl alone to talk somewhere else, and fortunately he's only half awake now.

"Einstein," Lepidopt said, forcing himself not to speak too quickly, "was involved in paranormal research, contacting the dead. This sounds incredible, I know—but remember that cartoon thing you just saw on the television. He, Einstein, was very secretive about it, but we want to know what he discovered." Lepidopt waved his free hand. "There are dead people we'd like to interview. And pioneers are careless—Humphrey Davy poisoned himself with fluorine, and Madame Curie killed herself by handling radium. Only later on did people discover precautions that those pioneers should have taken. Einstein exposed himself and his children to"—he glanced at Daphne, who was listening avidly—"to dangers. Your grandmother took a lot of precautions, but it may be that some of the consequences of her father's work caught up with her yesterday. And we can detect paranormal events; we believe, in fact, that one occurred yesterday afternoon at four-fifteen, in San Bernardino, within a small area that includes your house. Did you experience any kind of"—he waved his gloved fist toward the dark television set in the corner—"intrusion at that time?"

"Does paranormal mean witchy?" asked Daphne.

"Yes," said Lepidopt. He kept his eyes on Daphne, but she was looking at her father.

C an you," said Marrity, "make it stop?"

"If we can reproduce Einstein's work, I believe we can, yes. We can save—we can make this intrusion stop now, before it—goes any further."

Marrity was sure the man was being euphemistic because Daphne was listening. *We can save your daughter's life,* he had probably been going to say; or at least, *your daughter's sanity.* And *before it's too late.*

"I may have to—leave, abruptly," Jackson was saying now, and he pulled a business card out of his pants pocket. "Take this, and call us if you think of anything later, or—need anything."

Marrity took it—the only thing printed on it on either side was an 800 telephone number. He tucked it into his shirt pocket. "Do you speak German?" Marrity asked.

"Yes."

"What was the German thing the cartoon said, at the end?"

The NSA man appeared to consider not answering; then he said, "It meant 'Cut open her throat.' "

Daphne touched the stitches below her chin. "Again?" she whispered.

"No," said Jackson, "that was an echo of something it said this afternoon, when you were choking."

"An old woman said it," said Marrity, "in the restaurant. Were you there? What is all this? Was the old woman that thing on the TV? Tell me what's going on."

"I can't, until I know what's *gone* on. *Did* you have some kind of intrusion yesterday afternoon?"

"Yes," whispered Daphne.

"Yes," echoed Marrity. He rubbed his eyes. "Did you

have a woman approach me, a couple of hours ago? Primed with . . . knowledge of my tastes in books and liquor, to question me?"

"No," said the NSA man. "Where did this happen?"

"Outside St. Bernardine's, the first hospital we were at. She even smoked the same cigarettes I do."

"What did she look like?"

"Audrey Hepburn." He realized that he was describing her more to Daphne than to Jackson; they had watched *Breakfast at Tiffany's* not long ago. "Slender, that is, with dark brown hair in a ponytail. Sunglasses. Burgundy shirt, black jeans. About thirty."

"You have a pen and paper," said Jackson. "Let's conduct this conversation in writing, shall we?"

"You mean—not out loud," said Marrity.

"Right. I find it's easier to keep track of topics that way."

Marrity was surprised to see Jackson hurriedly twist a pair of earplugs into his ears. But probably they're miniature spy speakers, he told himself.

Marrity crossed to Daphne's table and tore off the top sheet of the pad and put it in his pocket.

Ten

Rascasse was snapping the fingers of his free hand as he listened to the scrambler telephone. He stopped in order to put his hand over the mouthpiece and bark at the driver, *"Ralentissez,* we are too late." The roaring of the bus's engine went down in pitch.

Finally he replaced the receiver in its box. To Golze, he said, "We should have put Charlotte at the second hospital, compromised though she was. Shaved her head and given her a fake mustache. Not wasted her on foolish Bradley."

"What happened?"

"An NSA man, or some fellow claiming to be of the NSA, talked to Marrity and the daughter at the hospital."

He sighed and dragged his fingers across his scalp, making his close-cropped white hair even spikier. "The dybbuk appeared on the TV set in her *chambre,* her *room,*" Rascasse went on, "trying to get her to let it into her mind. The NSA fellow and her father stopped her from consenting. An NSA man, knowing about dybbuks! We'll be getting a fax of the transcription of their talk, but Marrity mentioned Einstein, and the NSA man gave him a bunch of nonsense about wanting Einstein's work in order to talk to dead people. He hinted that Marrity's daughter is in big danger if Marrity doesn't cooperate."

"Well," said Golze, "she would be."

"He'd have dropped the hint in any case, to open Marrity up. And Marrity said he and his daughter experienced some kind of 'intrusion' yesterday at four-fifteen, which is precisely when we registered the Chaplin device as having been activated."

Rascasse had been looking at Golze, but now Charlotte saw her own face swing into his view. "*Then* Marrity asked if the NSA had set a *woman* onto him, primed with his tastes in books and liquor!" He paused, no doubt making some sort of face. "And he gave the fellow a good description of you too. And *then* the NSA man said they should conduct the rest of their question-and-answer session in writing! All we got was the sound of a pen scratching on paper! Luckily Marrity made the man leave after about five minutes. We should have had you in the room next to the girl's."

"True," said Charlotte in a level tone. She was one of the very few remote viewers who could read text while looking out of someone else's eyes—possibly because if she couldn't read that way, she wouldn't be able to read anything at all.

The scrambler phone buzzed, and Rascasse opened the case again and lifted the receiver. After thirty seconds he said, "'Kay." He replaced the receiver and shut the case.

"The San Diego detective who called the Shasta hospital yesterday is dead," he told Golze and Charlotte. "Before he died, our people asked him who told him to track down Lisa Marrity. The detective, who was Jewish, said he was doing a favor for a friend—and under duress admitted that he believed his friend was with the Mossad."

Beside Charlotte, Golze gulped audibly. "Then that wasn't an NSA man in the girl's hospital room—he didn't sound like NSA, what with the dybbuk and all." Behind the disordered tangle of his black hair, his glasses winked in the overhead light. "Could the Mossad be on to *us, here,* because of the New Jersey branch's pass at the Tel Aviv mainframe on Saturday?"

"They're here for the same reason we are," said Rascasse. "They want the thing Lieserl Maric had."

After a moment of bafflement, Charlotte remembered that Lieserl Maric was Lisa Marrity's real, Serbian name.

"We've got to get the thing, both pieces of it, and close this down," said Rascasse. "We're on alien turf here, our strength is all in Europe. This is still Einstein's defended exile island. Tomorrow," he said, staring at Charlotte so that she had a good view of her own face, "early morning, you kill Marrity. Gunshot."

Charlotte watched her eyebrows and mouth, keeping them in straight lines.

"He's the Mossad's source now," Rascasse went on, "and we don't want them to get any more out of him than they did tonight. This will isolate the daughter, and we might be able to work on her with help from the dybbuk and our *tête* friend in the cabinet."

Her face swung out of Rascasse's view as he looked out the window at cars in other lanes. "You've been due to kill someone for a while, you know, Charlotte," Rascasse went on, not unkindly. "Can't get favors from the Devil unless you do some favors for him."

"Okay," she said flatly. She thought about her younger self, the pre-1978 Charlotte who could still see. *I have done nothing but in care of thee,* she thought forlornly.

"Paul," Rascasse went on to Golze, "tell the field men to bring in that old man who has been driving the green Rambler. He hasn't done anything worth watching yet, but we need to prevent the Mossad from getting hold of him too. And I think we need to take another look at the Einstein cluster on the freeway."

Charlotte was estimating how many steps it would take her to get to her coat and purse at the back of the bus, and the bottle of Wild Turkey.

"The freeway" was the Vespers term for the five-dimensional state outside of time, the region where the ghosts existed and where a person's whole lifetime could supposedly be seen as something like a long rope curling through a vacuum abyss; though sometimes they described the lifetimes as sparks arcing across a vast gap, or as standing waves ringing some inconceivable nucleus.

From any point on a person's lifeline, such as right now, the person's future was contained in an invisible cone expanding away forward in time. Like everybody, the Vespers could largely control their futures; but Charlotte knew that they hoped to work in the other direction too, so that even their pasts would be expanding cones of changeable possibilities, opening out backward.

Charlotte needed it to be true.

They were hardly the first natural philosophers to hope to do this—the Holy Grail was a picture of their ambition: a chalice made of two opposite-facing cones, one opening upward and the other opening downward.

Already they could project their astral awarenesses "onto the freeway," out into the bigger space of the fifth dimension, but they could only hang in one place out there and look around. They couldn't do anything that could by analogy be called moving. And they could do even just this much only by summoning the beings that existed in that region, and . . . *paying* them.

With the device Lieserl Maric had possessed, they believed they would be able to *travel* through the fifth dimension, into the past and the future—and they would probably be able to dispense with the diabolical escorts.

And they would be able to change the past, with surgical precision.

Right now the Vespers were pretty sure they knew how to "short out" a person's lifeline, how to make someone never have existed. Einstein had supposedly left a device in a tower in Palm Springs that could delete a person's lifeline from the universe, but among the Vespers it was generally believed that the device had never been used since Einstein created it in 1932.

They couldn't be certain, because in the resulting world—the world in which the shorted-out person had never existed—only the person who had performed the "erasure" would have any memory of the erased person or the world that had included him or her. And so far no one had claimed to have done it.

Charlotte had heard Golze joke about a person known as Nobodaddy, who was evidently the mythical founder of the Vespers. According to the story, at some point the Vespers had shorted out the founder's lifeline, erasing him from the memories of everyone in the world except the one person who had done the erasure, and leaving the Vespers as an organization that nobody had founded.

"We should call it a tollway, not the freeway," said Rascasse through closed teeth. "Fred!" he called to the driver. "Pull over when you see somebody walking alone—tell him you need to know how to get to the 210 freeway. Get the person to come aboard the bus to show you on your map. Charlotte can do a scan to make sure nobody's watching, and when she says go, we'll subdue the person."

Charlotte could see her own face squarely in the center of Golze's vision; probably he was smiling at her. "People who would never get in a stranger's car will get into a bus," he said. "Everybody trusts bus drivers."

Eleven

W hat intrusion? yesterday
        my daughter watched a video, an old b&w—I
was in other room—reading d'ter's mind—and the video
scared her so bad that she set the VCR & her bedroom on
fire. Just with her mind, no matches
    wheres the video from?
    my grandmother's house, labeled Pee-wees Big Adv'ture,
but only first 5 min were Pee-wee—after, this b&w. Very old
movie, a silent—something about a woman eating the
brains out of a bald guy's head
    by the ocean?
    Dunno—ask her?
    later—video where now?
    burned up
    G'mother Lisa Marrity?
    yes
    what did she know about Einstein?

he was her father. She had letters from him
letters where now?
stashed. I cn make copies
need them now.
tomorrow. Bank safe deposit
What d u know about Einstein & yr g'mother? &
Chaplin?
Einstein, nada, she ne'r mentioned him. Said she knew
Chap in 30s, went t Switzerland in 77 after he died
G'ma ever refer to electric machine she &/or Einstein
made?
No
Where was yr g'mother last, in Calif?
? Airport, I guess?
Any certain reason to think so?
She took cab. Card here. Who was the woman who talked
t me?—books, liquor, cig'ts?
Not sure. Don't talk to her. Meet tomorrow—here, noon?
We'll compensate for time off work.
——ok

"Well," said Malk, slapping the sheet of paper onto the wooden table, "he didn't put those letters in any safe-deposit box. No bank was open yesterday, and we followed him all day today."

"We followed him yesterday," said Bozzaris. "It's Tuesday now." He was crouched on the floor at the shadowed opposite end of the little twelve-sided motel room, dialing the telephone that was mounted on the low vertical section of the white wall; above elbow height the walls slanted inward to a flat ceiling panel.

The ringer coil and clapper had been taken out of the telephone, and the two brass bells themselves had been carefully wrapped in tissue paper and stashed in separate places. Lepidopt wasn't worried about the cellular phone, which Marrity would reach if he called the number on the card Lepidopt had given him—the premonition had palpably been about telephone bells, not the electronic tone of a Motorola cellular phone.

"The letters must be at his house," said Malk. "We could go look for them right now."

"No," said Lepidopt, who was sitting on the bed. "There's a thousand places in that house to hide letters; and he's being cooperative, considering his crash recruitment. Incidentally, Bert, I want you to go through his trash cans, before dawn, and find that burned-up VCR and videocassette."

"Okay. Does he believe his daughter's in big danger, and that you can save her?"

"Partly. Mostly."

"Odd that he wouldn't give you the letters right away. Why does he want to make copies of them?"

"So he can sell the originals, I imagine," said Lepidopt. If it were my son who was in danger, he thought, I would not be thinking first of making money from selling the Einstein letters.

It's afternoon in Tel Aviv right now, he thought; Louis is probably with Deborah, maybe having lunch. If I were there he would want to go to Burger Ranch for lunch, and get one of those disgusting Spanish burgers, with the watery tomato sauce on it.

Lepidopt remembered riding on the old Vespa scooter with Louis through the quiet evening streets of Tel Aviv, stopping to feed the many stray cats and watch lights come on behind the shutters and awnings and planter boxes that residents had hung all over the balconies of the 1920s Bauhaus apartment buildings, breaking up and humanizing the once stark architectural lines.

He pushed the tormenting thoughts away.

Lepidopt and Malk and Bozzaris were in one of the tepee rooms of the Wigwam Motel in San Bernardino, on what had been Route 66 until two years ago but was only Foothill Boulevard now. The neighborhood, right across the highway from the train yards and the towering Santa Fe smokestack, had already begun to deteriorate. Luckily the Wigwam Motel was still in business—nineteen conical cement tepees arranged irregularly across three weedy acres, each tepee twenty feet tall and painted white with a pastel zigzag line around the middle. To see their cars, Lepidopt would have to get down on his hands and knees and peer out through one of the two diamond-shaped windows.

The safe-house apartments were more conveniently located, and had garages and closets, and were certainly much *bigger,* but these concrete tepees, with steel-pipe "lodge poles" crossed at the narrow top, had the virtue of being largely free of right angles—a hostile remote viewer would find it difficult to get preliminary reference bearings.

And Lepidopt was in no danger from telephones in nearby rooms!

"My *sayan* is dead," said Bozzaris harshly, hanging up the telephone. "The detective in San Diego. The police down there found his body an hour ago. Apparently he was tortured."

Lepidopt's face was cold. Another *sayan* dead, he thought. "How could our, our *adversaries* have found out about him?" he asked.

"He called the LAPD about Lisa Marrity yesterday," said Bozzaris. "And then he called the hospital in Shasta. Probably the adversaries were monitoring calls to the hospital. Fuck." He was still crouched beside the telephone, his head lowered and a lock of his black hair hanging across his face.

Malk shifted in his chair at the little table. "You figure the 'adversaries' is the crowd with the dark-haired sunglasses girl?"

"For now I figure that." Lepidopt stood up from the bed and leaned against the slanted wall beside the front door. He dug a pack of Camels out of his pocket and shook one loose. "And clearly they're not just Einstein scholars, or Charlie Chaplin fans. We should have roped in the old guy in the Rambler when we had the chance. They're likely to get him next, whoever he is." He struck a match and puffed rapidly on the cigarette.

Two *sayanim* dead, he thought. Sam Glatzer was a heart

attack, but this one sounds like plain execution. Tel Aviv would not be pleased—*sayanim* were sacrosanct. There would have to be retribution for this.

"Bert," said Bozzaris, straightening up and stepping away from the wall to stretch, "at the Italian restaurant, you *did* pick up those two beer bottles from the old man's table, right? The Rambler guy?"

"Yes," said Malk.

"Then Frank Marrity must have approached him in the restaurant, shortly after he and his daughter arrived. The fingerprints on the bottles are all Frank Marrity's."

Lepidopt could feel the skin tighten on his face. He exhaled a stream of smoke, and then said, "For sure?"

Lepidopt's voice had been strained, and Bozzaris stared at him curiously. "Yes."

"Bert," said Lepidopt, feeling again the tension he had felt in the wrecked lobby of the Ambassador Hotel in Jerusalem, on the night before they had besieged the Lion's Gate in June 1967, twenty years ago now. "You've got your half of the orders?"

Malk looked startled. "Yes."

"Haul it out." He dug a set of car keys from his pocket and tossed them to Bozzaris. "Ernie, get the can of Play-Doh out of my car."

Bozzaris also looked disconcerted, but only said, "Right, Oren."

"Tel Aviv told us not to do anything," said Malk as Bozzaris unbolted the door and stepped outside, letting in a lot of chilly night air that smelled faintly of sagebrush and diesel exhaust. Lepidopt could briefly see a diamond-shaped lozenge of yellow light from a tepee in the middle distance. "That would include reading those orders now."

"This supersedes what Tel Aviv said." And I'm glad it does, Lepidopt thought; I want to see what we're supposed to do, before the arrival of the Prague *katsa,* who outranks me.

"What, all our *sayanim* dying?"

"That too."

"Does Tel Aviv know about your 'never again' premonitions?"

Malk and Bozzaris hadn't known, until the necessity of insulating himself from all telephone bells had made Lepidopt explain it to them.

And I must not hear the name of the actor who starred in True Grit. *Don't say it!*

For members of the Halomot branch of the Mossad, they had seemed very skeptical.

"Yes," Lepidopt answered. Tel Aviv took it seriously, he thought. Now Admoni probably intends this new *katsa* to replace me, if he didn't intend that already.

Lepidopt heard a car trunk slam shut, and then Bozzaris hurried back inside and closed and bolted the door. In his hand was a yellow can of Play-Doh with a blue plastic lid.

"Don't open it yet," Lepidopt told him, "it starts to dry out pretty quick." He reached into his shirt and pulled up the inch-wide steel cylinder that he always wore on a cord around his neck, while Malk was doing the same. Each of the cylinders was lathed to resemble a stack of disks, with the gaps between each precisely as wide as the disks, and the edges of the disks were visibly engraved with tiny figures.

Lepidopt held out his hand for Malk's, and Malk lifted the chain off over his head and stood up to pass it across to him.

"This is premature," said Malk.

Lepidopt shook his head decisively. "Should have done it Sunday."

He held the two cylinders up next to each other, with their top and bottom faces exactly parallel—the disk edges of one precisely matched the grooves of the other, and it looked as if he could have pushed them together to some extent, like meshing two combs.

"The engineering branch seems capable of precision machining, anyway," Lepidopt said. "Let's hope they remembered to do the text in mirror image." He pulled the cord off over his head, untied the knot in it, and slid it out through the ring in the top of the cylinder.

Malk had sat down again and was lighting a cigarette of his own, with shaky fingers. "Even if they didn't," he said impatiently, "there's a mirror in the bathroom."

"True, true. Okay, Ernie," Lepidopt told Bozzaris as he unsnapped the chain on Malk's cylinder and drew it free of the ring, "open the can and roll me out a flat sheet of the stuff."

As Bozzaris was prying open the can's lid, Malk asked, "What's the movie, that the girl watched? That made her burn up the VCR?"

"Almost certainly it's a thing called *A Woman of the Sea*," said Lepidopt, "filmed in 1926 by Josef von Sternberg. There were a couple of versions, and this would be the one edited by Charlie Chaplin, with scenes Chaplin shot. The brain-eating bit is supposed to have been only implied, subliminally. This Daphne is obviously a sensitive girl; and tough—*I* wouldn't want to watch it." He looked at Malk and shrugged. "And I guess I won't. It was never shown in theaters, and Chaplin burned all the prints and negatives in '33, on June 21, the first day of summer. Three years ago there were still two people living who had seen the film, but Paul Ivano died in '84, and Georgia Hale died in '85."

"Obviously Chaplin didn't burn every copy," said Malk.

"True. This was certainly his own copy, secretly kept in spite of Einstein's advice."

Bozzaris blinked at him. "Einstein said burn 'em all?"

"Right," said Lepidopt. "This one was buried with Chaplin, but Lieserl got it anyhow. You remember Marrity said she went to Switzerland after Chaplin died. I'm sure it's gone for good now, though—Chaplin would have destroyed the original film reels when he'd got it transferred onto VHS tape."

"Dangerous thing to leave lying around, apparently," said Malk.

"Very."

Malk spread his hands. "So what's it . . . *good* for? What *was* it good for?"

Lepidopt stared from fortyish Malk to late-twenties Bozzaris. Twentieth-century men, he thought; Jews, at least, so they know about more centuries and perspectives and philosophies than just the local ones they were born into, but still men who grew up swimming in the complacent default assumptions of the twentieth century.

"You're Halomot," he reminded them. "Call to mind your training, call to mind some of the things you've seen."

Bozzaris grinned. "We expect it to be weird."

Lepidopt nodded, frowning. "Chaplin meant it to be a device that would let a person travel in space-time. It's not, quite, just by itself, but it apparently turns out to be—to have been—a useful *component* of such a device. Like a catapult to help get jets up to speed coming off an aircraft carrier. The movie by itself would get you up to speed but wouldn't provide an airplane. It—"

"Is that like a time machine?" interrupted Bozzaris.

"The complete device that Lieserl had would be more than that. But yes, it would be a time machine too."

There was no expression on Bozzaris's face. "You mean like so a person could go into the future or the past."

"Yes," said Lepidopt levelly, "and change things. In 1928 Einstein built the prototype, which could only travel up and down, to points in the operator's future and past, not sideways to points outside of his future and past. And it was primitive—apparently Einstein almost killed himself when he used it in 1928—but over the years Lieserl added expansions and improvements, some of which were apparently provided by the movie. The Chinese Theater slab was probably a supplemental component of it too."

Malk nodded and waved his hand for Lepidopt to continue.

"Chaplin," Lepidopt went on, "apparently meant the movie to be a working time machine all by itself, just like he did with his later movie, *City Lights*. He had noticed that movies could evoke tangible energies out of the psyches of their audiences, and in these two movies he tried to direct those energies. He met Einstein in January of '31, and attended some séances with him, and when Chaplin went to London later in '31 he stood up the prime minister—a dinner to be given in Chaplin's honor at the House of Commons—to run to Berlin and confer with Einstein again. It seems that Einstein didn't so much say it couldn't be done as that it would be a very bad idea."

"Why did Chaplin want a time machine?" asked Bozzaris.

Lepidopt pursed his lips. "His first son died three days after being born, in 1919. Two weeks later Chaplin started shooting the movie *The Kid,* in which his Tramp character has adopted an orphan boy who the authorities are trying to take away from him. But apparently that . . . vicarious cinematic resurrection wasn't enough. Chaplin wanted to go back and—somehow—save his actual son."

Bozzaris had used a water glass to roll a chunk of the blue Play-Doh into a sheet on the tabletop. "Ready for you here." He looked up and frowned. "Wasn't Chaplin's body dug up again, and held for ransom?"

"Yes," said Lepidopt, stepping away from the wall. "By two idiots who wanted money to open a garage. They were caught, and Chaplin's coffin was restored to the Vevey Cemetery, but the police never caught the woman who had coerced the two men into it, and of course she got away with the videocassette that had been in the coffin."

Malk frowned at the sheet of Play-Doh. "If the movie and the footprint slab are improvements Lieserl added," he said, "what's the basic engine?"

Bozzaris got up from the table, and Lepidopt sat down in his chair, across from Malk.

"It's a machine," Lepidopt said absently, hefting the cylinders, "small enough to fit into a suitcase, apparently. Einstein referred to it as his *maschinchen,* little machine, and from his papers we gather that part of its function—God knows why—is to measure very tiny voltages. Whatever it is, I think it's in Newport Beach, or was, on Sunday. Tomorrow at dawn Ernie and I will go look for it."

"The cab," said Malk. "The card."

Lepidopt smiled and nodded. "Right. I called the cab

company and pretended to be LAPD, aiming to find out which airport Lieserl went to, which airline. But the cab-driver reported taking an old woman with one suitcase to Newport Beach, not to any airport. Balboa and Twenty-first, right by the Newport Pier. It may still be there, some pieces of it anyway, these thirty-six hours later."

"That's *this* morning," said Bozzaris.

"Young people don't need much sleep," said Lepidopt absently.

Now, carefully, he pressed one of the cylinders into the soft blue surface of the Play-Doh, and then he rolled it slowly away from him, maintaining the pressure. After he had rolled it across four inches, he lifted it away—imprinted on the blue surface now were five sunken bands, with frag-ments of raised letters visible in them. Then he lined up the other cylinder and just as carefully rolled it across the same area, and its disk edges imprinted the raised lines that had been left untouched by the first cylinder.

When he lifted the second cylinder away, the Play-Doh showed a one-by-four-inch impression with tiny raised char-acters on it; the top rows of figures were repeated at the bot-tom, for he had rolled out more than one full turn of the cylinders, to make sure he got everything. The figures were Hebrew letters.

"Do you need a magnifying glass?" asked Bozzaris.

"Yes," said Lepidopt, though already, squinting, he had managed to make out the Hebrew characters that spelled "1967" and "Rephidim stone" and "change the past."

The Rephidim stone again, he thought. Where Moses struck the rock to get water for the Israelites, in the Sinai desert—the original destination of the 55th Parachute Bri-gade, during the Six-Day War in 1967, for which we were issued the radiation-film badges that were actually amulets.

He sighed and flexed his maimed hand. "So get me a magnifying glass, would you, Ernie?" he said.

ACT TWO

Ye Shall Not Surely Die

And he walked in all the sins of his father,
which he had done before him . . .

—1 KINGS 15:3

Twelve

Derek Marrity wasn't going to go near Arrowhead Pediatric Hospital—no, sir—even though he knew that's where Frank Marrity would be right now.

He needed to see Frank Marrity one more time, to tell him some things to do—and if Frank paid attention and did even some of what Derek would tell him, it should make the difference between living comfortably, on the one hand, and living in a twenty-four-foot trailer in a chain-link-bordered trailer park, on the other. But tonight would not be the night to approach him about it.

He rolled his left hand on the steering wheel to look at his watch, then with his right hand pushed the stem to light its face. Nearly 1:30 in the morning. Not a good time to be driving drunk, and with no believable driver's license, past the empty floodlit lots and the stray dogs and the dark car-repair garages of Base Line Boulevard in San Bernardino.

The conversation between Daphne and Frank Marrity would have ended at least an hour ago, and Frank Marrity would be asleep by now in his truck in the hospital parking lot.

Derek knew vividly what had taken place at the hospital. Frank Marrity had fallen asleep over *Tristram Shandy* in a chair in Daphne's room, but he had awakened when a man peeked in at the door of the room; the man had apologized and walked away down the corridor, but by that time Daphne had been awake too.

She had been uncommunicative before she'd gone to sleep, presumably woozy from the anesthetic; but now she had seemed alert, and not happy to see her father in the room.

There was a pad on the desklike table by her bed, Derek knew, and Daphne had written on it, *u cut my throat* in letters that tore the sheet of paper in a couple of places.

Frank Marrity, poor doomed soul, had said something like, "I had to, you were choking." *coughing,* she wrote. "Daphne," Marrity had protested, "no, you weren't coughing, you were *choking.* You would have died. I love you, I saved your life." She'd had to tear off the torn sheet of paper to write more, and then she had written: *I was OK—u cut my throat—dont want to be alone w u.* And of course after he had protested again that he had done it to save her, that he loved her, she had written *I hate you.*

At that point, Derek knew, Frank Marrity had stumbled blindly out to his truck and eventually gone to sleep on the seat, with some serious drinking indicated in the near future.

Probably one gang or the other had put microphones in the hospital room, and taped Marrity's half of the conversation. Derek Marrity didn't need to hear a recording of it.

One pair of taillights shone on the dark highway a hundred yards ahead of him, and in his rearview mirror two swaying headlights were coming up fast. It didn't look like a police car—probably a drunk. Good, thought Derek as he steered into the slower right-hand lane, any cops who are out here tonight will go after him, and ignore this sedate old Rambler. If it *is* old. I forget.

Then a new white Honda came up fast from a dark street on the right and rocked into a squealing right turn directly in front of Derek; he wrenched the wheel to the left, but suddenly the car that had been a hundred yards ahead was braking hard, and looming up fast in front of him in the left lane; and the car speeding up from behind swung wide to the left, as if to pass Derek, but instead of shooting on past in the empty oncoming lanes, its hood dipped as it abruptly slowed.

Derek stamped on the brake and the tires screeched as he braced himself against the wheel. The old Rambler rocked to a halt, shaking on its suspension. His vodka bottle tumbled out from under the seat and rapped his left heel.

His face was cold with sudden sweat. They've got me bracketed, he thought tensely—I could shift to reverse, but I know I wouldn't get away in this old wreck. I can talk to them, I can make a deal with them—they won't be rough, they've got no reason to be rough with an old man—

The Rambler was still shaking, in fact it was shaking so rapidly that the motion was a harsh vibration now, accompanied by a loud rattling hiss like a rain of fine gravel on the roof and the hood and even in the ashtray, though the windshield showed empty black night; only because it moved so fast did he notice the needle on the temperature gauge swing to the right.

And somehow he was getting an electric shock from the plastic steering wheel.

Derek's heart was racing, and he kept his foot pressed on the brake as he would cling to a tree trunk in a hurricane.

Then the shaking and the noise and the electric current were gone, and he almost fell forward against the wheel as if they'd been a pressure he'd been leaning against.

The Rambler was stopped, though the engine was still running. He made himself uncramp his hands from the wheel and focus his eyes out through the windshield, and he saw that his car was positioned diagonally across the center divider lines in the middle of the highway.

No other cars were visible at all, up or down the wide light-pooled lanes; no lighted signs, just an anonymous band of blue neon far away in the dark. The night was perfectly silent except for the grumble of the Rambler's idling engine.

Shakily he reached for the key to turn it off, then noticed that the temperature-gauge needle was back down in its usual ten o'clock position.

Did I pass out? he wondered, his forehead still chilly with sweat. And did the guys in those other cars just *leave*?

Derek started the engine and cautiously lifted his foot from the brake and stepped on the gas pedal, and the car jumped forward. For a moment he thought the stress must have knocked a valve or lifter back into its proper position, and that the car was running uncharacteristically well; then he realized that it was his right leg that was performing smoothly.

His heart was still hammering in his chest, and he tried to take deep breaths. When he had straightened the car in the left lane and got it moving steadily at thirty miles per hour, he reached down and pressed his fist against his right thigh.

It didn't hurt at all.

He steered the Rambler across the right lane to the curb in front of a lightless cinder-block thrift store, clanked the shift lever into park, and cautiously climbed out of the car, leaving the engine running.

In the chilly night air he took two steps out into the street, then two steps back. Then he stood on his right foot and hopped around in a circle.

His teeth were cold, for his mouth was open; he realized that he was grinning like a fool.

He did three deep-knee bends, then crouched and crossed his arms and tried to kick like a dancing Russian. He tumbled over onto his back on the cold asphalt, but he was laughing and bicycling both legs in the air.

At last he rolled lithely to his feet and slid back into the driver's seat.

"I'm as giddy as a drunken man," he panted, quoting Ebeneezer Scrooge.

He took a deep breath and let it out, staring at the dark low buildings and roadside pepper trees that dwindled with perspective in the big volume of night air in front of him.

But in fact he wasn't drunk. This was sobriety—not the shaky, anxious sobriety of a few hours or days, but the easy clarity of months without the stuff.

She must have died after all, he thought. I can go to the hospital now. And—and I no longer have any reason to hate hospitals! And there are lots and lots of things I've got to tell Frank Marrity—he's going to be a very wealthy, healthy, contented man.

N orth of the San Bernardino city limits, Waterman Avenue becomes Rim of the World Highway as it curls steeply up into the mountains around Lake Arrowhead. The turns are sharp and the drops below the guardrails are often precipitous; the steep mountain shoulders are furred with towering pine trees, but at 3:00 A.M. the only view was of the lights of San Bernardino, far below to the south, dimmed and reddened now by veils of smoke. Forest fires on the other side of the mountain lit the fumey sky like a Hieronymus Bosch painting of Hell. Aurora Infernalis, thought Denis Rascasse.

The bus was pulled off the highway at Panorama Point, a wide sand-paved rest area, and Rascasse and Golze stood in the smoky darkness outside the bus, a yard back from the knee-high rail. The abyss below the stout railing was called Devil's Canyon, East Fork.

Golze glanced back toward the bus. "How's our boy, Fred?" he called.

From one of the opened windows in the dark bus came the driver's voice: "Breathing, through his nose."

"No obstruction to closing the lid, if somebody pulls in here?"

"Nothing's in the way," said Fred. "He's entirely in the bin, and I can close it quietly."

They had picked the young man up at Foothill and Euclid an hour ago. He was a student at one of the Claremont colleges, and he had stepped up into the bus with no hesitation when Fred had asked him to point out the 210 freeway on a

Thomas Brothers map-book page. Now he was bound and gagged with duct tape.

Golze nodded and peered down at the glowing criss-crossing dotted lines that were San Bernardino's streets. "Where's your focus?" he asked Rascasse.

Rascasse pointed slightly west of south, toward the largely unlighted patch that was the California State University at San Bernardino campus. "Right behind the library."

Half an hour ago he had carefully laid on the grass down there a square of oiled glass with his handprints and a few of his white hairs pressed onto the slick surface of it.

Soon Rascasse would kneel down by the railing here, step out of his body, and let his astral projection partly assume the sensorium of the Rascasse focus down there behind the college library. At the same time he would still be aware of kneeling up here beside the bus—like a beam of light split by a slanted half-silvered mirror.

Rascasse would then be occupying two finitely different time shells—the minutely slower time three thousand feet below and this infinitesimally accelerated time halfway up the mountain. He would, briefly, be disattached from the confines of the four-dimensional continuum.

Golze would then cut the throat of the young man in the bus, and the fresh-spilled blood—the end-point of one of the lifelines on the freeway, the release of the young man's accumulated mass energy—would in that instant have drawn the hungry attention of one of the Aeons who existed in the five-dimensional continuum; and that creature would be aware of Rascasse, who for the distance of a second or two would be protruding out of the "flat" four-dimensional fabric like a thread pinched up out of a sheet of cloth.

And Rascasse would leap and cling to the bodiless spirit, mind to incomprehensibly alien mind, and look out at the unphysical landscape that he would then perceive surrounding him; and since space and volume didn't exist there, it would be just as accurate to call it the landscape he would be surrounding. Lifescape, fatescape.

He would be out of his body for no more than a second by

his watch, but time didn't pass on the freeway—an hour out of his body, a day, a year, wouldn't give him a better comprehension of that non-space.

For that timeless moment Rascasse's perspective would be freed of things in the way—viewed from this bigger space, nothing in the normal four-dimensional continuum could be in front of anything else, or under it, or hidden inside it; and seeing a man or a car at one moment would not make it impossible for him to see them simultaneously at other moments too. Golze had said once, when he had stepped back down into sequential time, that it was nearly the perspective of God. And he had seemed both wistful and angry to have to say *nearly*.

The cold wind from over the top of the mountain behind Rascasse smelled of pine sap and wood smoke, and he was shivering when the radio on his belt buzzed softly. He unsnapped it and said, "Prime here."

"Quarte here," said a voice from the radio, frail and tinny under the vast night sky. "You said it might get surreal, and not to hesitate to tell you about crazy things happening. Uh, man and superman."

Rascasse switched the frequency-selector dial on the radio. "Right," he said into the microphone. "So what happened?"

"I was in the lead car," came the voice from the radio, "and after the number three car swerved in from the south, number two came up from behind and blocked him on the north. Then in my rearview I saw the Ra—the—"

"The subject car, the quarry, go ahead."

"Right. It suddenly accelerated toward me faster than . . . any subject car like that should be able to. And he didn't hit me, he should have, but he didn't, but I heard a huge bang, like an M-80. Uh, Caesar and Cleopatra."

Rascasse switched the frequency again, impatiently. "Go on," he said.

"Well, then he was gone. I mean, the car was just gone,

not visible anywhere up or down the highway, and not in any of the lots to the sides. The scanner says the subject car is about three miles northeast of us right now. But the weird thing is, the guys in the number two and three cars got out, and it turns out each of them saw the, the subject car suddenly accelerate toward *him*! Like the subject car split into three cars, each shooting straight at one of us!"

"Arms and the man," said Rascasse quietly, almost absently.

On the new frequency, Rascasse went on, "Find him again, but this time wait until he's out of the car, and then ghosts."

Rascasse switched frequencies again, but after several seconds realized that the field man had not caught the cue. "Dammit," he whispered, and switched back to the previous frequency.

"—try that," said the field man, and then his signal was gone.

"Shit." Rascasse switched the dial back to its previous setting, and the man was saying, "Are you here? Was that a cue? There's no ghosts on the list."

"Never mind," snapped Rascasse, "we're here now. Hit him with a trank dart when he doesn't know you're on to him."

"Okay. What was it about ghosts?"

"It's—a Shaw play that wasn't on your list. Never mind. Just bring him to me. That's all."

"'Kay. Later." And the signal was gone again. Rascasse hooked the radio back onto his belt and took a deep breath of the cold, smoke-spicy air.

"*Ghosts* is by Ibsen," said Golze.

"I know, I know. Shut up."

"I guess that old guy in the Rambler isn't just some relative in town for the funeral."

"Shut up, I said." Rascasse exhaled, almost whistling. "What happened there? When our fellows tried to grab him, and his car disappeared."

"It wasn't bilocation," said Golze. "Trilocation, that is—because the car went in three directions too, not just the man . . . assuming the man was in the car; he might have 'ported away an instant before. I would have, if I was him, if I'd had that option. But that wouldn't explain three apparent cars."

"Does it sound as if he's used the Einstein-Maric artifact?"

"That wouldn't explain the multiple cars either, or at least I can't see how it would. Maybe Charlotte shouldn't kill Marrity. He could know some things."

"A decision made is a debt unpaid," said Rascasse. "And the Mossad will have briefed him, with compulsions, on what to tell other agencies. The daughter will be more valuable to us isolated. And," he added, waving at the bus behind them, "it wants this offering from each of us—our dues— and Charlotte has been in arrears."

"Our souls."

Rascasse shrugged. "Anything that would interfere with our chosen polarity."

"Does it really count as binding payment if you're drunk when you pay it?" Golze asked. "The rest of us don't drink alcohol. Charlotte does."

"For some people, and Charlotte's one of them, drink is a valuable disassembly factor. But once it's disassembled her, she'll have to leave it behind too."

"That'll be a day. You were kind of sweet on her once, weren't you?"

"Irrelevantly."

Golze pulled a lock-back knife from his pocket and opened the blade. "She thinks she'll be allowed to go back, remake her life."

"Do you care what she imagines?"

Golze laughed fondly. "Care? No. Note." He waved the knife toward the bus. "My dues are paid up. Fred!" he added, speaking louder.

"Yo," came Fred's voice through the open bus window.

"Ask your boy if he's a Christian."

"He nods," called Fred after a moment.

"Aw, too bad. Tell him he's gift-wrapped for the Devil."

"Cruelty is another good disassembly factor," remarked Rascasse. "But it will eventually have to be given up too."

"Don't anthropomorphize me," said Golze with a laugh. "Have to be given up? 'Man can't will what he wills.' I'm a roulette ball."

Rascasse shook his head. "Schopenhauer. Philosophy will be left behind too. Even rational thought, eventually."

"Can't wait."

"You'll go far. It's time for you to get aboard the bus."

Golze laughed softly and trudged away across the packed sand and disappeared around the lightless front of the bus. A few moments later the bus shifted perceptibly as he stepped aboard on the far side.

We need to succeed at this soon, Rascasse thought as he began taking deep breaths in anticipation of stepping outside his body. I need access to the bottom half of the chalice.

He shuffled to the guardrail and knelt in front of it. It was a horizontal wooden pole supported at every ten feet by a steel stanchion, and he leaned his chest against it, draping his arms over the far side.

He had been twelve, the first time he had left his body; he had simply got out of bed one morning and looked back and seen his body still lying in the bed. Terror had driven him back into it, and for the first time he had experienced re-entering his body: like a tight bag being pulled over his head and sliding down his arms and legs and eventually closing over his toes. A few years later he had experienced it again, while breathing through the ether-sprinkled mask during a dental operation. And by the time he was twenty, he had been able to step out of his body at will, with only the faintest reflexive twitch of vertigo.

He felt a flash of cold now, and then he was standing beside his kneeling body, carefully noting that it was balanced and leaning firmly against the guardrail. He flexed the fingers of his right hand, and saw the kneeling body's fingers spread wide.

He leaped forward into empty space, and then he could

not only still feel the guardrail against his chest, but also smell the grass of the college lawn and feel oily glass under his fingers—and then he was rocked by the explosion of energy sweeping through higher dimensions as the young man on the bus gave up the ghost, and Rascasse was on the freeway.

Here time was distance, and he was unable to move anything but his attention.

By a perception that did not involve light he could see the bus, and Golze and Fred and the dead boy inside it—and he could see them from all sides at once. Even their organs and arteries, and the valves and crankshaft of the bus, and the secret sap and inner bark of the surrounding trees, were as clearly visible as the mountain. And he could see all sides of the mountain, the fires on the northern slopes and the compacted gravel under the asphalt of the roads.

He moved away from this close perspective, and saw the men now as zigzagging lines, their recent actions and their future actions laid out like rows of tipped dominoes, blurring out of focus at the far ends; the moon was a long white blade in the sky. Golze was beside Rascasse's body, telling him "Ibsen," and Golze was also climbing into the bus, and cutting the young man's throat, and leaving the bus and talking to Rascasse again, and the bus itself was driving out of the Panorama Point rest area, making a loop with the trail of earlier versions of itself driving in.

This was the perspective of the crows in the Grimm brothers's fairy tale "Faithful John"—flying high above the surface-bound characters and able to see things previously encountered and things still to be met.

The young man in the bus was a line of blended figures like Marcel Duchamp's *Nude Descending a Staircase,* and the line ended at the point where the young man's astral body made a turbulence that spread into the sky.

It was a motionless shock wave, and Rascasse's attention followed it outward, away from the precise time and place of the young man's death.

And Rascasse wasn't alone. A living thing that seemed to

consist of buzzing or corrugations was with him, its thoughts as evident to him as the inner workings of the bus but far more alien to him than the courses of the stars or the repetitive patterns of cracks in the stone of the mountains.

Rascasse knew at least that it was summoned by the human sacrifice.

The living thing occupied a region that extended far in a dozen directions from the early morning hours of August 18, 1987, and Rascasse's disembodied self overlapped the thing's self.

Lines like arcing sparks or woven threads stretched across a vast vacuum, and he could discern the thread that was his own time line, with several exploded segments along its extent; he was occupying the cloud around one of the ruptured sections now, just as he was occupying the others in his previous and future excursions onto the freeway.

Just as a photograph of lunar craters can seem to show domes and ridges until the eye's perspective shifts to see craters and cracks, the arcs or threads were also visible as tiny, tightly wound coils, like knots in an infinitely tall and wide stack of carpets.

In the shorter wavelengths of his attention, the lifeline of Albert Einstein was discernible—extending from the band that included Ulm, Germany, in the region of 1879 to the band encompassing New Jersey in 1955.

Rascasse had paid attention to the Einstein line before, and knew what he would see. Even viewed as a stretched-out arc rather than a coil, the Einstein line was a tangled mess; it intersected with a number of other lines, one of which showed branches near the intersections—looked at from another perspective, these branching lines could be seen as two lines merging into one, but Rascasse was imposing time's futureward arrow onto the vista—and so the branches were childbirths, offspring.

Einstein's second wife was his first cousin, whose maiden name was Einstein, and their lifelines from 1919 through her death in 1936 were a hopelessly interconnected hall of mirrors; and from the midst of that confusion a third thread emerged in 1928, in the region of the Swiss Alps, though it didn't seem to arise from one of those branchings that indicated a childbirth.

Rascasse's attention was on that spontaneously arising thread. It went on to intersect with another thread at several points, and showed two offspring branches—close focus indicated that these two were the lifelines of Frank Marrity and Moira Bradley—and then the strange thread ended in 1955, in New Jersey, so close to the end of the Einstein thread that they almost seemed to have merged. They were, in fact, extraordinarily similar.

Rascasse shifted his attention forward in the direction of increasing entropy, to Frank Marrity's adulthood.

Marrity's thread intersected with another in 1974, and the daughter's resulting branch was distinct for a distance of a dozen years; but in 1987 a new thread was in *their* cluster too, and Rascasse's attention couldn't make out where *that* new thread had come from either. Whatever it was, whoever it was, it made a confusion of Marrity's lifeline— just as the cousin-wife's line had made a confusion of Einstein's. There appeared to be a rupture in Marrity's lifeline there in 1987, or perhaps the rupture was in the newly intruding thread; they were so close and so similar that Rascasse couldn't be sure.

Rascasse occupied the tight-focus end of his attention, and he saw the Marritys' newcomer as a zigzagging line in San Bernardino in a narrow section of 1987; and, sampled at several points, the newcomer's line was in a sequence of cars that were all the green Rambler station wagon. But even in the car the newcomer was hard to follow—at least once the Rambler seemed to end and then begin again in a different place.

None of this was easy to perceive. The whole 1987 region was chaotic, with thousands of lifelines blurring into a cloudy unity, especially at the bands that were Mount Shasta and Taos, New Mexico. This haze was the Harmonic Convergence, turbulent with virtual personalities that arose as points in the psychic fog but that extended no farther in time.

Lieserl Maric's time line bent impossibly in this cloud:
Instead of moving forward in the direction of time, it bent
sharply *sideways,* perpendicular, and simultaneously occupied miles and acres of space, and then ended in the static
tornado around Mount Shasta. She had jumped out of the
four-dimensional fabric, but to move through space instead
of through time.

Somehow it seemed that she had ridden a golden helix
from Pasadena to Mount Shasta; and Rascasse realized that
in cross section the helix would be a swastika shape.

Rascasse's focus on the 1987 maelstrom had tilted him
back toward that time, and he could feel his attention losing
scope, narrowing down. The bus was a looping track through
the area that was late summer, like a particle of dust enact-
ing Brownian motion in a glass of water, and he could see
the little loop in its track that was its stop halfway up the
mountain at Panorama Point.

He let himself fall back into specific spatial locality and
the conveyor belt of sequential time.

He was on his knees, and his arms were clinging to the
railing post. He had been in this position for so short a time
that his knees didn't yet ache from pressing against the hard,
sandy surface.

He got to his feet, and was standing, staring out at the
lights of San Bernardino when Golze came trudging up
from behind.

"Did you see my tattoo?" Golze asked.

"I saw our man in the green Rambler," said Rascasse
shortly. "He doesn't appear to have been born—he simply
showed up here and now within the last few days."

Golze whistled, all flippancy gone. "Now *that* could be the
old lady's device at work. I thought he was Frank Marrity's
father."

"No, he's not. I can't imagine who he is. But speaking of
Marrity's father, he *also* doesn't show a mother or a birth—it
looks as if he simply appeared in 1928, in the Swiss Alps—but
he died in New Jersey in 1955. I remember it. We killed him."

"So Derek Marrity's dead? Been dead for thirty-two years?"

"Right."

"And he had no mother or birth? I thought he was Lisa Marrity's son. Lieserl Maric's. Einstein's grandson."

"No, Lieserl . . . adopted him."

"So why did you kill him, in '55? You keep killing all these interesting people, rather than talking to them. You sure you don't want to call off Charlotte?"

"Yes, I'm sure. We did talk to him. We concluded that he would be more use to us dead than alive—though in fact he has not been much use so far."

"How did we *think* he would be of use to us dead?"

"As a guide, an oracle, because of his origin. And he might yet serve as that." Rascasse turned and started back toward the bus. He paused in front of the folded-open door. "I think we should dump the body of our . . . toll, right here."

"Sure," said Golze, grinning, "we leave a trail of corpses. Like Hansel and Gretel, so we can find our way back."

Thirteen

Frank Marrity awoke in the hospital-room chair when the aluminum-framed window had just begun to pale with dawn. Daphne was asleep under the thin-looking blankets, the IV tube still taped to her elbow, and he was impatient to get her out of here.

He reached into his shirt pocket for the NSA man's business card, and pulled out two cards. One was the NSA man's, blank except for the 800 telephone number, and the other was Libra Nosamalo Morrison's. Veterinary Medicine.

I should have given her card to Jackson, he thought, along with the taxi company's card. Or maybe I should give Jackson's card to her. Who are any of these people? Libra Nosamalo—*deliver us from evil.*

He stood up and stretched, then crossed to Daphne's table and wrote on the top sheet of her pad, *Went for a smoke— back in five.* He laid the pad on her blanket.

He walked past the nurse's station to the elevators, and as he was crossing the carpeted ground-floor lobby, nodding to the bored-looking woman behind the desk, he already had a pack of Dunhills and a Bic lighter in his hands—and he was surprised to see Libra Nosamalo Morrison herself, outside the window glass, standing beside a blocky concrete bench and smoking again. She was looking away from him, out toward the still dark parking lot.

He shuffled to a stop.

She was at St. Bernardine's yesterday afternoon, he thought. What is she doing at *this* hospital now, this *children's* hospital? Well—Dunhills, Milton, Housman, Laphroaig scotch—obviously she's here to talk to me. At about five in the morning.

Don't talk to her, Jackson had said.

Marrity took two steps backward, then turned to go back to the elevators.

But behind him he heard her voice call, "Frank?" and he stopped, and then turned around.

She had stepped inside, and as soon as he looked squarely at her she turned her head toward him and waved, smiling. She was still wearing her sunglasses—in fact she was still wearing the black jeans and the burgundy blouse. Her right hand was in her purse, possibly groping for a pack of cigarettes. Was she going to ask him to go outside and smoke with her?

A man was pushing through the door behind her, but Marrity's attention was on the woman, who now pulled a big steel revolver out of her purse.

As Marrity watched, the gun was raised to point at his face.

"Frank!" screamed the man behind her, lunging forward and apparently punching her in the back; her arm swung wide in the instant that Marrity's ears were shocked by the hard *pop* of a gunshot. Glass broke and clattered behind him.

The man behind her was his father, and the old man was staring hard at the blue carpet. "Don't *look* at her, Frank!" the old man yelled, nearly as loud as before. "She's blind if you don't *look* at her!" Derek Marrity spun to face the woman behind the reception desk. "Get down!" he shouted at her.

Marrity crouched and looked toward the hallway that led back to the elevators.

"Frank!" called the woman in sunglasses. "Look at me!"

It reminded Marrity of what the cartoon figure had said to Daphne a few hours ago—*Say I can come in, Daphne!*— and he looked instead at one of the dozen blue couches and dove behind it.

She fired two shots anyway, and one of them made the couch jump.

"Somebody look at me!" she yelled.

"You're facing the elevators!" shouted Derek Marrity, apparently at the Libra Nosamalo woman. "We're behind you!"

"Liar," she said, and two more shots shook the lobby air.

If she steps around this couch, she'll have a clear shot at me, Marrity thought. He braced himself to sprint for the hallway, but in that instant he heard the doors clack open, and then his father called, "She left. She couldn't see. Go to the elevator hallway without looking back."

Marrity got to his feet and made himself look only toward the elevator doors as he hurried out of the lobby. His father was beside him, hardly panting. He seemed much less sickly now than he had yesterday.

"And out the back," the old man said. He even had a suntan now.

Marrity hit the 2 button. "No, I've got to get Daphne."

"Frank, she's dead, there's nothing you can do for her. You've got to get out of here."

. . . she's dead . . .

Marrity's heart froze, and the next thing he was consciously aware of was jumping up the stairs two at a time. Behind and below him he heard his father bang aside the stairway door, which hadn't had time to close.

Marrity slammed open the door to the second floor and raced past the nurse's station to Daphne's room; and then he sagged in relief when he saw her sitting up in bed and blinking at him in alarm.

"You're—all right?" he said breathlessly. "Nobody's been in here?"

"I'm fine," she said hoarsely. Then she whispered, "Was a woman shooting at you, or did I dream that? No, nobody's been in here."

"Daph," he said, "I think it's time you checked out." He turned to the closet and began yanking her jeans and blouse off the hangers. His face was cold with sweat.

"Right now?" she whispered. "I've got an IV!"

"We'll get a nurse to take it out. Or I will. If I can do a tracheotomy, I can—but we're not—"

Footsteps slapped on the hallway linoleum, and Marrity stepped back to stand in front of Daphne, but it was his father who strode into the room.

"They'll have moved her—" the old man began, and then his eyes focused on Daphne.

"I don't understand," he said clearly.

And then Marrity turned and threw himself across Daphne, for his ears had been concussed by a deafening bang, and his father had collapsed against the door frame and begun to slide to the floor.

No further explosions followed, though over the ringing in his ears Marrity thought he heard a crisp roar, like a TV set on a blank channel with the volume turned way up.

Marrity looked fearfully over his shoulder—but though his father had tumbled apparently unconscious onto the linoleum floor, nobody had appeared behind him. The roaring had stopped, if it had ever been a real external noise. His father's slack face was pale and old.

With trembling fingers Marrity peeled the tape off Daphne's forearm and drew the IV needle out of her wrist. She was probably deafened too, so he just shoved her clothes into her hands.

She started to sit up, then winced and said, "Ribs! Help me up!"

He got an arm behind her shoulders and lifted her to a sitting position, and she quickly slid out of her hospital gown and scrambled into the jeans and blouse with no further hindrance from her cracked ribs. She knelt by the closet to pick up her shoes in one hand, and then nodded at Marrity.

Nurses were shouting questions, but Marrity held Daphne's elbow and marched her toward the far-stairway exit door.

"I'll fetch the truck," Marrity said loudly as they scuffed down the steel-edged cement stairs. "You wait by the door and hop in when I pull up."

Daphne was ahead of him, nimble on her bare feet. In something like her normal voice she asked, "Shouldn't we do something about your father?"

"Like get him to a hospital?"

At the bottom of the stairwell, Marrity pushed open the door and peered out; no one was in sight along the brightly lit carpeted hall, so he led Daphne to the exterior door at the near end of the hall.

"One minute," he told her.

He stepped outside and glanced in both directions, but he didn't see the woman in sunglasses, and so far there were no police or security guards in sight. There were no shadows yet, but the sky was bright blue over the mountains in the east. He took a deep breath of the chilly air and then ran across the parking lot to the Ford pickup truck.

It started on the first twist of the ignition key, and without giving it a moment to warm up he banged it into reverse and swung out of the parking space; then he had pulled the lever down into first and gunned the truck across the empty lanes to the door, and only when Daphne had burst out of the door and hopped up into the passenger seat did he realize that he had been holding his breath.

"What's going on?" asked Daphne, slamming her door.

"Somebody tried to shoot me, a few minutes ago," Marrity said as he made a right turn out of the hospital parking lot. His hands were trembling again, and he gripped the steering wheel tightly. He was panting. "You didn't dream it. Put your seat belt on, and keep it away from your neck. A woman, with sunglasses—"

"The one you told Mr. Jackson about." Daphne pulled the spring-loaded strap across her chest and fumbled beside her for the buckle. "He said don't talk to her. Headlights?"

Marrity pulled out the headlights knob, though it made no difference in visibility. "That's the one. I didn't say a word to her, she just started shooting. And then my father said you were dead, and he was—you saw—real surprised to see that you were alive. He saved my life," he added. "Knocked her gun aside."

"I hope he's not dead."

"I do too, I guess."

W here do we go?" Daphne hummed a few rising and falling notes. "My voice seems okay."

"I don't know." Marrity looked into the rearview mirror as he made a third right turn, onto westbound Highland Avenue now, and saw no cars at all in the shadowed lanes under the brightening sky, just a couple of big grocery-delivery trucks receding away ahead of him. "Nobody's following us. Yes, you sound like your usual self."

"Maybe home?"

"Maybe. Or—I'm gonna turn south now, and see if that new car back there turns left too."

The light was red at D Street, but he turned left into a doughnut-shop parking lot, drove diagonally right through the lot and made a left onto D Street. The truck rocked on its springs.

Daphne was twisted around under her seat belt, kneeling on the seat to look behind them through the camper shell's back window.

"He turned south too, Dad," she said quietly as she sat down again. "I think there's two people in the car."

"Yes," agreed Marrity, forcing himself to speak calmly. And the passenger, he thought, is wearing sunglasses.

His father had said, *She's blind if you don't look at her.*

"Don't look at them, Daph," he said tightly.

There was a police station five or six blocks ahead, he remembered.

He could see now that the car behind was a tan Honda—it was gaining on them, clearly meaning to pass. Marrity

could believe that the person in the passenger seat would
have some kind of full-automatic gun this time. He tromped
on the gas and the truck surged forward, but the Honda was
still gaining, edging to the left.

There was no way that Marrity would be able outrun it
to the police station.

"Daph," he said quickly, "can you picture the radiator of
a car?" The truck's engine was roaring, but he didn't want to
shift to third because in that gear it tended to slack off for a
few moments before regaining power.

"Sure. Are they going to shoot us?"

"Yes. Can you *grab* the radiator of their car, without
looking at it, the way you grabbed Rumbold on Sunday?"

Daphne frowned and screwed her eyes shut, then after a
moment opened her eyes and peered uncertainly over her
shoulder.

The Honda was nearly even with them, but swinging out
wide into the empty oncoming lanes—to prevent Marrity
from sideswiping them, presumably, and to have a clear shot
even if Marrity braked hard.

Which he did. In the same instant that he straightened his
leg to force the brake pedal all the way down, the hood of
the Honda exploded up in a huge starburst of white steam.

Marrity had to concentrate on his own vehicle. The truck
was shuddering and fishtailing as the tires screamed on the
pavement, and even in the confusion Marrity remembered
to pull the gear shift lever down into first, so that he was
able to let the brake up and steer quickly through the cloud
of tire smoke into an alley on the right, and then speed down
the alley with his exhaust battering back from a row of
closed garage doors.

He glanced sideways at Daphne, but the sudden hard
pressure of the seat belt didn't seem to have hurt her ribs,
and the stitches in her throat weren't bleeding.

"They had a gun!" she said shrilly. "I had to look! It was
pointed right at both of us!"

Smoke swirled under the windshield—the ashtray was
on fire.

"Just push it closed," Marrity said, "it'll go out on its own. And don't yell through your patched throat."

At E Street he made a left turn fast enough to set the tires chirruping, and accelerated.

"I had to grab something here to brace against," said Daphne more quietly as she pushed the ashtray closed with her foot. Marrity was glad to see she had managed at some point to pull her sneakers on.

"I think the ashtray's kind of melted," she added.

"That's okay. You were smart to think of grabbing the ashtray."

"I'm sorry I looked, when you said not to."

"I'm glad you did. We've got to ditch the truck." Marrity turned right, into a tree-lined street of quiet old bungalow houses. His mouth was dry, and peripherally he could see the collar of his shirt twitching with his rapid heartbeat. "I think they've got a radio beacon on it somewhere, is how those guys found us."

"Okay," said Daphne. "Anything we need out of it?"

"Just my briefcase." Marrity braked to a stop at the curb in front of an apartment complex and trod on the parking brake. He took a deep breath and exhaled before unclamping his hands from the steering wheel and switching off the ignition. In the sudden quiet, he said, "It's got a bunch of Albert Einstein letters in it, along with my students' Mark Twain papers."

"Really!" Daphne opened her door and hopped down to the sidewalk. "That was smart of you."

Marrity opened his door and shivered at the chilly dawn air in his damp shirt. "Let's find a bus stop."

"Do you have your Versatel card?"

"Yup." He climbed down onto the asphalt and walked around the front of the truck to join her on the sidewalk. "Only about two hundred dollars in the savings, though. And about eighty in my pocket."

"All we need is enough money to get there. Then we'll have a whole lot of gold."

"I'll give you a hundred," he said, taking her hand as they began walking west along the sidewalk, "and then I think I should drop you off at Carla and Joel's. I'll pick you up again once I've been to Grammar's house. Then we—"

"No, I have to go with you."

He looked down at her earnest upturned face and shook his head. "There's people shooting at me, Daph. I can't duck them and watch out for you too, worry about you too."

"They're—" Clearly she was thinking fast. "They're after me as much as you. It was me that the cartoon thing wanted, wasn't it?"

"Yes," he admitted. He was nervously watching the traffic moving back and forth on E Street a hundred feet ahead, hoping not to see the tan Honda.

"And they'd probably find Carla and Joel's place. From your phone book, easy. Everybody we know, they'd be watching their places." She scratched her nose. "And anyway, what if that cartoon guy can tell where I am, the way they can tell where the truck is?" She gripped his hand tighter, and he could tell she had scared herself with the thought.

And it scared him too. I sure can't say that's not possible, he thought.

"And," Daphne went on with a brave show of nonchalance, "Carla and Joel put Velveeta cheese on everything."

"They could make you a Velveeta soufflé," he said, matching her tone. "Let's cross, and go down that alley."

Hand in hand they sprinted across the street, then resumed walking, south now, between backyard fences and little old wooden garages.

"They wouldn't call it a soufflé," said Daphne.

"Velveeta Puddle."

" 'And it's got Rice Krispies in it!' " she mimicked, pronouncing *rice* as *rahss.*

"Okay," he said, "good point. I guess you'd better come along with me at that."

Fourteen

If something's going to be on the radio," said Ernie Bozzaris, "why didn't you save a radio for us?"

"She wouldn't have done it right here, where we're standing," said Lepidopt. "And the only thing that's going to come over the radios—one or two of them, anyway, I hope—is interference fringes, alternating patches of noise and silence."

The early morning sun was already bright on the pastel nylon windbreakers of the fishermen out on the Newport Pier, but Lepidopt and Bozzaris stood in the chilly shadows of a closed Thai restaurant up on the damp, sand-gritty sidewalk. Lepidopt looked enviously at the handful of surfers bobbing in the dark blue swells out beyond the surf line—since his premonition that he would never again swim in the ocean, he didn't even dare go out on the pier. He and Bozzaris were both wearing jeans and sweatshirts and tennis shoes.

Lepidopt felt free to dispense with the earplugs out here. He couldn't even see a pay telephone anywhere.

"This is awful public," said Bozzaris. "Why would Lieserl have come here to work the machine?" They had parked across Balboa Boulevard in the ferry parking lot, and at Bozzaris's insistence they had stepped into a bakery on the walk over here, and now he fished a powdery jelly doughnut out of the paper bag he was carrying. "Is this where she did it before, in 1933?" He was blinking around uneasily. "I don't suppose you want any of these," he added, waving the doughnut bag.

"Peace, youth," said Lepidopt. "This wouldn't have been where she set it up in '33, no—but it would be a reliable place for her to have set it up two days ago, since I believe she did not mean to survive that jump. This is a place where time and space might be reliably kinked, you see." He raised an eyebrow at Bozzaris's doughnut. "No, thank you."

"Kinked," echoed Bozzaris around a mouthful that probably contained lard, from pigs.

Lepidopt nodded and waved at the nearly empty parking lot and the pier. "This—right here—was the epicenter of the 1933 earthquake. March tenth, at five fifty-four in the evening. You notice all the buildings are modern! Einstein was at Cal Tech at that moment, actually discussing seismographs, in fact. We believe he was afraid Lieserl had tried out the *maschinchen,* the time machine, the day before. There had been a foreshock on the ninth, which probably *was* Lieserl trying it out.

"But she wouldn't have been here, then," he went on. "Not her physical body, at least. I gather time travel—*travel,* that is, as opposed to just getting out there and looking around from the perspective of the *Yetzirah* world—actual time *travel* is most safely done with two remote astral projections of yourself, one on a mountain, one lower down, with the physical *you* somewhere between. Sea level is the best for the low one, in the Los Angeles area, unless you wanted to project one all the way out to Death Valley." He glanced up and down the row of seaside shops and rental houses; already, in spite of the morning chill, there were young people in scanty bathing suits riding bicycles along the sidewalk, through the patches of shadow and sunlight.

"But two days ago," he continued, "Lieserl Maric—our Lisa Marrity—wasn't concerned with her safety, I believe. She meant it to kill her. So jumping from sea level would have been fine, and she might well have set up the *maschinchen* right here. I don't believe it's a very complicated apparatus—she apparently carried it here in a taxi, in a suitcase, after all."

Bozzaris squinted around at the parking lot and the more distant green lawn by the foot of the pier.

"Wouldn't she have needed the movie?" Bozzaris asked. "She left that at home."

Just before dawn Malk had crept into Marrity's yard and silently sifted through the contents of his trash cans, and carried away the VCR with the remains of the tape cassette still in it. As if to make doubly sure the thing was destroyed, Marrity had apparently doused it with gasoline and set it on fire. It was just barely possible to ascertain that the remains of a videocassette were in the ruin.

Lepidopt shrugged. "She added improvements, over the years—the movie, the footprint slab. She might have figured out others, more portable."

"So what will it look like? This *maschinchen*?"

"A gold-wire swastika, for one thing," Lepidopt said, "about three feet across, laid flat for her to stand on—just like what they found at her arrival site in Shasta. She would have concealed that—with luck she buried it here somewhere, and it's still buried. We need to see the wiring, and ideally the whole construction."

"There wouldn't have been any of the—two days ago, none of the virtual babies would have appeared here, right?"

"No. And apparently they only last a few seconds, so they wouldn't still be around anyway. You can quit worrying about stray babies stuck under the pier."

"Were there reports of . . . virtual babies, in that meadow on Mount Shasta, on Sunday?"

"No, but she didn't use the *maschinchen* to travel through time on Sunday—just instantaneously through space, sideways out of the cone of her possible future. Not like when she jumped in 1933. On Sunday I think she was trying to scrape something off of herself, something like a psychic barnacle—jump in a direction it couldn't follow—die clean, without it."

Bozzaris laughed, though he seemed to shudder too. "Psychic barnacle—and the friction of it has caused all the fires in the mountains." Looking out at the water, he asked, "Did Lieserl change the past, when she jumped and returned in 1933?"

Lepidopt spread his hands. "How would we know? If she did, we live in the world as she remade it. Did Einstein change the past when he jumped in 1928? Only Lieserl Marity and Einstein would know the answers to these questions."

His answer didn't seem to cheer Bozzaris. "And they're both dead," he said. "But even in '33, when she'd have returned to '33 from the past, none of the spooky babies would have appeared *here*—right?" He shook his head. "That's too weird, about the babies."

"No, they wouldn't have appeared here—quit fretting about them. According to Levin at the Technion in Haifa, the virtual infants appear where the physical body arrives, and even then only briefly. When you lose five-dimensional velocity after traveling in time—decelerate back into sequential time, back down to our constricted *Asiyah* world from moving in the bigger *Yetzirah* world—the excess energy is thrown off as virtual replicas of yourself, and it's more economical for the universe to throw a lot of very young replicas than a few maturer ones; just as a heated brick throws a lot of low-energy infrared waves rather than anything in the higher-frequency visible range."

Bozzaris rocked his head, clearly not comprehending the metaphysics of it. "Are they real babies, though? When it does happen? Or are they just, like, mirages?"

A blond girl on a bicycle slowed to toss a little red plastic transistor radio to Lepidopt; he caught it with his left hand.

"Normal reception, and boring," she said, and accelerated away, her tanned legs flashing as she rode out of the shadow toward the beach.

"*Sayanim* are getting prettier all the time," noted Bozzaris.

"You are a beast." Lepidopt had not kept the plastic Sears bag the radios had come in, and after he had peered at the tuning dial to verify the frequency, he tucked the radio into the pocket of his sweatshirt.

"What are they tuned to?" asked Bozzaris.

"A hundred and eight megahertz," said Lepidopt, "the highest frequency FM goes to. I believe it's a Christian broadcasting station." He sighed. "If Lieserl *did* jump from here, less than forty-eight hours ago, the space-time fabric should still be kinked enough to put some wrinkles in high frequencies. The signal should interfere with itself."

He squinted around impatiently at the beach and the parking lot, then went on, "One time an infant was taken out of the reentry field, before the field collapsed. That infant lived at least seven years. So yes, they seem to be real babies."

"Am I allowed to know about this?"

"It's relevant to our business. Lieserl was with her father when he went to Zuoz, in the Swiss Alps, in 1928. She was twenty-six then, and Einstein was forty-nine. Later he told her that he had gone to Zuoz to undo a sin he had committed some years earlier—and that he had wound up committing an even greater sin. Anyway, when his mysterious machine was prepared and he stood on the mountain in Zuoz and . . . flickered for a moment, I suppose . . . he immediately collapsed, unconscious, since he had used only one astral projection of himself, which was in the valley below Piz Kesch, and so the shock of reentry was not distributed, not balanced. And Lieserl found herself not only confronted by her unconscious father, but surrounded too by . . . what, several? dozens? . . . of naked infants lying in the snow. She snatched up one of the babies and ran to the nearby house of a friend of Einstein's, Willy Meinhardt; there she got people to come help, but when they returned to the spot, only Einstein lay

there. All the other infants had disappeared, though the one
Lieserl had rescued was still fully present at Meinhardt's
house. Before that, Einstein liked mountains—he used to go
hiking in the Alps with his wife and Marie Curie. After that
he couldn't stand the sight of a mountain."

A teenage boy glided past on a rumbling skateboard and
called, "Goofy station but clear reception!" He tossed a
green plastic radio, and Lepidopt caught it and waved.

"We know all this," he went on to Bozzaris, "from a
Grete Markstein, who was an old girlfriend of Einstein's
and who took the impossible infant and raised him—it was
a boy, of course—for the next seven years. Here, you hold
this radio; keep it for your own. Apparently Einstein didn't
make child-support payments, so in 1935 Grete went to several colleagues of Einstein's, in Berlin and Oxford, asking
them to tell Einstein that she was his daughter and the seven-
year-old boy was his grandson, and that she wanted finan-
cial help; she told us that she knew Einstein would understand
who she really was, and who or what the little boy was. The
Oxford man, Frederick Lindemann, happened to give the
woman and the boy a drink of water when they visited his
office, and after they had left he saved both glasses, for fin-
gerprinting."

Lepidopt paused to look up at half a dozen seagulls sailing in the sunlight overhead, bright white against the still
dark blue sky.

"Isser Harel," he went on, "got hold of those two glasses
in 1944, four years before he became head of the Shin Bet
and six years before he became director general of the
Mossad. Harel verified the woman's prints as Markstein's,
but of course he was very intrigued by the boy's prints. The
secret archive Harel built behind a false wall in his Dov Hoz
Street apartment in Tel Aviv, during the days of the British
Mandate, was mainly to hide the boy's water glass." He
shrugged. "Not that it *proved* anything—it was just an old
glass with a child Einstein's fingerprints on it, and there was
no proof that the prints weren't put on the glass in the

1880s—but with its admittedly hearsay provenance it was evidence that Einstein had something Israel needed to know about. Harel concluded that it was time travel, that somehow the young Einstein had been brought forward to 1935; in fact it *was* time travel, but the boy was only a quantum by-product, not the real Einstein."

"So why are Frank Marrity's fingerprints identical to that old man's, the guy who was driving the Rambler? Is Frank Marrity a surviving duplicate of the old guy?"

Malk had found the Rambler this morning in the Arrowhead Pediatric Hospital parking lot, though the old man who'd been driving it had not been seen. Shots had been fired in the hospital lobby, and Marrity and his daughter, both apparently unharmed, had fled.

"That's possible," Lepidopt told Bozzaris, "if the old man at some point time-jumped to 1952; though Marrity has a valid-looking birth certificate from a hospital in Buffalo, New York. One of these virtual babies wouldn't legitimately have a birth certificate."

Lepidopt stared hard at Bozzaris. "It's more likely," Lepidopt went on carefully, "that the old guy *is* Frank Marrity, having jumped back to here, to 1987, from the future."

Bozzaris blinked. "Wow."

"That's probably what killed Sam Glatzer," Lepidopt added. "When the old Frank Marrity drove the Rambler into his younger self's driveway on Sunday afternoon, Sam found himself seeing the same guy in two places. Remote viewers are out on a wire when they work, precarious, and that might have been a badly disorienting shock."

A young policeman in blue shorts and T-shirt rode up to them on a bicycle and braked to a halt in front of Lepidopt. "No interference anywhere within a hundred yards of the pier," the man said. "I dropped the radio."

Lepidopt waved magnanimously. "No problem. Thank you." After the policeman had nodded and pedaled away, Lepidopt shrugged at Bozzaris.

"We should just grab the old guy," Bozzaris said, "the older version of Marrity, and find out everything he knows about the future! He looks sixty—he must be from about 2012!"

Lepidopt shuffled north along the damp, gritty sidewalk, staring down at his sneakers. Bozzaris stepped after him.

"We'll grab him all right," said Lepidopt quietly. "If necessary we'll kill him to keep the other crowd from getting what he knows. But the future as he's experienced it won't necessarily be relevant, if I carry out the orders that were on the Play-Doh last night."

"Oh, yeah." Bozaris frowned. "And not just the future—nearly my whole life, if you go back and change something that happened in '67. I was born in '61."

"It's unlikely to alter your life story at all," Lepidopt muttered, aware even as he spoke that what he said was a lie.

What if the changes he provoked should alter or somehow prevent the Yom Kippur War of 1973, when Egypt and Syria attacked Israel by surprise on Yom Kippur, the Day of Atonement, when most of the country's reserves were in the synagogues or praying at home? And how could any deliberate change *not* be aimed to affect that?

Lepidopt had been at the Mossad headquarters in the Hadar Dafna building on King Saul Boulevard in Tel Aviv during that two-week war, overseeing the Mossad remote viewers nearly twenty-four hours a day as they desperately tried to track the Egyptian tank divisions in the Sinai desert. Israel had managed to defeat the Syrian and Egyptian armies—and some opportunistic Iraqi and Jordanian forces too—but in the first week of the war, things had looked very bad indeed for Israel. Many, many lives had been lost. Changing the course of that disastrous war would inevitably change Bozzaris's life, in any number of ways. For all Lepidopt knew, Bozzaris's father was killed in the Yom Kippur War; plenty of men were, in the Sinai, on the Golan Heights, in the skies and at sea. Or maybe he wasn't, but *would* be killed in a new reality's version of the war.

At least Bozzaris had already been born by 1967. Lepidopt's son, Louis, had not been born until 1976.

He remembered the amulet that had been exposed onto

the strip of film in the radiation-exposure badge he'd been given in 1967. *Your life story be sacrosanct, and all who are in your train. Unchanged, unedited.* He wished it hadn't been taken away from him, and that he had given it to young Louis.

"Which is bullshit," said Bozzaris, smiling as he dug in the bag for another doughnut. "At least—at the very least—you and I will never have had this conversation. I'll never have eaten this doughnut." He took a quick bite, as if the universe might even now try to prevent it.

Lepidopt thought about the orders the three of them had read in the damp Play-Doh last night at the Wigwam Motel:

Use Einstein's maschinchen *to return to 1967 by way of your lost finger. Tell Harel, 'Change the past'—he has been ready for that recognition sign since 1944. Give him a full, repeat full, report. Get to the Rephidim stone and copy out inscription on it (which as things now stand is obliterated in 1970 by Israeli scholar who kills himself immediately afterward). Deliver inscription to Harel, with your full story. You will be returned to Los Angeles in resulting 1987, if desired.*

After they'd all read it, Lepidopt had rolled the blue Play-Doh into a ball, and then had filed off all the incised figures on the steel cylinders that had pressed the message into the Play-Doh. And Bozzaris had thrown the defaced cylinders off the end of the pier an hour ago.

I wonder, Lepidopt thought, what the inscription on the Rephidim stone was . . . or what I'll discover it to be, if I can get back to 1967. I wonder if I'll sympathize with the man who killed himself to make sure it was lost.

He remembered the passage in the second-century *Zohar*:

. . . but when Israel will return from exile, all the supernal grades are destined to rest harmoniously upon this one. Then men will obtain a knowledge of the precious supernal wisdom of which hiterto they knew not.

"True," Lepidopt sighed, "it's bullshit."

Bozzaris grinned. "How do you figure you'll go back in time?"

"I have no idea. Ideally the elder Frank Marrity will tell me how. If not, maybe the Einstein letters will explain it; maybe we'll summon ghosts, and ask them; maybe the thirty-five-year-old Frank Marrity knows, and will tell me."

"Not if the sunglasses girl gets near him again."

"I suppose the likeliest outcome is that I won't figure out how to do it at all."

That would be very good, he thought; we *did* manage to decisively win the Yom Kippur War, after all, and Syria and Egypt had been hugely relieved, as usual, when the UN had finally imposed a cease-fire.

But I must go back if I can, and try to save as many as possible of the Israeli men and women who died in that war.

"How would it be 'by way of your lost finger'?"

"I can't imagine. I suppose my aura still has ten fingers, one of which now contains no actual physical finger. An astral projection would still have ten fingers."

By way of your lost finger.

An enormous thought welled up in Lepidopt's head: What if all my "never agains" —never again touch a cat, never again hear the name John Wayne, never again hear a telephone ring—apply only in this time line? If I go back to 1967 and simply prevent the twenty-year-old Lepidopt from touching the Western Wall, then I won't get that first premonition! And maybe—surely!—in that time line I won't then get *any* of them!

He seized on the thought. Of course that's been the explanation for them all along, he thought eagerly—they've simply been oracular clues that this is not the time line that's to prevail. This isn't the destined course of my life.

Everything, including that first premonition at the Wall, has been provisional, subject to an eventual revision. When I return here to 1987, having saved the Rephidim inscription in 1967 and given Harel my full report, I'll find myself in the *real* time line, free of those too close boundaries to my life.

He thought of the uprooted Jewish tombstones he had seen bridging ditches in Jerusalem. Perhaps the tombstone he'd been picturing lately—the one with *Lepidopt* incised on it, with 1987 as its second date—could be uprooted too.

He looked coolly at Bozzaris. You'll be all right, he thought. You'll be safely born by the time I switch the tracks ahead of history's locomotive—

—but Louis won't be.

He remembered what he had thought, last night in the Wigwam Motel, about Marrity's apparent intention to copy the Einstein letters so that he could sell the originals: *If it were my son who was in danger, I would not be thinking first of making money from selling the Einstein letters.*

Not of money, no, he thought now. But of a life that extends past the next time a telephone rings in your vicinity?

But Louis would still be born in 1976, as in this present time line, assuming the twenty-five-year-old Oren Lepidopt married Deborah Altmann in 1972, which there was no reason to believe he would not. That was the year before the Yom Kippur War, so nothing would be likely to change it; he'd see to it that nothing impinged on that story.

If that young Lepidopt and Deborah conceived Louis on a different night in 1975, this time, though—would he still be the same boy Lepidopt knew? Would he even be conceived *as* a boy? What was the biological mechanism that decided whether an embryo was to be a boy or a girl?

What if the Yom Kippur War goes differently, because of this mission, and the young Lepidopt is *not* assigned to the Mossad headquarters, but instead is sent into combat and killed before he fathers his child? But surely that was very unlikely! Lepidopt recalled that there had been no one else who would have been likely to take charge of the remote viewers.

But would they *need* remote viewers, this time around, if they had prevented or controlled the war because of forty-year-old Lepidopt's report from the future?

Well, I can make sure my younger self doesn't go into combat before Louis is conceived in '76 . . . or go into *any* dangerous work, before then. Or step carelessly into traffic, or fail to wear seat belts? Or drive at all, maybe? Can I make the younger Lepidopt see the urgency of all this, for a son he's never seen?

Lepidopt was sweating, though it was still chilly here in the shadows of the beachfront houses.

A tanned boy in swim trunks and with white zinc oxide sunscreen on his nose scampered up to them barefoot and said, "Forgetting him, you see—" and paused, panting. He was holding a cardboard tube of Flix chocolates.

Something from Malk, Lepidopt thought. Something he thinks might be urgent, to send it by *bodlim, sayan* couriers. This boy looked flighty, but certainly there was an adult nearby who was watching to make sure the handoff took place.

"—means you've forgotten me," said Lepidopt, "like my forgotten man." Bozzaris had chosen their recognition signs from the lyrics of old musicals—Lepidopt hoped Bozzaris's tastes would turn out to include old musicals, again!—and this, he believed, was from *Gold Diggers of 1933*.

The boy held out the cardboard tube, then ran away when Lepidopt had taken it.

"Could be a bomb," said Bozzaris lightly.

"I bet it's not."

Lepidopt tore away the Scotch tape that sealed it and un-folded the piece of paper crumpled in the top; in Malk's handwriting was the message, *Just came, FedEx, from home. Gross.*

Lepidopt peered inside, then stared more closely—and he almost dropped it.

"Now that's disgusting," he said hoarsely.

"What is it?"

"It's—I believe it must be my finger."

Bozzaris stepped back, then laughed nervously. "Can I see?"

"No. Shoot off your own finger, you want to look at a

finger." With his maimed hand he pulled a handkerchief out of his back pocket and wiped his face. "They—*saved* it! They knew, even back then—" Lepidopt peered again into the cardboard tube. "There's—a couple of holes in the tip, one through the fingernail—and crossways scratches on the nail! They had a label or something *stapled* to it!"

Bozzaris shrugged. "Twenty years. Tape would have dried out."

Lepidopt gingerly tucked the tube into his sweatshirt pocket next to the radios. One of the radios fell out and cracked on the sidewalk, and he kicked it out onto the parking lot pavement.

"Business card!" he said harshly. "Cab company! Suitcase!"

Bozzaris stared at him. "Hmm?"

"The time machine isn't here. She didn't do it here. This was a feint, a bluff. Lieserl carried an empty suitcase down here in that cab, or no—more likely paid some *other* old lady to do it. I don't need to be standing here looking at the fucking *ocean*."

Bozzaris's eyebrows were raised as he fell into step beside Lepidopt, hurrying toward the short street that led back to Balboa Boulevard. Lepidopt nearly never used bad language.

"She left the card on her kitchen counter, and—" Bozzaris began.

"To waste our time, or the *other* crowd's time—*whoever* might be alerted by the psychic noise of her departure— CIA, the press, the Vatican! Listen, she hid out all these years—she was as secretive as her father, she had a child too, she didn't want the thing to be found, and used. She would *never* have left that card on her counter if she really had come down here to do the jump! The cab company and the old woman with the suitcase, whoever she was, were a move to delay anybody looking for the machine—not stop, just *delay*. If it was worth the trouble to decoy us away from the search even for just a couple of hours, then a couple of hours must be important, it must make a difference. She must have set up—of course she *would* have set up!—some chain of events that would destroy the machine after she used it."

Lepidopt was practically running now, and Bozzaris pitched his bag of doughnuts at a trash can as they hurried past it. "So where do we look?"

"We have one clue: The machine isn't here."

Fifteen

Bennett Bradley stood up as the two men nodded to him and halted in the restaurant aisle beside his booth. One was short and pudgy and darkly bearded, and the other was tall and effeminate with a white brush cut, and they both wore dark business suits. And by the morning light shining through the windows across the room, they both looked tired.

"Mr. Bradley," said the white-haired one, bowing sketchily. "You can call me Sturm."

"Drang here," said the bearded one with a smile, blinking behind eyeglasses.

"Please sit down," Bennett said. It was barely nine in the morning, and one of these—Sturm, he thought—had called him at seven this morning. Bennett was tired too—he would have liked to sleep later, after having flown home from Shasta last night, and taken the remote-parking shuttle to the car, and then negotiated the freeways to home.

He had left the house this morning without waking Moira.

The two men sat down in the booth, bracketing Bennett.

"We spoke," said Sturm, on Bennett's right, "to your brother-in-law, Francis Marrity, on the phone this morning; and we told him that we had called you last night. We mentioned that we would have to deal with both of Lisa Marrity's heirs to finalize our sale—that is, you and your wife as well as him. He, ah, said that possession is nine-tenths of the law, and hung up. He has checked his daughter out of the hospital, and they have not returned to their house in San Bernardino."

"Hospital? What was she in the hospital for?"

"A tracheotomy. She choked on some food, apparently."

"Kid eats like a pig," said Bennett. "She'll probably need it again, they should have installed a valve."

"Just coffee, for all of us," said Drang to the waitress who had walked up with a pad. When she had nodded and moved on, he said to Bennett, "The price is fifty thousand dollars, and we would like to consummate this transaction as soon as possible. Today, ideally." The fat man's breath smelled like spearmint Tic Tacs.

"If your brother-in-law absconds with the items," said Sturm, "he could sell them to somebody else; and there's very little we or you could do about it. Afterward he could plausibly claim never to have had them. Total ignorance, stout denial."

Bennett's stomach was cold. "But you could go to the police, couldn't you, with your, your list? Your correspondence with his grandmother? I mean, *you* know what the items are . . . as well as I do, *better* than I do, since you know specifically what the old lady wanted to sell." He wished the coffee would get here. "Right?"

Sturm stared at Bennett for a moment. The man's eyes were very pale blue, and the lashes were white. "It's not really a matter we'd like to get the police involved in," he said at last. "You notice that we haven't identified ourselves to you at all. You have no phone number nor address for us. If the transaction doesn't work out, we'll shrug and . . . disappear. Keep our money."

Great God, thought Bennett. What was that crazy old woman dealing in? Crates of machine guns? Heroin? Whatever this is—fifty thousand dollars!—no identification!—it's obviously illegal. Suddenly and irrationally he was very hungry, and very aware of the hot smells of bacon and eggs at nearby tables.

"Do you know where Marrity and his daughter might have gone," asked Drang, "after hanging up on us?"

"When would I be paid?" asked Bennett. "And how? Since this is—such an off-paper transaction." I should walk out of here, he thought. I know I should. What good would a check be? And if they gave me cash—how could I know it wasn't counterfeit? I have no business dealing with this sort of people. I'm glad I didn't wake up Moira this morning.

Sturm said, "The Bank of America branch on California Street is holding six cashier's checks, each made out in your name for $8,333.00. That adds up to two dollars short of fifty thousand, actually, but we'll pay for your coffee here. As soon as we have the property, we'll drive you to the bank, pick up the cashier's checks, and hand them to you. You can cash them or deposit them wherever you please, at any time during the next three years."

That would work, thought Bennett. He could feel a drop of sweat running down his ribs under his shirt.

"You could split it with your brother-in-law, if your conscience dictates," said chubby Drang with no expression.

Bennett could feel his mouth tighten in a derisive grin.

"Do you know where Marrity and his daughter might have gone?" Drang asked.

"Yes," said Bennett. "But let's pick up the cashier's checks first."

"We can do that," said Sturm, getting to his feet.

"You can owe me for the coffee," said Bennett, with frail bravado, as he stood up too.

I'm not an old man, I'm a young man something happened to. He believed that was a quote from Mickey Spillane.

The man who called himself Derek Marrity stared at the crystals hanging from the switched-off ceiling light in the increasingly sunlit room, unable to sleep in spite of having been awake for more than twenty-four hours. He was lying on Lisa Marrity's narrow bed, where he had slept Sunday night; he had got up at seven on Monday morning, to go to Marrity's house. Now, on Tuesday morning, he wished he had slept late and not visited the poor Marritys at all.

From the bedside table he picked up a battered cigarette butt with a bit of Scotch tape wrapped around it. The filter had once been tan, but was now faded to nearly white.

Look anywhere but homeward, angel.

He dropped the cigarette butt back onto the table.

The crystals were turning in the breeze coming in through the open window above his head; he could smell Grammar's jasmine flowers, and refracted morning sunlight was making dots of red and blue and green light that raced and paused on the book spines and paintings.

The lace curtains were swaying over him. He recalled that Grammar had used the phrase *voio voio,* which was from the German word for "curtain," to describe empty pretense, portentous talk with no substance, ambitious plans that were impossible. Useless endeavors.

This whole expedition, he thought as he shifted his twisted and aching right leg to a more comfortable angle on the bedspread, has been *voio voio.*

I can still give young Frank Marrity investment advice, I suppose, but what could really *help* him, at this point? Would there be any use in telling him the crucial things? *Don't drink? Don't let Daphne drink?* Useless, useless.

The Harmonic Convergence has undone me. Earnest, well-meaning young Frank Marrity has undone me.

Daphne was supposed to choke to death, yesterday, on the floor in Alfredo's.

Marrity reached behind his head to turn the hot pillow over.

He had two recollections—three, now—of that terrible half hour in the restaurant.

Originally he had kept on trying the Heimlich maneuver, and kept on trying it, until he had simply been shaking a pale, dead little girl. He could still remember the cramps in his arms. The paramedics had arrived too late to do anything. He had grieved over Daphne, but he had got through the funeral, and the furtive interviews with various secret organizations, and the horrible lonely months afterward, without "taking the Daughter of the Vine to Spouse," as Omar Khayyam had described alcoholism. Two years later he had married Amber, who had been a student in one of his University of Redlands classes in 1988: that is, who would be in one of Frank Marrity's classes next year. He and Amber had not had any children, but they'd been very happy, and had eventually bought a house in Redlands in the mid-'90s. A good time for it, before the prices of houses went up out of sight for a college teacher and his eBay-dealer wife. By 2005, at the age of fifty-three, he had been thinking about early retirement.

He thought of that life as Life A.

And then in the early months of 2006 he had begun to have vivid hallucinations of a different life, a Life B. In this *other* life he had not married Amber, and Daphne was still alive, still with him, and the two of them were living in a trailer park on Base Line. Moira, a widow by this time, had long since bought out his share of Grammar's house, and was living in it, and had got restraining orders against both him and Daphne. Daphne was thirty-one, and an alcoholic, and she hated her alcoholic father. And, truthfully, by that time he had hated her, and himself too.

In both lives twelve-year-old Daphne had watched Grammar's movie, helplessly, all the way through, while he had been up the hall in his office grading papers; when he had eventually come down the hall to make dinner he had found Daphne still staring at the blank screen. He had ejected the tape and hidden it. That night Daphne had begun to have difficulty swallowing her food.

And though in his original life, Life A, Daphne had choked to death on the floor of Alfredo's the next day, in the intrusive hallucinatory Life B he had punched a hole in her throat, and she had not died; but when she had recovered from the surgery she had written *u cut my throat . . . i hate you* on the pad beside her hospital bed. And from then on she had seemed to be possessed by a spiteful, hateful devil.

He could see now that it had been merciful, in the original story of his life, that she had died on the restaurant floor.

The Life B hallucinations had become so frequent and prolonged that he had had to take a leave from teaching, and eventually he honestly didn't know which life was his real one.

He was the single father of the adult Daphne as often as he was the childless husband of Amber.

Then he was simply living with Daphne in the trailer, and the life with Amber was a less and less frequent dream. And by April 2006 those dreams had stopped. He was stuck in the drink-fogged trailer life with his angry, drunk, adult daughter—though he could still remember his original life.

Why would my past change, in this way? he wondered. Why did this 1987 Frank Marrity *do* the tracheotomy yesterday, when in my original time line I did *not* do it?

It must be that the Harmonic Convergence, that sudden drop in worldwide mind pressure, caused a crack in the continuity, allowed a brief gap—like an unstable seam between two pours of cement—in which some new variable could make things resume in a different way.

So in this skewed history, Marrity did not marry Amber; by the time Daphne was twenty-two, she was a dedicated alcoholic, and so was he; and when she was twenty-seven, in 2002, she took his car keys and he blundered out of the trailer to stand behind the battered Ford Taurus to prevent her from taking it.

He shifted his bad leg now to a new position on Grammar's bedspread. Standing behind the car had been a mistake.

And so he had made a desperate bid to save Daphne, and himself—to start an entirely new life, a Life C, a third roll of the dice.

He had remembered the questions the secret agencies had asked him in both previous lifetimes, and those questions had led him to the discovery of who his great-grandfather had been—and had then led him to the study of quantum mechanics and relativity and Kabbalah. He had stolen some Einstein letters from Grammar's house, which by then had been Moira's.

And then he had actually used the machine in Grammar's Kaleidoscope Shed and jumped back in time and intruded on his thirty-five-year-old self and the twelve-year-old Daphne, and pretended to be his own lost father.

Pretending to be his own father had been even more difficult than he had imagined it would be—claiming to be gay had been much easier than claiming to be that evil old man.

Daphne had noted the resemblance between them: the old and young Frank Marritys! He had hoped that Daphne might survive this time, as the sweet child she had been, if there were no choking and therefore no throat cutting. And he had got his younger self to promise not to go to an Italian restaurant on that fateful day.

And of course he had gone to Alfredo's himself, ready to chase them away if they nevertheless tried to eat there—but when they hadn't arrived at noon, as he clearly remembered doing, nor at 12:30 or 12:40, he had relaxed and sat down and had lunch and a few beers. Fate had evaded him by sending them in an hour late.

And then Daphne choked, and her young father did the tracheotomy.

The old Frank Marrity rolled to a new position on Grammar's bed. He should have . . . broken Marrity's leg, set his truck on fire, called in a bomb threat to the restaurant.

Last night—it tormented him now to remember it—last night he had been certain that Daphne must have died at the hospital—a hemorrhage, error in anestheic, a mis-prescription, it didn't matter. The feeling of deliverance had been overwhelming.

He had been sure she had died because he had experienced half an hour of restoration, starting when the three cars had bracketed him on Base Line, and the Rambler had behaved so oddly—for a blessed thirty minutes after that, his right leg was strong and free of pain, and he was healthy, not weakened by years of heavy drinking.

After the incident on Base Line, he had found that he was on another street entirely, but he had got his bearings when he'd come to Highland Avenue, and he had driven to the Arrowhead Pediatric Hospital full of bubbling optimism.

He had been ready to begin prepping Marrity for the next nineteen years—marry Amber, bet on the winners in the NFL and NBA and the Stanley Cup, buy stock in Dell and Cisco and Microsoft and Amazon, and get out of it all by 1999 and then put the money in T-bills and insured securities—buy many copies of the first edition of *Harry Potter and the Sorcerer's Stone,* and don't be in New York City on September 11, 2001. To this 1987 Frank Marrity, 9/11 still meant the emergency phone number.

It wouldn't have been precisely the same as the happy life with Amber that the old man remembered, but it should have been acceptably close. And it would have been affluent.

Of course neither of the Marrity-lives the old man had experienced had included a visit from his long-missing "father." And in neither of the remembered lives had the semiblind woman tried to shoot him!

And there were a couple of other discrepancies too between this young Marrity's life and what the old man remembered. In neither of the time lines he had lived through, the happy one or the miserable one, had Grammar's VHS tape burned up. He had been surprised to see the scorched VCR lying in the grass outside Marrity's kitchen door, yesterday morning. And neither Daphne nor this young Marrity should know anything about a connection with Albert Einstein yet; he had not learned of it until 2006. But somehow Frank and Daphne did already know about it.

And why had they been an hour late for lunch yesterday? Urgent housework that couldn't wait?

And then at the hospital he'd seen that Daphne was still alive after all, and decrepitude had fallen onto him again like a waterlogged plaster ceiling. When he had struggled weakly to his feet, Daphne and Marrity had been gone,

Daphne's IV tube swinging free and dripping dextrose and sodium chloride onto the floor, and he had had to curse his way past the shouting nurses and limp out of the hospital.

He hoped to be able to find the foreign crowd, the sunglasses girl and her friends, and make a bargain with them—to get them to leave Marrity alone. He could tell them priceless facts about future events, in exchange for that. Even give them Grammar's time machine, for that.

He could try to do that much for his younger self, at least.

Lying on Grammar's bed now, he sniffed—then hiked himself up on his elbows. The raw reek of gasoline was overpowering the scent of the jasmine, and for a breathless instant he thought some recoil effect was pulling him back to the moment of his arrival in the gasoline-fumey Kaleidoscope Shed—with the dozen impossible infants waving their arms in the weeds outside—and then he heard young Frank Marrity's voice through the open window behind his head.

"There's a cigarette in it!" Marrity said.

Then the old man bared his teeth and winced, for twelve-year-old Daphne said, "What, in the gasoline?"

"Right, see, that's the filter, and that's the paper that used to be around it."

"Who'd throw a cigarette in a gas can?"

"Somebody who thought it would set it on fire. I bet she laid a lit cigarette across the open mouth of the can, figuring when it burned down it'd fall in. Which it did. But then it just went out."

"You shouldn't pour it into the dirt. I think that's illegal. Why didn't the cigarette set the gas on fire?"

"The can was nearly full. I guess there wasn't enough vapor. We can't just leave it sitting here; and we can't take it to a gas station for, for whatever the proper disposal is, on a bus." The old man heard the clang of the empty gas can being put down on the concrete of the patio. "I wouldn't have taken bets on it *not* catching fire, though," Marrity's voice said. "I can see why she *thought* she had reliably burned down the shed. She must have left too fast to see that it hadn't worked."

The old man in the bedroom shivered in sudden comprehension—if Grammar's makeshift incendiary device *had* worked, he would have been jumping straight into the middle of an inferno, at noon on Sunday, instead of just into a heady reek of gasoline fumes. Even the fumes had made him scramble out of the shed as fast as he could.

"Poor old Grammar," said Daphne. "I wonder what was going on."

"I think we've got to figure *out* what was going on, before somebody else tries to shoot me."

"Let's go look at the shed," said Daphne, her voice moving away from the window.

Old Marrity swung his legs off the bed. In both his previous lifetimes he had eventually dug up the gold wire, and in horrible Life B he had sold his trailer to get gold wire to replace it and rewire the time machine, but he couldn't let them disassemble it *now*—they might just wreck it, and if the machine was gone, could he still have jumped back here? He couldn't figure out the logic of it, but he didn't want them fooling with the machine.

"Wait!" he shouted, limping toward the bedroom door.

He hobbled past the washing machine and wrenched at the dead bolt on the back door; finally he got it back and pushed the door open, squinting at the bright sunlight in the yard. It occurred to him that he hadn't shaved in two days, and his jowls must be bristling with white stubble.

Daphne and his younger self were standing in the weedy yard gaping back at him.

"Wait," he said again. And then he took a deep breath, not having any idea what he could say next.

Sixteen

Sturm and Drang had driven Bennett to the Bank of America on California Street and led him inside, and there they really had given him six cashier's checks, each for $8,333; Bennett had tucked the envelope into his inner jacket pocket, feeling dizzy and anxious. The bank happened to be only a couple of blocks from Grammar Marrity's house.

Then they had driven out of that neighborhood, north to the cedar-shaded parking lot at the Holiday Inn by the Civic Auditorium. Sturm had parked next to a big brown Dodge van with a sliding door in the side, which had rolled open when Sturm got out of the car and knocked on it. From the passenger seat of the idling car, Bennett had been able to see three burly young men and a dark-haired woman in sunglasses in the van; white-haired Sturm had conferred with them for a few moments, then had got back into the car and driven out of the lot, eyeing the rearview mirror to make sure the van was following. The air-conditioning was uncomfortably cold, and somehow the car smelled of burnt fabric.

"Where are we going?" Sturm asked now, without looking sideways at Bennett.

"Uh, 204 Batsford," said Bennett. "It's two blocks south of the bank we were just at. What burned in here?"

In the backseat, Drang lifted a shoe box from beside him and held it forward, lifting the cardboard lid.

Bennett hitched around in his seat to look, then recoiled from the little blackened figure inside. "What the hell is that?" he barked. The burnt smell was gagging him now.

"Your niece's teddy bear, we assume," said Drang, clearly pleased with Bennett's reaction. He put the lid back on the box and set it down on the floor by his feet. "It was buried in Marrity's yard. She apparently burned it up."

"When we get there," Sturm went on, "don't mention any of this about the sale of the grandmother's property. Just get Marrity and his daughter, both, to come to the van. Tell them you've got a bicycle for the girl or something."

From the backseat, Drang said cheerfully, "We can take them from there."

Sturm glanced at Drang in the rearview mirror. "When we get there," he told the fat man, "you go back and wait in the van."

Drang raised his eyebrows. "You think I look alarming?"

"Better that they see only one stranger."

Bennett shifted uncomfortably under the front seat's shoulder strap, wishing he could lean forward and put his face into the cold air coming from the dashboard blowers. "Why did you bring the, the burned-up teddy bear?"

Sturm scowled, as if he wished Drang had not shown Bennett the bear. "It might mean something to the girl," he said.

Bennett realized he was nodding, and he made himself stop it. "You could just let me go—I mean, I can get a cab to get back to my car, then. After." He rubbed his hand over his mouth, feeling sweat in his mustache. "When you've—"

"Okay," said Sturm.

It occurred to Bennett that they were now paying him just for the delivery of Marrity and Daphne, and not for the things Grammar had wanted to sell—if in fact these men were going to *let* him keep the money, or even let him go.

I should have awakened Moira, he thought. She'd have stopped me. Why the hell couldn't she have woken on her own?

Daphne stared at her grandfather, who was standing in the shade of the trellis looking like a bum. His white hair was all shoved up in the back, and she knew that when her father's hair was that way it meant he'd been napping.

She was glad to see that he'd mostly recovered from whatever had happened to him at the hospital this morning. Over the door behind him was the wooden sign that read, *Everyone Who Dwells Here Is Safe.* She wondered if that sign was why he had come here.

"Wait?" said her father beside her. "Wait for what?"

Her grandfather was swaying in the patchy trellis shade.

"Don't—go," the old man said. "I was asleep, and I heard your voices. I—"

"Who was that woman who shot at me," her father interrupted, "in the hospital lobby?"

"I don't know—"

"You said, 'She's blind if you don't look at her.' Which was true. And she tried to kill Daphne and me an hour ago. Who is she?"

"Ach! She did? She's a—a psychic. I haven't spoken to her in years, I truly can't imagine why she tried to kill you. I saved your life."

Daphne's father shifted his feet in the weeds. "It's true, you did. Thank you. How do you know her?"

"She—she was part of a team that interviewed me once, after a, a bereavement—she's with a secret agency—"

"Not a United States one," said her father. "We talked to a man from the National Security Agency last night, and he told me not to speak to her."

"You did? I never did, not the NSA. I—only want what's best for you."

Daphne noticed that he said it directly to her father. How about what's best for me too? she thought.

"What sort of secret agency?" her father asked.

The old man sat down in a shaded wicker chair against the outside bedroom wall. "They were interested in something a . . . family member of mine had previously picked up, which didn't belong to her." He waved his spotty old hands inexpressively. "A family member who had in fact just died. I gave it to them, and they went away. They were psychics, they had a head—anyway, I didn't argue with them, so I didn't learn anything about them."

"When was this?"

The look the old man gave her father seemed defiant. "I was thirty-five."

"You're not saying you met that woman then," Daphne's father objected. "She's only about thirty now."

"I've met her," said the old man. "Leave it at that."

Marrity shook his head impatiently, then asked, "What did your family member take, that you gave to these people?"

The old man exhaled. "Call it a book. Call it a photo album. Call it a key." He glanced at Daphne for the first time, then quickly looked away. To her father, he said, "Next time I'm inclined to save your life, remind me of how grateful you were this time."

Her father paused, and Daphne looked up and saw him nodding. "Sorry, sorry. But you need to tell us *all* these things, not just the things you think we'll believe. Why did you think Daphne was dead, this morning?"

"A nurse, I must have misunderstood what a nurse said. I don't hear very well. Leave me alone."

Marrity relented. "Okay. Do you want a beer?"

"They're gone, if you mean Grammar's."

"Well, *I'd* like a beer," Marrity said. He put his briefcase down on the cement porch slab to reach into his pocket. "Where's Grammar's car? I can drive it."

"It—broke down. I took a bus here."

Daphne doubted that. She and her father had taken a bus, and had got here a few minutes ago; her grandfather had been here long enough to have taken a nap. What did he do really, she wondered, steal a car? There's an old car parked by the garage with the hood up. Do you need to open the hood to steal a car? Or to stop it, once you've driven it somewhere?

"I want you to know," said the old man abruptly, "that *I* hate my father *too*."

"Why do you want me to know that?" asked Marrity.

"It's something you and I have in common. For a father to just leave his poor wife and children—what excuse could there be?"

Marrity laughed in evident surprise. "Well, you tell me, old man. I can't think of one. Not blackmail and the threat of imprisonment, for example. I wouldn't abandon Daphne to avoid those things."

"No, I know you wouldn't. Not even to save your soul. I know you wouldn't."

"To save my—" Her father seemed to consider getting angry, then just relaxed and laughed. "No, not even to do that."

The old man spread his shaky hands and frowned. Daphne wondered if he was quite awake yet, after his nap.

"Eventually it winds up costing everything," he said. "But remember I hate the old man as much as you do."

Marrity was frowning. "Which old man? Your father, or . . . *my* father?"

"That one," the old man mumbled, nodding.

Daphne heard the front door slam inside the house, and then there were footsteps coming through the kitchen.

"Who's here?" came her uncle Bennett's voice from the dimness beyond the open back door. "Why is the door unlocked? Frank? Daphne?"

"Out back, Bennett," said her father loudly. He gave Daphne a look, and she knew he meant *Good thing we didn't start prying up the bricks.*

She imagined the two of them on their knees in the shed—covered with mud and with a treasure chest full of gold coins half exposed in a hole under the bricks, blinking up in confusion at her grandfather and Uncle Bennett—and her father smiled at her before looking back to the back door.

Daphne wondered if her uncle Bennett would yell at her father again about coming here without him and Aunt Moira—but, in fact, he didn't seem upset.

Bennett was standing there on the back step, blinking and smiling nervously. "Well, this is lucky!" he said. "I got a free bicycle from an ad shoot, and I was going to give it to you next time I saw you, Daphne! But I've got it right outside, in a van!"

A van, thought Daphne. A free bicycle. If this was a stranger, I'd run away as fast as I could. She could feel reflexive caution in her father too.

But, "Okay," she said. "Thanks!"

"I'll go look too," her father said, stepping forward. Daphne stared hard at his briefcase on the cement, and he hurried back to pick it up. "Thanks," he muttered.

"Yes," said Bennett eagerly, "you come look too, Frank."

"I'll come too," said her grandfather, and Bennett jumped, clearly noticing the old man in the shadows for the first time.

"Who are you?" Bennett asked.

The old man didn't answer, and didn't seem to want to look at Bennett.

"He's my father," said Marrity.

Bennett frowned at the old man. "Moira's father?"

Marrity nodded. "Probably he inherits the place, actually. All Grammar's stuff."

Bennett touched the lapel of his jacket. He started to say something, then just said, "Fine! Let's go look at the bike!"

Daphne and her father followed Bennett through the musty-smelling kitchen and living room to the front door. As Bennett pushed aside the creaking screen door and stepped out onto the porch, Daphne saw two vehicles parked in the shade of the big old curbside jacaranda: a brown van and a gray compact car. A man with a white brush cut sat in the driver's seat of the compact.

"That's the—producer, in the car," said Bennett, almost babbling. "His name's Sturm."

Daphne's grandfather had followed them out onto the porch. "Sturm?" he said gruffly. "Where's Mr. Drang?"

Daphne knew that *Sturm und Drang* was some kind of German literary term, but Bennett blinked at the old man in confusion. "How do you know them?" Again he slapped at the lapel of his jacket, as if to be sure something was still in his pocket. "Have *you* made a deal with them?"

"Relax, Bennett," the old man said, still not looking at him. "Life—trust me—is too short."

As Bennett led the group from the house down the walkway, the Sturm man was getting out of the car, smiling like a chef on a label, and Daphne noted that the man's gray suit looked expensive but didn't really fit his figure. Bennett stepped ahead of the others, apparently wanting to talk to him.

Daphne's grandfather was staring at Sturm, and his mouth was open in evident dismay.

He turned to Daphne and her father. "Run," he said quietly. "This is the crowd that tried to shoot you this morning."

Peering around the old man's shoulder, Daphne saw Sturm squinting at them, ignoring Bennett, and he reached into his jacket and opened his mouth.

Daphne's father had grabbed her hand and yanked her back, but she saw Bennett brace himself and then drive his fist very hard into Sturm's stomach.

"Wait, Dad!" she yelled. She heard her father's heels tear the grass as he halted.

The white-haired man folded and tumbled facedown onto the sidewalk pavement, and Bennett was right on top of him, fumbling inside the man's jacket.

The door to the van rumbled back, and two younger men in T-shirts hopped down to the sidewalk—then stopped. Bennett, crouching above Sturm, was holding a pistol, pointing it at them.

"Get in the car!" Bennett screamed. He hammered the butt of the pistol down onto the back of Sturm's head, and Daphne flinched at the sudden hard *pop* of a gunshot.

But her father was pulling her toward Sturm's now empty
gray car, and Bennett was on his feet and running around
toward the driver's side. As if the accidental shot had taken
away his inhibitions, Bennett paused before getting into the
car and fired the gun three times at the van; Daphne saw
dust fly away from the left front tire and then the van sagged
on that side.

Her father had yanked open the back door and bundled
her and his briefcase into the backseat and slid in behind
her. Bennett was in the driver's seat, and without even closing the door he twisted the ignition key and jerked the engine into gear.

The car's back door was still open, and Daphne struggled
up to look out at her grandfather, but the old man was backing away, toward the house.

"Wait for my grandfather!" said Daphne. "Get in!" she
yelled at him over her father's shoulder.

The old man shook his head. "No," he said clearly.

A slim, dark-haired woman in sunglasses had stepped
out of the van and seemed to be staring very hard at the
people in the car.

Her grandfather saw the woman too. "Go!" he yelled, waving them on.

The tires screeched as Bennett gunned the engine and
steered away from the curb. The back door swung shut.

Though her ribs were aching, Daphne was craning her
neck to look out the back window. The woman held up a
hand, either waving or signaling the men in the van not to
shoot. Daphne didn't wave back.

"Did *you* make a deal with those people?" Bennett yelled
as he pulled his door closed. He turned right onto the wider
street at the end of Batsford. "Sell them something Grammar had?"

"No," said Marrity, helping Daphne straighten up on the
seat. "Belt, Daph!" he said. Acceleration pressed them both
back against the vinyl upholstery. Daphne fumbled for her
seat belt, noticing a burnt smell in the air. Maybe it was the
tires.

"They paid me," panted Bennett, "they want you and Daph real bad. I think—I saw he had a gun—I think they want to *kill* you! Shit. *Shit.* Now they'll want *me* real bad! Maybe I can just give 'em back the money." Daphne saw his eyes in the rearview mirror, glaring. "What did you *do*?"

"I don't know," Daphne's father said, tucking his briefcase down in front of his knees and groping to find his own seat belt, "but there's a guy I've got to call. Are you heading for the police station? Take a left on Colorado."

"Yes. No." Bennett was breathing hard. "Do you want to go to the police? Your father's back there."

"He knows them," said Marrity. "And he didn't want to come with us." He bit his lip, and Daphne got a quick vision of the old man pushing the sunglasses lady from behind, in the hospital lobby. "He didn't want to come," he said again. "Actually I should call this guy, before we go to the cops."

There was a familiar shoe box by Daphne's foot, and she kicked the lid off it—and squeaked in surprise. Bennett swerved in the traffic lane, then angrily said, "What now?"

"Rumbold!" she said. "Daddy, they've got Rumbold here!"

Her father peered over her at the open box on the floor, and his face went blank with surprise. "What the hell?"

"You mean the teddy bear?" Bennett's voice was loud. "Burned up?"

"Yes," said Daphne's father, "her teddy bear. We buried it. Why do *they* have it?"

"They probably saw you bury something." Bennett sped up as they passed a Holiday Inn. "They want *something* from you."

It took Daphne a moment to realize that her father was picturing the videocassette she'd taken from Grammar's VCR, because she was picturing it too. And her father was also picturing a sheaf of creased yellowed papers. The Einstein letters, she was sure.

"I've got to stop and call Moira," said Bennett as he made a rocking left turn onto Colorado. "Tell her to leave work right now and meet us at the Mayfair Market on Franklin, in

Hollywood. We'll be there before she is, we can wait for her. We're all in some real trouble, I hope you know that."

Daphne wondered how he could imagine that they might not know that.

"And then what?" asked Marrity.

"I know a place where we can all hide, and decide what to do. Hollywood Hills, panoramic view with Hollywood sign and easy access." He sighed. "I've still got the keys to the place."

Bennett had turned right, onto a street called Garfield, but now he sped right past the police station and the high red dome of City Hall, and made a left turn onto a broader street.

Daphne stared out the left-side rear window at the white headstones of a cemetery wheeling past. For a moment she thought of asking Bennett to stop so that she could bury Rumbold there, but she just sighed and kept silent.

C harlotte could joggingly see herself standing on the sidewalk, and Rascasse lying facedown on it, as Golze hurried up, staring.

"Backup car says sixty seconds," Golze panted. "Bradley *shot* him?"

"No," said Charlotte, "he hit him with the butt of the gun, and the gun went off. The bullet went into the tree, I think." Through Golze's downward-staring eyes she noted the red blood trickling down through Rascasse's spiky white hair to puddle on the sidewalk pavement under his chin. She was mildly surprised to find that she didn't feel anything at all about him.

"Have the boys be ready to lift him," Charlotte said.

"I may do that," Golze snapped, "or I may leave him right here. I think he's dead."

Golze's vision shifted to the right, and focused on the old man who had refused to get into Rascasse's hijacked car with the Marrity family.

"Who are *you*?" Golze asked.

"He's the guy who was driving the Rambler," said Charlotte. "Frank Marrity's father." *And he gave me an awful shove,* she thought, *this morning at the hospital.*

The old man smiled, though his face went blank again when Golze said, "Bullshit, we killed Marrity's father in '55, in New Jersey. Who are you?"

The old man licked his lips. "Do you have Frank Marrity's fingerprints?"

"Yes," said Golze.

The old man visibly took a deep breath. "Good, you'll want to check this. I'm Frank Marrity, the same guy who just drove away in that car, but I'm from the year 2006. I want to make a deal with you people."

For several long seconds Golze's gaze was fixed on the old man, and Charlotte stared right along with him. Her face tingled, but she couldn't tell if it was hot or cold.

I knew *it was possible,* she thought breathlessly, *I knew Rascasse and Golze were on the track of something that could be attained. I can save my young self, save her vision, save her soul from all my sins . . . if this guy isn't lying.*

The old man who claimed to be Frank Marrity licked his lips again. "*Killed* my father?—in 1955! Why?"

Charlotte's view of him was blacked out for a moment: Golze had blinked heavily. "Ask the dead guy on the sidewalk there," Golze said. His gaze swung back toward the van, and one of the men who had been inside it was growing in apparent size as he strode up to them.

The man waved back over his shoulder. "Car's here."

"Frisk this guy," said Golze, nodding toward the old man, "then get Rascasse into the car. Charlotte and Hinch and the old guy come with us in the car, you and Cooper stay with the van. Tell the cops one of those guys was shooting at the other, missed and hit the van's tire. You don't know who they were. Give a bad description of them, and of the car. Say *we* were just strangers who stopped to help, and drove off with this injured guy to find a hospital. You don't know who anybody was. You're bewildered and angry, right? Toss your guns in the car trunk right now."

Golze turned to the street, where a white four-door Honda was slanting in ahead of the van, so Charlotte switched her attention to the man Golze had been talking to, who now proceeded to pat down the old man.

She was still dizzy. As she watched the hands slap and slide over the potbellied torso and the new-looking clothes, Charlotte wondered if this could really be Frank Marrity from . . . nineteen years in the future. If he was, the years had not been kind. How was *your* light spent, Frank? she thought. In what dark world and wide? You're a nice-looking guy in '87—what happened?

A hand grabbed her elbow from behind, and she reflexively switched attention—Golze was looking at her, pulling her toward the car.

"You in back on the left," Golze said to her, "Marrity in the middle, Rascasse on the right. Hurry."

Rascasse wasn't dead—when he had been hoisted up and was being folded into the Honda, he raised his blood-smeared face and muttered something in French.

"Oh la la," said Golze, shoving the old man's head down to get him into the car, then wiping his hand on the shoulder of Rascasse's suit.

As she hurried around to get in on the other side, Charlotte was thinking about the little girl she had waved to in the fleeing car. Charlotte had seen her through Golze's eyes and then jumped to the girl's viewpoint—and it had *been* the girl's viewpoint, because Charlotte had seen herself behind the car, on the fast-receding sidewalk—but suddenly she had glimpsed a quick image of the little girl herself, up close, in profile.

It only seems to happen with Frank Marrity and his daughter, thought Charlotte as she slid into the seat next to the old Frank Marrity and pulled the door closed, this falling into one viewpoint from the other. What does that mean?

And why did I wave at her?

Seventeen

S hit," said Bennett shrilly, "a cop."

In the backseat next to Daphne, Marrity didn't look around. "Has he got his lights on?" They were driving north on Fair Oaks Avenue, over the bridge that spanned the 210 freeway.

The stolen car rocked as Bennett hit the brakes.

"No, but he's right behind us! How fast was I going just now? What if he pulls us over? I haven't called Moira yet! And I've got fifty thousand dollars in my pocket! My God, what have you people *done* to me? You fucking Marritys—"

"Lay off the brake and just drive straight," Marrity said sharply.

"This car is stolen! I've got a gun in my pocket! And it was fired only a few minutes ago! Oh Jesus—" His hands were visibly shaking on the steering wheel.

Beside Marrity, Daphne turned around and knelt on the seat to look out the back window.

A moment later Marrity heard a muffled *boom*, and with

a sudden cold chill in his stomach he guessed what had happened. He twisted around to look, and sure enough there was a car receding behind them, its hood up and billows of steam whipping around it in white veils.

"Make the first—" Marrity began.

"The police car blew up!" interrupted Bennett.

"I know. Make the first right turn you can, and pull over. I'll drive." Marrity smelled burning plastic.

"Jesus, now the car's on fire!"

"It's just your ashtray," said Marrity, feeling ready to vomit. His own hands were shaking now. "It'll—"

"It's the stereo," said Daphne. "There isn't an ashtray."

"Get off this street and park, dammit!" said Marrity loudly.

"Dad, I'm sorry," said Daphne, "I thought I had to!"

"Maybe you did, Daph." They swayed on the seat as Bennett wrenched the car into a right turn. Marrity wasn't sure his anger and dismay were justified, and he tried to keep them out of his mind, where Daphne could sense them. "Are the cops all right?"

Daphne was crying now. "Y-yes, I just grabbed the radiator!"

Bennett had turned right on Villa, and now steered the car to an abrupt stop against the curb. Black smoke was pouring up from the dashboard and curling under the windshield.

"I think we just abandon this car," said Marrity, levering open the right-side door and grabbing his briefcase. "Come on, Daph."

"I've got to bring Rumbold!"

"Sure, bring Rumbold."

Bennett climbed out of the car, and Marrity took Daphne's free hand and began striding away up the sunlit Villa Street sidewalk.

"Did Daphne blow up the cop car?" Bennett demanded breathlessly, catching up with them.

"Bennett, that's crazy," snapped Marrity. "Don't go crazy now." He peered ahead, not wanting to look back at the car.

"I see some stores. Is that fifty thousand dollars of yours in cash?"

"Of course not," said Bennett. "But you asked her if the cops were all right, and she said—"

"Then I'll give you a quarter to call Moira with. She still works at the dentist's office in Long Beach, right? I'll give you a couple of quarters. We can stop for a drink after you call and still have plenty of time to get a cab and meet her in Hollywood."

"Or an ice cream," said Daphne humbly, trotting along beside him.

"Or an ice cream," Marrity agreed, squeezing her hand. "There used to be an ice-cream place up here when I was a kid." He cleared his throat. "Bennett," he added awkwardly, "I think you saved our lives back there. At Grammar's house."

"And probably got myself killed doing it," said Bennett. "I'm not joking." He slapped his pockets. "I left my sunglasses in the car."

"You can afford another pair. The guy I'm going to call is with the National Security Agency. He'll believe what we tell him, and I think he'll arrest your—Sturm und Drang, and the woman who tried to kill Daphne and me this morning." And I hope they'll rescue my father, he thought, who also saved my life today. Marrity looked at Bennett, for once not focusing on the scowl and the bristly mustache. "I'm—grateful to you for saving me, and for saving my daughter," he said.

"Fuck you and your daughter," said Bennett, hurrying along. "And the NSA can't arrest people, they'd have to get the FBI to do it."

"Do you really have fifty thousand dollars in your pocket?" asked Daphne.

"I think it's two dollars less than fifty thousand," said Bennett gruffly. "I—shouldn't have said 'Fuck you.'"

"That's okay. Anybody who saves my dad's life can say anything he wants."

"Anybody who saves your dad's life should get a checkup from the neck up." He squinted at Marrity. "What does the National Security Agency have to do with all this? And

Daphne said she grabbed the radiator—after you asked her if the cops were—"

"Grammar's father was Albert Einstein," interrupted Marrity. He was sweating, and his mouth still felt too full of saliva. "Grammar had something she got from Einstein, some kind of machine, I gather. The NSA wants it, and I imagine this crowd who tried to kidnap us just now wants it too." How much should he tell Bennett about all this? The man deserved to know something about what he had got tangled up in. "Grammar probably used it on Sunday, and that got everybody's attention, got all these people on to . . . us, her descendants. They all think we have it, or know where it is."

"Bullshit her father was Einstein."

Marrity blinked at him. "Does that really strike you as the most . . . today, the most implausible thing you've . . ." He waved and let the sentence go unfinished.

"Did Daphne use this machine to blow up the police car?"

"No. I don't know." Marrity spat into a hedge, and for a moment thought he would have to crouch behind the hedge to be sick. "In a way, maybe," he added hoarsely, taking a deep breath and stepping forward into the breeze.

His briefcase was getting heavy, and he could sense the ache in Daphne's arm from carrying Rumbold in the shoe box. She was about to explain, and he decided not to stop her.

"I watched that movie that I stole from Grammar's shed," she said, looking down at the sidewalk as she skipped to keep up with her father. "*Pee-wee's Big Adventure,* except it was actually another movie, an old silent movie." She blinked up at Bennett, squinting against the sun. "The movie scared me so bad that I burned up the VCR and my bed. Rumbold was on my bed."

"Poltergeist," said Bennett.

Oh that's all we needed, thought Marrity.

"Poltergeist?" asked Daphne in dismay. "Like the ghosts that came out of the TV, in that movie?"

"No, Daph," Marrity said, trying to project reassurance, "real poltergeist stuff isn't like the stuff in that movie at all.

Poltergeist is when a teenage girl sets things on fire, at a distance, when she's upset. Nothing to do with ghosts or TV sets."

"Well," said Bennett, "it's supposed to be children around puberty, both boys and girls, though admittedly most recorded cases involve girls; and it's not just starting fires, by any—"

"Bennett," said Marrity. "It's a girl this time. And it's fires, this time."

"I was only—"

"There's a phone booth," interrupted Marrity, nodding ahead. "And there's a drive-in burger stand that probably sells ice cream."

It wasn't the place he remembered from his childhood—he and Moira had ridden their bicycles to an A&W root-beer stand that used to be here, in the early '60s. But this was the place that time had left them, and it looked as if it would do.

'm only going to eat the ice cream," said Daphne, "not the cone."

Bennett, and then Marrity, had talked to Moira on the pay phone, and had managed to convince her to leave work at once and drive to the Mayfair Market on Franklin, in Hollywood. Marrity had then phoned for a taxi, and had been told that one would pick them up in half an hour. Now they were at a picnic table in the roofed patio behind the hamburger stand, not visible from the street.

"Why not the cone?" asked Marrity. "Did he touch it?"

"Yes! He's supposed to take it from the bottom of the package, with the little paper holder, but he took it out of the top, with his fingers."

"His hands are probably clean."

"He handles money."

"Oh, yeah—good point."

Bennett had ordered a cup of coffee, but pushed it aside on the picnic table after one sip. He wiped his mouth on the sleeve of his white shirt, since all the paper napkins Daphne had pulled out of the dispenser had blown away when her father moved Rumbold's box, which had been holding them down.

"Those Sturm and Drang guys," said Bennett, "told me they were in negotiation with you to buy something Grammar had—this machine, apparently. They said you were going to keep the money, even though Moira should get half."

"That was a lie," said Marrity, sipping a cup of coffee of his own. "I've never spoken to Sturm und Drang, and I only met the sunglasses girl yesterday afternoon. We just talked about Milton, but then this morning she tried to shoot me, and a few minutes after that she tried to shoot me and Daphne both."

"Are you serious? *Shoot* you? Did she have a gun?"

"Yes, Bennett," said Marrity patiently, "and she fired it too. Several times. At me."

Bennett frowned and shook his head. Then he asked, "Who's Milton?"

"A poet," said Daphne. "Dead for a long time."

Bennett waved impatiently. He was squinting fiercely at the cars in the shopping-center parking lot. "Why would your father have stayed with that crowd?" he asked Marrity.

"He knows them, I gather," said Marrity. "I don't know anything about him—we only met *him* yesterday."

"Moira hates him."

"So do I, probably. Though he saved my life this morning, at the hospital."

"You didn't tell us Daphne was in the hospital," said Bennett. "I had to find out from Sturm and Drang, this morning."

"It was very sudden," said Marrity.

"My dad did a tracheotomy on me, on the floor of Alfredo's restaurant," said Daphne proudly, "on Base Line. With a knife."

"They gave you fifty thousand dollars?" asked Marrity.

"I guess so. You did a tracheotomy yourself? An emergency tracheotomy? Wow." He wiped his mouth on his sleeve again. "Originally the fifty thousand was for whatever it was that your grandmother had, this machine, I guess. But then it was just for handing over you and Daphne."

Marrity shuddered. "I'm glad you didn't hand us over to them." He didn't ask Bennett whether he had intended to split the money with him.

Daphne had by now eaten all the ice cream off the cone. "Don't you think the germs would be dead by now?"

"What germs?"

"From the ice-cream man's hands. Wouldn't the open air kill them?"

"I suppose it might."

She held the cone up and blew on it, turning it to catch all sides. "They'd blow off, wouldn't they? Germs?"

"Yeah, I bet they would. Be sure to chew it, thoroughly."

"You're supposed to say, 'Absolutely.' "

"Absolutely."

"Well don't say it if you don't mean it."

"Daph, I have no idea whether they'd blow off or not."

"Well, he didn't touch the tip," she said judiciously, and bit the point off the end, and melted ice cream spilled down her chin and onto her blouse.

She dropped the cone onto the table. "I need clean clothes," she said. "So do you, Dad. We've been wearing these since yesterday. And toothbrushes."

"There's our taxi," said Marrity, getting to his feet.

"I think there's a washing machine at this house we're going to hide out in," said Bennett.

Charlotte was looking out through the eyes of the old fellow who claimed to be Frank Marrity from the future.

In the rearview mirror she could see the blue eyes of young Hinch, who she recalled had been a theology student at a Bay Area seminary before his progressive, urbanely skeptical instructors had driven him to look elsewhere for a true supernatural power. The Vespers had picked him up with the promise, as she privately thought of it, that "ye shall not surely die: for God doth know that in the day ye eat the fruit thereof, then your eyes shall be opened and ye shall be as gods, knowing good and evil."

Denis Rascasse, slumped unconscious now on the far side of the Marrity guy, would probably have said something like *efficiency* rather than *evil*. And *cowardice* rather than *good*.

Over the headrest of the passenger seat she could see a few curls of Golze's disordered dark hair.

The radio on the dashboard clicked and hissed, and then a voice said, "Tierce."

Golze picked up the microphone. "Seconde."

"We found Prime's car, guns of Navarone." Golze impatiently switched frequencies, and the voice went on, "On Yucca. Nobody relevant visible in the neighborhood. The stereo was burned up, car full of smoke."

"Does it run?"

"Yes, runs fine."

"Meet us at Santa Monica and Moby Dick." *Click.* "And Van Ness. We'll switch cars, you take this one."

"Gotcha," said the voice, and Golze hung the microphone on its hook.

"Take us to Santa Monica and Van Ness," he said to Hinch.

Charlotte wondered why the stereo of Rascasse's car should have caught fire.

Abruptly she found herself seeing her own right-side profile; she was alarmed by the stress lines around her mouth and eyes. She turned to look toward the Marrity man, and was glad to see that in the full-face view, the sunglasses hid the crow's-feet at the corners of her eyes.

"Why the hell," he asked her, "did you try to kill Frank Marrity—my younger self—this morning?" She wished she could see his expression.

"I think," said Golze quickly, "that we've all been working under some misunderstandings." He shifted his bulk to peer back around the headrest at the old Marrity.

From the constriction at the top of Marrity's vision, Charlotte guessed that he was frowning.

"Soon enough," Golze said, "we'll all be able to ask and answer all the questions." Golze's eyes were blinking behind his glasses, and Charlotte saw him glance to the far right side of the rear seat, toward the slumped figure of Rascasse. "I think Rascasse is dead," he added. "Dying, anyway." He turned and looked ahead again.

Charlotte tried switching to Rascasse's point of view—and found herself seeing Golze and Hinch head-on, and old Marrity in the rear seat behind them; apparently her viewpoint now was from the dashboard, looking backward. Faces and hands were unnaturally bright, as if this image were seen by infrared radiation. Rascasse was evidently out of his body, but not far out of it.

She switched back to the Marrity view. "I don't think so," she said.

On her right, the old Frank Marrity cleared his throat, jiggling her vision. "Really, why did you kill him?"

"It was that Bradley guy," said Golze, "he hit him on the head with a gun butt. Your brother-in-law, if you really are Frank Marrity."

"I mean my father, in 1955. I—that doesn't make any sense."

"How do you know it doesn't make any sense? You were what, three years old? Anyway, I don't know, *I* wasn't even *born* yet. Rascasse said your father was more useful to us dead than alive, whatever that might mean, if anything." Golze hitched around in the seat again and smiled back at Marrity. "So give us a sample. What's some news from the future?"

"Are you *sure* you killed him, then?"

Golze shrugged. "Rascasse says we did. He seemed pretty sure. Why, did you hear from him after '55?"

"No—that's been my—we hated him for that, my sister and I. For leaving and not ever getting in touch with us."

"Well," said Golze, "any hate is good practice, even if it's baseless, as in this case. Better, in fact, more pure. So tell us something that happens in the future."

Frank Marrity blinked several times. "Uh, the Soviet Union collapses in '91. The Berlin Wall comes down before that, in '89. No war, the whole Communist thing just collapsed from inside, like a rotten pumpkin." He took a deep breath, and after several seconds let it out again. "I want to make a deal with you people. Something I can do for you, something you can do for me. But first you need to buy me a bottle of vodka."

"Vodka after talk," said Golze.

"No," said Marrity. "You people killed my father, and . . . and I don't know where that leaves me. I've hated him all my life for what he did, and now he's gone, and he *didn't* do it—and I'm afraid—"

He broke off and laughed weakly, and for a moment, before he blinked his eyes again, Charlotte could see the blur of tears around the edges of his vision. His voice was flat when he went on, "So I insist on a bottle of vodka before we proceed."

Charlotte saw Golze shrug. "Okay," he said. "Charlotte, the guy who's driving Rascasse's car will take you home in this one." Knowing her ways, he stared straight into Marrity's eyes as he added, "You haven't slept in thirty hours, and I don't think we'll catch up with our fugitives within the next ten hours. Get a shower, get some sleep, eat something."

You don't want me to hear you interview the Marrity guy, she thought. But in fact her eyelids and eye sockets were stinging, and she could smell her own sweat.

"Okay," she said.

To her right, she could feel old Marrity relax. He's afraid of me, she thought, and she wondered whether to be amused or annoyed.

She leaned back in the seat, her left elbow on the door's armrest, and again she reached out mentally for the unconscious Rascasse's view—and then she smothered a gasp, though her fingernails reflexively scrabbled at the door and her right hand gripped Marrity's knee, doubtless to his alarm.

Rascasse was fifty feet above Colorado Boulevard—his astral projection was, anyway. Only after a bewildered moment did Charlotte realize that the motionless streamlined train in the lane below them was simply the car their bodies were in—it looked like an impossibly long limousine, stretched from one block to another, right through an intersection—and at the intersection, other elongated vehicles were stuck perpendicularly right through it.

We're a bit outside our time slot, she told herself firmly. We're looking at several seconds at once. The black strings of pearls hanging in the air are probably flapping birds, crows.

Then either Rascasse descended, or he narrowed his focus; she could see Golze in the front passenger seat head-on, nearly level with her and only a foot or so away, and his blurred head became clear, frozen, grinning in a candid moment.

Then she could see inside Golze, by God knew what light; she could see his ribs, the slabs of his lungs, and the veiny sack that was his motionless heart; somehow in this impossible light it appeared to be black.

Then Rascasse's gaze entered the heart, with such a tight focus that the motionless valves were mouths caught pursed or stopped in midsyllable.

Charlotte switched back to Marrity's view, and involuntarily let out a sharp sigh of relief to see the back of Golze's head rocking in the passenger seat in front of her, and brake lights flashing through the windshield.

Golze turned around again to look at her, his eyebrows raised.

"I'm going to sleep right here," Charlotte said, speaking too loudly. "You know the way you think you're falling, right as you go to sleep?"

"Jactitations," said Golze, returning his attention to the traffic ahead. "Common in alcoholics."

Oh yeah? thought Charlotte, genuinely too tired to take offense. But I bet my heart will outlast yours.

Eighteen

When the taciturn young man dropped her off at the corner of Fairfax and Willoughby, Charlotte waited until she heard him drive away and then, since no one was looking at her, she listened to the traffic. Vehicles were growling from left to right in front of her, so she waited until that noise stopped and engines were accelerating back and forth to her right. She stepped confidently off the curb, and used the engine volume to keep herself from slanting out of the crosswalk that she couldn't see.

Stepping off the curb, she thought. I did that, all right. That experience with Rascasse's viewpoint in the car might not have been all the way out to what those boys call *the freeway,* but it was . . . pretty far up an on-ramp, at least! A good distance above the surface streets I live in.

Her hands were shaking, and she clenched them into fists.

There was bourbon in her apartment, but she wasn't sure about cigarettes, and right now she needed a cigarette. Up the far curb, she shuffled tentatively across the 7-Eleven parking lot, listening for cars suddenly turning in or backing out of parking spaces, and finally someone was looking at her.

She saw herself from a viewpoint inside the store, through the tinted window, but it was clear enough for her to walk briskly. She smiled and waved toward the viewpoint, just to keep the person looking at her until she reached the doors.

The action reminded her of having waved at Daphne, possibly half an hour ago. What was that all about? she wondered again. Hello? Here I am? Daphne Marrity is *not* my younger self!

Once inside, she switched to the point of view of the clerk behind the counter, without even having seen if it was a man or a woman. The clerk didn't look at her wallet as the pack of Marlboros slid across the counter between the displays of Bic lighters and little cans of cold-sore balm, so she had to feel for two one-dollar bills—she kept ones folded into squares, to distinguish them from the fives that were folded twice lengthwise, the tens that were folded once lengthwise, and the twenties that were not folded at all. She could see the two quarters the clerk gave her in change, so she didn't have to feel for the milled edges of the coins to know what they were.

Outside again, she paused in the hot, smoggy breeze, scanning the nearby viewpoints for a view of herself; over the years she had become very good at picking herself out even in very crowded scenes. And after a few seconds she located herself in the view of a man—she could see the edges of a mustache at the bottom of the view field—at the roofed RTD bus-stop bench across Willoughby, and he obligingly watched her as she walked the dozen yards to the gate of her apartment building. He even kept her in view as she stepped along the grass-bordered pavement to the front door of her apartment, so she didn't have to drag the fingers of one hand along the walls and windows of the other ground-floor apartments, as she sometimes did.

By touch she fitted the key into the front-door lock, and bolted the door behind her once she was inside. Through the eyes of the man across the street, she could dimly see her silhouette inside the apartment through the always uncurtained windows, but that view was of no use, and she let it go.

Her apartment was chilly with air-conditioning, and the faint smells of upholstery and damp plant soil were a relief after the aggressive exhaust-and-salsa smells of the street.

She hung her keys on the hook by the door and took three strides forward across the carpet, and with the fourth step her left rubber-soled Rockport tapped the linoleum tiles of the kitchen floor.

She peeled the cellophane off the pack of Marlboros and tapped one out. Several lighters were in the drawer under the counter, glasses in the cupboard above, the bottle of Wild Turkey on the Formica-top table, and in ten seconds she had sat down at the table and poured a couple of inches of bourbon into the glass and was waving the fingers of one hand over the lighter to be sure it had lit; then she slowly brought it toward the end of the cigarette, puffing until she could taste the smoke.

She inhaled, then put the lighter down to take a sip of the bourbon; a moment later she exhaled smoke and bourbon fumes, and a lot of the tension in her shoulders went with them.

But her heart was still going faster than usual, and she knew it was because of her brief vicarious experience of being outside the boundaries of one-second-at-a-time. It's actually true, she thought cautiously, trying out the shape of the idea; you really can get into a higher dimension, from which the four dimensions we ordinarily live in can be viewed from outside. She had taken their word for it before, but now she'd actually seen what Rascasse and Golze had been talking about all along.

If one of them's got to kill the other, she thought, I hope it's my poor old Rascasse who survives. Especially if he goes along with Golze's evident decision that I no longer need to kill the young Frank Marrity. Obviously the situation's changed since I was given that order. This crapped-out old Marrity, who has information we need to have, might just evaporate if I were to kill his younger self. Who knows? It all seems to be real, the old guy seems actually to be a visitor from the future.

As I will be.

She took another drag on the cigarette and another mouthful of the whiskey, and as she swallowed she let the shiver shake through her all the way to her fingertips, probably throwing the ash off her cigarette. And she realized that the nervousness she felt was relief and anticipation.

This is going to work, she thought. I don't have to kill Marrity, and this thing is going to work. I'll be able to ditch this life, like a paper towel you cleaned up some nasty mess with. Throw it away and then wash every particle of memory off your hands.

She recalled helping Golze lure a young man aboard the bus in Pasadena last night. Golze had used a stun gun on him once he was inside, and then had duct-taped his mouth, wrists, and ankles. She had been dropped off at the Arrowhead Pediatric Hospital in San Bernardino about half an hour later, and in all that time the young man had not moved. Perhaps Golze's stun gun had killed him—Golze hadn't referred to the incident today.

She drained the remaining couple of ounces of bourbon in one swallow, and welcomed the depth-charge effect, the unfocusing warmth spreading through her whole body.

She stood up and crossed to the sink, where she put down the empty glass and ran water over the cigarette, afterward dropping the soggy filter in the wastebasket.

As she walked back across the living room carpet, she was remembering Ellis, her last boyfriend; he had said that Elizabeth Taylor didn't seem attractive to him in old movies like *Cat on a Hot Tin Roof* or *Butterfield 8* because the image of her present-day self kept getting in the way.

She stepped sideways onto the linoleum of the bathroom floor, into the faint smells of Lysol and rust. She opened the medicine cabinet and took down a hand-size plastic bottle of baby shampoo and squirted some into her palm and

began washing her hands, rubbing her fingertips. Before the
shampoo had been entirely washed from her fingers, she
several times brushed warm water over her eyelashes, from
the bridge of her nose outward.

She had only *seen* the young Frank Marrity twice, briefly,
both times through the eyes of his twelve-year-old daughter:
yesterday at 1:00 P.M., when he had been sitting across from
the daughter at the Italian restaurant, and five hours before
that, when he had been sitting at his kitchen table next to the
old version of himself. The old one had been drinking something brown, brandy or whiskey.

Did the young Marrity imagine that the older man was
his father, as Charlotte had? Would that be what the old man
had told him?

Charlotte called up young Marrity's face—lean and kind
and humorous under the disordered dark hair, very different
from the defeated, pouchy face of the old guy. And the voices
had nothing in common—young Marrity's was a clear tenor,
while the old guy's was hoarse and raspy. She didn't see them
as the same guy—no perceptible Elizabeth Taylor effect.

She lowered her chin as if to whistle a deep bass note,
opening her eyelids wide; then drew her left forefinger along
her lower eyelid until she could feel the bottom edge of the
plastic scleral shell. And with a gently gouging push, she
popped it right off the coral sphere implant and onto the palm
of her hand.

A moment later she had done the same with the right eye.
She rinsed the prosthetic eye shells, rolling the flexible plastic between her still slick fingers.

When they were clean, she dried them on a towel and
carefully laid them in a silk-lined glasses case and snapped
it shut and slid it onto the shelf above the toilet.

She kept her eyelids open wide to let the coral spheres air
out. *Of her eyes are coral made,* she thought.

She was aware of a viewpoint not far away, and she focused on it. The young student in the next apartment was
staring at his television screen, on which Clark Gable and
Vivien Leigh were sitting on a veranda, watching a little girl

riding a horse sidesaddle; and Charlotte had taken a step toward the living room, to turn on her own television set and get audio to go with the clairvoyant picture, but then she noticed that the lights were glowing on the student's VCR, on top of the television set—*Gone With the Wind* wasn't being shown on a TV channel, he had rented a tape of it.

The student always watched the news on Channel 7 at 7:00 A.M., and sometimes Charlotte set her alarm so that she could watch it through his eyes, listening to the sound on her own set. Usually, though, she would rather sleep.

Ellis had been good with movies, generally paying pretty close attention. She had made a show of keeping her eyes pointed toward the screen to encourage him to do the same. And he had been a great reader, never skimming or skipping pages—often she had just sat beside him on the couch, her eyes closed, reading along through his eyes. He had liked John D. MacDonald and Dick Francis mysteries, which were fine, but she wished she could meet a man who liked the Brontë sisters. Charlotte had only read *Wuthering Heights* and *Jane Eyre* before being blinded. Frank Marrity probably liked the Brontës.

She sighed and picked up her purse and the towel and counted her steps into the bedroom. She sat down on the bed, spread out the towel across the bedspread, and then pulled her .357 Smith & Wesson revolver out of her purse.

With her finger outside the trigger guard and the gun pointed into the corner of the room, she pushed the cylinder-release button and swung the cylinder out to the side. She tilted the gun up and pushed the ejector rod; one heavy cartridge fell into her palm, along with five empty brass shells.

Five shots! she thought with a shiver. And apparently all I did was break a window. She was glad now that she had not killed him.

If Marrity had looked at her, she had planned to see herself facing him squarely and pointing the gun a bit below his eyes, so that she would not quite be able to see down the barrel. That ought to have had the gun aimed at his chest. And then squeeze the trigger. She had wondered if he would look down at the wound in himself or keep staring at her.

In spite of her intimacy with Ellis, her recollections of him were nearly all of his profile at restaurants, as people at other tables had glanced over at him and Charlotte.

When they had made love he had hardly ever looked at himself—not surprisingly, she thought; he wasn't a narcissist—and so all her recollections of their passion were views of her own naked body. And of his hands.

She had had perhaps half a dozen lovers during the nine years since the exploding battery had blinded her in the missile silo in the Mojave Desert; and her memory of every one of them was of her own body and a pair of hands.

It still seemed odd to her that she and Denis Rascasse had never been lovers, not even when he had first recruited her three years ago.

Involuntarily she found herself recalling old Robert Jerome, the Fuld Hall custodian at the Institute for Advanced Study at Princeton, in New Jersey. She had seduced the amiable old man in order to get access to the restricted Einstein archives—and then had convinced him that she loved him, to get his help in robbing the extra-sensitive files still kept in the basement of Einstein's old house on Mercer Street.

Even with Robert Jerome, all she could remember was her own face and body, and his wrinkled, spotty hands.

The pebbled-plastic gun-cleaning kit was in the bedside table drawer, and she lifted it out carefully and opened it on the blanket, by touch separating the rods and brushes and sharp-smelling bottles of solvent and oil.

Was *she* a narcissist? If so, it was by default. She couldn't help but always wind up looking at herself, through someone else's eyes.

But no, that wasn't the way it was—she didn't care about this blinded body, nor even about the twenty-eight-year-old woman who animated it.

If I'm a narcissist, she thought, it's in the same way that the crapped-out old-man Marrity probably is. We want to go back and rescue our younger, more innocent selves from some bad thing that threatens them. *I have done nothing but in care of thee.* We're willing to throw ourselves away—make ourselves into things that *ought* to be thrown away—if by doing so we can save that one precious person who by our disgraceful actions will be spared our disgraces.

She looks like I used to.

According to Rascasse, it's possible to leave *now* and go back and change your past, then return in Newtonian recoil to *now* again, with your memories intact—with, in effect, two sets of recollections: memories of the original-issue life and memories of the revised one too. Einstein apparently did that in 1928, and Lieserl Marity probably did it in 1933. But I won't do it that way, Charlotte thought. I won't come back.

Throw it away and then wash every particle of memory off your hands.

Robert Jerome had used those old hands she remembered to make a noose out of his own shirt, not very long after Charlotte had impatiently explained to him that she had never loved him, that she had only seduced him to get the papers she had stolen. He had been in jail for being an accessory to burglary, his job and pension lost, when he had killed himself.

He had also been guilty of perjury, in absolving Charlotte of all blame; through a Vespers decoy address she had eventually received a letter that he had written to her from the jail, but she had never asked anybody to read it for her.

I won't impose these memories on the redeemed Charlotte Sinclair, she thought as she began screwing the .38-caliber brush onto one of the rods. I'll save her and then just go away, with all my sins unshared.

Nymph, she thought, reflexively misquoting Hamlet, *in your orisons be all my sins forgotten.*

Bennett and Moira had walked ahead as the four of them made their way up the steep curves of Hollyridge Drive, with Marrity and Daphne trudging along behind, all of them crowding against a fence or garage door whenever a car slowly moved up or down the narrow lane. Marrity couldn't imagine what happened when two cars needed to pass each other.

Mockingbirds made sneering calls from the aromatic eucalyptus trees overhanging the embankment to their right, and the one resident who noticed the four of them—a blond woman who was hovering with a watering can over a row of tomato plants in red clay pots—stared at them with evident unease. Pedestrians who weren't jogging or walking dogs were apparently unusual. Marrity wasn't surprised—the noon sun was a weight on his shoulders, and this hike would have been strenuous even if he were not carrying his jacket and his briefcase and Rumbold's shoe box. Bennett was holding a paper bag that had a bottle of scotch whisky in it—he'd bought it at the Mayfair Market on Franklin, one block north of Hollywood Boulevard.

Moira had finally driven into the market parking lot about an hour after Bennett had called her. They had all got into another taxi then, while Bennett and Marrity both tried at once to explain to Moira why they were all fugitives, even she; and then, when they had driven no more than half a mile up through the narrow, twisting lanes that curled like shaded streams down the Hollywood Hills, Bennett had told the driver to stop.

Now Moira halted and kicked off her shoes, so Bennett stopped too, and they waited for Marrity and Daphne to catch up.

"So are these *spies,* Frank?" Moira asked, standing on one foot to rub the sole of the other. "Soviets, KGB?"

"I don't know," Marrity said, pausing to switch his briefcase to his left hand and cradle his jacket and Rumbold in his right arm. "I guess if the NSA's after them, they probably are."

"Bennett says they . . . *shot* at you and Daphne?"

"Shot at me, aimed a gun at me and Daph. Serious both times." He lifted his briefcase to wipe his forehead on his shirtsleeve. "This is all true, Moira."

"Bennett says you told him Grammar's father was Albert Einstein." She smiled at him. "I could lose my job over this, not going back after lunch."

Marrity was tempted to open his briefcase and show her the Einstein letters; but he still didn't trust Bennett with knowing about them. "The NSA man we met last night said her father was Einstein," Marrity told her. "So did our father, yesterday morning."

Beside him Daphne nodded solemnly.

Moira's smile had disappeared. "Our *father*? Who do you mean?"

Marrity looked at Bennett, who shrugged and rolled his eyes. Clearly he had not told Moira about seeing their father.

"My father. Your father. He's back. He—"

"*Our* father?" Her shoes fell out of her hands and clattered on the asphalt.

"*Yes,* Moira," said Marrity patiently, "he came back because he heard Grammar died, and *he* wants to make a deal with these—"

"You've *talked* to him? Where is he?"

Daphne crouched to pick up Moira's shoes.

"He's with these people who are after us," said Marrity, "who shot at me. He—"

"*Where?*" She swayed on the narrow black pavement, and Marrity and Bennett each reached out to grab one of her arms. Marrity dropped his jacket.

"I don't know where he is now!" said Marrity. "He was standing on Grammar's lawn when we drove away, an hour and a half ago. We wanted him to come with us, but he waved us off, said, 'Go!' We couldn't wait."

"He had amnesia," said Moira, "all these years. I'm sure of it." Very slowly, supported by Marrity and Bennett, she sat down on the asphalt. The skirt of her brown linen suit was knee length, and she had to sit with her legs stretched out in front of her. Daphne frowned and crouched again to press her palm against the street surface, and Marrity knew she was checking to see if the tar was sticky.

"You can't just *sit* here," said Bennett anxiously. "Get up, it's only a few steps to this key I have the, house I have the key to."

"Come on, Moira," said Marrity.

Daphne was crouched beside Moira, her face level with the woman's. "We should get in out of the sun," Daphne said. "We'll all get skin cancer."

Moira blinked at her. "Of course, dear," she said, and let Marrity and her husband help her back onto her feet.

Daphne picked up her father's jacket and carried it and Moira's shoes the rest of the way. They were nearly at the top of the hill, where Hollyridge made a hairpin turn to the left to become Beachwood, and the street was narrow and steep between the eucalyptus trees.

Bennett waved at a shaded one-story house that was crowded up to the street pavement on their left. Red bougainvillea blossoms clustered over the door and two windows. "This is it," he said tiredly, pulling a set of keys from the pocket of his slacks.

Entering the house was stepping out of shadow into sunlight, for the entire west side of the house was windows facing the Beachwood canyon. Frank Marrity and Daphne followed Bennett and Moira inside, blinking around at the blank white walls of the spacious interior; they had entered at street level, but stairs led down to a lower floor with a balcony outside the glass. The afternoon sunlight gleamed on polished wood floors, and Marrity noticed that the faces of his companions were underlit, as if by reflecting water. He put down his briefcase and the shoe box by the door.

"Lock it, Dad," said Daphne.

"Right," said Marrity, twisting the door's dead-bolt knob.

"This would have been perfect for filming," muttered Bennett. "Camera on the balcony and on the street out front, lots of room inside for everybody's gear."

The kitchen was on the upper, entry level, and Marrity noticed a telephone on the wall by the counter.

"The phone work?" he asked, starting toward it. His footsteps echoed in the empty house.

"It's supposed to," said Bennett, following him as Moira and Daphne moved to the rail to look down into the broad lower level. "I think Subaru is paying the bill. Let me see your man's card."

Marrity was already tugging his wallet from his hip pocket, and when he pulled the card out he handed it to Bennett.

Bennett looked at the phone number, which was all that was printed on one side of the card, and then at the other side, which was blank.

"Who says this guy is with the NSA?" he asked. "Besides him?" He clunked his bagged bottle down on the counter. "I should have bought plastic cups," he said, his voice lower. "We'll have to drink from the bottle."

"I don't really care if he's NSA or not," said Marrity, taking the card back. He was speaking more quietly too—the echoes seemed to amplify volume. "He's against the crowd who keeps trying to shoot us, which makes him somebody I approve of."

Daphne had joined her father by the counter. "Eugene Jackson was a nice man," she said.

Moira turned around and leaned back against the rail, so that she was just a silhouette against the brightness behind her. "Why not just call the police, Frank?"

Marrity remembered the cartoon thing that had spoken to Daphne from the turned-off television at the hospital, late last night. The Jackson person had appeared to know how to handle it—and Marrity was certain the police would not.

And he remembered Bennett's fifty thousand dollars. Was Bennett anxious to talk to the police?

"We'll probably call the police," he told her. "But I want to call this NSA guy first, and then you need to hear the full story. *Then,* if you like, we can call the police."

"Can I call my office?" Moira went on. "Tell them I'll be late coming back?"

"You should have done it from a pay phone down the hill," said Bennett. "You haven't seen these guys, Moira, they're scary."

Moira laughed incredulously and stepped away from the

railing, into the kitchen area. "You think they've tapped the phone at the dentist's office?"

"Let's see what our NSA man says about you calling your office," said Marrity. He laid the card down on the tile counter with a faint slap, and then took a deep breath and flexed his fingers.

They all stared at him.

"Who," Bennett asked, squinting, "was the Greek philosopher who practiced rhetoric by putting pebbles in his mouth?"

"Demosthenes, I think," said Marrity.

"They probably didn't have scotch, in those days." Bennett pulled the bottle of Ballantine's out of the paper bag. "You want a mouthful before you call?"

Moira muttered, "Oh for God's sake," but Daphne nodded at her father as solemnly as if she were advising sunscreen or seat belts.

"Good idea," Marrity said. Bennett twisted off the cap and took a generous sip of the liquor before passing the bottle to Marrity.

Marrity took several scorching swallows, then handed it back.

Bennett nodded. "*Damn* good idea," he said breathlessly.

"We didn't get any Cokes," said Daphne.

"Sorry, Daph," Marrity said, exhaling, "we'll get some later. But you can't have warm scotch right out of a bottle."

"Nor even in a glass with ice and soda, I hope!" said Moira.

"No, no," agreed Marrity, who in fact had been thinking that if they'd had glasses he could have given Daphne a very watered-down drink. "Here goes," he said, picking up the telephone receiver and dialing the number.

The phone at the other end rang only once, and then a man's voice said, "Yes."

"This is—"

"I know who it is," interrupted the voice.

"Okay. I think we need rescue."

"Yes you do. I gather you and your daughter weren't injured this morning? Let's not use names."

"Okay. No, that's right, neither of us was injured. But two hours ago that crowd tried to kidnap us in front of my grandmother's house. It's the woman with the sunglasses and her friends, I mentioned her to you last night."

"Yes, we're aware of them. Where's the last place your grandmother was standing, on Sunday, in Pasadena? As far as you know? I *don't* think she went to Newport Beach, do you?"

"No, she didn't go to Newport Beach. Who said she did? She went to the airport. We have information you need, and if you don't rescue us this crowd will find us again."

"And kill us," added Daphne. Marrity frowned and touched his forefinger to his lips.

"We'll pick you up immediately," said the man on the phone, "and you'll be safe. Did you use a radio, or the telephone, at your grandmother's house, Sunday or today?"

"No." Marrity frowned impatiently. "Yes, on Sunday, I called my sister from there. Why, was it tapped?"

"How was the connection?"

"It was a bad connection, it kept fading out, with static. We can tell you all this—"

"But where's the last place your grandmother was standing in Pasadena? To the best of your knowledge?"

Marrity reminded himself that this man was their only hope. "At the curb, waiting for the cab. Or on the porch."

"No, I mean while she was still in the house."

"How could I possibly—in her kitchen, I imagine, or in the shower, or in her shed. How should I know? Listen, my father is *with* these people, the people who tried to kidnap—"

"Voluntarily?"

"My father? Yes, he could have driven away with us, but he decided to stay with them. He says he's met them before, when he was thirty-five, though most of this crowd is too young for him to have met them then."

"I daresay. Why her shed? What's in the shed?"

"Uh—lawn mowers."

"Plural?"

Marrity was sweating. Actually there wasn't even one lawn mower in Grammar's shed; it had just seemed like a plausible answer.

The man went on: "Is there any unusual machinery in her shed? Is this the decrepit old shed in her backyard?"

"Yes, that shed." Marrity saw Moira raise her eyebrows. "Well, she's got a VCR out there."

"A VCR. Is there a gold-wire swastika on the floor? Maybe under the floor?"

Marrity opened his mouth, but couldn't think of an answer to give the man.

"I'll take your silence as a yes," said the man's voice. "And I bet she was barefoot."

Marrity remembered the tire-soled sandals he and Daphne had seen on the brick floor of the Kaleidoscope Shed. "Uh . . ." he began.

"Stay right where you are, I'll send somebody to pick you up. For right now just tell me your nearest big cross streets— call this number again in half an hour to give me your exact location."

"Nearest . . . ?" said Marrity, trying to remember. "Uh, Franklin and Beachwood, I guess. We're up in the hills." He glanced at Moira. "Can we call the—what do you think of the idea of us calling the police? Or my sister's employer?"

"Don't call anyone else. Repeat, *do not*. Just sit still and call me again in half an hour."

Daphne was tugging at Marrity's sleeve. "Something you've got to tell him!" she whispered.

"One second," said Marrity into the phone; then he covered the mouthpiece and said, "What, Daph?"

"They've got to feed the cats!"

Marrity nodded and took his hand off the phone. "You still there?" he asked.

"Yes."

"We have one condition, for our cooperation. A . . . gesture of good faith, on your part."

"What is it?"

"You people need to put a twenty-pound bag of Purina Cat Chow in my kitchen. Lay it down flat, like a pillow, and then cut the whole top surface off. It's stiff paper, there're knives in the drawer to the right of the sink. They'll be all right for water, they all drink out of the toilets."

"Your house is certainly under hostile surveillance."

"That's why I'm asking a pro to do it, not one of the neighbors."

The voice laughed. "Fair enough. We'll do it. Talk to you in thirty minutes."

Nineteen

Lepidopt switched off his portable telephone and tucked the bulky thing into its carrying case. He shifted in the passenger seat to look around; they were on Fairfax, not far south of Hollywood Boulevard.

"Ernie," he said to Bozzaris, "get to Lieserl's house right now—204 Batsford Street, in Pasadena—take the 101 south to the northbound Pasadena freeway, it ends very close to her place."

Bozzaris visibly decided on the quickest way to the 101, then made a fast right turn onto Santa Monica Boulevard.

"And when we get there," Lepidopt went on, "you go into the shed in the backyard and find the gold swastika on the floor. It might be under whatever the floor is, which I hope isn't concrete. Photograph the swastika, trace any wiring or machinery and photograph that, and then take it all out; we'll want to reassemble it at the Wigwam Motel. That other crowd has got the old twenty-first-century Frank Marrity.

He's with them voluntarily—he'll probably want to delay telling them about the machine in the old lady's shed until he's made some deal, got some assurances, but they might abbreviate that. So be quick."

"The old guy knows this stuff about the shed?"

"It's got to be how he came back here, from the future."

"Ah. You'll want me to drop you off somewhere."

"No, I'll wait in the car, outside her house. None of that crowd has seen me before. If they arrive in the middle of your work, I think we'll kill them."

The portable phone buzzed again, and Lepidopt thought Marrity must have thought of some other task like feeding the cats; but it was an old man's voice on the line.

"What?" said the reedy old voice.

Lepidopt's chest was suddenly cold, for he thought he recognized the voice. Easy enough, he thought, to make the phone ring again. Just push some electrons around, reactivate the circuitry that was activated a moment ago.

"Uh," said Lepidopt hoarsely, "Sam?"

Peripherally he could see Bozzaris glance sharply at him.

"I don't know what it is," said Sam Glatzer's voice. "But it's in a cement tepee. And it's also in a truck. This thing."

"What is, Sam?" A moment later Lepidopt bared his teeth, belatedly remembering that it's no use asking ghosts questions before they've given the answers.

He was sweating. He had talked to a ghost only once before, and that had been during his training in Tel Aviv in 1968, in the trailer, with an instructor and other students—and the ghost hadn't been anyone he had known.

Another ghost voice intruded on the phone line now—a younger man, possibly drunk: "Two days I sat beside my body, staring at the holes in my chest." Looking out the car window, Lepidopt noted that they were driving past the gray stone walls of the Hollywood Cemetery.

"Not that," said Sam, "but a place that looks like that."

"Okay," said Lepidopt helplessly.

"I went to my grandfather," said the other man's voice; a moment later the voice added, "to find out who I am, where I came from."

Lepidopt gritted his teeth. The intruding voice was certainly a ghost too, so there was no point in telling him to be quiet.

"And it's in the Swiss Family Robinson tree house at Disneyland," said Glatzer's voice, "in a manner of speaking."

"Right," Lepidopt said. *What* is, Sam? he thought. He tried to remember everything Sam had said so far.

"At the Chinese Theater," Glatzer went on. "It's in a lot of places."

"But I have no mother, really," interjected the other voice, "Only children."

"You know what a capacitor is, right?" said Glatzer. "Put the hand in when the cement was wet. It's more like a capacitor."

"My mother will hide them," said the other ghost voice, "or try to. Everyone who dwells here is safe."

"The thing I thought was a gravestone," said Glatzer.

Lepidopt sighed and wiped his forehead.

"Tell me about it, Sam," he said, to pave the way for the things the old man's ghost had already said; for he had it now.

"They'll try to find my children," said the other voice unhappily.

"Oren," said Glatzer, "listen . . ."

Oren Lepidopt held the phone to his ear, but neither of the ghosts said anything more.

Lepidopt supposed that was the last thing he would ever hear Sam Glatzer say: *Listen . . .*

Lepidopt switched off the phone. "That was Sam Glatzer," he told Bozzaris. "His ghost. He says we've got to get the Charlie Chaplin footprint slab too. It's apparently part of the machine, and it's apparently in the shed too. It's a capacitor, he said." He began punching numbers into the phone. "I'd better get some *sayanim* with a truck."

Bozzaris's eyebrows were up, and he was nodding as he

watched the glittering lanes ahead of him. "How did Sam sound?"

Lepidopt laughed harshly. "Good. Rested."

Denis Rascasse's body was stretched across one of the bunks at the back of the parked bus. He was breathing through his open mouth, in ragged snores. The gash in his scalp had been rubbed with Neosporin and bandaged, but he was still unconscious and there were no plans to take him to a hospital. Young Hinch sat up front in the driver's seat, twisting a Rubik's Cube on each square of which he had painted a Hebrew letter.

Rascasse's attention was several miles away, at Echo Park. He had long since lost the body habit of seeing from two close-set points as if he were using organic eyes, and his perspective was broad—sunlight was gleaming off the lake in a million directions like a fire, and at the same time the lake was a placid jade green with no reflections at all; he could see all sides of every one of the trees around the lake and the undersides of the lotus lillies on the western shore. Nothing was "in front of" anything else.

But he couldn't focus on one of the rental boats on the lake.

He knew why. Golze and the elderly Frank Marrity were in that boat, and Golze must have removed the Chaplin's-hat ribbon from the Baphomet head and buttoned it around his own neck—almost certainly with a twist to make a Moebius strip of it.

Chaplin had made a lot of movies at Echo Park for Keystone Studios, back in the nineteen-teens. Chaplin had been a magician who took extensive masking precautions, and his lifeline was a tangle here; every time a director had said, "Cut!" there was a jig in his line, and in 1914 Chaplin had even made a movie in which he had completely submerged in the lake, as if in a baptism. Lots of kinks and false stops.

And Golze had now lit up that old spiderweb camouflage

pattern by wearing Chaplin's hat ribbon. Whenever Rascasse tried to focus on the boat, he found that he was instead
looking away from the boat, in all directions at once. Even
for a person as experienced in out-of-body perspectives as
Rascasse, it was jarring and disorienting.

The elderly Frank Marrity squinted around in the sunlight at the palm and yellow-flowered acacia trees that
ringed the little lake. From the boat on the water, he could
see here and there a homeless person sleeping in the shade
beside a shopping cart, and children and ducks on the asphalt walk that ringed the lake.

"Last time we talked," he said, "it was on a bus. Do you
still have that bus?" He leaned forward as he spoke, to be
heard over the clanging and squeaking of the mechanical
toy animals Golze had set into motion on the curved boards
below their feet.

"Yes." Golze rested on the oars, having propelled the
orange-painted rowboat a good ten yards out from the shade
of the roofed rental dock. He had loosened his tie and laid
his tweed jacket across the blue vinyl cushion on the thwart
between them, but his white shirt was already dark with
sweat. For some reason the fat man was wearing a black ribbon choker, barely visible below his beard.

"When was this?" Golze asked.

A tin ape with a pair of cymbals had run down, and
Golze picked it up and wound the key in its back. Luckily
most of the toys were battery operated.

The old Frank Marrity shrugged as Golze set the rackety
toy back down among its fellows. "It might have been right
now, this date and this hour," Marrity said. "I don't recall,
exactly. For me, subjectively, it was quite a while ago—I was
thirty-five years old." He took a sip from his can of 7-Up, to
which he had added enough vodka to dispel its coldness, and
shuddered. The lake smelled like moss and algae and the
breeze smelled like roof tar.

"I see," said Golze. "Things, events have deviated, from

the way they originally happened? You can help keep these toys wound up."

"Of course they've deviated." Marrity carefully set his 7-Up on the thwart and then bent to pick up a dog with brown-and-white nylon fur and begin twisting its key. He wished he'd brought a hat; the sun overhead was hot on his scalp through his thinning gray hair. "For one thing, in my original experience of August 1987 my elderly father didn't visit me. That's who I've told my younger self that I am. My father. Our father. He believes it—I'm close enough to the right age, and of course I look like him, and I know the family history."

"So he hates you?"

Marrity frowned as he put the dog down. "I think he does. Though he's more civil than *I* would be, if I met the old man." Then with a shiver of loss he remembered that his father had been killed in 1955. "But of course the old man turns out not to be the bad guy we always thought he was." And who is now? he asked himself rhetorically. Got to have a bad guy.

"What did we talk about," Golze asked, "in the bus, when you were thirty-five?"

Marrity thought: You wanted Grammar's VHS movie, and I sold it to you. But the movie is gone, this time. And you also asked about Einstein's machine, which I didn't know about, then. Aloud he said, "You said you wanted to buy a machine my grandmother had, which had been designed by Albert Einstein."

"And?"

"And I sold it to you, for fifty thousand dollars." Close enough, he thought—I sold him the movie that time. "I want something else, besides money, this time."

Golze smiled, obviously pleased. "And there was the movie too."

"You mentioned a movie, but I didn't have that, whatever it was." He picked up a big red plastic ant that had stopped moving.

Golze's good cheer was gone. "The *movie,* it was watched

at your house at four-fifteen P.M. two days ago! Before there were any divergences between your lifeline and your younger self's!"

That's right, thought Marrity, forcing himself not to reach for the 7-Up can. Instead he nervously twisted the key in the ant's belly. "Daphne—may have watched a movie—I was working—"

"Why are you lying? Your younger self has described it as a paranormal 'intrusion' that occurred at four-fifteen on Sunday." He leaned forward across the oars and smiled at Marrity, widening his eyes and showing his yellow teeth. "Why are you lying?"

Marrity exhaled. "Because it's *gone,* the movie's destroyed," he said, relieved to be admitting the truth. "In my original life nineteen years ago, I sold it to you, but in this time line the VCR burned up with the movie in it when Daphne was watching it."

"Burned up? You *know* it was burned up?"

"I saw the VCR in my, his, front yard. It was charred." The ant had begun writhing mechanically in his hands, and he hastily set it down.

"And her teddy bear was burned too," said Golze quietly. "And the stereo in Rascasse's car! Was this poltergeist? Telekenesis? Did she grab these things psychically?"

"I don't know. I wasn't there. She didn't have any psychic powers when she was *my* daughter."

"Poltergeist!" Golze shouted it like a curse.

The fat man picked up the oar handles and rowed furiously to a spot several yards farther out. Then he let go of them and rubbed his red face with both chubby hands as the boat surged on for a yard or two and then rocked to a stop on the green water.

Marrity peered around at the distant new apartment buildings beyond Alvarado Boulevard, and in the other direction at the rental dock's little lighthouse, which looked as if it dated from the 1920s. And a man from the twenty-first century sitting in a boat between them, he thought.

Finally Golze said, "I believe you," through his fingers.

"All our remote viewers reported that it simply disappeared; not just stopped being used, but dropped out of their perceptions entirely." He lowered his hands and stared at Marrity. "Why would she have poltergeist powers in this time line?"

"I can't imagine. It's new to me."

"Tell me the truth about our meeting nineteen years ago."

"I *can* give you the machine."

"The meeting."

"Well, the blind girl was there, and after I gave you the movie, she stopped bothering to pretend she could see out of her own eyes. There were some vulgar jokes, when one of the men would go to the bathroom. She was pretty drunk, as I recall! And you had—I'm glad not to see it here—you had a mummified human *head,* which appeared to be alive." He squinted at Golze, but the fat man didn't seem surprised, so they must have it in this time line too. "It made noises and wiggled its jaw, anyway." He picked up the ape with the cymbals, which had run down again. "Like one of these toys. Why didn't you get all battery-operated ones?"

I'm talking too much, he thought as he wound it up. He put the ape down and took another sip of the lukewarm, fortified 7-Up and shifted on the blue vinyl cushion. He wondered if the cushions were supposed to serve as life preservers if the boat sank.

"The wind-up ones provide discontinuity," Golze said shortly. "So you gave us the Chaplin movie, when you were thirty-five."

"Right. A videocassette, labeled *Pee-wee's Big Adventure,* though that's not what the movie in the cassette was."

"Had you watched the movie?"

"No. My daughter did. Practically put her in a coma."

"I can imagine. And we asked you about the machine too?"

"Yes, but at that time I didn't know anything about it. This is the truth. I only learned about it years later, from hints you dropped about Einstein and my grandmother. I had to read up on quantum mechanics, and consult Ouija boards and spiritualists, all sorts of screwy research. I still don't exactly know how it works."

"But you figured out how to *work* it. You came back in time by means of it."

Marrity smiled smugly. "Right." .

"Then we can use it to go back in time from here, and prevent the destruction of the movie."

It seemed to Marrity that Golze was acting as if the movie was the important thing, and discounting what Marrity had to offer. "What do you even need the movie for?" Marrity asked. "The machine lets you go into the past and future, all by itself."

"You sound like Rascasse," said Golze. For a moment he was silent, staring out at the water. Then, "Yes," he went on irritably, "the machine would let me go into the past and future—the past and future from wherever I *am,* from whatever specific little volume of cubic space the universe has permitted me to occupy. But I—we—want to be able to travel in *now.*"

"Now?" asked Marrity in bewilderment. "You can already travel in now. Anybody can."

"I can be in one compressed, predestined point of it, not travel in it. My whole possible future is contained in a cone that expands into the future from here, this constricted now point. And my past is locked into a cone that extends backward in time from now. That's the Grail, those two cones, and Einstein's machine will let me travel in them. But all the time and space outside those cones is an extension of *now,* it's every place and time general relativity says I can't get to. Getting out there would be . . . moving *sideways* in the time-space hypercube; your grandmother did it, to get to Mount Shasta—she got there instantaneously."

"But—obviously I've read up on this—the bits that are outside the cones right now will be included in the widening cone of your possible past, if you just wait. And anyway, the boundaries are expanding at the speed of light, and the entire earth can't be more than one light second from end to end! What's the big deprivation, what are you afraid you'll be excluded from?"

Golze wasn't looking at him, and Marrity wondered if the fat man somehow aspired to eventually be in all places and moments at once. Would that, Marrity wondered, make him God?

If it did, he would always have been God—he would have been occupying every place in every moment since the beginning of time.

Marrity forced himself not to smile at the thought; then he remembered the twitching black head he had seen nineteen years ago, and the hateful woman little Daphne had grown up to be, and the babies he had seemed to see in the weeds two days ago; and he considered the nature of any God that could have created this world—"This dreary agitation of the dust, and all this strange mistake of mortal birth," as Omar Khayyam had written—and the impulse to smile was gone.

Golze had been looking at the water, but now looked directly at Marrity. "So where is the machine now?"

Marrity sat back, to put as much distance as possible between their faces. "That's my merchandise, telling you that. But first you've got to pay me."

"Okay." The black steel oarlocks clanked as Golze pulled on one oar and pushed on the other, and the boat rocked on the jade water as the bow began to move to the left. "What payment do you want?"

Marrity took a deep breath and let it out, glad of the breeze in his sweaty hair. "Why are we doing this in a boat?" he asked. He looked around at the grassy banks and the arching red wooden footbridge. "This is where a scene in *Chinatown* was filmed, right?"

Golze frowned, either at the evasion or at the question itself; and at first it seemed he wouldn't reply. Then, "Yes, Jake Gittes was in a boat here, in that movie, photographing Hollis Mulwray and Mrs. Mulwray's daughter."

Golze opened his mouth to go on, but Marrity impulsively said, "Jake didn't get the daughter away in the end, did he?"

"No," said Golze with exaggerated patience, "the horrible old man took her away. But this is a relatively good spot for this particular confidential conversation. The jangling toys, and the fact that the boat keeps turning, make it difficult for anyone on the shore with a shotgun microphone to monitor our talk."

He bent to fetch up the dog again, and he squinted at Marrity as he slowly ratcheted the spring tight. At last he put it down and scratched at the black ribbon choker around his neck. "And the lake's got associations with Charlie Chaplin. In certain ways it's a deflection, for any psychic trying to track us. What payment do you want?"

That was a short delay, Marrity thought forlornly.

"Three things," he said at last. "First, you leave Frank Marrity, the younger one, alone. No more shooting at him, no more anything at all, ever. You just forget about him and let him live to a ripe, untroubled old age."

"Okay. I don't know how we can prove we've done that until he *has* died of old age, but I can tell you that I don't know why we bothered to try to kill him in the first place. And I suppose if we killed him, your younger self, *you* might just disappear! I'm not sure of the physics on that." He tugged at one oar, and the boat jostled around to the right, swaying in the water. "What's the second thing?"

"You let me use the . . . time-travel procedure to return to 2006, where I can resume my life. Oh, and there's a house you've got to buy."

"A house? Okay, after we put you through a very thorough series of interviews, probably under narcohypnosis. What's the third thing?"

There was a long pause before Marrity answered, and Golze shifted the boat again.

"I could tell you in three words," Marrity said finally. "Two. And I certainly don't care what you think of me. But I want to explain what it *is*, anyway."

"Fine. What is it?"

"It's the way the universe originally played out, the way my real life played out. I had a life, and I want it back."

"What took it from you?"

"The damned Harmonic Convergence took it from me. An incident in this year, here in 1987, *changed,* even though it was in my past—imagine having something in your past change on you, so for instance you and some friends were shooting a gun when you were seventeen, and nothing went wrong, and you've grown up to happy middle age—but now suddenly you find yourself in a life in which you've been a quadriplegic since the age of seventeen because one of your friends accidentally shot you in the neck, way back then!" He mopped his face with the sleeve of his windbreaker. "And you still remember the original happy life! You'd want to go back, right?—and tell your seventeen-year-old self not to go shooting with those friends."

"How did the Harmonic Convergence do this?"

"All these zombies—blanking their minds on the mountaintops—pressure drop—they've made a crack in the space-time continuity. Things resume on the future side of the crack, but not quite the same, a bit of quantum randomness has seeped in, like groundwater into a cracked foundation. Hell, *you* might soon get a visit from *your* future self, trying to put *your* life back on its original track."

"You're not a quadriplegic. What *is* it you want us to prevent from happening?"

"Well, it already happened. Yesterday. And I want you people to undo the change, undo the *error,* put my life back into its original . . . configuration."

"Okay. What happened yesterday that shouldn't have happened?"

For a few seconds the only sound was of some children playing around the snow-cone vendors on the north shore. Marrity stared out across the lake surface, with its patches of tiny, fine-hatched ripples among the glassy low swells.

"My younger self . . . Frank Marrity . . ." Marrity was dizzy, and wondered if he was going to vomit. "He saved my daughter's life, at that restaurant, yesterday. He did a tracheotomy on her. She was supposed to choke to death, she *died* there, in my original lifeline. In the *real* world."

Golze's eyes were wide behind his steamy glasses and a smile was baring his yellow teeth and pulling his beard up on the sides. The choker ribbon was fully visible around his fat neck.

"You want us to kill your daughter?" he said. "What is she, twelve?"

"Yes, she's twelve. But by the time she's thirty, she's a monster. And no wonder—she's unnatural, living past yesterday; like a dead body walking around and talking."

"But you told her to run, this afternoon. We'd have her now, maybe, if you hadn't told her to run."

"I wasn't telling *her,* I was telling my younger self! This morning you people tried to *kill* him! Which . . . obviously isn't what I want."

Golze bent down to pick up the red ant. "You get the ape," he said. And when the toys were buzzing and clattering away again, he slouched back on his seat and said, "So you want us to kill your daughter."

Marrity felt hollow, a frail shell around a vacuum, as if he might implode into himself. Why did the fat man have to ask for a yes or no answer? he thought. I can't say *yes* to him.

The horrible old man took her away.

But all I want is justice! My real life, not the nightmare life that grew out of the crack in reality, like a weed, like a nest of scorpions. What I'm saying *yes* to is reality!

Marrity opened his mouth—but he was sure that if he said *yes* here, now, he would not ever be able to go back to being the man who had not said it.

But I want the life the universe originally gave me. It's mine.

He took a deep breath.

Twenty

Yes," Marrity said hoarsely. The boat seemed very un-steady, and he gripped the hot orange-painted wood of the gunwales.

Golze was staring at him curiously. "Not just—kidnap her, sell her to Arab slave traders in Cairo? Get the duck."

"No, I think there's a . . . a Law of Conservation of Re-ality, that would bring her back." Marrity was sweating—drops were running down his forehead and he could feel them crawling over his ribs under his shirt as he obediently bent over and picked up the toy duck. "We'd still wind up in that twenty-four-foot trailer, and she'd still back the Ford over me in 2002. I can't risk her coming back. And killing her would be"—he was panting with the effort of trying to believe what he was saying—"would be more merciful."

"Okay, we'll do it. So where's the machine?"

"You don't have her. She's escaped from you. And as far

as I can tell, your blind woman still means to kill Frank Marrity."

Golze jerked the oars in opposite directions, splashing drops of water into the air and jarring the boat. "Where is the machine?"

"I'd need some assurances—"

"We'll give you what you want if you tell me now. If you don't tell me now, we'll give you what you don't want, abundantly. Where is the machine?"

Marrity's shoulders slumped and he shook his head. "It's at my grandmother's house. In her backyard shed."

"Can we move it? Get it into the car?"

"No!" Marrity involuntarily looked at his hands, to be sure they were still solid enough to twist the key in the duck. "If you *move* it, how will I use it in 2006?"

"We'll move it back later, don't worry. We need you to have come back to tell us all this, after all. We don't want to screw up your time line. But we need to move it *now,* because *other* people are going to try to take it, and they *won't* care if it interferes with you or not."

"Okay, right." I've lost all control, Marrity thought. "No, you can't get it in the car. Part of it is the cement slab from the Chinese Theater, with Charlie Chaplin's footprints and handprints on it."

"Good lord. That's part of it? But she didn't have that in 1933, did she?"

"No, the slab was still out in front of the theater then. My grandmother had Chaplin himself, in '33, and he wound up getting temporally dislocated too, at least an accidental astral projection of him did, though he meant to just be a, a nonparticipating observer. It scared the daylights out of him—well, there was the earthquake too—and that summer he burned all but one of the prints of *A Woman of the Sea.*"

"And we'll get that back," Golze said. "Burned up by a twelve-year-old girl! But we'll get it back." He had begun rowing strongly toward the dock. "Got to get to a radio," he panted. His glasses were opaque white, reflecting the sun. "We're going to need some help, and a truck."

The elderly Frank Marrity gripped the edges of the car seat and wondered if he was going to be sick. Golze was driving Rascasse's car, too fast around corners, and the car reeked of melted plastic. What had been the stereo was a blackened crater in the middle of the dashboard.

They were nearly at Grammar's house, and Golze had driven up the 110 to get here, so they were approaching from the south, and Marrity's excursions during these last three days had been by way of California Street, to the north; he hadn't seen these streets for many years, and there was more of his childhood than of his adulthood clinging to these old trees and pavements.

Moira and I rode our bicycles up and down Marengo Avenue, he thought, in the 1950s and '60s. The old bungalow houses were rushing past in a blur now, but he remembered each one; there's where we used to jump from roof to roof with the Edgerly boys, he thought, and there's where Moira fell off her bike and cracked her head and I had to carry her all the way home, three blocks.

Golze made a leaning right turn onto Batsford Street, and Marrity could see Grammar's house ahead on the left—and he remembered riding his bicycle up the sidewalk here on many late afternoons in the winter rain, his canvas newspaper bags empty and slapping wetly against the front wheel fork, and the olive oil taste of Brylcreem in his mouth from the rain running down his face.

It was tears he tasted now, and he quickly cuffed them away.

Grammar's old gray wood-frame house was on the northwest corner of Batsford and Euclid, and Golze turned left onto Euclid—but he drove straight on past Grammar's back fence and garage.

Golze was saying, "Fuck fuck fuck," in a quiet monotone.

"You passed it," Marrity said.

"I know," snapped Golze, peering into the rearview mirror. "There's a U-Haul truck parked at the curb." He was biting his lip. "Our truck won't be here for another couple of minutes, at least."

"You think these guys are here to take the stuff out of her shed?"

"Maybe." Golze drove past half a dozen houses, then slowly turned into an old two-strip driveway and backed out again, facing south now. He pulled in to the curb and put the engine in park, but didn't turn it off. Fifty yards ahead they could see the truck and the cars by Grammar's back fence.

"They may just be family," Golze said, "getting furniture out of the house. But we can't go in while they're there. Give me the binoculars from the glove compartment."

Marrity opened the glove compartment and handed Golze a pair of heavy olive-green binoculars. "They don't look like my family," Marrity said. They must not take the machine away, he thought.

"Hired movers, maybe." Golze lifted the binoculars. "Shut up."

The gate in the fence opened, and two men in overalls walked out holding faded lawn chairs. Behind them several men were carrying a flat tarpaulin-draped square with table legs visible under it.

Marrity noticed that the men with the draped table took short steps, planting their feet carefully, and that the table didn't swing at all.

"Stop them," he said, leaning forward, "they *are* taking the machine."

Golze lowered the binoculars to squint at him. "It's chairs and a table."

"They've got the Chaplin slab on a table, dammit! If they set it down, the legs would collapse—look how heavy it is!"

The radio was mounted below the dashboard, and had apparently survived the fire that had wrecked the stereo above it. Golze lifted the microphone.

"Seconde," he said.

"Tierce," came the reply from the speaker.

"Come north on Euclid, and when you're just past the house, I want you to park on the wrong side of the street, north of a U-Haul truck you'll see there. Kix." He adjusted the setting of a dial on the radio, then went on, "Let the guys out to run alongside, and then I want you to drive south, in reverse, and ram the U-Haul truck as hard as you can, Wheaties."

"No," said Marrity loudly, "part of it's glass! They'll break it!"

"Frosted Flakes." Golze changed the frequency again. "Never mind that, do not ram them," Golze said into the microphone. "Do not ram the truck, understand?"

"We won't ram it. Just park where you said? Special K."

The men down the street had carried the tarpaulin-covered object to the rear of their U-Haul truck, and had laid it on its side on the hydraulic lift.

Golze changed the frequency again. "Right. Guns ready. I'll be right behind you. How soon?"

"I'm just passing Dodger Stadium," came the reply. "Five minutes if I crank."

"Crank."

Golze hung up the microphone.

"I guess these guys will run if they see guns," ventured Marrity. He clasped his hands between his knees; he wasn't shivering, but all his muscles felt poised to start.

"If they're Mossad," said Golze, "they'll have guns of their own. Our only chance would be to surprise them."

"I hope they realize there were some gunshots fired here just a couple of hours ago," Marrity went on. His mouth was dry. "The cops are likely to respond extra quick if there's any more."

"If they're Mossad, they know and don't care." Golze was staring through the soot-smeared windshield at the men down the street. He exhaled and hitched around on the seat as if to reach into his pocket for his wallet; but what he pulled out was a heavy stainless-steel .45 automatic, and with his thumb he clicked down a little lever on the side of it. "Busy day," he said.

Marrity was just narrowly glad that he was still able to see, and clasp his hands, and make a dent in the car seat. Can I continue to exist, he wondered, if these people make it impossible for me to use the machine in 2006?

The hydraulic lift at the back of the U-Haul truck had risen to the level of the truck bed, and the four men were now wrestling the tarpaulin-covered square into the shaded interior. Another man, dark haired and wearing a blue sweatsuit, closed the gate to the old woman's yard and trudged toward the passenger side of the truck cab.

"Got to follow them," snapped Golze, "can't wait for our guys. The slab was obviously the last of it." He jerked the gearshift lever into drive, but slammed it back into park again when the man by the truck fifty yards ahead scattered a couple of handfuls of glittering objects across the asphalt of the street behind the truck.

"Ach!" exclaimed Golze.

He opened the driver's-side door and crouched behind it, bracing his right forearm in the V between the door and the slanting doorpost. Sunlight gleamed on the .45 in his chubby fist.

The bang of the gunshot was stunning, and the ejected shell spun across the empty driver's seat and landed in Marrity's lap; it was very hot, and he brushed it away with a shudder.

Golze fired three more shots, hammering the air inside the car, and Marrity batted away the hot brass shells as they spun toward him—then Golze paused, and only then did Marrity think to look through the windshield toward the truck.

The man who had been walking toward the truck was lying down now, mostly on the grass but with one arm draped over the curb onto the street. All Marrity could see inside the truck's back compartment was the square tarpaulin-draped bulk that must be the Chaplin slab. On the other side of the street, across from the truck, a man had stepped out of a white Honda that had been parked at the curb.

Then the car Marrity was sitting in was thumping and quivering as flashes winked around the edges of the draped square in the truck and a staccato popping echoed between the old bungalows on either side of the street. The loudest noise was a sharp smack as tiny bits of glass stung Marrity's cheek and the windshield was suddenly a glowing white grid, and as he ducked he heard Golze tumble back into the driver's seat.

There was bright red blood spattered on the fat man's hand as he shoved the gearshift lever into reverse, and then Marrity was flung forward against the diagonal constriction of the seat belt as the car accelerated backward, the engine roaring. Golze was twisted around to look out the back windshield, which was still clear. Marrity managed to raise his head, and he saw that the left shoulder of Golze's jacket had a pencil-size hole in it; the white shirt underneath was already blotting with red.

Something crunched under the back wheels and thumped under the car, and Marrity saw a section of chrome handlebar with a green rubber grip on the end spin away to the curb as the car's front end jumped briefly—then they were on past, and Golze had backed the car to the far curb and slammed the gearshift lever into drive, and after punching out a section of the opaque windshield with his right fist, he was driving rapidly north up Euclid. Marrity was as stunned as if he'd been shot himself, and he could not shake the idea that Golze had run over a phantom of Marrity's childhood, preserved and projected by these unchanged streets until now. He clasped his hands together more tightly.

"Caltrops," said Golze, speaking loudly to be heard over the head-wind that was blowing his beard around his ears. His face behind the beard was so pale that it seemed almost green. "This hurts—a lot."

"I—beg your pardon?" Marrity said.

"My shoulder hurts!" With his right hand Golze slapped the wheel around in a right turn onto California Boulevard.

"I meant—'caltrops'?"

"What that guy scattered on the street. Like jacks that

little girls play with—but bigger and with pointed ends.
They don't brush aside, they dig in, you gotta pick 'em up
one at a time—I *couldn't* follow—not on flat tires." He was
breathing fast, almost whistling with each exhalation. "They
got the machine—we gotta get the Chaplin movie."

But it's burned up, thought Marrity, and you can't go
back in time to rescue it, now that those guys took the machine. He was feeling nauseated himself; it was just beginning to dawn on him that Golze had probably run over a
child a few moments ago.

"The movie isn't burned up," said Golze, "if Daphne
Marrity never existed."

With conscious care and deliberation, Oren Lepidopt
reversed into a driveway and followed the U-Haul
truck as it lumbered south on Euclid Street. It would be his
job to divert any further attempts to interfere, whether they
came from this rival crowd or from the police.

His ears were ringing. Ernie Bozzaris was dead.

Lepidopt had been standing in the street, still holding his
little .22 automatic, when he had caught the eye of one of the
sayanim who had picked up Bozzaris's body from the curb;
and just before sliding the body into the back of the truck
and climbing in to pull down the sliding door, the man had
given Lepidopt a thumbs-down.

Lepidopt watched the traffic in all directions as he drove.
There didn't seem to be any cars, police or otherwise, speed-
ing up toward the truck from ahead or from side streets, and
Lepidopt let his aching fingers relax on the steering wheel.

Bozzaris was dead, but Lepidopt had to concentrate on
driving. He would think later about his young friend who
now would not see today's sunset.

Baruch Dayan Emet, Lepidopt thought. Blessed is the
Righteous Judge.

The *katsa* from Vienna would be landing at LAX in—he
rolled his wrist to see his watch—in about an hour. Lepidopt
had lost two *sayanim* and one agent, and had disobeyed the

order to do nothing until the senior *katsa's* arrival. But he had got Einstein's machine.

His telephone buzzed, and he pried the receiver away from its case and switched it on.

He took a deep breath and let it out, then checked his mirrors and made sure he was following the truck closely. "Yes," he said.

"It's me," said Frank Marrity's voice. "You said to call after half an hour."

"Good," said Lepidopt. "Now call again a half hour from now."

"How long are we supposed to—"

"You'll be picked up soon," interrupted Lepidopt. "Be patient. Call me again in half an hour."

He had to hang up because he needed a free hand to wipe his eyes.

R ocking in the passenger seat as Golze drove, old Frank Marrity had to remind himself to breathe.

The movie isn't burned up if Daphne Marrity never existed.

Golze was speeding east on California, passing cars. Marrity could hear him breathing, deep and wheezing, over the battering flutter of the headwind through the broken windshield. After a couple of blocks, he cut across the right lane into another residential street, and slowed down.

"But Daphne *does* exist," said Marrity, talking loudly even though the headwind had now diminished.

"And you and I are having this discussion," said Golze impatiently. "In your previous lifetime—lifetimes, I guess— we never did, did we? Nothing's . . . written in stone."

"You'll go back in time and kill her as a baby you mean? But you don't have the machine."

"We don't need the machine to do this. This is Einstein's other weapon, the one he couldn't bring himself to tell FDR about. The atom bomb was within Einstein's conscience, but he couldn't tell Roosevelt how to . . . unmake people, delete

them from reality entirely. Not even if it was to be Nazis."
Golze started a laugh, but choked it off with a fierce scowl
after one syllable. "Einstein was okay with *ending* people's
lives, but he had qualms about making them never have had
lives at all—never born, never conceived."

Marrity's eyes were squinting and watering, and he
wished he'd brought sunglasses. The car was still moving
slowly down the block, passing old houses and lawns that
stirred his memories.

Can these people do that? wondered Marrity. If Daphne
never existed . . .

But even as of 1987, twelve years of Marrity's life had
been tied up with her; even in his previous good life, he had
been her father. Who would he be, if he had never had a
daughter?

And Marrity hated Daphne, the one he knew best, the
one he had known *since* 1987, the one who had backed the
car over him, but did he really want to condemn her to . . .
never having existed at all? Not remembered by anyone?
Did the little girl he had seen on Grammar's back porch this
morning deserve that?

And even though Lucy, Daphne's mother, was dead, he'd
be depriving *her* of Daphne too. Suddenly Lucy's termi-
nated life would never have included a child, that particular
little girl.

What would become of Daphne's soul? he thought.

What will become of mine?

"It's risky," said Golze, his eyes half closed, possibly
talking to himself. "Even with a twelve-year-old who hasn't
ever done much of anything. These past three days, at least,
will turn out to have happened differently, since she'll never
have been a player. Risky. But ahh—" He exhaled gingerly.
"I'm shot, Rascasse is probably dead, the movie's burned,
the Mossad has the machine—if there was ever time for a
re-deal, this is it."

The radio sputtered. "Prime," said a voice. It was oddly
flat, with no resonance behind it.

Golze's white face jerked toward the radio, and though he

instantly looked back at the street ahead of him, his hand moved only very slowly toward the receiver.

At last he lifted it off the hook. "Seconde," he said.

"Get back here to the bus," said Rascasse's synthesized voice. "We need to get—the Daphne child right now, which only can—be done from here." The voice became louder, as if a volume knob had been turned up: "And bring the hatband too. Don't lose it! And get Charlotte here as well. And—mother's little helper—do it fast."

Golze peevishly leaned forward and changed the frequency setting and didn't take his hand off it. "I can't get Charlotte. You get her. I need a doctor, I've been shot, sympathy for the Devil." He switched to the next frequency and leaned back, clearing his throat gingerly. The car was moving at barely five miles an hour now.

"Take off the—hatband," said the depthless voice on the radio.

"I'm driving, I can't—"

"Take it off. Or have—the old man take it off, if you cannot."

"For Chrissakes—" Golze reached up behind his ear and tugged the black choker, and with a snap it came loose. He tossed it into the backseat. "I wasn't getting blood on it," he began, but Rascasse's voice cut him off.

"Be quiet now," Rascasse said; then, "The shoulder blade itself is fractured; but the artery below—subclavian—is fine. Infection is of course a likely outcome, but before that happens, all this time line will be gone."

Golze paused, his mouth open as he stared at the street through the hole in the windshield. Then he smiled, exposing yellow teeth. "Well, good point. It'll be a long drive to—can't always get what you want." After changing the frequency again, he said, "To Palm Springs. But you have to pick up me and my companion, this car isn't driveable. I'm at—"

"Don't bother changing frequency, my sight includes you. Park the car. We'll pick you up."

Golze hung up the microphone and squirmed on the seat,

his face gray. "I hate it when he looks *inside* me," he muttered. "I swear I feel *heat* when he does it." He steered the car to the curb in front of a house with a real estate sign in the front yard, and shifted into neutral. "He doesn't have a French accent when he's not speaking through his actual mouth, did you notice? Odd phrasing still, but American pronunciation. Accent must have to do with the tongue muscles."

The car was stopped. Marrity clasped his hands to keep them from trembling. "If Daphne—" he began.

"You won't have to worry about her anymore," Golze said, wincing as he leaned back in the seat. "And we won't need to bother you at all—in this new time line, you'll never meet us."

"Won't you still need to learn about the machine?" asked Marrity. "From me?"

"Rascasse will manage to interrogate you somehow before we do it, and *he'll* remember this time line, even after it's collapsed to nonexistence. He'll be the only one who does. I think he's the one who erased Nobodaddy, if there ever really was such a person, in any time line. Though how an organization can exist if its founder didn't is a puzzle."

"I—won't remember her?"

Golze was sweating, and his face was gray, but he stared at Marrity with evident curiosity.

"Not a bit," he said. "Not even as much as a hard drive remembers what was on it after a magnet gets rubbed on it. You'll be a, a whole *new* hard drive." He started to reach his right hand toward his wounded left shoulder, but let it fall back onto his lap after getting no more than halfway. "And so will I. I won't even appreciate not getting shot, since this experience won't be part of my lifeline. Today is a Tuesday in the August of Never."

Marrity relaxed in the car seat, and he realized that he had not relaxed since using Grammar's device to come back to 1987; in fact, it seemed to him now that he hadn't been really relaxed for years.

He ran a word in his head, and then permitted himself to say it out loud: "Good."

"Better than the Catholics' Confession, isn't it? You just snip off the sinful yards of tape and start over. No repentance required."

"Nobodaddy," said Marrity, to get past that subject. "Like in Blake?"

"Who's Blake?"

"Poet. Late eighteenth century, mostly."

"Oh, William Blake, sure. He wrote a poem about somebody called Nobodaddy? I thought it was beatnik slang, like Daddy-O."

"It was Blake's name for the demiurge, the crazy god who created the universe. Not the eternal God—that one's too remote to have anything to do with the universe."

Golze's sweaty face was expressionless, and his mouth opened and closed without speech. At last, "Rascasse," he said hoarsely. "*That's* who Rascasse kills?"

Marrity remembered wondering, in the boat on the lake in Echo Park half an hour ago, if Golze aspired to be in all places and moments at once, and if achieving that would make the fat man God.

Marrity shrugged, an action Golze couldn't perform. "If it was the Nobodaddy that Blake was talking about. Where did you get that term?"

"I think Rascasse was the first to use it." Golze looked around at the street and the houses and the old eucalyptus trees along the curbs in the sunlight, and Marrity thought he seemed to be frightened of the whole landscape.

"August of Never," Golze said, weakly but defiantly. "He's still . . . monitoring my vital signs, I can feel his attention inside my chest. It's as if Mr. A. Square of Flatland had somebody leaning down over him with a flashlight, peering at his innards. Worse than being naked. How does it work?"

Marrity thought it was a rhetorical question, but a moment later Golze shifted to peer at him irritably.

"How does it work?" said Marrity. "I don't know. I guess if he's working in a bigger group of dimensions—"

"Not Rascasse," Golze said. "I know how *that* works, don't I, Denis?" he added, addressing the headliner above him. "He can hear all of this. No, I meant how does the time machine work? Do you need to kill somebody, to get past the Aeons?"

"Well, I hardly traveled aeons—"

"I mean living things, living categories, called Aeons, didn't you study this stuff? Didn't you read the *Pistis Sophia*? All the old Gnostic and Kabbalist literature talks about the Aeons, time and space as demons. And they are demons, believe me."

Marrity blinked at him. "Well, I didn't have to kill anybody," he said.

Golze shifted on his seat as he tried to peer down at his wound. "It's gonna be a long drive to Palm Springs," he said tightly. "Maybe you *become* one of the Aeons, when you can travel in time. Maybe I sacrificed a guy to *you* last night. August of Never. So how does it work?"

"You—use up your accumulated mass energy, you spend it, to propel yourself right out of your predestined time line. Einstein said that gravitation and acceleration are the same thing—there's no difference between us sitting in this car with gravity pulling us down against the seats, on the one hand, and being away from any gravitating body in a car that's accelerating upward through space at thirty-two feet per second per second, on the other hand. Let go of a pencil, and it doesn't make any difference whether you say it rushes down to the floor or the floor rushes up to it."

Golze made an impatient beckoning gesture with the blood-spotted fingers of his right hand.

"So every person on earth," said Marrity, "has been accelerating at thirty-two feet per second per second all his life. Before he was a year old he would have exceeded the speed of light, if that were possible; but of course he can't quite do that, so he's been accumulating mass energy instead. I spent all my accumulated momentum when I broke out of sequential time."

And it has left me feeling empty, he thought.

For several seconds Golze didn't speak, then, "I hope California still exists, nineteen years in the future," he said slowly. "It sounds as if you might have blown it off the continent, releasing that kind of energy."

"It was a, a shaped charge, it all went outward, out of our four dimensions—strike a match on a painting and you haven't really hurt the painting—with me riding it like a guy fired out of a cannon." Marrity smiled nervously. "Switzerland still existed when Einstein came back to it, after having exited this way, in 1928."

Golze seemed to have forgotten his gunshot wound. "You came back nineteen years. How far back *could* you have gone?"

"I don't know. Not farther back than my birth in 1952, I think, unless I could jump over to my mother's lifeline." His leg was aching, and he tried to shift to a more comfortable position in the passenger seat. "Certainly no farther back than whatever date it was when that configuration was assembled—the Chaplin slab and the *maschinchen* itself. I think Grammar put the machine together in 1931, and added the Chaplin slab in the 1950s."

The radio hummed, and then Rascasse's unaccented and unechoing voice said, "How did you work it, the *maschinchen* thing?"

Marrity reached for the microphone, but Golze shook his head. "Just talk," the fat man said. "He's just using the radio speaker now, he's not actually on the air."

"It's a—" Marrity sighed deeply, but he still felt empty. He took a deep breath and started again. "Among other things, it's a very sensitive voltmeter," he said, "and it amplifies tiny voltage differences. It's ten rotating condensers set up in series, so that each beefs up the voltage into the next, up to where you can feel the current, if you're standing barefoot on the two tiny gold posts that stick up through the bricks. They're set flush with the bricks on the floor, no bigger than nail heads. This is in Grammar's shed I'm talking about, and the condensers themselves are in a big dusty glass cylinder under the workbench—though I suppose those guys have it now! It was dusty in 2005, anyway, maybe Lieserl was

Windexing it back here in 1987. And it looks fragile—the condenser plates apparently hang from a glass thread."

"And we could build this," said the flat voice on the radio. "Not so difficult."

Marrity shook his head. "I said 'among other things.' Anyway, what you do is, you press your hands into the Chaplin handprints and then you send two astral projections of yourself to targets you've set up—one on a mountain, one at sea level or lower, while your body stays in the middle ground somewhere, standing barefoot on the gold electrodes. You guys know about astral projections, right? That way you're existing in three time shells at once—they're only slightly different, but the *maschinchen* amplifies tiny differences and imposes a combined-wave signal through the electrodes in the floor. You're not in any one time shell anymore at this point, see, you're smeared across three of them. And for your safety you *need* three of, of 'you'—to spread out the recoil that's coming up soon. Einstein only had two, in 1928: himself on a mountain in the Alps and a projection in the valley below him. It was enough to spread him across some time shells, but the recoil still nearly killed him."

Through the ragged hole in the windshield Marrity could see a sidewalk shaded by jacaranda trees. It all seemed a lot farther away than it could really be.

" 'Among other things,' " said the Rascasse voice. "What other things?"

Marrity wished he could get out of the car. In spite of the fresh air blowing in through the torn windshield, the smell of burnt plastic was making him sick, and his bent leg ached all the way up to the hip.

"In 2006 I wiped some of the dust off the glass cylinder the condensers are in," he said hoarsely, "and looked in it with a flashlight. Einstein, or Lieserl, had painted Hebrew letters on the ten condensor plates. I couldn't rotate them, or see the letters in toward the axis, but in several places I saw the Hebrew word *Din,* which is the name of one of the ten *Sephirot,* the ten world emanations of God. In his letters to

Lieserl, Einstein seems to have equated *Din* with determinism. Judgment with no mercy mixed in, I gather. No indeterminacy, no uncertainty. Anyway, I couldn't have copied out all the letters on the plates without taking the thing apart."

"And now the Mossad has it," said Golze. His voice was frail, and when Marrity looked at the fat man in the driver's seat beside him, he wondered if Rascasse's optimistic diagnosis was correct; Golze appeared to be dying. Perhaps Rascasse knew he was, and wanted him to die. Maybe Rascasse won't need to have killed Nobodaddy, Marrity thought—maybe he can just *prevent* him.

"And," Marrity went on, "you couldn't build the Chaplin slab."

"Are you close?" wheezed Golze irritably. "We're sitting in a parked car with the windshield—fuck—broken out."

"Five minutes since we left from Echo Park," said Rascasse's voice, which seemed to be just shaking the air now, independent of the radio's speaker. "We're on the 101 now, soon to hit the Pasadena freeway junction. Just a few more minutes. What's the Chaplin slab? Why wouldn't . . . Shirley Temple's do as well?"

Marrity realized what had been nagging him about the way Rascasse was speaking—it was all in iambic pentameter.

"The slab," he said, "is a sort of kink in time—in conjunction with the machine, it works like a catalyst, it makes it easier to get out of the time stream. My sister, Moira, took out a restraining order against me, in 2003—claimed I was a dangerous drunk!—but one day when she wasn't home, I broke into her stupid house and found some letters from Chaplin to Grammar, written in 1933 and '34." He smirked, distracted by the memory. "They may have been romantically involved! Grammar would only have been thirty-one in '33, and Chaplin—"

"Goddammit," said Rascasse's voice, "how's the slab a kink in time?"

"Right, right." Marrity frowned but went on, "Well, Chaplin was with Grammar in '33, when she jumped back in time, and he got dislocated too, for a moment. He found

himself occupying his 1928 body, kneeling next to Mary
Pickford and Douglas Fairbanks in the Chinese Theater
forecourt, pressing his hands into wet cement. A moment
later he was back in the Kaleidoscope Shed and it was 1933
again, but"—Marrity shrugged—"it was the 1933 Chaplin
who made those handprints in 1928. The slab, just by existing, is a violation of sequential time."

"We're on the Pasadena freeway now," said Rascasse's
disembodied voice.

Still in iambic pentameter, Marrity noted. His hands were
trembling, and he clasped them together as if in prayer.

Twenty-one

After the bus had pulled up alongside the battered car and Marrity had helped Golze climb aboard, Rascasse's voice from the bus radio had told the driver to go back to Hollywood and pick up Charlotte Sinclair; and again Marrity had noticed that Rascasse spoke in iambic pentameter.

Now the bus was parked in streaky palm-tree shade in a remote corner of the Alpha Beta parking lot at Pico and La Cienega, idling with the air-conditioning running, and Charlotte was sprawled across the left-side seats just behind the Baphomet head's cabinet, blinking sleepily and seeing through old Marrity's eyes on the other side of the aisle. Golze was slumped next to Marrity, against the window frame, and when Marrity glanced at him she saw that the fat man's face was deadly pale behind his sparse beard. She assumed that Rascasse's body was still lying on a bunk in the back of the bus, but nobody had looked there and she hadn't the energy to ask.

She was about to feel in her purse for the half-pint of Wild Turkey when, through old Marrity's eyes, she saw the pointer on the electronic Ouija board swoop up to the letter *T* in the upper-right corner. Nobody remarked on it.

Rascasse's voice rang out of the empty air behind the driver. "Paul's right. We need to take the Daphne girl."

Charlotte had jumped in surprise and now she wished someone would look around. Take it easy, she told herself—if Rascasse can project his awareness, it should be no trick for him to project his voice. She took a deep breath and let it out.

Today the bus smelled like a slum restroom: bleach and excrement. She didn't let herself think about the young man she had helped lure aboard, last night; instead she recalled what the bodiless voice had just said.

"Why the child?" she asked.

Nobody answered her, and then Marrity's view swiveled around to her. She couldn't tell if she needed lipstick—nobody had looked squarely at her when they'd picked her up, and now her head was just a silhouette against the bright window at her back.

"Daphne," Marrity said, "burned up the Chaplin movie." His voice was a hollow monotone, and she wished Golze would look at him.

But Golze was just staring at his curled hands in his lap. "We *need* the damn *movie*," he said. "We need sideways too, not just up and down."

"These two are going to take her to Palm Springs," Marrity went on, "and somehow cause her never to have existed. I won't remember her, or any of this, after."

Charlotte just said, "Ah." And neither will I, she thought. I suppose that's another thing that's actually possible—deleting people from the universe.

She looks like I used to.

Charlotte recalled the stories she'd heard about the anomaly Einstein had supposedly left in a tower in Palm

Springs—an anomaly that could short out a person's lifeline, so that person had never existed.

And I waved at her, this afternoon, because she looked
like my . . . my "little daughter": my uncorrupted younger
self. Two little girls—one to disappear, literally without a
trace, the other to finally get a life.

"Now, Mr. Marrity," said the disembodied voice from the
air, "if you would please just open up the cabinet you see in
front of you." Rascasse's voice didn't really sound organic—
it was like someone using a violin bow to play a xylophone.
"Go on, it isn't locked."

"Damn head never knows anything," muttered Golze
from beside Marrity. "How many times did we ask it to find
Einstein's daughter?"

Marrity's viewpoint ascended jerkily as he got to his feet
and focused on the pairs of opposed brass cones that were
the cabinet's handles.

"Last time I was here," Marrity said, sounding shaky,
"nineteen years ago by my watch, this is where you kept that
black head."

"It still is," said Charlotte, and she shifted her perspective to the driver, who was metronomically switching his
gaze back and forth between the rearview mirrors and the
empty pavement in front of the parked bus. It was much
more restful than seeing the damned head.

But the cabinet behind the driver was still right in front
of her, and she heard the latch snap and the doors creak
open, and she caught the shellac and spice and old shoes
smell of the thing.

"Thank you," said Rascasse's ringing voice. "And would
you now say 'Find me,' please."

"Find me," said Marrity in a baffled tone.

And Charlotte could hear the head whispering again. It
was only one voice this time: "Two days I sat beside my
body, staring at the holes in my chest."

It had said this before, she recalled.

"Thank you for letting us know where they are," said
Rascasse's voice. Charlotte frowned in puzzlement, then

remembered that ghosts existed backward; presumably Rascasse was trying to get an answer to a question before asking it.

She sighed and switched to Marrity's perspective.

Through it she could see the afternoon sunlight glinting on the polished black brows, and on the silver plates tacked to the cheek and jaw. From the height of Marrity's vision she could tell that he was still standing.

Surreptitiously she felt in her purse for the bottle.

Marrity took solace in the faith that he would soon forget all of this. No, not forget it—never have experienced it.

"I went to my grandfather," came the whisper from the forever slightly parted coal lips, "to find out who I am, where I came from."

"Thank you for telling us where they are now," said Rascasse again. If he was impatient, his high-pitched inorganic voice didn't reflect it.

"But I have no mother, really," came the whisper, more faintly now. "Only children."

"You've told us where your children are," said Rascasse, like a hypnotist. "Where are your children now? Thank you for telling us."

Your children? thought Marrity; but he had to strain to hear the whisper now: "My mother will hide them," it said, "or try to. Everyone who dwells here is safe."

Everyone who dwells here is safe.

Marrity's breath had stopped. That was the sign over Grammar's back door. What else had the thing said? *I went to find my grandfather . . . holes in my chest . . . children . . . my mother will hide them . . .*

Abruptly the skin on his arms tingled and his vision narrowed to include only the glittering black-and-silver head, as his body understood before his mind permitted itself to.

A moment later he was out of his seat and halfway down the aisle, gripping the bar on the back of one of the seats, gasping for breath and ready to vomit.

"That's my *father!*" he yelled hoarsely. He was facing the back of the bus and blinking rapidly. "That's—what am I—that's *my father's head.*"

"Shit!" muttered Golze at the front of the bus.

"Turn it off!" Marrity shouted. "Can he *see* me?"

Rascasse's voice seemed to come from right in front of Marrity. "The ghost is gone. The imbecilic thing gave us no clue to where to find your self—your younger self. I'd hoped that when *you* asked, it might tell us—I guess it doesn't know."

"It did tell us," came Golze's weak voice. "The Ouija board pointer moved before Marrity said, 'Find me.' Before is after, for ghosts. Hinch, back the truck around to face south."

"It pointed to the letter *T,*" said the woman in sunglasses, whose real name was apparently Charlotte.

"No," grated Golze, "it pointed in a direction."

The bus vibrated as Hinch started the engine, and then the shadows and light moved across the seats as the bus backed around in a wide circle in the parking lot, and Marrity saw the supermarket swing past outside the left-side windows. The bus slowed to a halt, facing south now.

The Ouija board pointer now rested on the pin at the letter *A*.

"The young Frank Marrity," said Golze distinctly, "is now behind us. Northeast of here."

"He's in the hills, I'll bet," chimed Rascasse. "This vehicle is far too big and slow. Hinch, radio to Amboy—tell them we need full support."

T here's no towels," said Daphne meekly.

Frank Marrity was sitting on the floor against the kitchen cabinet, next to Bennett, and he looked up and saw Daphne shivering in the hall entry in her old jeans and blouse, which were now visibly wet.

He got to his feet, leaving the bottle beside Bennett. "Not even any curtains," he agreed. "Sorry, Daph, I should have thought of that before I said you could take a shower. You could sit downstairs by the windows, it's sunny there."

His voice echoed in the empty house. Until Daphne had spoken, the only sounds had been from outside: birdcalls, faint sounds of car motors, a helicopter thudding over the hills.

"It's been half an hour again," said Moira. She was leaning against the rail, her back to the sloped ceiling of the living room on the lower level.

Marrity peered at his watch. Sure enough, it was 12:35. He turned to the telephone as Daphne pattered barefoot down the stairs.

As soon as he had dialed the number, the Jackson man said, "Hello?" apparently before the phone had even rung.

"It's me, it's been—"

"Right. Where are you?"

Daphne's voice echoed up from the living room behind and below Moira: "Dad, can I lay out on the deck? You can see the Hollywood sign real close!"

"It's inaccessible," said Bennett, still sitting on the floor. "And the only street it overlooks is across the canyon."

"Go with her, would you, Moira?" said Marrity. Into the phone he said, "We're at the top of—" And then he paused to ask Bennett, "Where are we?"

Moira sighed and pushed herself away from the rail.

"Go up—give me that." Bennett stood up and took the phone. "Go up Beachwood till it loops sharp to the right and becomes Hollyridge, which heads back downhill. I'm his brother-in-law. The sister, correct. We're the third house downhill after the Hollyridge dogleg, on your right." He paused, listening. "Yes, I'll turn it on." He hung up the phone. "The porch light. He wants us to turn it on."

"Do you know where the switch is?"

Bennett turned toward the door. "Gotta be by the—*hey!*"

Marrity had grabbed the pockets of Bennett's coat and yanked the pistol free and then lunged down the stairs, mostly sliding along the banister.

His attention had been caught by a sharp pain in Daphne's cracked ribs, and in the same instant he had experienced her sensory impressions of a cloth pressed over her mouth and the breath driven out of her nose from hard constriction around her arms as she was abruptly lifted up backward; Daphne's jerky field of view was only of the converging treetops overhead, but she heard Moira grunt sharply. Marrity felt Daphne's bare heels kick at the aluminum-pole railing as she was hoisted over it.

When Marrity burst out onto the sunlit deck, a young man in a sweatshirt was outside the northside railing, facing him but leaning away; the man's tan-gloved hands gripped a rope moored to the railing, and he was clearly about to slide down to the dark slope below. Moira was sprawled on the deck planks behind Marrity, her hair over her face.

Daphne was gone.

Marrity lifted the pistol and fired it straight into the man's chest.

Marrity saw the man jerk his blond head forward and fall away from the balcony, and as the ejected shell flew through the open door into the living room, Marrity sprang to the rail and swung one leg over it, tucking the hot pistol behind his belt and grabbing the rope with both hands as the echoes of the shot rapped back from the far side of the canyon. The sound of the helicopter was louder out here.

He tried to go down the rope hand over hand but mostly slid, with the bristly rope burning the skin off his palms, his legs flailing uselessly in the rushing, empty air. He landed jarringly, sitting down on the body of the man he had shot, and rolled off and began crawling up the leafy slope even before he could suck air into his shocked lungs. His vision was dimmed, but he could see figures scrambling up the slope above him.

You said the girl and the woman were safely out of sight of the men," said Hinch, opening the driver's-side door of the black BMW and swinging his legs out. "This is a mess." The drone of the Bell helicopter that had landed on the cleared ground beyond the fence a hundred feet behind the car was louder now, and hot, dusty air blew away the car's air-conditioned chill.

The driver's-side door slammed and Hinch was gone before Charlotte could answer. Through his eyes as he ran forward she saw three of Rascasse's men scramble up from the shadowed slope to the sunlit street pavement, carrying a flexing canvas bundle that would be the little girl.

Daphne was wrapped up, but Charlotte knew what she looked like.

The men with the bundle, squinting in the rotor wind, hurried up the sloping road past where Charlotte sat in the idling BMW. Through Hinch's eyes she had glimpsed herself in the passenger seat, and then he had run on past; now she saw the open gate on the far side of the road's crest, and the open door in the helicopter's bright blue fuselage, and a man inside waving. The tail rotor was a silvery blur, and the helicopter was bobbing on its landing-gear dampers.

When the men had tumbled Daphne into the cabin of the helicopter and slid the door shut, Hinch turned back toward Charlotte—and so she could see, beyond the front of the car, a man come clambering up the slope and then stand shielding his eyes from the glare and the rotor wind. He was holding a handgun and he was the thirty-five-year-old Frank Marrity, and Hinch's view was suddenly jolting as the back end of the black BMW increased in apparent size.

When I consider how my light is spent—

Blindly Charlotte lifted her feet and slid them under the steering wheel; her right foot hit the gas pedal, and the engine roared for a moment, then she had slid over into the driver's seat and by touch pulled the gearshift lever from park down into drive.

Through Hinch's fast-approaching perspective from the rear, she could see that the car was aimed at the slope beyond the road, and she pulled the wheel to the right and was glad to see that she would miss the edge. Hinch saw Marrity step in front of the car, so she hit the brake. She banged her head against the closed driver's-side window, then impatiently opened the door and yelled, "Get in if you want to save your daughter!"

Through Marrity's eyes now, she saw the BMW's headlights and bumper, and her own face leaning out above the slant of the opened door, and Hinch sprinting up from behind.

"Last chance!" she yelled.

She heard the drone of the helicopter increase in pitch, and knew it must be taking off.

M arrity saw the helicopter tilt and lift from the clear patch beyond the fence at the crest of the narrow road, and he guessed that Daphne was in it. A man was running toward the BMW in front of him, clearly meaning to stop the driver; and now an orange compact car nosed around the bend at the top of the road, probably allied with these people.

Last chance! the woman had yelled.

All he sensed from Daphne was fright and constriction and blackness.

Marrity threw himself forward across the pavement and pulled open the passenger-side door—he tumbled in and yanked the door closed just as the man caught up with the car and opened the right-rear door.

The woman behind the wheel stepped on the gas and the car shot forward; the sudden headwind blew the back door closed.

Marrity looked back, and then was jolted forward against the dashboard as the right fender grated against a parked car.

"Look ahead!" the woman screamed.

Marrity turned and blinked out through the windshield at the green Porsche they had sideswiped, and at the clear blacktop lane stretching away on the left, and she straightened the wheel and stepped on the gas again. He could still hardly get breath into his lungs, and his abraded hands stung.

"Look at the road, don't look away," she said, a little more calmly. "I can't see except through you."

Marrity ached to look back and try to see which way the helicopter went. "Can you," he gasped, "follow that helicopter? Is my daughter—on it?"

"Yes, she's on it. I know where they're going. Keep watching the road or we're dead."

"You're . . . Libra Nosamalo." Marrity stared wide-eyed at the curving asphalt lane ahead of them. He thought about groping for the seat belt, then tensely decided it might momentarily interfere with his view.

"Charlotte Sinclair," she said. "The other name was to be cute. Tilt the rear view mirror so you can see behind us through it."

"Okay, but—slow down a second." Without looking away from the rushing road, Marrity felt for the rearview mirror with trembling fingers and then bent it around to a likely-feeling position. He darted a glance at it, bent it some more, and then glanced at it again. Back at the crest of the hill he could see the man who had tried to get into the car sprinting back now toward the orange car.

"The orange car—" he said.

"I see everything you see," Charlotte Sinclair said. "They'll try to catch us."

He managed to take a deep breath. "Where's the helicopter going?" The gun was jabbing painfully against his lower ribs.

"Palm Springs. Eyes front, dammit!" She wrenched the car back onto the road, but not before it had run up onto the shoulder and snapped off a post with a birdhouse mailbox on it. "Here's a curve, up ahead," she said, though in fact she speeded up. "Rearview."

Marrity flicked a look up at the mirror; the orange car was behind them now, only a hundred feet back and gaining fast.

"Thanks," she said. "Hang on."

The road curved to the left around a steep, rocky outcrop, and as soon as the BMW was around the bend, Charlotte stomped on the brake; the car came to a shuddering halt almost instantly, with no screeching of tires. "Look back!" she yelled, and then she clicked the gearshift to reverse and floored the gas pedal.

Marrity pushed himself away from the dashboard and shifted around in the seat just in time to see the pursuing orange car flash into view around the rocky shoulder—and then with an almighty *slam* the cars smashed into each other and he was nearly pitched into the backseat.

The black trunk lid was buckled and the orange car's hood was folded up so sharply that he couldn't see the windshield. Both cars were stopped, still rocking.

"Front, front!" Charlotte was yelling, so he wrenched himself around to look ahead. She clicked the engine into low and pressed the accelerator, and the car quivered for a second and then pulled free. Metal and plastic clattered on the asphalt.

She clicked it into drive and sped on down the road. Marrity couldn't hear any bad noises from the car. "Antiskid brakes," she said. "Standard on the new BMW Sixes."

For several seconds they drove downhill in a ringing silence. Marrity kept his eyes in a wide, unfocused stare through the windshield and concentrated on getting breath in and out of his lungs.

"Aren't you *with* these people?" he asked finally, forcing his voice to stay level. "Is Daphne a hostage?"

The BMW was swerving smoothly down the canyon road, flashing in and out of the shadows of overhanging trees.

"Rearview," she said.

Marrity glanced up at the mirror; there were no cars visible behind them. He reminded himself that he didn't have to tell her that.

"I'm not with them anymore," Charlotte said, "I guess. God help me. Probably they wouldn't have given me a new life anyway. I guess I knew that." She exhaled, almost whistling, and Marrity was sure that if he could look at her he would see tears in her eyes. "You have some kind of overlap

with your daughter's mind, is that right? A link? *You* screwed
up the smooth snatch back there, though I know they're
blaming *me*."

"*Where* in Palm Springs?"

"Dammit," said Charlotte, leaning into a turn while Marrity stared tensely at the road, "this is what might save her.
When I look through one of you I get a bleed through from
the other. Have you got some kind of psychic connection
with her or not?"

Marrity glanced at her, and he did see a glistening line
down her right cheek, and a moment later the off-side wheels
were thumping on dirt. "Watch the road!" she yelled.

He looked up to see a shaggy green oleander bush with
white flowers rushing at them; Charlotte stood on the brake
and the car stopped short of it, half on the shoulder. Dust
swirled around the windows.

"You can drive now," she said, opening the door on her
side and stepping out. "Watch me."

Marrity kept his eyes on her as he slid across the seat,
and when she had shuffled around the front of the car to the
passenger side and climbed in, and he had steered the car
back into the lane and begun driving too fast down the
road, he said, "Yes, for the past couple of days Daphne and
I have been able to see into each other's minds. It's happened before. Usually lasts about a week. Where in Palm
Springs?"

"That's good," she said, feeling for the seat belt. "I don't
know where. I've got to call them, my former employers
back there. What a mess that operation turned out to be."
Having fastened the seat belt, she leaned back in the passenger seat and closed her eyes. "Did somebody get shot?"

The backs of Marrity's hands tingled, and he gripped the
wheel more tightly, ignoring the sting of his scraped palms.
"I shot a guy. One of the guys who grabbed Daphne."

"Shot dead?"

Marrity remembered firing the gun directly into the
man's chest, and remembered the man falling. "I—I imagine so."

"Steady, slow down!" Charlotte said, her eyes still closed.

Marrity hastily took his foot off the accelerator. They were down out of the hills now, and the street was two lanes each way, but there were more cars to watch.

He tried to estimate what emotion killing that man had roused in him—it wasn't triumph, certainly, but it wasn't guilt or remorse either. He could hardly separate his own feelings from the tolling misery he sensed in Daphne's mind.

"Tell me the truth," he said. "Do they mean to kill her?"

"No," said Charlotte. "And there isn't any information they want out of her either. And they're going to find out that what they *do* mean to do with her can't happen while you're still alive."

"What do they mean to do with her?"

"They want to make her never have existed. Short out her lifeline. You'd never have had a daughter."

Marrity realized what emotion the shooting had left him with: depression. He thought of asking Charlotte, *Why?* but it seemed too hard; instead he said, "They can't do it unless they kill me first, though. You say."

"Right. You're her psychic Siamese twin right now. To, to *unmake* her, they'd have to isolate her, and they can't isolate her from you." She flinched, though her eyes were still closed. "Watch it."

He had been coming up fast on a station wagon that was moving too slowly in the left lane, and now he swerved around it to the right. "If you saw it," he said irritably, "you know *I* saw it."

"I'm paying better attention. We've got to—"

"My sister's back there, unconscious. Will they hurt her?"

"They don't care about her, or her husband, now. He can call paramedics. But we've got to figure out a way to hide from the—from your father. He can track us on this electric Ouija board they've got. It's in one of their other cars now, not the orange one we just smashed."

The helicopter, Marrity told himself, the guy you shot, the NSA man, the cartoon creature that talked to Daphne from the hospital television last night. Daphne setting Rumbold on fire. Serious people are taking this stuff seriously. Electric Ouija boards.

"My father saved my life. From you."

"That's not your father. We need a drink. Do you know—"

"Oh, bullshit. Excuse me."

"He's not. Now—"

"If *he's* not my father, who *is*?" Marrity shrugged impatiently. "You said we've got to hide from my father."

He glanced sideways at her and saw her frown. "Your father is somebody *else,* okay?" she said. "Do you know where the Roosevelt Hotel is? The lobby bar there has a million exits, and it's generally crowded, lots of eyes, I can monitor the whole place."

The next big street ahead of them was Hollywood Boulevard. To get to the Roosevelt Hotel he would turn right. "We should go straight to Palm Springs," he said. To get to Palm Springs he would turn left, and get onto the 101 south.

"I've got to call the guys who have your daughter. They don't know yet that they've got to kill you before they can do anything to her, and I've got to point that out to them. And I need three fast drinks. *In vino immortalitas.*"

He sighed and clicked the turn signal up, for a right turn. "Can you remember a phone number?" he said. "I can remember it right now, but I might not remember it when we've got to a phone."

Racing east, the twin-engine Bell 212 helicopter had skimmed between Mount Hollywood and the domes of the Griffith Park Observatory and over the dry-brush hills of Eagle Rock and was now following its shadow along Colorado Boulevard, a few hundred feet below.

Denis Rascasse's body lay stretched out on the rearmost bench seat, right over the fuel tank. He was still breathing, though his consciousness was now focused in a couple of giant pink banksia flowers and an orange-glowing rocket-shaped lava lamp, all belted into a bracket on the starboard bulkhead.

Gray-haired Frank Marrity sat in a forward-facing seat, across from Golze, who was looking sleepy and red-faced since giving himself a shot of morphine from the bus's first-aid kit. The air inside the cabin smelled of something like burnt peanut butter.

On the floor between them was the duct-taped canvas bundle that contained Daphne.

Nobody had spoken in the minutes since the helicopter had lifted away from the cleared area at the top of Beachwood Canyon, but now the banksia blossoms vibrated, and Rascasse's voice rang out over the drone of the turbine engines on the helicopter's roof: "Now Mr. Marrity, you'll please explain—exactly how you worked the time machine."

In apparent response to the voice, Daphne's knees and head dented the canvas, and Marrity heard her muffled voice.

"Open the canvas at the head end," said Golze. "We don't want it smothering."

Marrity shook his head. "Soon," he whispered, "she won't exist anyway!"

"If it smothers," said Golze, shifting uncomfortably on his rear-facing seat, "it'll exist forever as a corpse. Open the package, dipshit."

Marrity's face was hot. It seemed to him that he must somehow protest *dipshit*—that if he didn't, there would be ground lost that he would never recover.

"We're taping this," said Rascasse's voice. "What were the steps you took?"

"Uh . . ." Marrity began, but Golze scowled and pointed at the canvas bundle.

Marrity had to unbuckle his seat belt to lean down over the bundle, and with shaking hands he tore away the duct tape over Daphne's head, then unfolded the grommeted edges of the canvas.

In the shadows between the seats, Daphne's face seemed to be just wide green eyes and disordered brown hair.

"You!" she said, blinking up at him. "Where's my father?" Then she was looking past him at the quilted silver fabric that lined the ceiling and at the fiberglass bulkhead panels with their inexplicable inset round and oval holes. The cabin swung like a bell, and then extra weight told Marrity that they were ascending. "Are we in an airplane?" asked Daphne.

"Helicopter," said Golze, staring out the port window at the San Gabriel Mountains. "So don't *do* anything."

"Oh." She seemed to let out her breath.

"You're the dipshit," said Marrity to Golze, belatedly.

"What did you do," said Rascasse's voice, "to make the damn thing work? How do you stop at one specific time?"

Marrity glanced at the bracket and saw that the flowers were shaking and the red blobs in the lava lamp's tapered cylinder were all clustered at the top.

"How I did it—I was improvising, but it worked—was to tape right against my skin a thing that had undergone a decisive change at the time I wanted to get to. I found one of my grandmother's old cigarette butts between the bricks of the shed floor, and used that. It wasn't precise to the minute, but it landed me in the right day, at least."

"*Your* grandmother?" said Daphne.

Marrity just kept staring at the flowers. He could feel sweat rolling down his chest under his shirt.

"A cigarette butt?" said the silvery voice. "Nothing more than that?"

"That was it," said Marrity hoarsely. "It sort of shivered and got hot when I had slid back in time along the gold swastika—which looks like a quadruple helix in that perspective—to the right day. And then you just sort of—stretch, flex, step out of your astral projections. You can feel the rest of your momentum go rushing on without you, into the past."

After a pause, Daphne asked Golze, "Where's my father?"

"Dead, I suppose," said Golze, still looking out the window. "Probably wrapped around a tree in the Hollywood

Hills. He took off down the canyon in a car driven by a blind woman."

For a moment Marrity thought of telling her that *he* was her father, but the banksias were shaking their narrow petals.

"But you can still go back?" said Rascasse. "It's not one way?"

"You can go back," said Marrity, speaking to the flowers and the lamp. "The return—and both my great-grandfather and my grandmother did it—is apparently prepaid. Plain Newtonian recoil, in a lot more dimensions. If I stand on the gold swastika again, I think I'll shoot straight back to where I was in 2006. Though I'll be arriving," he added, careful to keep looking at the flowers and not at Daphne, "in a very different life."

"How much came back here with you," said Rascasse's voice. "Clothes, the air?"

Marrity was glad of the distraction of the questions. "It's apparently everything within the boundaries of the aura that goes," he said. "I thought it would be a bigger volume; a lot of stuff I was going to bring along got left behind in 2006—my Palm Pilot, an iPod, a Blackberry."

"Sounds like a salad," said Golze.

Glancing down at Daphne peripherally, Marrity noticed that she hadn't reacted to Golze's statement about her father probably being dead—she was still glancing around at the interior of the helicopter. Already she doesn't care about her father, he thought. Just as I remember.

A shrill buzzing sounded from below Golze's seat. "Could you get that?" said Golze. "It's the cell phone."

"It's my father," said Daphne.

Marrity's shirt clung to his sweaty skin as he leaned down across Daphne to lift the telephone case. He unsnapped it and pulled out the bulky telephone, then raised his eyebrows at Golze.

"The button at the top," Golze sighed, "puts it on speaker. Then just set it down on the seat."

"Modern ones are no bigger than a bar of soap," said

Marrity defensively. He pushed the button and laid the brick-size thing on the vinyl seat.

"Hello," called Daphne.

"Hello," came a woman's voice, loud enough for everyone in the cabin to hear, even over the steady whistle of the turbine engines overhead.

"Hello, Charlotte," said Golze. "You're lucky this time line is about to be canceled."

"Put my dad on," said Daphne from the floor.

"He's not here, Daphne," said Charlotte's voice from the mobile telephone on the seat, "but he should be back anytime. Now I want to talk to the grown-ups alone, can we—"

"He's standing right beside you," Daphne interrupted, "I can hear you through him. Oof! And his mouth's full of beer."

For a moment there was silence from the phone. "Who believes that?" asked Charlotte finally.

"I do," said Golze.

Marrity nodded sourly.

"I'll know it soon enough," said Rascasse's voice from the flowers. "Your signal's clear."

"Okay, dammit, yes, he's right here," Charlotte said, "and young Daphne brings me to my point. I'm holding a gun on him—"

The flowers in the wall bracket shook. "You're not," said the metallic voice. "It's in your purse. I don't see him."

"What else you got, Charlotte?" asked Golze wearily, leaning back and closing his eyes.

Rascasse's voice said, "I look for him, but see this girl instead." For once the artificial voice seemed to express an emotion—bafflement.

"Dad!" called Daphne from her cocoon on the floor plates. "Don't let them catch you!"

The young Frank Marrity's voice came out of the phone's speaker now: "I won't, Daph, and I'll come get you soon. These people aren't planning to hurt you." After a moment he added, "It smells like peanut butter there. Don't eat or drink anything they give you, Daph."

"That's just how this helicopter smells," said Daphne.

"We bought it from the Comision Federal de Electricidad," said Golze, "in Mexico City. Maybe they use peanut butter for insulation."

Marrity's voice from the phone said, "Don't *do* anything in the helicopter, Daph!"

"I already told her," said Golze.

"Denis," said Charlotte's voice, "I bet you could sense the Marrity I'm with if you look at the girl there."

Old Marrity noticed that the blobs in the lava lamp were breaking up into strings.

"It's true," said Rascasse's violin voice, "I sense him there—but not enough to see him. I can hardly see this girl."

"Okay," said Charlotte, "I'm not bluffing now, here's some truth: The young Frank Marrity and that girl have a psychic link—as Denis says, their minds overlap. They'll look like an X from the freeway, not separate lines. You can't negate her, you can't isolate her time line, while he's still alive."

"This is bullshit," said old Marrity quickly, rocking on the seat as the helicopter swayed under the rotors. "I never had any, any *psychic link* with her, in *either* of my lifetimes." He wiped a hand across his mouth. "I'm not telling you another thing until my younger self's safety is . . . assured."

Frank Marrity found that he had leaned back against the brown tile wall of the telephone alcove. A moment ago he had been leaning in over the pay phone with his ear to the receiver Charlotte held, but now he felt as if he were wrapped in some coarse fabric and rocking supine on a hard floor, and he realized that in his shock he had mentally fled his physical situation and retreated to Daphne's.

That's no help, he told himself, and he took a deep breath of the smoky gin-scented air that was actually around him and looked out at the fountain and balconies of the Roosevelt Hotel lobby. The tables on the tile floor around the fountain were crowded even at this afternoon hour, and he made himself hear the babble of voices and clink of glasses rather than the drone of the helicopter's engines.

"If we do this my way," said Charlotte into the phone, "his safety will be assured. Denis, if you try to stop his heart, you're just as likely to kill the girl."

Marrity pushed away from the wall and stepped up beside Charlotte again. On the little wooden counter below the pay phone was the pad on which she had written Eugene Jackson's number, and now Marrity picked up the hotel pen and scribbled, *MY YOUNGER SELF?* and then, *THE YOUNG FRANK M?*

Charlotte covered the mouthpiece. "I told you he wasn't your father," she said impatiently. "The thing that was in your grandmother's shed is a time machine."

Marrity was still holding a glass of beer, and he drained it in one long swallow now. And he looked again at all the people sitting in the lobby.

He could feel Daphne in his mind—it wasn't a sensation or a thought, just the mental equivalent of holding his hand. He returned the psychic pressure. *You and I will come out of this okay,* he tried to project to her. *The rest of these can go their own ways, whoever they are.*

"I'll tell you," said Charlotte into the phone, "if you'll shut up."

He looks like me, thought Marrity, an older version of me. Daphne said so, right away. He told us not to go to an Italian restaurant. He claims to have met this crowd when he was thirty-five; I'm thirty-five. On Grammar's back porch this morning he said, *I hate the old man as much as you do,* and when I asked him if he meant his father or mine, he nodded and said, *That one.*

He believes it, at least, thought Marrity, and so do these people, apparently—

—and they don't seem to be fools—

—but I can simply acknowledge that they all believe it, and work from there.

"Okay," said Charlotte. "With Frank's help, I wrote out a

letter and xeroxed it, and got envelopes and stamps here, and we just got done dropping three copies in different mailboxes. The envelopes are addressed to the FBI, and the Mossad care of the Israeli embassy, and to the LAPD—all Los Angeles addresses—and the letter includes an account of your murders of that San Diego detective and that kid last night, the two shootouts today on Batsford Street, your passport numbers, the New Jersey and Amboy locations, and the license-plate number of the bus." She paused, clearly listening. "You've both used your passports when I've been with you. You know me, I didn't exactly have to lean over your shoulders."

After another pause, she went on, "So listen, listen! The plan is the same as before, except that it's *me* you short out, *my* lifeline that you erase from the universe. No, dammit, think about it—without me in the picture, Frank Marrity wouldn't have got spooked so you decided we had to kill him, and without me he wouldn't have fled the hospital this morning and told the Mossad about the thing in his grandmother's shed. You only missed getting the machine today by a couple of minutes—do it this way and you'll be at least a day ahead of the Mossad. And without me, this letter wouldn't exist, wouldn't be in the mail right now."

Charlotte was leaning in close over the phone. Marrity remembered seeing tears in her eyes during the wild drive down the canyon. She had said, *Probably they wouldn't have given me a new life anyway. I guess I knew that.*

And he remembered the name she had originally given him: Libra Nosamalo. *Libera nos a malo.* Deliver us from evil.

"Denis," she said now, "it'll take you forever to track Frank Marrity, the young one, with his—with your horrible head, if Marrity knows to get away from me and keep running and changing direction. With those letters in the mail, you don't have the time. I'll call you back and arrange a trade—me for the girl."

She hung up the telephone. Without looking around, she reached one hand back toward Marrity. "Got another quarter?" she asked.

ACT THREE

Baruch Dayan Emet

Whose daughter art thou? tell me, I pray
    thee: is there room in thy father's house
    for us to lodge in?

—GENESIS 24:13

Twenty-two

"Could I bum one of those?"

Lepidopt raised his eyebrows, then held out the pack of Camels toward Bennett. "Sure. You decided you need a new vice?"

The two of them stepped across the sidewalk away from the glass doors of the Hollywood West Hospital emergency room. There were spots of blood on Bennett's wilted white shirt and on his jacket, and he looked as if he hadn't slept in days; his fingers were shaking as he pinched a cigarette out of the pack.

Moira had been diagnosed as having a concussion, and at best it would be several hours before she would be released.

"I used to smoke," Bennett said, "but it's a stupid—well, today."

Lepidopt put the briefcase down on the grass while he lit his own cigarette, then he handed the lighter to Bennett. Out here in the warm breeze he couldn't light one without using two hands, one to cup around the flame, and he didn't want to invite remarks about his missing finger.

"That's," Bennett began, then sucked hard on the cigarette. "That's Frank's briefcase," he said, exhaling smoke.

"I picked it up when we got you and Moira out of that empty house. Didn't seem right to leave it there."

"Those people—with the helicopter—they grabbed Frank and Daphne."

Lepidopt sighed. "Evidently," he agreed.

"I should have the briefcase. That is, Moira should have it."

Lepidopt stepped back, then crouched and reached out to pick up the briefcase. "I'm likely to see Frank sooner than you are," he said with a smile as he straightened up. "I'll give it to him."

Bennett scowled, then shrugged.

They walked out of the building's shadow into the late afternoon sunlight, and Bennett slapped his jacket pocket and then just squinted. "Is anybody going to come looking for *me,* is what I want to know," he said. He waved his cigarette back toward the emergency room. "Or my wife."

Lepidopt could see the white Honda, with Malk behind the wheel, parked idling a dozen yards away. "These people wanted Marrity and his daughter," he told Bennett without looking at him, "and now they've got them. I don't imagine they'll bother with you anymore."

"I should—I should call the police."

"Go ahead."

A man had walked up beside the driver's side of the Honda—a white-haired old fellow, in a dark suit—and Malk was talking to him now. "You should go back inside," Lepidopt said. "Your wife seemed upset."

Bennett's shoulders slumped. "Her father's with that gang," he muttered. "She thinks he had amnesia, all these years. She'll want to try to get in touch with him."

Lepidopt saw the Honda's headlights flash twice, fast, then once. *No problem here,* that meant. "She won't be able to. Get back inside."

Bennett followed Lepidopt's gaze, then nodded and hurried back to the glass doors and disappeared inside the hospital. They'd yell at him for smoking in the building.

As Lepidopt strode toward the car, he didn't have to pat his waistband over his right hip pocket; he could feel the angular jab of the .22 automatic concealed by his jacket. He had sewn two steel washers into the jacket hem so that it would flip aside quickly.

The old man in the suit saw him coming and smiled, placing both his hands flat on the roof of the car. "Oren," he said, in a voice that carried just far enough across the pavement for Lepidopt to hear it. "I think you've strayed from the established plan." His accent was perfect American newscaster.

It must be the *katsa* from Prague, Lepidopt thought. But how on earth did he track us here? The finger. They put something in the finger.

And when he had walked up to within a few paces of the car, he realized that he wouldn't need to ask for identification, for he recognized the old man—this was the instructor who had taken the young Halomot students into the desert north of Ramle in 1967, and summoned the Babylonian air devil Pazuzu, which had whirled ferociously around them but had at the same time been profoundly motionless.

Lepidopt wasn't reassured by the man's smile. "Every plan is a basis for change," he said gruffly. That was an old Mossad saying, reflecting the fluid nature of field operations. "New developments indicated—"

"And you can't rely on *sevirut*," the old man interrupted. *Sevirut* meant "probability," and after Israel's general staff had used the term to dismiss the likelihood of a surprise attack from Egypt and Syria in 1973—a surprise attack that had occurred twenty-four hours later—Golda Meir had said she shuddered every time she heard the word.

Lepidopt thought of old Sam Glatzer, and Ernie Bozzaris, and Bozzaris's *sayan* detective in San Diego. There had been no evident probability that any of them would die. "True," he said, exhaling.

"You through here?" the old man asked, and when Lepidopt nodded, he said, "Let's look at the situation."

Lepidopt got into the backseat, and the *katsa* walked around to open the passenger-side door. "I understand you've got Einstein's machine," the *katsa* said as he folded himself into the seat and pulled the door closed, "but you don't know how to work it. I'm Aryeh Mishal, in case you don't remember the name from that day in the desert."

"Get us out of here, Bert," said Lepidopt, "the Bradleys can find their own way home."

He stretched his legs to the side and leaned his head back on the seat, heedless of disarranging his yarmulke-toupee. "And head for the Pico Kosher Deli, I'm starving." To the white-haired head in the front seat, he said, "That's right. The only living person who has worked the machine is now with the other team, whoever they are, and they've captured a source of mine. Two of our *sayanim* and one of our agents are dead. Altogether it has not been a—a textbook operation." He hefted Marrity's briefcase and set it down on the seat beside him. "We do have some letters Einstein wrote to his daughter. They might be helpful."

"I'll salvage what can be salvaged," said Mishal in a contented tone. "First I want you to—"

He was interrupted by the electronic buzz of the cellular phone. Only one person had the number to that phone, and Lepidopt straightened up and reached between the front seats to lift it out of its case.

He took a deep breath and then switched the telephone on. "Yes."

"You guys were too slow," came Frank Marrity's voice from the earpiece. "They've got my daughter now."

"Where are *you* now?"

"At the Roosevelt Hotel, in the lobby. They—"

"How did they find the two of you?" Lepidopt asked.

"I'm not sure—apparently my father—who isn't the—"

Lepidopt tensed when he heard fumbling at the other end of the line, but relaxed a little when a woman's voice came on.

"They've got his father's mummified head in a box," the woman said. "It's not quite dead, and it can point to Frank here via an electric Ouija board. We shouldn't stay here."

Marrity's voice came from farther away: "What the *hell* are you *talking* about?"

"Put him back on," said Lepidopt. A moment later he could hear heavy breathing. "Frank, who is she, the woman with you?"

"Her name's Charlotte something. She's the woman who tried to shoot me this morning, sunglasses, apparently she's changed sides. Listen, it's crazy to say my father's head is—'not quite dead'!—in a box, tracking me."

A defector from the other side! thought Lepidopt. He covered the mouthpiece with his palm and whispered to Malk, "The Roosevelt Hotel, *now*." Lifting his hand away, he said, "Listen, Frank, we can save your daughter. We need to meet. We're only—"

"But that's crazy, isn't it? Daphne's kidnapped and I'm standing here with a crazy woman."

Lepidopt spoke carefully. "Have you experienced supernatural or paranormal events, in the last three days?"

"You know I have. You were there when that thing showed up on the TV last night."

"And you know something about Einstein, and your grandmother's shed. Has this Charlotte woman been involved in this stuff longer than you have?"

"Yes, obviously."

"Then just *maybe* she's not crazy. Reserve judgment. Will Charlotte talk with us?"

"She wants to, yes."

"Good. We're only ten minutes away—stay there in the lobby. It's public. Okay? Your daughter's life is at stake."

"Okay."

Lepidopt turned off the phone and leaned forward to put it back in its case. "That was the agent I thought had been captured. He's in the lobby at the Roosevelt with a woman who was on the opposing team. Apparently she's switched sides and wants to talk to us."

"All *right*," said Malk, hunched over the wheel.

"The opposing team," Lepidopt went on, "has—according to the woman—has my man's father's head in a box, and it can lead them to him."

"I can hide him from that," said Mishal, facing forward again. "You're going to have to buy a couple of bottles of whisky, Oren."

Lepidopt pressed his lips together. He remembered how whisky had been used in some of the demonstrations in his training.

"This agent," Mishal went on, "how did you recruit him?"

"I false-flagged him, told him I'm with the NSA. It was a hasty recruitment, but his daughter was about to invite a dybbuk into herself."

"A dybbuk." Lepidopt saw the white head nodding. "How would you guess you'll rate this agent in your eventual *Tsiach* report? Hardly blue and white, I imagine," the old man added with a chuckle.

Blue and white, the colors of Israel's flag, indicated an agent who was totally committed to the Israeli cause.

"I think he'll work out as a B," Lepidopt said. "Maybe a B minus. He initially lied to us about where he had stashed the Einstein letters, but all agents lie about something."

"And ideally they never find out they were agents," said Mishal. "But at least he imagines he's working for the NSA, albeit an NSA that foils dybbuks. Right?"

"That's right."

In the rearview mirror, Malk gave Lepidopt a sympathetic glance.

"I hope you remember," said Mishal mildly, "that you're—we're—operating outside normal channels here. We have no diplomatic immunity; if we're caught, we go to prison as spies."

"I'd like to know who they'd say we're spying *on*," said Lepidopt.

Mishal laughed. "I imagine impersonating an NSA officer would suffice to get you arrested. And then they'd look at your American passport. You've played very fast and

loose here so far. I'm here to rein you in and save your mutinous hide."

Lepidopt nodded tiredly, though the old man couldn't see
it, and he wondered what he might find suitable to eat in the
Roosevelt bar. There wouldn't be any *glat kosher* sand-
wiches, for sure. Maybe celery and carrot sticks. A lot of
them.

H e's actually Mossad," said Charlotte quietly, "not NSA."
She held out her hand, and Marrity glanced at the glass-
topped table so that she could see where her martini glass
was. "Thanks," she said, reaching down and curling her fingers around the stem of it.

The Roosevelt Hotel lobby was enormous, with a second-
floor balcony on all four sides and an ornate ceiling high
overhead, and it echoed with talk and laughter and the rum-
ble of wheeled luggage. Marrity and Charlotte were seated
next to each other on a small tan couch that faced away from
the Hollywood Boulevard entrance, not far from where a
black stone statue of Charlie Chaplin sat on a bench for
tourists to have their pictures taken with. Charlotte had said
that with all these eyes moving around, she didn't need to
put Marrity in a good vantage point.

"He said you're not crazy," Marrity ventured.

"Good to hear." A brass ashtray lay on the table next to
her purse, and she leaned forward and pulled a pack of
Marlboros and a lighter out of her purse.

"My father's . . . mummified head?" Marrity cleared his
throat. "They've got?"

"They say they killed him in 1955. I don't know why."

"That's when he disappeared. That's why he never came
back to us. That *would* be why, if it's true." He sat back on
the couch, not believing it but considering it. "I've hated
him all these years."

How can I let go of that? he thought in bewilderment.
Hating him has been the basis of my resolve to be the opposite sort of father to Daphne.

After a moment Charlotte asked, "You on the wagon?"

"Hmm? Oh, no, sorry." Marrity picked up his third beer and took a deep sip. When he put it down again he said, "'Drink, for you know not whence you came nor why— drink, for you know not why you go nor where.'"

Charlotte laughed and lifted her free arm and draped it over his shoulders. "'A flask of wine, a book of verse, and thou,'" she said. He looked into her face—he could see himself mirrored in the sunglasses—and she quickly leaned forward and kissed him on the lips.

He reached up and touched her cheek, and suddenly he was kissing her in earnest, and she had opened her mouth and her hand was gripping his shoulder. He tasted gin on her tongue. There were hoots from nearbly tables, but he didn't care.

A flash of sudden astonishment made him close his lips and lean back.

Her face was still very close. She raised one eyebrow.

"It's Daphne," he said hoarsely.

Charlotte actually blushed as she pulled her arm back and folded her hands in her lap. "Oops! She doesn't need this."

Marrity closed his eyes to concentrate, and he projected an image of himself hugging Daphne; and in return he got a clear impression of . . . cautious amusement, like a wink through tears.

"It's okay," he told Charlotte. "She didn't mind. We've *got* to get her back."

"We will. These people aren't stupid." She sighed deeply and gulped her martini. "I didn't mind either."

Marrity could still taste her gin. He was shaky. It had been two years since he had kissed a woman, and a whole lot longer than that since he had kissed a woman he didn't know well. "I didn't either," he said quickly. Then he took a deep breath and changed the subject: "Mossad, you said— that's Israel's secret service?"

"Shoot at you in the morning, kiss you in the afternoon. What's left?" She sighed and he watched her light a cigarette. "Yes, Israel. They've apparently kept close track of all things Einsteinian. Did you know that after the first president of Israel died, in 1952, they asked Einstein if he'd be president? It wasn't just a gesture—the Mossad knew that Einstein had made some unpublished discoveries."

"Like a time machine." Marrity shook his head. "I think you said—Jesus—that that's *me*, that old guy, that old drunk guy! Who claimed he was my dad? Like, me from the future?"

"One future, not *the* future. There isn't any *the* future. He used this machine in your grandmother's shed to come back here to 1987 from 2006. His life—"

"2006? Then he's only . . . if he's me . . . fifty-four. He looks older."

Marrity tried to summon skepticism, and found he didn't have any. He believed it, believed that the pouchy-faced old man was in fact himself, and he hated the thought of that querulous old fool walking around and talking to people. Marrity had never been drunk enough to have done and said things he couldn't remember later, but he felt as if it was happening now. What might he be *saying,* Marrity wondered helplessly, what personal secrets of mine might he be blabbing to these people?

Marrity could feel his face getting hot. "Is *Daphne* talking to him?"

"I don't imagine he's eager to talk to her," said Charlotte quietly. "He's experienced two lifelines already—one broke somehow, and spilled him into the other. In the original happy one, Daphne died yesterday, in that Italian restaurant. He wants to make sure that in *this* time line she doesn't grow up—doesn't go on living."

Marrity was dizzy, and couldn't make himself look at Charlotte. "He's not me, I could never want that. What could Daphne ever do—"

He was staring down at his clenched fists, and Charlotte took hold of one of them. "There is no *the* future," she repeated. "When you get free of this, you and Daphne can do anything you choose to do." She squeezed his hand. "But he told Golze that in his second lifeline, you—he, that is, he and Daphne were both alcoholics, living in a trailer somewhere, and they hated each other. Daphne tried to take his car at one point, and he tried to block her, and she backed it over him."

"Those weren't us. Those weren't us."

"Make them not be."

She was facing him, so he couldn't see her eyes. "What do you—" he began, then halted uncertainly. When she cocked her head, he went on: "It's none of my business, but what do you want to use the time machine for?"

She took a deep drag on her cigarette and exhaled a long sigh of smoke. "True," she said, almost absently, "it's none of your business. But none of your life is my business—*I* am *not* Daphne's keeper—but somehow I'm knee deep in it anyway." She stubbed out the cigarette in the ashtray. "You've got an advance warning to go easy on the booze, haven't you?"

"Yes, I guess I have."

"Did you plan to start going easy today?"

"No, not today."

She picked up her empty glass and half stood up—then sat back down again. "I want to go back," she said quietly but quickly, "and prevent my younger self from being blinded in 1978. All I've worked for is to save her. I don't even think of that little girl as *me* anymore, I think of her more as my lost daughter who needs rescuing. If I can save her I can disappear, and she'll be a new person, born out of me like—" She waved her empty glass.

"Like parthenogenesis," said Marrity.

"Exactly. Identical body, but not *this* person." She took hold of his empty glass in her free hand and straightened gracefully to her feet. "Same again?"

"Same again."

T he Roosevelt Hotel was right across the street from the banners and green copper roofs of the Chinese Theater forecourt, and Lepidopt shifted to stare at the ornate old structure as Malk turned off Hollywood Boulevard at Orange and found a parking place at the curb, avoiding the Roosevelt's valet parking.

Do they wonder what's become of their Charlie Chaplin slab? Lepidopt thought, rocking in the abruptly stopped car. Who'd imagine it's in the Wigwam Motel in San Bernardino now?

"APAM, gentlemen," said Mishal as they got out of the car and blinked in the heat and late afternoon sun glare of the summer Hollywood sidewalk.

Lepidopt had had enough. APAM, short for *Avtahat Paylut Modienit,* meant securing operational activity, and it was the first thing a Mossad *katsa* was required to learn.

"We're *katsas*," he said shortly.

"Of course you are," said Mishal with a smile.

Mishal had paused in the shadow of a shaggy magnolia that draped its branches over the wall of the Roosevelt Hotel parking lot, and Malk and Lepidopt scuffed to a halt beside him.

"Remember that all we want is information about this opposing group, and any information either of these people might have about Einstein's machine. We will appear to care about this man's daughter, and whatever terms this woman may want, but in fact we will not care about them. Everyone is either target or enemy."

"We're *katsas*," Lepidopt repeated. "We know this."

"Oh?" Mishal squinted at him. "Wouldn't that dybbuk, articulate in the girl's body, have been more useful than the girl inviolate?" He held up one thin hand. "Well no, since you let the opposing group capture the girl. Point withdrawn."

Malk glanced at Lepidopt and rolled his eyes for a moment before sauntering ahead to do a route of the hotel lobby, identify Marrity and the woman and make sure no one else was watching them.

At a more leisurely pace, Lepidopt and Mishal tapped up the hotel's back steps.

"No offense," said Mishal.

"Of course not," said Lepidopt. In fact he was wondering if the elder *katsa's* criticism had been valid. Did I, he wondered, jump in to recruit Marrity too quickly, just because the little girl was in danger of being inhabited by that thing?

And he remembered again being in her bedroom, and wondering if she would like his son Louis.

I'm too old for this, he realized; but one way or another I'll be out of it soon.

Malk was on the second-floor balcony on the far side of the lobby when Lepidopt and Mishal walked in; he was holding a newspaper in his right hand, which meant there was no sign that Marrity and the woman were being watched, and then he leaned against the railing and opened the paper, pointing the fold of it downward and slightly to his right. Lepidopt followed the implied line and saw Frank Marrity sitting on a couch with an attractive dark-haired woman on the Hollywood Boulevard side of the lobby.

In any meeting, he recalled, the agent must be there and sitting down before you enter; you never wait for him at a meeting place.

Lepidopt stepped forward across the tile floor while Mishal hung back, and he walked the long way around the fountain to approach Marrity from in front.

Marrity saw him and stood up. "Mr. Jackson," he said. "This is Charlotte, uh . . ."

"Charlotte S. Webb," said Charlotte, smiling quizzically and not getting up.

Lepidopt grinned, and noticed that Marrity did too. Anybody with a book-loving child, he thought, would recognize that title. He wished he could remember the name of the pig in *Charlotte's Web,* to be able to make a clever reply.

"Do you have any children?" he asked her.

"With luck a little girl," she said. "Parthenogenesis."

Lepidopt stared at her for a moment, then pulled a metal chair across the tile to the opposite side of their table and sat down, slightly in profile to Charlotte and with the tail of his jacket hanging away from his belt.

"I'm Eugene Jackson," he said. "Shortly we'll be joined by another man, possibly two. We want to get the pair of you away from here to a safe place."

"I want some terms agreed on before I go anywhere with you," said Charlotte. "I've proposed a deal to my former employers, and I'm going to go through with it unless I can make a different deal with you people."

Mishal stepped up to the table, carrying a chair in one hand. He put it down facing away from the table and sat down straddling it, one forearm lying along the chair back. With his other hand he pulled two folded sheets of ragged-edged paper from his inside jacket pocket and laid them on the table.

"What are the deals?" he asked cheerfully. "Would each of you take one of these papers? Don't get them wet. Oren, do you have matches?" Charlotte pointed at her lighter, but he said, "No, we need matches."

"I've got some," said Marrity. He shifted on the couch and pulled a matchbook out of his pocket and tossed it beside the ashtray, then picked up one of the sheets of paper and unfolded it impatiently. It was blank, and felt oddly coarse.

"Handmade," said Mishal.

"If I lead you to my former employers," said Charlotte, "and tell you everything I know about them, you rescue Daphne and I get to use the time machine." She smiled. "And since it's a time machine, I get to use it before I lead you to them."

Mishal laughed and pulled another folded sheet of paper out of his pocket. This one seemed to be plain typing paper, and it had markings on it in black ink. "No, not before. Oren, you remember this exercise, help them get some matches burned. I want each of you to copy onto your sheet of paper the symbols drawn on this." He unfolded the third sheet and laid it out flat on the table.

Lepidopt recognized the curves and circles—they were *kolmosin,* also known as "angel pens," or "eye-writing" because the arrangements of the figures often made them seem to be childish drawings of eyes. He picked up Marrity's book of matches, tore one out and struck it. The head flared bright purple and yellow.

Marrity was staring at the six lines of complex figures. "Couldn't we just xerox that sheet onto these blank sheets?"

"No," said Mishal, "it's got to be in your own hand, and you've got to use burnt matches to draw it. And note that on this original, none of the lines touch each other! They can't in your copies either."

Lepidopt shook out the match and lit another. "Break the heads off," he said to Marrity. "It's easier to draw with just the cardboard stick." His nose itched with the smell of sulfur.

"What is this," Marrity asked, pushing the burnt match with his finger, "a test of coordination or something?"

"It's an amulet," said Mishal. "Don't sneer, your great-grandfather invented this one. In 1944—for the war effort!— he made a handwritten copy of his 1905 paper on relativity, and auctioned it off. Among all the pages of arcane symbols for reference frames and constant acceleration, nobody noticed this sheet of *kolmosin,* though the FBI was watching him closely. And by the time the manuscript got to the Library of Congress we had lifted the sheet anyway. As he meant us to do." He glanced at Lepidopt. "You didn't lose your remote-viewer's holograph talisman, did you?"

Lepidopt could feel the disk against his chest, with the fragment of Einstein's manuscript sealed inside it. "No," he said. But I'm not the remote viewer Sam Glatzer was, he thought.

He struck another match.

W hat," said Marrity, "will be different after we've done this than is the case now?"

"Nicely put!" said Mishal.

"He's an English lit professor," said Charlotte smugly, linking her arm through Marrity's.

"Ah." Mishal squinted at Marrity. "These, when you have folded them correctly and put them against your skin, will make you un-trackable by the people who have your daughter. We'll be able to sneak up on them. Right now you're both occulted by proximity to me"—he pushed back the jacket and shirtsleeve above his right wrist, and Marrity saw the black lines of part of a tattoo on his forearm—"but you might not always be with me."

"Okay." Marrity freed his arm from Charlotte's and picked up one of the matches Eugene Jackson had laid out for him. Peripherally he saw that Charlotte had picked one up too, but she paused, humming some old half-familiar tune.

Of course, he thought, she can't do it unless someone *watches* her do it!

"This is some kind of magical stuff," he said, dropping his match. "I'll watch her do it first. See what happens."

He stared at the sheet with the printing on it, and then at Charlotte's blank sheet. She picked up a match and, as he continued to shift his gaze from one sheet to the other and back, she began copying the curves and circles.

"He wants to see if I turn into a toad," she said.

"Well," said Marrity in a tone he tried to make sound defensive, "it's like tasting food. If it's poisoned, better if just one person tries it."

"You also serve who only stand and watch," she said, and Marrity could hear the amusement in her voice as she went on copying the figures. She was already on her third match. Belatedly Marrity recognized the tune she'd been humming—it was "Bye Bye Blackbird."

"We'll talk to both of you at length this evening," said Mishal, "in a safer place, but right now—where are they now, the people you were with until today?"

"In Palm Springs; on their way there, anyway." Charlotte was biting her lower lip as she moved her eyes up and down—which was just for show, Marrity realized. "There's a thing my pal's great-grandfather made, there—I don't know the whole story, but allegedly you can twist somebody's lifeline right out of existence with it. It uses some energy—having to do with the great-granddad's cosmological constant? It's way bigger in other dimensions, which is why it measures nearly zero from here, to us. Like a big beachball has a footprint that's only the size of a dime on a two-dimensional sheet of paper. The old guy said it was the worst mistake of his life, figuring it out."

Marrity heard old Mishal shift in his chair. "Do you mean," Mishal said, sounding interested for the first time, "they can make someone never have existed at all? No record or memory of that person?"

"Yep." Charlotte finished the final circle and dropped the last match onto the glass tabletop. She turned to Marrity and spread her hands. "No ill effects!" she said cheerfully, though Marrity thought her voice was shriller than she had meant it to be.

"And this is *located*, somehow," said Mishal impatiently, "this . . . *tap* for the vacuum energy?"

"Yes," said Charlotte. "One of my employers said it was 'a singular object.' "

Lepidopt had struck several more matches, and Marrity picked one up and began copying figures onto his own sheet of paper. He was pleased to see that his scraped palm wasn't leaving blood on the paper—God only knew what effect that would have.

Mishal nodded. "I imagine he said 'singularity.' Einstein made a few oblique references to a thing like this in his notes, and we've wondered for years whether it might have been something he actually figured out. We have to look into this—though I wonder if even I have the math for it." He squinted at Charlotte. "Have they ever used it?"

Charlotte shrugged. "Who'd know?"

"Of course, of course. Where is it, where in Palm Springs?"

"Well, that's my bargaining chip, telling you that," she said. "I'll tell you, in exchange for use of the time machine. We—they—know you've got it. One of their guys got shot this afternoon when you took it out of Frank's grandmother's house."

Marrity was glancing at Lepidopt as she said this, and he thought Lepidopt's eyes narrowed slightly—in satisfaction?

"You said you've proposed a deal to them," said Mishal, "and that you'll go through with it if you can't make a deal with us. What did you propose to them?"

"They want to negate Frank's daughter, so that she won't have burned up their movie and generally made a hash of their plans. But Frank and Daphne have a psychic link, like mental Siamese twins, so these people can't isolate her and erase her while Frank is still alive. Of course they'd like to just kill Frank and get on with it, but the deal I proposed to them is that they negate *me,* instead."

Marrity had paused from his copying to look at her. She was staring across at Mishal, so Marrity could see her eyes behind the sunglasses; but when he noticed the glitter of tears on her lower lashes, and her impatient blink, he quickly looked back down at his paper.

She went on, "I screwed up their operation badly enough so that if I never existed, *they'd* have got the time machine, not you fellows. I've proposed a trade—me for Daphne."

"But that won't do," said Mishal, shaking his head, "if this singularity is real. If you're negated you'd never have told us about it."

Lepidopt leaned forward, frowning. "Miss, uh, Webb," he said. "You proposed that they erase your existence? No one remember you, nothing you've ever done leaving any slightest mark—this would be worse than death."

"Or better," said Charlotte. "But if you'll let me use the time machine, then I won't have to follow through with it."

"There's something you did," said Lepidopt quietly, "that needs to be undone."

Marrity had finished his copy of the strange diagram. Mishal took it and Charlotte's and frowned critically over them.

"You can't use the time machine," Mishal said absently. "But if, after I've done some math, this singularity looks plausible—and if the time machine works and we get our priority tasks out of the way—and if the change you want to make meets with our approval—we'll dispatch an operative to make the change for you." He put the papers down, pursing his lips. "These are good enough."

"I don't know if your operative could do it," said Charlotte. "It'll involve getting onto a secret U.S. Air Force base in 1978."

Mishal looked up from the papers and gave her a frosty smile. "Oh, I think we can manage."

He held out his hand, and Charlotte shook it.

"And you'll get my daughter away from those people," said Marrity.

"Yes," said Mishal. "Of course."

Lepidopt caught Marrity's eye and nodded slightly. Then he waved at the papers they'd marked up with the burnt matches. "Fold those in half, top to bottom, with the marks on the outside, without smearing the carbon, and press them against your skin under your shirts, top side outward. They'll smear soon enough, but it's the initial burn that counts. You can make fresh ones again later."

Charlotte took hers and started to get up, but Lepidopt raised his hand. "I'm sorry, Miss Webb, but you've got to do it here. We can't let either of you out of our sight, and I'm not going to escort you to the ladies' room."

Marrity began unbuttoning his shirt. He noticed Lepidopt look up at the balcony over their heads and touch his chin, and then look back down at the table. Signaling a watcher? thought Marrity. I bet we'll be leaving here soon.

When he had pressed the paper against his chest and buttoned his shirt over it, and Charlotte had rearranged her blouse over her own copy, Marrity cocked his head and opened his mouth to speak, then hesitated.

Lepidopt raised an eyebrow.

"Nothing," said Marrity, "I just—" He turned to Charlotte. "Do you get any . . . ?" He waved vaguely at his rebuttoned shirt.

She touched her blouse over the hidden piece of paper. "Yes," she said, "The paper, as if it's . . ." She giggled, then bit her lip. "I think I'm getting your heartbeat."

Marrity grinned in embarrassment. That was it—the paper

was faintly pulsing to a heartbeat that was not his. "And I guess I'm getting yours," he said. "Cheaper than stethoscopes."

Mishal had shifted in his chair to look at the crowd behind him. "That's a common effect," he said to Marrity over his shoulder, "when the papers are prepared at the same time." A sandy-haired man in a business suit was walking toward their table, and Mishal seemed to nod slightly in recognition.

Marrity was aware of curiosity from Daphne, and he was glad that wherever she was she had the leisure to notice things like this. He crossed his arms and then patted the couch on either side of himself, hoping this would show her that he was not actually pressed skin to skin against Charlotte.

Charlotte was looking at him, her eyebrows raised above the frames of her sunglasses.

"Clarifying it for Daphne," he explained.

"Ah! Your chaperone!"

The sandy-haired man had paused by the fountain a dozen feet from their table and was watching the people in the lobby with no apparent interest.

"You'll tell us all you know," said Mishal to Charlotte, confirming it.

"Yes," she said.

"Where is the singularity located?"

"I'll tell you as soon as I know. And I'll know as soon as I call them. Where they propose to do the exchange, that's where it is. They'll want to be ready to negate Daphne instantly if things go wrong."

"Fair enough," said Mishal, getting to his feet. "Right now we're going to take you both to a safe house. Or is it a safe tepee, Oren?"

"Tepee," said Lepidopt. "Well, wigwam."

Twenty-three

The twin-engine Bell helicopter had touched down at a shadowed plateau high in the rocky San Jacinto Mountains southwest of Palm Springs, and when its passengers had climbed or been carried out, it had taken off again, the late afternoon sun lighting up its blue fuselage as it climbed above the level of the peaks.

The plateau was a couple of hundred feet wide, crowded up to the mountain shoulder and slanting down to the northeast, and an old flatbed truck was parked next to a gray wooden cabin on the eastern edge. A new-looking black tent was set up on the truck's bed.

Three young men in olive green park ranger uniforms had wheeled two gurneys and a wheelchair across the dirt, and Golze sank shakily into the wheelchair while the young men lifted the bundle that was Daphne onto one gurney and Rascasse's unconscious blanketed body onto the other. Even at three thousand feet, the breeze was stiflingly hot, but the cabin at the east end of the plateau had a clattering air-conditioning unit on its shingle roof, and when they had all walked or been lifted up the wooden steps, the air in the big kitchen proved to be cool.

The tape was stripped off Daphne's canvas sack, and she kicked it away and hopped down off the gurney and brushed off her jeans as the other gurney, the one with the blanketed body on it, was wheeled to a corner by the front door. One of the uniformed young men, blond haired and with no expression in his pale blue eyes, bolted the door and then, with a kind of indifference that was scarier than rudeness would have been, marched Daphne across the room and handcuffed her to a rusty vertical water pipe against the east wall.

The cabin was mainly a kitchen, and the white refrigerators were at least as old as Grammar's and the wide stoves had ceramic knobs on them. None of the equipment seemed to be hooked up anymore, and the place smelled faintly of motor oil. A lot of rust-brown utensils hung on the wall over the stoves—bottle openers, spatulas, whisks—and Daphne tried to make out the labels on the dusty boxes and cans that were crowded on a shelf above them.

A door in the far wall opened, and a lean white-haired man in a red flannel shirt scuffed into the room, his hands in the pockets of his faded jeans. Behind him Daphne could see a smaller lamplit room, and she noticed that there were two more doors in that wall. She hoped one of them was a restroom.

"I don't see my favorite girl," the man drawled. His face was very tanned and wrinkled, and he had a bushy white mustache.

"She switched sides," rasped Golze from his wheelchair in the middle of the floor. "Took a car and ran off with the young Marrity, and now she's invisible to Rascasse—she couldn't have done that on her own, she must be dickering with the Mossad."

The white-haired newcomer widened his eyes and laughed, then crossed to where Daphne stood against the far wall, his boots knocking on the floor. "Then I've got to find a new favorite girl! What's your name, sugar pie?"

In the corner on the other side of the door from Rascasse, the old Frank Marrity shook his head and said, "I was told there was liquor here," then began laboriously lowering himself to a sitting position against the wall.

"Daphne Marrity," said Daphne.

"Well, Daphne, I'm Canino, like in canine. I'm the old dog around here. I'm guessing you could use a chair."

"I'd like to be driven to a town, Mr. Canino," said Daphne, "where I could call somebody to pick me up. I've got quarters."

Marrity had managed to sit down on the floor, his right leg extended straight out. "Dream on," he muttered.

Canino's eyes were bracketed with wrinkles that deepened when he squinted sideways at old Marrity. "You'll get your bottle as soon as I'm satisfied you can keep your mouth shut. Right now I've got my doubts." To Daphne he added, "If any of these sumbitches give you any sass, you tell me, hear?" He smiled and patted her on the shoulder. "We'll be turning you loose soon enough, child. But not right now. We need to find out who these people are that your dad's hooked up with. We got no business with your dad or you, but these people will come after you, and we got to talk to *them*."

"Can I use the bathroom?"

"Good lord yes! I'm sorry. Fred, free her and take her to the bathroom. Wait outside the door."

The same expressionless young man who had handcuffed her now released her and led her by the elbow across the booming wooden floor to the middle door in the far wall. Daphne went in and closed the door behind her.

It was a narrow room, lit only by the early evening light filtering in through a small cobwebbed window high up in the wall.

The ancient toilet proved to be in working order, and the sink, almost invisible in the dimness, produced a trickle of water. As she dried her hands on her blouse, Daphne looked at the window wall.

Her father had said, *I won't let them catch me, and I'll come get you soon. These people aren't planning to hurt you.*

He had also said, *Don't do anything in the helicopter!*—meaning, don't try to burn up the engines.

Then her father had kissed that woman Charlotte. Charlotte had told these people that they should not try to kill her father, and that they should "negate" her instead of Daphne.

Daphne hoped the woman wouldn't be killed, if negated meant killed. Sometimes at night, even these two years later, Daphne would be awakened by intrusive images of her mother, and a droning undercurrent of bewildered loss.

I'm not enough, loving him by myself, she thought. I need help.

She opened the door before the Fred man might start knocking on it. Fluorescent lights now glowed whitely below the ceiling in the big room.

The box with the portable phone in it began ringing, and old Canino picked it up from the floor and carried it to Golze. "Here you go, chief," he said, unsnapping the case and lifting the phone out.

Daphne jumped then, and even felt a twitch too in Fred's restraining hand on her upper arm, for a cluster of ancient whisks on the wall over the stove had begun buzzing and vibrating, throwing off a cloud of dust. Old Marrity's bad leg drummed on the floor planks as he made an abortive scramble toward the front door.

A voice came shaking out of the ringing whisks, with a baritone quality provided by the resonance of the wooden wall. "It's Charlotte. Go along with what she says."

Golze nodded irritably and switched the phone on. "Charlotte!" he said. "What's the good word?"

Charlotte's voice was scratchy under crackling static. "Oblivion, Paul," she said. "You know you want it too. Meet me at dawn somewhere and we'll do the switch. Daphne walks out first from your side, then I walk out from mine and you take me in exchange for her."

"Okay, that works for us," said Golze. "El Mirador Medical Plaza, at Tacheva Drive and Indian Canyon Drive. That's, uh, in Palm Springs."

"Duh. I'll be armed, and if anything goes funny, I promise

you I'll be able to kill both myself and Daphne, as well as anybody else who might be standing nearby, and you'll be left with nothing. Right?"

"Well, not with nothing," said Golze. "We've got the directions on how to use the time machine. We've debriefed old Marrity thoroughly, and we'll kill him at the first sign of any trouble from your side. So don't let your new pals imagine they can just wipe us all out like the pope did at Carcassonne. You know *they* have no interest in this exchange."

"I've got no pals. 'But I will go where they are hid who never were begot.' And I don't care about the time machine. You can all fight about that in a world that never included any Charlotte Sinclair."

"I hope they don't negate you!" piped up Daphne.

"You be me, kiddo," came Charlotte's faint voice. "Go easy on the sauce." There was an enormous click, and the line was dead.

Golze turned the phone off, then said to the ceiling, "She's sincere. If the Mossad is running her to get to us, she doesn't know it. Fred, cuff the girl to the pipe."

"She's with them," said the Rascasse voice, sounding to Daphne like a bowling ball rolling over broken glass, "or I'd see her, and I don't. They've given her a masking amulet."

"Speaking of which sort of thing," said Golze, "get the girl's prints."

Canino nodded and touched his forehead, then crossed to the stoves and lifted a foot-square pane of glass from a white enameled pan. Clear oil ran off the corner of the glass in a long, glittering string, and he wiped the front and back surfaces with an ancient towel and then turned to Daphne, holding the square of glass out toward her.

"If you would press your hands on that, sweetie."

Daphne did, and then accepted the towel from him and managed to wipe most of the oil off her hands on its stiff fabric.

"And," Canino said, "I'll take just the tiniest bit of your

hair." He clicked open a switchblade knife and cut off a pinch of her brown hair. "Thankee."

Then Fred took her back to the vertical pipe and ratcheted the handcuff onto her wrist again.

"I think we can assume Charlotte's with them," said Canino, pressing the hairs onto the oily glass and then wiping his hands too and tossing the towel into a corner, "and that they'll come with her, acting like backup but ready to push her aside and take *you*." He pointed at Golze. "Or Denis. Is he still alive?"

"Fred," said Golze, waving toward the gurney in the corner, "if you would . . ."

Fred walked to the gurney in the corner and flipped back the blanket.

"Shit!" he exclaimed. "This is a woman!"

Canino burst out with a surprised laugh. "Now where did you clowns leave poor old Denis?"

"That's me, you fools," said Rascasse, managing to make the whisks and the wall almost roar, "I was a woman once." After a pause the voice went on, more quietly, "I see I've now reverted back to that."

"I'm not sure this can be said to be . . . *going well*," said Golze thoughtfully.

Daphne was horrified to realize that she was about to start giggling, though not in merriment. She clamped her teeth together hard and didn't look toward Canino.

"Some magical procedures," rang Rascasse's voice from over the stoves, "can't be done by women. I found certain alchemists who reconfigured all my elements, and fixed me in the masculine estate."

Canino shook his head, frowning sympathetically. "Looks like you've come unfixed, old buddy."

Daphne snorted, and then she was laughing hysterically, trying to stifle it by biting her handcuffed fist.

Fred turned to her and, still with no expression, slapped her cheek stingingly hard.

Rascasse's voice went on, "I'm losing my attachment to

this place and time. I never quite came back to here, I think, from last night's freeway trip. But I can last until we close this time line out. Paul, radio for reinforcements now. Three cars—we'll want the helicopter too."

Daphne had noticed that he was speaking like someone in Shakespeare, the same cadence. Rubbing her cheek, and with a cautious glance at Fred, she asked, "Why are you speaking in iambic pentameter?"

"I need to keep my thoughts straight, little girl," rattled the whisks, "and meter is an aqueduct for them." After a pause, they went on, "I was a little girl myself, you know."

Daphne just nodded, wide-eyed.

"I sure signed on with the winning team," said Marrity. "Where's that bottle?"

"I'll dig one out for you," said Canino, looking at a watch on his tanned wrist, "as soon as I get back from taking my favorite girl for a little walk."

He signaled Fred to unlock the cuffs, and then Canino unbolted the door and waved Daphne ahead of him, outside. To Fred he said, "Watch us."

As she tapped down the two steps to the dirt, she listened to Canino's steps behind her over the alien buzz of cicadas, and she considered running. The sky was dark blue already, with a few shreds of clouds showing pink over the mountain's shoulder, but the breeze was still warm. Could she outrun Canino and Fred and hide, somewhere among all those rocks up there?

A puff of dust sprang up from the ground a dozen feet ahead of her, simultaneous with a breathy *snap* from behind her. She spun around.

"I wasted a dart," said Canino, grinning as he lowered a pistol, "but you see it works. Tranquilizer darts, Fred has one too. You'd fall down—bloody nose, torn clothes—we don't want that, do we?"

"No," said Daphne. Mentally she reached out for the gun, but she knew she couldn't get away before Fred could shoot her with a dart. The cicadas sounded like a hundred dentists' drills.

She sighed, and followed Canino around the corner of the cabin to the flatbed truck that had a tent set up on its bed. The tent was hardly bigger than a ticket kiosk at a carnival.

"Now this tent!" said Canino, putting a hand on the edge of the truck bed and lithely vaulting up onto it, his boots knocking on the wood, "is where you're going to be spending the next couple of hours. Girl needs her privacy. Gimme your hand." He leaned over the edge and took hold of Daphne's hand and then lifted her up onto the boards. Up close, Daphne could see that the tent was made of some thick black cloth.

Looking back, she saw that Fred was leaning against the corner of the cabin. She looked the other way and almost gasped—far below the edge of the little plateau, the lights of what must have been Palm Springs lay in lines and squares against the darkness of the desert-valley floor.

Canino pulled the tent flap aside and reached into the darkness; a moment later she heard a click over the rattle of the cabin's air-conditioning unit, and an electric bulb was glowing on the end of a wire swinging from the tent's peak. Below it in the narrow space, a kitchen chair was bolted to the truck-bed boards, and a silvery roll of duct tape lay next to one of the legs. In front of the chair, a section of white plastic pipe was mounted like a telescope on an aluminum pole, and the far end of the pipe stuck outside the tent through a close-fitting hole in the fabric. Behind the chair were stacked a lot of metal boxes with cables connecting them, and at the top were what seemed to be two car headlights.

"This here's sort of a deprivation chamber, though not sensory," said Canino with a squinting smile. "I've got to tape you in, but you'll have fresh air"—he clicked a switch with the toe of his boot, and a motor hummed and air was being blown into the tent—"and music." He touched a dial, and faintly she could hear recorded strings and woodwinds now—vaguely classical in a comfortless "easy-listening" way.

"Deprivation of what?" she asked hoarsely, and in spite of the hot, acid-smelling air her jaw was tingling as if her teeth might start to chatter.

"Trouble," said Canino kindly. "Sit down."

Daphne took what felt like her last look at the world—the rock-crusted mountains against the darkening sky—and then sat down in the chair.

Canino picked up the roll of tape and began pulling off strips, cutting them free with his teeth.

"You ever hear the old rule, 'Love thy neighbor,' Daphne?"

"Sure."

Her right ankle was farthest from him, and he reached in under the chair to loop tape around the cuff of her jeans and the chair leg.

"How are you supposed to do that, really?" He pressed the edge of the tape down firmly. "Lots of neighbors aren't very nice."

"Well, you can love them without liking them, my dad says."

With a ripping sound, he unrolled another length of tape, and she heard his teeth click as he bit it off. He taped her left ankle to the chair leg.

"Your daddy's right. Did you ever have a cat or dog die, that you loved? Well, your mom died, didn't she?"

"Yes." Daphne took a deep breath and let it out.

"But God loves us, right? That's what everybody says." He pulled her right wrist down until it was against a slat of the chair's back, and grunted as he worked a piece of tape between the slats.

"Right," said Daphne. "God loves us."

"But He kills our cats and our dogs and our mothers. Pretty cruelly too, sometimes! Why is He always doing shit like that? I'll tell you a secret."

"I don't want to hear any secrets." Daphne was keeping her voice steady only with an effort.

Now Canino was holding her left wrist against the outside chair-back slat, and he was able to tape it down more quickly.

"It's like neighbors. God loves us, but He doesn't like us. He doesn't *like* us at all."

Suddenly Daphne was aware of her father's love and

urgent concern, and she knew he had been radiating these for at least the last several seconds.

I'm okay, Dad, she thought, hoping he could catch the thought. She told herself not to be afraid, since her father could sense her fear. God might not like her, as Canino had said, but her father did.

Canino straightened up. "I'm going to have to turn off the light," he said, "but you can look through that length of pipe at Palm Springs. See?" He switched off the overhead light-bulb and stepped back, out of the tent.

Daphne peered into the plastic tube, and there were the distant lights of the city, far, far below.

"I'll come out and see how you're doing in a while," Canino said. He let the tent flap fall closed, and then she heard his boots scuff on the truck-bed boards, crunch into the dirt, and recede away.

Daphne stared longingly at the remote lights of restaurants and theaters and homes, and clung to her father's mind.

F red was leaning against the cabin wall in the gathering darkness. Canino stopped beside him and pulled a pack of Camels from his shirt pocket.

"What with that music and the synchronized lights and all," Canino said, "she'll be pretty dissociated, come dawn. Have a couple of the guys get that piece of oiled glass down the hill. You stay here." He stretched. "I'm gonna get a beer, you want a beer?"

"I don't drink. The plan is to proceed with negating her?" Fred waved toward the truck and the tent.

"Oh shit yes. We can't negate Charlotte—she's been involved too long, we'd lose years. She's stupid, or she thinks we are. Hell, she's the one who fucked over that old guy in New Jersey, to get us the Einstein papers from Princeton! Remember, the old guy killed himself in jail afterward? Would we have got those papers anyway, without Charlotte?

Maybe, maybe not. And negating Charlotte wouldn't stop this kid from having burned up the Chaplin movie. Nah, it's gotta be the girl."

"Kill her father?"

"Sure, why not? There's no way he won't be coming along with Charlotte tomorrow morning, so that should be easy. But," he added, laughing softly, "by tomorrow noon he'll be alive again, in a brand-new world. He just won't ever have had a daughter."

Twenty-four

The twelve-sided motel room was crowded. Frank Marrity and Charlotte sat on the double bed with an ashtray on the bedspread between them, Lepidopt and Malk sat on the carpeted floor, and old Mishal was rubbing his eyes at the lamplit desk by the bathroom door. On the far side of the bed, blocking one of the knee-level windows, stood the concrete block Marrity had last seen in his grandmother's shed. Somebody had apparently been shooting at it since then—it was pocked and cracked in the right handprint and in the imprint of the cane, and the *S* in *Sid* had almost entirely been chipped off. Alongside the block were stacked four cardboard moving boxes with old cloth-insulated wires trailing out of the tops. The light in the narrow ceiling threw an antiquating sepia radiance over everything.

Marrity's Einstein letters lay on the table in front of Mishal, each page now in a clear plastic sleeve.

"I've read the letters," Mishal said, leaning back from the desktop lamp that had made his face look like a skull.

"They're supplemental. Valuable, but Einstein assumed his reader already knew a lot of things we don't know."

"I notice he gives page numbers for something called *Grumberg's Fairy Tales*," said Lepidopt. "I could look that up."

"His handwriting was no good," said Mishal. "That's 'Grimm bros,' and I know what story he's referring to. It's 'Faithful John,' in which crows are represented as being able to see the past and future. Sequential events are on the ground, along roads the characters have to travel, but the crows live in a higher dimension, and can see what's in the future and past of the characters. He's explaining higher-dimensional perspective to his daughter." He stretched. "Bert, did I see you making coffee?"

Malk leaned forward to look into the bathroom. "It'll be ready any minute."

"We won't be having any for a while yet. *And*," Mishal went on, "Einstein mentions having told Roosevelt—Einstein calls him the king of Naples in the letters, it's all in terms of characters out of *The Tempest*—having told him about the atomic bomb, but he says he didn't tell Roosevelt about this other thing he's discovered, which is the time machine. Or maybe it's the singularity you told us about," he said, nodding to Charlotte. "Most likely they're both parts of the same thing. Right before his death in 1955 he writes that he's talked to 'NB,' who visited in October, and he says NB fortunately has no clue about the time-machine possibility inherent in the math. Niels Bohr visited Einstein in October of '54." He squinted at Marrity. "Basically all he does in the letters is tell your grandmother why she should destroy the machine in her shed."

"She tried to," said Marrity, "at the end."

"And he mentions 'the Caliban who is your chaste incubus,'" Mishal said. "That's the thing that showed up on your daughter's hospital-room TV set?"

"Maybe," said Marrity. "It quoted one of Caliban's lines from *The Tempest*. You heard it," Marrity said to Lepidopt.

Lepidopt nodded. "And it was trying to get your daughter

to let it into her mind. It said, 'the mountains are burning,' and 'when the fires are out it will be too late.' It's what your grandmother died to get rid of—she jumped sideways, as it were, across space instead of time, and she scraped the Caliban thing off, like a psychic barnacle." He remembered that poor Bozzaris had been amused by the phrase, when they had talked in Newport Beach—only about twelve hours ago! "And the so to speak friction of it started all these fires in the mountains."

"Caliban," said Marrity. "What *is* it?"

"It's pretty clearly a dybbuk," said Mishal wearily. "More correctly *dybbuk me-ru'ah ra'ah,* the cleaving of an evil spirit. More correctly still, it's an *ibbur,* the spirit of a man who has no proper place in the world, and has to find a host to cling to, to live in." He looked at Lepidopt. "Are the fires still burning in the mountains?"

"They were today."

"Then the *dybbuk* is still stalking your daughter," Mishal said to Marrity. "But she's in no danger unless she invites him in; he can't penetrate her mind forcibly."

Marrity probed for Daphne's mind, but sensed only her ongoing attention to him, and uneasy boredom. Faintly he thought he could hear Muzak. He tried to project a smile and a clasping hand.

"How soon is dawn?" he asked.

"Hours yet," said Malk. "We won't even leave here for hours yet."

"We should *go* there," said Marrity desperately, clenching his fists. "I should go there."

"Go where?" asked Malk, not unkindly. "They won't be at that hospital until dawn, and they might be anywhere now. They could be holding your daughter in Cathedral City, Indio, Palm Desert—not to mention all the mountains around there. We've got to wait till dawn."

"What do we do in the meantime?" asked Charlotte. Her

sunglasses were incongruous in this dimly lit little room, but nobody had commented on them. She was chewing her fingernails—Mishal had said they couldn't smoke tonight because it would repel ghosts.

"We need to know more than we know," said Mishal. "And so we will mine some old science."

Marrity saw Lepidopt frown for a moment.

"Nobody," Mishal said, "saw any use in Richard Hamilton's matrix arrays until Heisenberg used them to work out his uncertainty principle seventy years later, right? And Fitzgerald's crazy guess that an ether headwind compressed objects in the direction they're traveling turned out to be an accurate description of what happened, though his explanation was wrong. The Riemann-Christoffel curvature tensor was considered a useless fantasy until Einstein needed it for General Relativity. In fact," he went on, looking at Marrity, "your great-grandfather renounced the cosmological constant he had originally put into his General Relativity equations—he said including it had been the biggest blunder of his life—but according to Charlotte here, it wasn't nonsense after all. Well, I think he knew that himself, all along. He was simply—justifiably—afraid of it.

"I'm a physicist," Mishal went on, "but I have to say that most physicists aren't comfortable with the reality they're supposed to be mapping. Most of them still start by setting up their problems in terms of Newtonian mechanics, and then only as they proceed do they shove in the quantum-mechanical concepts—like those old 'color' postcards that were black-and-white photographs painted over with watercolors. They should *start* with the quantum eye, that wider perspective. It's the same with the supernatural factor: We learned not to add it in after the problems were defined, but to have those crayons already in our box from the start, alongside the quantum crayons."

In a whisper Lepidopt asked, "Shouldn't we have been talking in whispers, all this time? And fasting?"

"You were a good student, Oren! But this time," said Mishal, standing up and nodding toward the slab and the boxes on the far side of the bed, "I think we're close enough already."

Charlotte was frowning. "Who'll come to us?"

"Ghosts," said Mishal. "We're going to have a séance. Oren, open the whisky, if you would, and pour each of us a full glass."

"First sensible remark all night," said Charlotte. "Why do we want ghosts to come to us? I've met them, they're pretty useless creatures."

"There's only four cups in the bathroom," said Malk. "Plastic."

"Frank and I can share," said Charlotte.

"I expect the ghosts you've met are the ones that were leaning in from their side," said Mishal, taking a freshly opened bottle of Canadian Club whisky from Lepidopt. "Talking backward and all. They make more sense if we visit them on their side."

Malk had got up to fetch the plastic cups from the bathroom, and now he peeled cellophane off one and handed it to Mishal.

"Thank you." Mishal poured amber whiskey into it and held the filled cup out to Charlotte, and Marrity watched it carefully so that she'd be able to take it without a fumble.

And why am I helping her deceive these people? he asked himself.

The old man filled Lepidopt's and Malk's plastic cups, then filled one for himself and clanked the bottle onto the table. "And," he said, "talking to ghosts on their own turf is much easier if one is not excessively sober." He raised his cup.

Charlotte took a deep sip and handed the cup to Marrity. I guess I'll start cutting back tomorrow, he told himself, and gulped a mouthful of the liquor; and when he had swallowed it and handed the cup back to her, he was grateful that Mishal's procedure, whatever it might be, required this.

Charlotte finished it and held the emptied cup out to Mishal.

"You're a good soldier," the old man said, tilting the bottle over the cup as Marrity made sure to watch.

Daphne was sleepy, but her ribs ached and the air being blown into the tent was colder now, and she wished she'd been wearing a sweater when she and her father had gone to lunch at Alfredo's yesterday. She was as aware of her father as if he'd been standing behind her chair; she tasted every mouthful of whisky that he swallowed, and she even felt that the alcohol was warming her.

The faint music from the speaker behind her seemed to have been lost in the airwaves for decades. It was some kind of brassy swing, but any liveliness in the melodies was dried out by the lifeless performance—she imagined a bandstand painted with glittery musical notes in a club out of an old Fred Astaire movie, with ancient, weary musicians in moth-eaten tuxedos swiveling their heavy saxophones this way and that.

The view of Palm Springs held her attention by default. White car headlights seemed to be streetlights that had come unmoored from their places in the ranks along the boulevards, and after a while she was able to make out the cycling pinpoints of red and green that were traffic signals. Houses were dots of yellow light, tormenting in their hints of families at dinner so far away.

A vocalist was accompanying the music now, and after a few moments Daphne was able to make out the nasally crooning words:

Now my charms are all o'erthrown,
And what strength I have's my own,
Which is most faint. Now 'tis true
I must be here confined by you . . .
Gentle breath of yours my sails
Must fill, or else my project fails.

Let your indulgence blot his sin—
Daphne, speak! And let me in!

Daphne knew it was the thing that had shown itself as a cartoon on her hospital TV set last night. The wind from the blower on her jeans felt like fluttering hands.

"Daddy!" she yelled, but the audible yell was just an involuntary echo of her mental cry.

In the cabin the upright pipe by the stove suddenly split, shooting a burst of steam across the room. Golze screamed weakly as the hot vapor whipped at the hair on the back of his head, and his right hand clawed the wheel to roll his wheelchair forward in a quarter circle across the floor.

He blinked tears from his eyes as he squinted back at the pipe, which was just leaking a trickle of water now from the split section.

"She's doing this," he snarled. "She's a poltergeist, she can set things on fire. You have to trank her."

"Aw, she's just grabbing hold of something, it's a reflex," said Canino, slouching forward to peer at the ruptured length of galvanized steel. "She was cuffed to that pipe, so vertigo made her grab it. It wasn't malicious."

"My head is scalded," Golze said. His right hand wavered up as if to feel the back of his head, then just fell to his lap. "She's dangerous."

"You'll be getting a brand-new head soon," Canino told him.

Marrity had choked and sprayed whisky across the carpet and the tan wall, and now, on his feet and coughing, he burst out, "Christ, that thing's after her again, the triffid or whatever it is! You've got to—"

"There's nothing we can—do from here," said Mishal solemnly. "She knows not to admit him."

Marrity closed his eyes and thought, *Don't let him in, don't say anything. Don't let him trick you.*

He was sweating, and he realized that a big part of his gnawing anxiety was the knowledge that his own older self was out there in Palm Springs, participating in this or at least not stopping it. Daphne's own father was letting this go on.

"Charlotte," he said, "you called them before—call them again. I need to talk to the, the old guy who's me." He focused his gaze on Mishal and made himself speak clearly. "Let her call them again."

Mishal just raised his eyebrows and stared at him owlishly.

"If that triffid thing gets her," Marrity went on, "she'll be linked to *it,* as well as to me." Or even *instead* of me, he thought with a shudder. "They don't want that. If I tell them—"

"But they're not going to negate Daphne," said Charlotte, "they agreed to negate me instead—"

"They'll still negate the girl, if they possibly can," pronounced Mishal. "It was the girl who wrecked the movie component of Lieserl's completed machine." He raised a finger at Marrity. "It's a dybbuk, not a tribb—not a triffid. And we need to be about summoning our ghosts."

"It might actually help," said Malk. When the others looked at him, he shrugged. "If we shake up the ghosts first, get their attention, by letting *young* Marrity call *old* Marrity, that's likely to help draw them when we do the actual séance. It'll be a curspic—a cons*pic*uous violation of normal reality."

"This Vespers crowd couldn't trace it," Lepidopt said. "The phone line is routed through half a dozen cutouts; and they can't psychically fix on us, especially here." He waved vaguely at the conical room.

After a pause, "*B'seder,*" said Mishal, "let's do it, we can begin the séance with that. We're all drunk enough. Here." He stepped back to the desk and turned the top Einstein letter upside down, and an envelope fell out of the plastic sleeve. Clumsily he shook out four more envelopes and handed them to Lepidopt, who passed one to each of the others. The envelopes were all tan with age, and each had Lisa Marrity's name and address on the front in Einstein's handwriting.

"Oren," said Mishal, "break open your . . . holograph amulet. And everybody's got to crowd over to the other side of the bed, by the cement block."

Charlotte and Marrity turned around on the bed while the three Mossad men shuffled around the foot of the bed and edged between the mattress and the block.

"One at a time, now," said Mishal, "everybody press your right hand into the handprint in the cement."

"It's cracked," said Charlotte as she leaned forward to spread her fingers in the indentations.

"Your old friends shot at it this afternoon," said Mishal.

Marrity was the last to do it, shifting across the bed to reach it, and he assumed that the warm dampness of the handprint had been imparted by the people who had touched it only moments before. When he lifted his hand away, a quarter-size flake of gray cement clung to his palm, and he closed his hand on it and shoved it into his pocket.

"Now," said Mishal, "everybody lick the glue strip on the Einstein envelope you've got."

"Ugh," said Charlotte after she had licked hers. "It's like French-kissing a guy who's been dead thirty years."

"Yes," said Mishal, grimacing over his own envelope. "It's likely to catch his attention, though."

"The envelopes were sticky," said Marrity, "when I picked them up, Sunday afternoon. My grandmother must have been licking them too."

"That's kind of touching, really," said Mishal. "I guess she wanted to have a last chat with her father."

Charlotte grimaced. "I French-kissed your grandmother too? This is getting revolting." Marrity could hear tension as well as drunkenness in her voice.

"Stop being disgusting, my dear," said Mishal. "Now if you would call your, ah, erstwhile employers again. I think

Bert's right, a conversation between Marrity and his older self might also help catch the old fellow's attention."

Charlotte rolled back over the bed and stood up unsteadily. Marrity followed her and stared at the portable telephone case on the little table by the Einstein letters, and she picked it up smoothly. Then he leaned over her shoulder and stared at the keypad so she could punch in the number.

She handed him the phone, and only at that moment did he realize that he was very drunk, and that he had no idea what he wanted to say to his older self.

Mishal stepped up and pushed a button on the side of the telephone, and then the background hiss was clearly audible to everyone in the room.

"I'll let you talk to him," Mishal said, "but not privately."

Marrity nodded and set the phone down on the bedspread.

A moment later a strained voice from the speaker said clearly, "Yes? I'm told that this is Frank Marrity the Lesser."

"Could I talk to myself, please," said Marrity distinctly.

"You don't have to lean over it," said Mishal. "Just stand and talk normally."

The person on the other end of the line laughed weakly and then said, "Why not?" and added, away from the microphone, "It's for you."

Marrity heard some furious whispering, and then heard again the voice of the old man who had spoken to him and Daphne in their kitchen yesterday morning.

"Hello?" the old man said belligerently.

"That dybbuk thing is bothering Daphne," said Marrity. "Go to wherever you've got her and say, 'Go away, Matt.' Don't let *her* talk at all. It might quote some lines from *The Tempest* at you—just respond with Prospero's lines. I assume you still remember them."

"I don't have any idea what the hell you're talking about. I've tried very hard to help you—"

"By eliminating my daughter from the universe! *Your* daughter! You should be putting your life on the line to *protect* her. How can you have got so . . . so *depraved* in twenty years?"

He could hear the older man breathing heavily. "You may very well find out. Don't stand in back of any cars she's behind the wheel of."

Marrity realized that the other man was drunk. Well, so was Marrity. The parallel frightened him. In what sense was the older man the "other" man?

He was aware of puzzlement from Daphne, and tried to project a reassurance he couldn't quite feel.

He said, "I could never decide to get rid of—"

"I couldn't either, at your age, with just the experiences you've had! Who do you think I *am*? The Harmonic Convergence cracked the continuity of our life, and in the *true* version of our life there was some, some variant stimulus and so you *didn't* do a tracheotomy! She died! She was *supposed* to die! When you get to where I am—"

"I'll never get to where you are. I'll make better choices."

"Choices! You don't get choices, you get . . . situations that you react to—the actual cumulative *you* reacts, with whatever half-ass wiring you've got at the time, not some hovering 'soul.' You're a mercury switch—if the spring tilts you to the right degree, you complete a circuit, and if it's got metal fatigue, it tilts you less, and you don't. You don't have free will, sonny."

"Of course I do, of course *you* do, what kind of excuse—"

"Bullshit. If—" The older Marrity was panting. "If a scientist could know every last detail of your physiology and life experiences, he could predict with absolute accuracy every 'choice' you'd make in any moral quandary."

Quandary! To Marrity the sentence sounded as if it had been prepared ahead of time. Not for talking to me, he thought, this old wretch couldn't have anticipated talking to me—he must have cooked it up for his own solace.

"Laplace's determinist manifesto," came another man's languid voice from the background. "It overlooks Heisenberg's uncertainty."

"Okay," said the older Marrity furiously, "then it's probability and statistics that dictate what we'll do! But it's not—"

"It's a sin," said Marrity, breathing deeply himself. To

Daphne he projected a vague cluster of images—hugging her, holding her hand—and he was able to have more confidence in his reassurance now.

"Said the fourth domino to the twenty-first!" exclaimed the older Marrity, laughing angrily. " 'Ah, wilt Thou with predestination round / Enmesh me and impute my fall to sin?' " The older man audibly took a deep breath. "But listen, you and I need to talk—there are things I've got to tell you—you'll be rich—"

"I wouldn't take them," said Marrity, "from you. What you can do for me is right now go to Daphne and say 'Go away, Matt.' "

"Ahh—go buy crutches now while they're cheap."

The phone clicked, and then there was just a buzz.

Marrity stared at the inert telephone on the bed. He couldn't bring himself to look at any of the others, especially Charlotte, who had volunteered to take oblivion in Dahpne's place. The horrible old man on the phone had been *himself*.

As if she'd read his mind, Charlotte said, "He's not you. He never was." She smiled, her eyes unreadable behind the sunglasses. "He never met me, for one thing."

Marrity tried to smile back. "He never kissed you, anyway, I'm pretty sure," he said gruffly.

"Tilt the block over onto the bed," said Mishal, "carefully, and then we all stand around it and hold hands."

Marrity shoved the Einstein envelope into his pocket so that he'd have both hands free.

Twenty-five

When the slab was lying across the bed with its anonymous back face upward, Marrity and Charlotte sat cross-legged on the pillows while Lepidopt hunched between the wall and the edge of the block, Malk stood on the door side, and Mishal crouched on the foot of the bed.

Mishal caught Lepidopt's eye and nodded toward the cement surface, and Lepidopt reached into his shirt and pulled a little piece of folded paper from a broken locket. He unfolded the yellowed paper and set it carefully on the cement.

"This is a piece from a letter Einstein wrote in 1948, which was auctioned off to support the Haganah—precursor to the Israel Defense Forces," he added to Marrity and Charlotte. He pulled Marrity's matchbook from his pocket and struck a match.

He held the match to the paper, and a ring of blue flame quickly circled the crabbed words on it.

"Hold hands, all," said Mishal. And when they were linked in a circle, he began reciting words in what must have been

Hebrew; Malk and Lepidopt joined in with some formal responses. Twice Marrity caught the syllables of "Einstein."

Suddenly Marrity wished he had not drunk so much of the whiskey—sitting on the bed, leaning back against the headboard in the warm room, he was falling asleep. Oh, let 'em do it without me, he thought. I should rest up anyway, for exertions at dawn. Dawn? Of what day, what year? I'm one of five people holding hands around somebody's gravestone, he thought, and his last blurry thought was, I wonder which of the five I am.

Lepidopt's right hand, clasped in Marrity's left hand, seemed to change—the skin was cooler and looser over the bones, as if it were suddenly an old man's hand—but Marrity didn't have the energy to look to his left. He closed his eyes.

He dreamed about Einstein, his great-grandfather. Einstein was young, with curly dark hair and a neat mustache, and he was sitting on the balcony of a second-floor apartment in Zurich with his friend Friedrich Adler. The sky was gray, and they were bundled up in coats and scarves, and with steaming breath they were discussing philosophy and physics— Schopenhauer and Mach—and Adler was very excited; he kept pushing his round glasses up on his nose, and his cold-reddened ears stuck out to the sides, and his mustache straggled over his mouth as he spoke. Both men were thirty-one years old, and Einstein's son and Adler's daughter were making a snow fort on the sidewalk below; Einstein could hear their happy shouts over the rattle of carriage wheels. Einstein had recently been hired as an associate professor at the University of Zurich, a post he had got because Adler, who had been the first choice of the Directorate of Education, had stepped aside and proclaimed that Einstein was the better man for the job. Adler's father was Victor Adler, leader of the Austrian Social Democrats, and what Friedrich actually hoped to do was follow his father into politics.

It was an idyllic several months, in Zurich in the winter of 1909. Adler and his family lived in the apartment directly below the Einstein family, and on Thursday nights after teaching a class in thermodynamics, Einstein would walk with the students to the Terrase café, and when the café closed he would take them back to his apartment with him, and Adler would join in the coffee-driven discussions.

But in the spring of 1910, Einstein began corresponding with the German University in Prague, which offered him the chair of mathematical physics, which for his sake they would rename the chair of theoretical physics. The Austrian Minister of Education and Instruction, Karl Count Sturgkh, opposed it, but Count Sturgkh's preferred candidate eventually withdrew; and so, after having taught only two semesters at the University of Zurich, Einstein moved his family to Prague in April 1911.

Count Sturgkh eventually became prime minister of Austria, resigning in 1918 and retiring with his family to Innsbruck after the war.

Einstein's friends were baffled by his decision to move—the German University in Prague wasn't one of the great universities, and Prague was divided into German, Czech, and Jewish quarters, mutually resentful. But Einstein had been working on his *maschinchen,* and had found that he needed to consult certain rabbis at the *yeshiva,* the Jewish school, in Prague.

Einstein had offered to let Friedrich Adler have the position at the University of Zurich after all, but by this time Adler was editing the Social Democrat paper *Volksrecht,* and he let the appointment go. But the paper failed to satisfy him, and his political ambitions seemed stalled, and he wrote to Einstein in October 1911, pleading with him to visit him in Zurich.

Einstein wrote back explaining that he could not come anytime soon, since he had committed to attend the Solvay Conference at the Grand Hotel Metropole in Brussels, where he would be meeting with all the great physicists of the world.

When he returned to Prague one evening in November, Einstein learned that Friedrich Adler had fatally shot himself in the head on Halloween. Einstein spent the rest of that night in his office at the German University, staring out at the untended walled cemetery below his windows.

Snow obscured Marrity's dream, and when it blew away in gusts, he saw Einstein again, walking on a mountain path with a dark-haired young woman—and Marrity recognized her as his grandmother. She was frowning and her lips were pursed as she trudged through the snow flurries behind her father, but Marrity thought she looked like Greta Garbo.

Einstein was older than he had been in the first vision— his hair was shaggier and beginning to gray, and the line of his jaw was sagging. Marrity knew it was 1928 now. Einstein was staggering along carrying something cylindrical wrapped in a blanket.

When he set it down and pulled off the blanket, Marrity saw that it was a big glass tube mounted on a board with a car battery.

They stopped, panting plumes of steam, and with gloved hands Einstein pulled a roll of gold wire out of his pocket and began straightening it and bending it, squinting against the wind as he peered down into the valley below.

When Einstein had bent and cut the wire into a swastika, he laid it on the snowy path and knelt to connect it to wires from the glass cylinder; and then he sat down and took off his boots and socks while his daughter, Marrity's grandmother, wrung her gloved hands. Finally the old man stood up barefoot in the snow and stepped onto the swastika. Something gleamed in his hand, and in the moment before he closed it in his fist, Marrity saw that it was a brass bullet shell. Einstein stared into the valley and closed his eyes—

—and for a timeless moment he was rushing through a limitless space where lifetimes were visible as static ropes or sparks arcing across a void—

—and then he was in Zurich again and it was the autumn of 1911, in the remembered attic where he and Adler had spent so many evenings talking by gaslight. Adler was sitting in a chair with a glass in his hand and a nearly empty bottle on the table beside him. Einstein hurried across the room to him, still barefoot, and began talking. They talked all night.

The next morning, comfortable in borrowed boots and confident that he had rid his friend of the idea of suicide,

Einstein waited until his young wife had taken their son out for a walk and his younger self had begun his two-hundred-yard walk down the Gloriastrasse toward the University of Zurich buildings. The older Einstein hurried up the stairs, broke the front-door lock, grabbed a gold chain of his wife's, and, snapping it in two, arranged it in a swastika on the balcony; then, taking off the boots and staring at the receding back of his younger self, he closed his eyes.

And the recoil hit him. He was back on the mountain in the gusting snow with Lieserl, but his heart seemed to have clenched shut and a pain like electrocution knocked him to the icy ground. His last sight was insanity—he seemed to see dozens of naked infants scattered across the frozen path.

He woke in the house of the friend he'd been visiting, attended by a doctor who had actually dedicated a book on heart pathology to Einstein; and on a regime of no salt or nicotine, Einstein slowly recovered from what the doctor had diagnosed as acute dilation of the heart.

But Einstein had two sets of memories now—in the original time line Friedrich Adler had shot himself in 1911; but in this new time line Adler had instead lived on, and in 1916 had assassinated the Austrian prime minister—fatally shot *him* in the head, as if he'd had to shoot *somebody* that way. And the man he killed, the man who was prime minister in 1916, was the same Count Strugkh who had given Einstein the professorship in Prague in 1911.

In prison Adler wrote an irrational treatise attempting to disprove Einstein's relativity theory.

Einstein, recovering in his sickbed in the Alps, was the only person on earth who remembered the original version of history—and so it was to Einstein that Strugkh's unconceived son came.

In the original time line, Strugkh had had a son in 1918, who would have been ten years old now—but the son's conception and birth were part of the time line that Einstein had canceled. Einstein met the dispossessed waif in his dreams, and, sickened with guilt at what his intervention had done, welcomed the lost creature into his mind.

Lieserl also had found a waif to care for. She had snatched up one of the impossible babies from the snow as she had run to get help for her stricken father, and though the other infants were gone by the time she got back, the little boy she had taken in was healthy—Lieserl said he was too fat, and she told her father that she was worried about the angularity of the back of the baby's head. Einstein felt the back of his own head, but said nothing. Lieserl named the boy Derek.

Einstein began to have terrifying dreams, often a recurrent nightmare in which he felt as if he were falling—not just falling from that Alpine mountain ledge but falling right out of existence, so that Hermann and Pauline Einstein never had a son named Albert. He realized that this was his subconscious applying to himself what had happened to the orphan who now had never existed anywhere but in his head.

In his dreams it said its name was Matt. Desperately Einstein told it stories, confided his mathematical speculations to it, played endless improvisations on his violin for its frail distraction—looked at the sky and told it about the sun and moon and stars.

And then one night it was gone from his dreams, and in the morning Lieserl told her father that all night she had dreamed of a boy named Matt who wanted her to let him in; but she had sensed that he was dead, and had not complied.

In horror Einstein had sent his daughter and the baby she had rescued to live with a woman he knew in Berlin, an old lover of his named Grete Markstein. For a while he sent money for their support.

Marrity snapped awake with an embarrassed grin, but nobody was looking at him. At the foot of the bed, Mishal was speaking softly in German, clearly asking questions and then pausing.

Marrity looked to the left—it was just Lepidopt who was holding his hand and staring at Mishal, but Marrity was sure it had been Einstein, or Einstein's ghost, who had been holding his hand for the last minute or two.

Charlotte squeezed his right hand, and he realized that she didn't have to look at him to know that his eyes had been closed for a while.

He didn't sense any alarm from Daphne. Maybe one of her captors had gone to her and said, "Go away, Matt!"

Marrity's face went cold, for now he knew what Matt was, what Caliban was. It was the boy whom Einstein had inadvertently negated in 1928, just as the Vespers meant to negate Daphne; and he wanted to tell Charlotte that negation wasn't necessarily the absolute oblivion she had volunteered for.

He tightened his hand on hers—but it wasn't Charlotte's hand. Big knuckles, a blocky ring—

Then he was dreaming again—he saw Lieserl and Einstein arguing in the familiar kitchen on Batsford Street in Pasadena. Lieserl was still as beautiful as she'd been in 1928, but Einstein's hair had gone white since then. They were speaking German in what he knew in the dream was a Swabian dialect, and Lieserl wanted her father's help in building another, better version of the machine he had used in the Swiss Alps three years earlier.

She had—Marrity knew with the certainty of dreams—become pregnant, and had abandoned the infant Derek to the care of Grete Markstein, and had then got an abortion in Vienna. But since then she had been having dreams like the ones Einstein had had during his recovery in 1928, and now she wanted to go back in time and persuade her younger self not to have the abortion done.

Einstein was emphatically refusing, and trying to convince her that the very physics of the machine was diabolical . . . and then the scene shifted, and Marrity saw the two of them and a third man, and they were seated around a table speaking English in what looked to Marrity like a medieval hall, with a beamed ceiling over second-floor arches high in the adobe walls. The third man was trim, full-lipped and handsome under prematurely gray hair, with prominent white teeth, and his gray suit, though it didn't fit perfectly, looked expensive.

The man's first son had died twelve years earlier, in 1919, at the age of three days; the man mentioned bitterly that the undertakers had pressed the baby's face into a smile, though in fact the little boy had never smiled while he'd been alive.

The man was a movie director, apparently, and he had just finished filming a movie that he hoped would summon the boy's ghost so that he could take the ghost into himself and let the boy experience *his* life, since the boy would never get one of his own.

In 1926 he had made a movie that had been crafted to accomplish this, by using "depth-charge symbols," as he put it, to evoke a powerful psychic response from audiences— but at the movie's only screening, a private one, several of the seats and some cars in the parking lot had burst into flame, and Chaplin—yes, Marrity realized, this was Charlie Chaplin!—had never released that film, *A Woman of the Sea,* commercially. The potent symbolism in this new movie, titled *City Lights,* was much less compulsive.

Einstein argued passionately against using this new movie in this way, and he hinted at the effect such an undertaking had had and was still having on himself.

He didn't convince Chaplin, but the premiere wouldn't be for another two weeks, and Einstein and Lieserl took a train to Palm Springs in the Mojave Desert, where they stayed with an old friend of Einstein's, Samuel Untermeyer. Palm Springs was a village scattered across a few dozen acres of the vast springtime desert between the Little San Bernardino Mountains to the northeast and the San Jacinto Mountains to the southwest, and its social center was the Spanish mission–style resort hotel El Mirador, with its square four-story tower that could be seen for miles over the pink sea of wild Desert Verbena blossoms.

Einstein had gone for long walks alone at dawn across the flat mountain-ringed landscape, and Tony Burke of the El Mirador had driven the old physicist far out into the Mojave Desert, as far as the desolate Salton Sea—and when Einstein appeared cheerful in the El Mirador at dinner one evening, even picking up a violin and joining the string trio

in the hotel lobby, Lieserl knew why. He had lost Caliban—
he imagined that he had exorcised the intrusive spirit in the
desert wastes.

But Lieserl knew what had become of that fugitive soul.
The thing had come to her in a dream, and in her childless
grief she had let it in.

At the premiere of Chaplin's movie, Einstein was able to
induce the theater's manager to interrupt the film at the end
of the third reel; the house lights were turned up while an
announcer asked the audience to pause and admire the theater's architecture. Chaplin lunged from his seat beside Einstein and charged up the aisle to force the resumption of
the film, but the escalating chain of symbols—the bald man
wearing the star hat, the man throwing himself into the
river, the blind flower seller whose sight would be restored—
had already been broken, and Chaplin's dead son had not
been summoned.

That had been on January 30, 1931. Chaplin didn't again
try to use the movie as an invocation, but that was because
Lieserl, with the help of the ghost in her mind, was assem-
bling a new version of Einstein's *maschinchen* in the shed
behind her house.

She did an exploratory run with it on March 9, 1933, and
dismissed as a coincidence the small earthquake that followed.
Then, with Chaplin as a nervous observer, she used it the following day. In her hand she was clasping the broken lens from
a pair of reading glasses she had had to replace in 1930.

And she found herself in Berlin, watching her three-
years-younger self feeding baby Derek by gaslight in a narrow upstairs kitchen.

Her younger self didn't know yet that she was pregnant,
and learning it while feeding a quarrelsome two-year-old
in a shabby apartment shouldn't have made the prospect of
motherhood look attractive; but the older Lieserl's tearfully
passionate description of the postabortion dreams, and the
impressive fact of her having come back through time just to
deliver this message, proved to be enough to convince the
younger Lieserl that she should not abort her child.

When Lieserl had arranged some gold coins on the floor and let the recoil take her back to 1933, she had stepped into noisy confusion.

Chaplin had experienced some kind of involuntary astral time-dislocation himself, and had found himself pressing his hands into the wet cement in front of the Chinese Theater in 1928—an event that had hitherto been a disquieting blind spot in his memory; this had panicked him, and so had the fact that the ground was still shaking and the power lines still swinging in a major earthquake, and even more so the fact that the yard was now scattered with naked infant girls.

Within seconds the infants had disappeared, but it took half an hour for Lieserl to get Chaplin calmed down, and only afterward was she able to call up the new memories of her revised time line, and remember that the baby she'd been pregnant with had miscarried in the late summer of 1930.

And even in this new time line, she remembered having let Caliban into her head in Palm Springs more than two years ago, in December 1930. In this time line she had had no abortion to atone for, but Caliban had come to her in a dream as a lost child, and she had not been in a state to say no to a child wanting to be let in.

She called Chaplin's chauffeur and got him to pick up his shaken employer. Early radio reports said that more than two hundred people had been killed in the earthquake. She was physically sick with guilt, but in her dreams that night Caliban was giddy and singing.

Marrity was leaning back against the headboard with his eyes shut, but the hand he was clasping was Charlotte's, smooth and warm.

Frankie, came his grandmother's remembered voice in his head. *Have I been talking in my sleep?*

Yes, Grammar, he thought. *Go back to sleep.*

Did I burn the shed? It was her voice, but she had no German accent now.

You did your best.

Okay. You take care of that little girl of yours.

The contact was gone, but he thought, I will, Grammar.

Marrity could still hear Mishal asking questions in German—but now Marrity could hear faint answers being spoken between the questions, and again it was Einstein's hand he was holding in his left hand.

Marrity opened his eyes and shifted them to the left. Between himself and Lepidopt was the old man himself, with the resigned pouchy face and the disordered white hair and mustache. Then it was the middle-aged man he had seen on the mountain trail in the snow, and then it was a bright-eyed, dark-haired child sitting beside him. Einstein's ghost was cycling through all the ages he'd ever been. When the figure glanced sideways at him and smiled, it was a young man in his late twenties, and the young man's face was that of Marrity's long-lost father, just as Marrity remembered him from the age of three.

Marrity had reflexively clasped the young man's hand before he remembered that he hated his father, and a moment later recalled that his father had been killed in 1955—and then he reminded himself that in any case this was Albert Einstein, the original of whom Marrity's father had been a copy deposited on a snowy trail in the Swiss Alps for Lieserl to rescue.

Old and white haired again, Einstein spoke in Marrity's mind, in English. *What seest thou else in the dark backward and abysm of time?*

It was one of Prospero's lines from *The Tempest.*

I need to rescue my daughter, thought Marrity, *from Caliban, the boy you brought back from oblivion.*

This thing of darkness I acknowledge mine, said Einstein. *There are yet missing of your company some few odd lads that you remember not.*

These too were lines of Prospero's.

How can I save my daughter? thought Marrity desperately.

But he blinked, and he was back at the El Mirador Hotel

in Palm Springs on a cool December evening in 1932. Everyone had climbed out of the green-lit pool or hurried out of the dining room and now stood around the cactus garden below the tower, for a young woman was up in the north arch of the tower's belfry, sobbing and waving a revolver that glittered in the last slanting rays of the sun.

Einstein, puffing and sweating in a rumpled white dress shirt, had climbed the three flights of wooden stairs inside the tower and now stepped up at last to the open fourth-floor belfry.

The girl had been looking down at the crowd on the pavement and the grass, but now she turned to look at him. Her fair hair was blowing around her face and her skirt fluttered in the evening breeze.

"You're Albert Einstein," she said.

"Yes," he panted. "Listen to me, you mustn't—"

"You're too late."

And she stepped out through the arch onto the narrow cornice, and leaned backward with her hips against the railing. Then she put the revolver barrel to her temple and pulled the trigger.

As a dozen voices screamed and the girl's body toppled backward, Einstein rushed to the railing and looked down— but he was not looking at the girl's body but at the chair by the pool where he had hung his dinner jacket.

When he spied the jacket, he projected himself to it, and touched the glossy fabric of it and felt under him the canvas straps and the rubber-tipped legs of the chair on the poolside concrete, and from this difference in height between his two points of view, he launched himself out into the timeless state in which lifetimes were streaks across a blank absence.

From this perspective the tower was a wall that extended into the past in one direction and into the future in the other.

In closer focus he could perceive the girl's lifeline curled up the tower stairs and abruptly dispersed at this point.

One or more of the entities that existed on this plane were now clustered around—had through eternity been clustered around—the end of her lifeline. Einstein couldn't help but be overlapped with the alien thing or things, and though he sensed life in the ridged or droning thoughts, and even something like hunger, he had no basis from which to understand them.

Einstein laid his attention across the girl's lifeline at a point *before* the dissolution that was her death, and by drawing on the energy latent in the total vacuum of this place, he was able to pry her lifeline out of the four dimensions it occupied—he hoped, in effect, to break off the section of it that was her death.

But instead, to his horror, her lifeline simply disappeared. The static arrangement of vast arching ropes or sparks didn't include her lifeline now, had never included it.

He recoiled back into sequential time.

Einstein was leaning over the balcony, looking down, but there was no crowd below. There had been no dramatic disruption of this evening, and the people in the pool were splashing around and laughing.

Before he collapsed and retracted the astral projection of himself that was still sitting in the chair by the pool, he stepped out again into the fifth-dimensional perspective, and there was a new feature now in the tower wall as it extended into the future: a kink like a ripple in glass in the arch where he had been leaning over the rail, a lens effect that didn't damp out as it receded into the blur of the future. The burst of vacuum energy he had pricked up here would apparently always occupy this volume of space, in the El Mirador tower's western arch. Mercifully it would be imperceptible and unusable by anyone not astrally occupying two time shells at once and focusing on this place.

He inhaled the projection by the pool. In the twilight nobody noticed Einstein up in the tower, and so he slowly trudged back down the stairs, knowing that he had left a blade, in the space back up there in the belfry, by which anybody could be cut right out of existence.

His mind was numb, thinking over and over again, But I was trying to help her.

Who was she?

Nobody, ever—not even imaginary.

What drove her to suicide?

Nothing that ever happened to anybody.

Beside Marrity, the ghost of Einstein sighed. *These our actors, as I foretold you, were all spirits and are melted into air, into thin air.*

Never born. Derek had never been born either, though he had lived and had children.

Einstein had always avoided the boy Derek, even though—or especially because—the boy was a physical duplicate of himself, created out of excess energy when Einstein had shed fifth-dimensional velocity in returning from 1911 to 1928. Lieserl had eventually adopted the boy from Grete Markstein in 1936, when Derek had been eight years old. By that time Einstein had settled in Princeton, never to return to California.

But Derek visited Einstein, in the Princeton hospital, in April 1955. Einstein was clearly dying then, of a burst aneurysm of the abdominal aorta.

Only days earlier Einstein had met with the Israeli ambassador to the United States and a man from the New York Israeli consulate. The state of Israel was to celebrate its seventh anniversary on April 27, and they feared some attack. Isser Harel, now director general of the Mossad, had not forgotten the water glass with the impossibly young Einstein's fingerprints on it—actually Derek's fingerprints—and wanted once more to ask Einstein about possible tactical uses of time.

Einstein had agreed to discuss it, but then the aorta had burst and he was taken to the hospital.

Derek had got in by claiming to be a son of Einstein's first wife, and after apologizing to the dying old man, he asked Einstein who had been his father and mother.

Einstein simply stared at the young man. "I don't know," he said finally, wearily. "Ask Lieserl. She is the person who found you."

"But I'm related to you," said Derek. He was pleading. "It shows in our faces. I have two children—who were their father's parents?"

"I am watched, all of the time," said Einstein. "The FBI

knows I am having more to tell, because Israel wants to hear it, so obviously. Another group, also, which has followed me into this exile of mine from Europe. I have ways, you do not, of pushing them away from myself." He sighed and closed his eyes. "They all have seen you now, and they want to know who you are. Even what you are. If they know you are no connection with me, you are safe—if you know no answers, you have no object in being questioned. Go home to your children."

Did he arrive home in safety? asked Einstein now, his frail hand barely tangible in Marrity's left hand.

No, thought Marrity bleakly. *No, he never came home to us.*

Oh weh. It was a sigh of despair.

Marrity looked at him, and again it was the dark-haired young man who was identical to Marrity's memories of his father.

Frankie, said this apparition, and Marrity knew that this really was his father, not another appearance of Einstein.

Dad! thought Marrity, squeezing the faintly felt hand in a convulsive grip. *Dad, I'm sorry! What did they do to you, why didn't you ever come back—*

Frankie, said the phantom of his father, *run, don't go to the tower in the desert. I had no birth, but you'll have no birth or death.*

Then Marrity found himself blinking tears out of his eyes and staring only at Lepidopt, who was looking back at him bewilderedly.

Mishal had climbed down off the foot of the bed and stood up to dig cigarettes and a lighter out of his pocket, and Lepidopt freed his hand from Marrity's. He was lighting a cigarette too now. Apparently the séance was over.

"We need some *sayanim,* with a couple of vans or trucks," Mishal was saying to Malk. "We need to get out to that tower, and we've got to bring our whole base; we can't afford to have this"—he gestured at the block and the boxes—"anywhere but with us."

He smiled frostily and added, "And after this is all secure and rolling, make some calls, rent a house somewhere, get a block of sidewalk pulled up and wrapped up tight, and have some unconnected *sayanim* take the sidewalk block to the rented house. Make it look as if all security measures are being taken with it, but use an open line and say a few key words like 'Marrity' and '*katsa*.' Nothing real obvious like 'Mossad' or 'Einstein.' Right?"

"Right," said Lepidopt, edging his way now between the block and the bed. "I trust we won't be putting these decoy *sayanim* in danger, guarding a chunk of sidewalk?"

Mishal waved again at the Chaplin slab and the boxes. "Israel needs this. And needs whatever it is that's in that tower too."

"The El Mirador Hotel is still standing?" said Marrity.

Mishal squinted at him through exhaled smoke. "You had a little séance all your own, didn't you? No, I doubt it is. But its tower is still there."

"Einstein was talking to you," said Marrity. "He told you how his machine works?"

"Yes. He always meant to. We're Israel." To Lepidopt he said, "Get a couple of pieces of glass, and some oil, and put your handprints on them. And some of your hair, you heard all that. *Right now.*" To Malk he said, "And likewise right now we need a couple of *sayanim* to take away the pieces of personalized glass, one up to the top of Mount Wilson and one out to Death Valley." Looking again at Lepidopt, he said, "You're to be ready to make your jump as soon as possible, understood?"

"Understood," said Lepidopt, though Marrity thought he didn't look happy about it.

Twenty-six

Daphne had fallen asleep in her chair in the black tent.

An hour ago Canino had walked around the tent, prodding the draped fabric with something that might have been a broom and calling, "Matt! Go away!" and "Scat, Matt!" Daphne had called out to ask what time it was, just to hear a human voice in reply, but Canino had simply trudged back to the cabin. At least the TV cartoon thing hadn't been on the speaker anymore.

But at some point the music had become louder, waking her up. It was an idiotically upbeat and repetitive melody now, like what a 1950s movie would have as the background theme while the lead couple mugged and clowned in a park.

Daphne stared through the plastic pipe at the city in the valley. There were fewer lights in the darkness now, and she wondered who the drivers were behind the few visible headlights, and what errands had them out at this hour.

Abruptly the whole world flared white, blinding after the

long period of darkness. The momentary glare had been silent, but so startling that it had seemed to crash in her ears.

And then she was in two places at once; her hands were still taped to the chair legs in the rebounding darkness, but she could feel one sheet of oily glass under all her fingertips, and she was sitting in the chair in the tent on the mountain, but she was also looking out through an airy arch of a tower at palm fronds waving in the night breeze.

She knew what had happened—she had caught a painfully bright beam of light from the city below her in the same instant that the lights mounted behind her chair had flashed. And it had apparently broken her mind in two.

The tower seemed to be falling—or else the truck's parking brake had broken, and the truck with the tent on it had rolled off the plateau's edge and was in midair—

Her wrists were taped to the chair, but without moving them she reached out through the tent fabric and across the expanse of gravelly dirt and grabbed the cabin, hard.

Golze's wheelchair lurched when the cabin rocked on its concrete-block foundations, and in the same instant the windows imploded and jets of orange flame burst upward out of the stoves. Golze's free hand clutched the armrest and he yelled, *"Canino, trank her!* Get out there, she's doing this!" He couldn't catch his breath again, and he waved at Fred.

Canino yanked the front door open, hesitated in the sudden bright glare of leaping flames, then hurled himself outside. Old Frank Marrity had dropped his bottle and was struggling to his feet.

"Fred," Golze managed to croak, and when the young man looked at him, Golze pointed to himself and then at the door.

Fred shook his head and dove out after Canino.

Already the cabin was full of red-lit smoke, and Golze didn't have the strength to cough, or even breathe. He began trying, with only one working arm, to lever himself out of the wheelchair so that he could try to crawl to the door. He heard Marrity collide with the door frame as he lurched outside.

Golze could hardly see through the smoke and his steamed glasses, but he could tell that it was a tall woman who appeared out of the smoke at the back of the cabin. She strode behind him, and then he felt the shift of strong hands on the grips of the wheelchair.

He nodded—but the woman began running powerfully forward, pushing him so fast that he was rocked back against the seat, and he was whispering, "No!" The wheelchair was moving at twenty miles per hour when the wheels clanked against the threshold and then spun free in midair.

He flew a good five feet and landed facedown in the gravel with the weight of the wheelchair and Rascasse on top of him.

Rascasse rolled off, and Golze tried to get air into his lungs. His face stung with abrasions and he was sure that several of his ribs were broken, but all his attention was centered on his right hand, which with all his determination he was barely able to move; he forced it to burrow under himself and close on the grip of his Army .45.

He heard a voice that was still recognizably Rascasse's say, "The wheelchair—get it off him, Fred. Right now."

The awkward bulk of the wheelchair was lifted away, and then a brusque hand took hold of his right shoulder and rolled him over on the flinty gravel.

Fred was facing the cabin, and by the orange fire glare Golze was able, even without his glasses, to see the blank expression on the young man's face. As much to change that as for every other reason, Golze tugged the gun free of his waistband, weakly lifted the barrel toward Fred, and pulled the trigger. The jarring explosion hammered his ears and the recoil sent a flash of pain from his wrist to his shoulder.

Fred's boots lifted from the ground and he sat down hard six feet behind where they'd been.

Footsteps scuffed in the dirt, and Golze could hear Canino's voice, though he couldn't make out words. "I told you guys,"

Golze gasped, though probably no one could hear him, "I told you she could do this."

Then Canino had grabbed him by the lapels and pulled him upright, and the pain in his broken left shoulder drove the consciousness out of him.

O ld Frank Marrity stood on the shadowed side of the tent on the truck; the heat of the burning cabin stung his face and hands if he stood anywhere else, and only out of its direct glare could he see what was going on. He had to concentrate to focus his eyes—he had been drinking rum in the cabin, and he was more drunk than he wanted to be.

The Fred fellow was lying on the ground, apparently dead; and Golze, being half-carried and half-dragged toward the truck now by Canino, seemed dead too. Marrity had heard a gunshot over the roar of the fire.

The person who had been Denis Rascasse was moving toward the truck too, behind Canino. The hair was still white and cropped short, but the body in the battered business suit was clearly a woman's now. She stared at the ground as she came through the smoke and orange light, and though her arms and legs swung back and forth, Marrity thought the gravel wasn't disturbed when her feet swept over it.

These are devils, he thought. I should hide up among the rocks, and then hike down to town tomorrow morning.

But I can't hike on this leg, he thought, staring angrily at the tent above him. They can negate Daphne. There's no "psychic link" to get in the way—Charlotte Sinclair made that up so that *she* could be negated instead.

Canino hoisted the limp body of Golze up into the truck cab, then walked back to the truck bed and hopped up onto it; and he saw Marrity crouching in the long shadow of the tent.

"We can fit four in the cab," Canino told him with a grin—his face gleamed with sweat—"since one's a little girl, but you'll have to hang on back here." He reached into the pocket of his jeans and pulled out what proved to be a switchblade knife when the blade sprang out. He disappeared into the tent, and a few moments later emerged again, carrying Daphne. She appeared to be dead too—her head rolled loosely in the crook of his elbow, and her free arm was swinging like a length of rope.

Marrity's breath caught in his throat. They killed her after all! he thought in confusion. That's good, isn't it? My younger self will be able to live without her—

But the sight of her lifeless body in a stranger's arms took him back nineteen years, to the remembered exertions of doing the Heimlich maneuver on a linoleum restaurant floor, finally watching through tears as one of the paramedics carried the body of his daughter away—

Canino laid her carefully on the far side of the truck bed, then hopped down and lifted her. "She's tranked," he called to Marrity. "She'll be out for an hour." He started toward the open passenger-side door, then paused and looked back over his shoulder. "Knock down the tent and toss all the stuff off onto the ground. And find a rope or a cleat or something you'll be able to hang on to—it's gonna be a bumpy ride."

Charlotte and Marrity were lying in darkness in the back of a roaring, rocking van, their ankles attached by cables and a padlock to a ring in the floor by the back doors. Malk was up front driving. The Chaplin slab and the boxed-up glass cylinder and gold wire from Grammar's shed were in another van with Mishal and Lepidopt, along with a bomb that Mishal assured them was powerful enough to completely destroy the entire Einstein machine, Chaplin slab and all.

Ten minutes earlier Charlotte had been sitting beside Frank Marrity on the Wigwam Motel bed, watching through Lepidopt's eyes as he and Malk draped blankets over the rectangular block of cement, looped canvas straps around it, and then taped two Styrofoam heads with toupees on them onto the top edge of it.

"When the vans get here," Lepidopt had told Malk, "we can walk this out to them. Whatever it looks like we're up to, it won't be smuggling a square from the Chinese Theater."

Malk had nodded. "And if somebody shoots at us, they're as likely to hit those guys as us," he said, nodding at the Styrofoam heads.

Lepidopt's glance had gone to the toupees, then resolutely away.

"You don't need a *lot* of yarmulkes," Malk had said.

Then Marrity had leaped up from the bed with a smothered yell. "Daphne is falling!" he had said urgently. "No—it's like on Sunday when she watched that movie—wow, she grabbed some building, and it's burning, completely on fire—" His arm had twitched then, and he'd winced. "And now—I can't sense her at all, she's gone! My God, did they kill her?"

"Gave her a tranquilizer," Mishal had said. "In the arm, from the way you jumped. Whatever the building is that she torched, they'll have to get out of there. They're moving. So are we."

And within minutes the vans had arrived and they were moving.

Marrity had asked why he and Charlotte had to be tied to the floor, but Charlotte had answered him. "None of us are really allies."

"What she said," Malk had agreed, snapping the padlock closed, then slamming the back doors and walking around outside to get into the driver's seat.

The interior of the speeding van smelled of potting soil and flowers, and Marrity guessed it was a florist's van when not commandeered for Mossad use. At least someone had thrown a couple of blankets over the plywood floor. It proved more comfortable just to stretch out and lie down than to try to sit up against the walls with their feet moored to the ring.

For Charlotte's sake as much as his own, Marrity craned his neck to look toward the front; the windshield was just a patch of lighter darkness except when a rushing streetlight lit the arched dust streaks on it, and he could just see the top of Malk's head above the driver's-seat headrest. Marrity and Charlotte were effectively restrained—even if Marrity had stretched, he wouldn't have been able to reach the back of the driver's seat.

In order to whisper, it was easiest to lie facing one another, with their arms around each other to keep from rolling back and forth. Marrity could feel the shape of a revolver against the small of Charlotte's back.

"I hope Daphne will be all right till we get there," whispered Marrity. He realized that he had said this already a few times, and grinned apologetically, though it was too dark in the back of the van for her to see, even if she'd been able to see. "And I hope my breath's not too horrible."

Charlotte kissed his lips lightly. "Your breath smells like Canadian Club," she whispered. "I like it. Daphne's fine. It's you they want to kill, and we won't let them do that." He felt her shiver in his arms. "Maybe they will trade me for her."

"We'll rescue her. And the Mossad will do the time-travel errand you want done."

"Right now they've got a bomb sitting next to that time machine. I'll have to decide when we get there whether or not I trust them to do what that Mishal guy promised. He sort of promised, didn't he?"

Marrity nodded in the rocking darkness. "Sort of," he added.

"I'd have a totally different life. I'd never meet you, or Daphne, and that's sad. I'd probably still be in the air force right now. Well, it was the army, really—INSCOM, Intelligence and Security Command, working originally out of Fort Meade in Maryland, though I was a little kid then. And I won't have been blinded in 1978. And I won't have done—*she* won't, the girl I'll be, won't have any memory of . . . people I've betrayed. I'd kill myself, but all the things I've done would stay done." She exhaled. Her breath smelled like whiskey too.

Marrity brushed her hair with his fingers, feeling the frames of her sunglasses.

She hugged him and pressed her forehead against his collarbone. "Or maybe," she whispered into his shirt, "I'll decide the Mossad can't or won't fix it for me, and just let the Vespers negate me. I'd never have met you then either."

He opened his mouth, but she put a finger on his lips. Pulling her head back and speaking loudly, she asked, "How much longer to Palm Springs?" Marrity could feel her heartbeat through the piece of damp paper against his stomach.

"Forty minutes," said Malk.

Marrity's hand was still in her hair; when she lowered her head, he kissed her on the lips.

"An hour from now we might all be dead," she whispered into his mouth, "or worse." He felt her lips smile under his. "Your heart is going like crazy."

They kissed again, and for a long time there was no more whispering in the back of the van that raced east down the dark 10 freeway.

Lepidopt was driving the other van, and Mishal was in the passenger seat. The taillights of Malk's van seemed motionless a hundred yards ahead in the freeway lane while the world rushed past, whistling in the wind wing by Lepidopt's left hand on the steering wheel.

The van belonged to a *sayan* who ordinarily lived in it, with a cat, and the interior smelled sourly of cat box.

"Whatever happens with this meeting," said Mishal, "this silly proposed trade of girls, you'll follow your orders today—this morning. I'll try to learn something about this singularity in the tower, and if possible I'll relay it over the radio for you to add to your report, but *you* have to use the machine to jump back to 1967. As soon as I've relayed all I can find out, or at the very first sign of any trouble, you *go*. You heard Einstein's ghost say how to do it. Right?"

"Right," said Lepidopt.

"And you've got your, your homing device?"

Mishal was referring to Lepidopt's dried finger, which was still in the Flix chocolate box in his pocket. In 1928 Einstein had been guided to his destination in the past by a bullet shell, which struck Lepidopt as a much more dignified sort of talisman.

"Got it."

"Can you feel your target sites yet, those pieces of glass? They should be set up by now."

Lepidopt tried to stretch his mind outward, past the haze of the whiskey, to a piece of oily glass on Mount Wilson and another in Death Valley. He didn't get any clear impression. "No," he said.

"Well, you probably have to be out of your body to sense them. You can still do an astral projection, I hope! You got good marks for that, in your training."

"I did? I hated it." Lepidopt shifted uncomfortably in the driver's seat at the memory of hovering weightlessly under some ceiling and seeing his limp body slumped on a couch on the other side of a room.

"Assuming it works," Lepidopt said, "do you want me to tell Isser Harel in 1967 that we've agreed to change some part of the past for Charlotte Sinclair, in exchange for her help?"

For a moment Mishal was silent. Then, "The thing the *Zohar* predicted," he said. "The 'knowledge of the precious supernal wisdom.' You want to use *that* to fix some divorce or childhood trauma or something for that woman?" He shook his head. "You don't throw what's precious to dogs."

Lepidopt asked, "What's precious to dogs?" Mishal didn't laugh, and Lepidopt flexed his maimed right hand on the gear-shift. "I'll be changing the past," he said. "From 1967 on."

"Right," said Mishal. "The Yom Kippur War will certainly go differently in the new time line you'll help initiate. A lot of things will."

"I, uh, got married in 1972," said Lepidopt, ashamed to be bringing it up. "My son was born in 1976. He's eleven now."

"That would follow, yes." Mishal sniffed. "I hope I don't smell the way this van does, when I meet these people."

"I wonder—if he'll still be born. That is, if *he'll* still be born. What if something I change—like a whole war— makes my younger self and his wife conceive the boy on a different night? What if the child is a girl, this time around? What if there *is* no child? My younger self in this new time line might die before fathering him."

"Unlikely—especially with you, the elder you, looking out for his safety. You can tell Harel that that's a condition of your cooperation."

"But I can't eliminate the *possibility* of my younger self dying. Much less eliminate the possibility that my son won't be conceived exactly as it happened originally." Lepidopt bared his teeth at the dark freeway lanes under the lightening eastern sky. "The boy I know might turn out never to have existed."

"All of us are at risk," said Mishal. "There might be a war six years from now in which your son will be killed, if you don't do this."

"But if he's killed, he'll at least have *existed*," Lepidopt said, knowing he was pushing a point Mishal considered settled.

"All our sons and daughters," said Mishal sternly, "and wives and parents, are at risk every day. Do you know what this thing in the Sinai desert *is*, at the Rephidim stone, that you're to copy out?" He laughed. "Well no, of course you don't. None of us does. But according to old manuscripts that never made it into the *Sepher ha-Bahir* compilation in the twelfth century, it's a way to travel in all the worlds of the *Sephirot*, not just in four or even five dimensions. It could make this time machine look like the Wright brothers's airplane."

"I see," said Lepidopt.

Mishal waved a hand, acknowledging Lepidopt's previous point. "God won't lose sight of any of us. Not of *us*. Do you think that machine can change God's memory? It would be disrespectful, as well as wrong, to think so."

Can I have that in writing? thought Lepidopt; but he simply kept the gas pedal pressed to the floor and watched the taillights of Malk's van.

Twenty-seven

Old Frank Marrity was glad to see the last of the flatbed truck as it turned left out of the hospital parking lot, heading south, though when its taillights had disappeared down Indian Canyon Drive he could still for a moment see the foolish chair mounted on the back of it.

He had managed to throw the tent and all the electronic equipment off the truck bed, in painful, sweating haste by the glare of the burning cabin, but that damned chair had been bolted to the wood. Canino had tied Golze's wheelchair to it, and Marrity had had to hang on to it, cursing and several times half sliding off the truck altogether during the bumpy half-hour drive down the mountain road to Palm Springs.

He had barely been able to crawl off the truck bed when they had finally stopped here in the hospital parking lot.

The few cars that whispered past now on the street beyond the sidewalk trees still had their headlights on, and the breeze was pleasantly cool, but the sky was already deep blue and in half an hour or so the sun would be rising over the distant Santa Rosa Mountains.

Across a sidewalk and a narrow lawn, the square, four-story tower loomed in gray shadow against the cloudless sky. Peering up at it, he could see a corner of the belfry ceiling through the west-facing arch at the top. The low tile-roofed building at its foot was medical offices now, but the tower had reputedly once been the highest structure in this desert village, the crown of the long-gone El Mirador Hotel.

Three Vespers cars had pulled into the lot ten minutes ago, and Marrity was leaning against the left-rear door of one of them, a brown-and-white Chrysler Fifth Avenue that was brand new but looked very old-fashioned and boxy to him. When will I see Saturns again? he thought. Lexuses? Geos?

The driver's-side door was open and the haggard-looking woman who was apparently Rascasse was sitting in the driver's seat, listening to the multiband radio. She smelled like stale bread this morning.

"We, uh, talked our way into the house," said a voice from the speaker, "and the cement block they had was just a section of sidewalk. Decoy. One of the renters there eventually directed us to a place called the Wigwam Motel, and the people we want had been there but have cleared out. Nothing in the room."

"Okay," said Rascasse in her new contralto voice. "Get here as quickly as you can."

Marrity couldn't see Golze in the passenger seat, but in the predawn quiet he clearly heard his frail voice: "They're working from a mobile base now."

"Indeed," said Rascasse, "and they'll be heading this way." She spoke into the radio again. "Prime."

"Tierce," came a tinny reply from the speaker.

"They're bringing Charlotte here to make the trade. But probably there'll be a vehicle accompanying them, a truck or van, that will be visible to human eyes but not to astral sight—not to my mind. Get—oleander." Marrity saw the old woman lean forward briefly, and then she sat back and went on, "Get the copter here, and have him circle and describe to me all traffic on the streets. Not models, just . . . 'a white van, a blue car ahead of it, a red car passing both of them' . . . like that."

"Right. Later."

The man who had driven up in the Chrysler was pacing the sidewalk a hundred feet away; the other two drivers were still sitting in their cars. Marrity wondered irritably what Vespers men did on their days off. Maybe they never got days off.

Marrity took a deep breath and then spoke. "You don't need to do this negation thing with anybody," he said. "You'll have the machine itself within the hour, and then you'll be able to go back and *fix* things, not just, just—start chronological avalanches! All you've got to do is kill D-Daphne, like you agreed to." He realized he was nodding like a monkey, and made himself stop. "That was part of our agreement, in the boat on the lake."

In this situation, he was certain, he was doing all that remained to be done for poor Daphne. If they killed her, she would at least have had a life; but if they negated her, there would never have been any Daphne Marrity at all. And how much of his own memories, his own *identity,* were tied up with her? He himself would become an entirely different person if she were negated, a person unimaginable to him now.

"We haven't got the machine yet," croaked Golze.

The two Mossad vans were parked in shadow at the end of West Tahquitz Canyon Way, in front of a house that was half hidden behind palm trees and honeysuckle and grapevines. A wrought-iron arch with an unlit lantern hanging from its curlicued peak opened on a stone stairway barely visible in the tree shadows beyond, and to the left Lepidopt could make out the two- or three-story house, with doors and windows deeply inset in thick, pale walls. A mailbox was mounted on one pole of the arch and a plastic rake leaned against the other. Mishal said Einstein had stayed here in 1931 and had hidden attention-deflecting stone amulets in the terraced garden behind the house.

They were seven blocks south of the El Mirador Medical Plaza, about half an hour short of dawn.

During the drive from San Bernardino to Palm Springs, the van had been a moving pocket of warmth and dashboard lights and a pair of glowing cigarettes in the lonely rock-studded hills in the predawn darkness, and the only signs of human habitation in the landscape of jagged ridges and remote, tilted alluvial deltas had been one line of half a dozen trailer trucks pulled off on the shoulder, and the twin red dots of Malk's taillights in the otherwise empty lane ahead. Lepidopt had been glad to turn off the freeway onto State Highway 111 and follow it into the sleeping town of Palm Springs, with its low, plain 1950s-style office buildings, its shops with aluminum foil covering the windows, and its dark ranch houses with gravel yards.

"It's about time to divvy the cargo," said Mishal now, unsnapping his seat belt. "Handcuff Marrity in here with the Einstein machine, where you can blow both of them to smithereens if worse comes to worse. Then you and Bert just circle around town in it, and try to stay in touch with me via the radio."

He tucked the Azden microphone-transmitter into his shirt pocket and clipped the microphone under his collar. The trouble with body microphones was that the crystal-controlled transmitters were as big as a deck of cards, and couldn't transmit farther than a few city blocks at the best of times, and a human body tended to block the radio waves.

"If you can't hear me," said Mishal, "just jump at dawn. You can at least bring Harel the news that the singularity Einstein. *appeared* to refer to *may* exist in that tower. Once you've jumped, all of this"—his wave took in the other van too, with Charlotte and Marrity in it, and all of Palm Springs—"won't ever have happened."

"Different courses for all of us," Lepidopt agreed in a level voice. He thought of being able to swim in the ocean again, and listen to Rimsky-Korsakov again, and then he thought of Louis back in Tel Aviv.

"Arm the thing," said Mishal, opening the passenger-side door. A puff of cool, sage-scented air dispelled the interior smells of cat box and cigarette smoke.

Lepidopt unsnapped his seat belt and stood up in a crouch to shuffle into the back of the van. He switched on the over-head bulb.

The Chaplin handprint slab was now bolted upright next to Einstein's big, dusty glass cylinder, and wires were stapled across the carpeted floor to a yard-wide gold swastika laid flat. On a linoleum counter closer to the back doors were a bottle of brandy, an ashtray already crowded with cigarette butts, and, screwed firmly into the counter, the "pressure-firing device."

This looked vaguely like a small floor jack, but the disk sticking up from one end of it wouldn't support anything—it was the pressure cap that would set off the bomb.

A copper tube—a nonelectric blasting cap—had been crimped onto the nozzle-like opening at the other end of the device, and the blasting cap was connected to a red plastic adapter that was screwed into the threaded cap well of a long brick of tetrytol explosive wrapped in tarry black paper.

A homely looking blue kitchen timer connected a dry-cell battery to a wire that ran into the tetrytol brick through a groove in the plastic adapter. If it came down to it, Lepidopt could either set the timer and run, or just smack the pressure cap.

A four-inch cotter pin was stuck through the barrel of the pressure-firing device, and Lepidopt now carefully pulled it out and laid it on the counter beside the ashtray.

"It's armed," he said.

From the pavement outside the van, Mishal called, "Good. I'll send over Malk and Marrity."

By the dim yellow glow of the overhead bulb, Lepidopt stared at the bomb and the time machine, and he tried to imagine what might go wrong. What if he and Malk and

Marrity were captured, and the bomb didn't work? There
was no bowl of dry macaroni here, but a gun available in an
unexpected place might be just as comforting a backup here
as it had been in the safe-house apartment on La Brea.

S till lying on the blanket-covered plywood floor of the
other van with her arms loosely around Marrity, Charlotte had been alternately looking through the eyes of the
three Mossad men; aside from Marrity's here beside her in
the darkness, there were no other viewpoints within several
hundred feet.

Malk was just sitting in the driver's seat in front of them,
peering into the shadows through the windshield and the
rearview mirrors. Mishal and Lepidopt had been talking
inside the other van, though of course she could not hear
what they had said, and now Mishal had got out and was
walking up toward this van. That other van was more interesting, though, with the Chaplin block and what looked like
a bomb, so she kept on looking through Lepidopt's eyes.

She saw him open a black plastic box and pull a small-
caliber automatic pistol out of the foam-rubber padding inside;
his glance swept the narrow interior of the van, then focused
on a plastic pan full of well-used cat litter in the corner. The
cat box became larger in his perspective as he approached it,
and then she saw his hands push the gun in under the gray
sand. His gaze narrowed a little, as if he were wincing.

Charlotte put her mouth to Marrity's ear. "In the other
van," she whispered, "there's a gun under the sand in the cat
box in the corner." She felt him nod.

"You two awake?" asked Malk as he saw Mishal approaching in the rearview mirror.

"Yes," said Marrity, stretching beside Charlotte. Mishal
was unlocking the back doors, and Marrity kissed Charlotte
quickly in the moment before the doors swung open and the
dawn breeze cooled her face and arms.

Then Mishal was unsnapping the padlock that moored

their ankles to the floor. "I'll be driving this van," he said, "and Charlotte, you'll be sitting up front with me. Frank, you go with Malk to the other one."

Charlotte groped her way forward, found the passenger seat and slid into it. She heard Mishal get in beside her, but she was looking through Marrity's eyes now as he was led to the back of the other van; he stepped up into the back of it, and as Mishal clanked the gearshift she saw Lepidopt handcuff Marrity's left wrist to a spare-tire bracket against the van's left wall, away from the machine and the bomb. She saw Lepidopt smile and say something, and Marrity's vision moved up and down in a nod. And as she felt the van she was in move slowly forward in a tight curve, Marrity's gaze fell on the cat box in the corner of that van.

That's it, she thought, and she let herself switch to Mishal's viewpoint so she could see where they were going.

The blue helicopter was visible in the south now, pursuing its endless rotating figure eight over the city.

"Fourteen minutes till dawn," said Golze.

His wheelchair was stopped on flagstones by the entrance to the clinic building at the foot of the tower. Old Frank Marrity peered at him—the bearded man's face was gray, and sweaty even in the dawn chill, and Marrity wondered if he was putting off taking another shot of morphine in order to stay alert.

I'm in more pain, thought Marrity defiantly, and not just the considerable throbbing ache in my abused leg. After all, I'm going to disappear from here within half an hour, and I don't know whether I'll reappear as a childless married man whose only daughter died ninteteen years ago, or as a total stranger—a stranger who might even have other children! I've had enough of *offspring,* thank you.

Marrity had to step back to make way for an elderly man in a three-piece suit pushing an aluminum walker like, Marrity thought, Sisyphus pushing his boulder. It took nearly a minute for the man to hobble past on his way to the hospital entrance, which was another hundred feet away. Luckily the hospital didn't seem to be very busy yet at this hour.

"You might still get shot, in this fresh time line," Marrity told Golze.

"Go have another drink, hero," said Golze.

Marrity hesitated for a moment, then limped across the grass and the pavement to the car Rascasse sat in.

The driver's-side door was still open, and Rascasse was listening to the radio, which was droning its endless list: ". . . city bus, green station wagon, motorcycle, white van, white van, red car . . ."

"I'm just gonna get—" Marrity began.

"Shut up, you idiot," snapped the Rascasse woman as she lurched forward in the seat. "Prime," she said; "was that two white vans or only one? Repeat it please."

"Tierce," said the voice on the radio, "two white vans, the northern one looks newer. The southern one just turned east on Alejo, the other is continuing north on Indian Canyon, toward you."

"Curare," said Rascasse. She adjusted something on the radio, and then went on, "Keep that eastbound van in sight."

"Got it." The radio clicked into silence at last.

Rascasse tapped the horn ring, and the man who had been pacing the street sidewalk came sprinting back to the brown-and-white Chrysler.

"You're looking for a white van," Rascasse told him, "now it's on Alejo, moving east. Take all three cars, and let the helicopter tell you where it is. And capture it and bring it here."

"—the bottle," said Marrity, opening the back door. The rum bottle was still on the backseat, and he picked it up.

"I don't sense any second van," said Rascasse, apparently to herself. "It must be them, and Einstein's time machine as well." She frowned back at him. "Don't take the bottle with you. Drink some here."

Rascasse stepped out of the car and stood up, and apparently caught Golze's eye, for she just raised a thumb and nodded. Marrity noticed that her feet seemed to slide slightly on the asphalt, like the bottom edge of a beaded curtain that just touches the floor.

Nine minutes till dawn," said Malk, rolling one hand on the steering wheel to glance at his watch. The ridgeline of the Santa Rosa Mountains to their right shone white with the imminent sun.

The van's windows were rolled down, and the breeze cooled Lepidopt's sweaty face. The soles of his bare feet were picking up grit from the van floor.

"Mishal will let us know when he's ready to go," he said. Assuming we can pick up his radio signal, he thought. And even if he does tell me to wait for some kind of report on the singularity, I doubt that'll take long. I suppose Mishal isn't too worried about getting killed here, since this morning's events are slated never to have happened. Probably within this next half hour I'll be doing the astral projection trick, and then—as if that weren't bad enough—jumping right out of 1987.

He thought of his first parachute jump, in 1965, from an old two-engine British Dakota circling over a patch of the Negev desert south of Beersheba—stepping out of the plane into nothing. The rip cord had been pulled automatically; and this time the rip cord would be his own dried finger, which was now under his shirt, taped against his sweaty chest.

He yawned, but not from tiredness.

"You okay back there?" called Malk.

"So far so good," came Marrity's voice from the back of the van.

"Stay away from La Bamba."

"I can't even reach it from here. Okay if I smoke?"

"Sure, fire won't hurt anything."

Malk had been keeping the van in the right lane, and now he said, "Fast boy coming up on the left." He had made a dozen similar remarks on the surrounding traffic during the last twenty minutes. Lepidopt once again braced his bare feet.

Then the white compact in front of them braked sharply and another car was braking right next to Malk's head in the left lane. As Lepidopt levered himself to his feet, he heard a pair of loud pops and saw dust spray from two spots on the asphalt ahead.

The van was shuddering to a halt. In the back of it, Lepidopt placed his bare feet on the gold swastika and leaned forward to press his hands into the handprints in the Chaplin slab.

Marrity was staring at him wide-eyed.

Two car doors slammed outside, and then a man's voice called, "Step out of the van, everybody."

Malk whispered, "Jump, goddammit!" and then said loudly, "We have a bomb aboard that will wreck your cars too. Dead-man switch. Nobody's getting out."

Lepidopt's heart was pounding in his chest. Almost more clearly than he could see the scrawls in the cement slab in front of his eyes, he could see Louis's face, and the boy seemed to be staring at him earnestly, as he had so often in the past.

"One of us will ride with you," said the voice outside.

"Nope," said Malk. "Bomb."

"Then we escort you, two of us behind and one leading. If this isn't acceptable, I advise you to detonate your bomb."

"We'll go with you," said Malk. The car doors slammed again, and then the van was moving forward. After a moment Lepidopt could hear the turn-signal indicator clicking.

"Are you still there?" asked Malk furiously. "Marrity, is he still there?"

"I'm here," said Lepidopt, blinking sweat out of his eyes.

"Doesn't it work? If it—"

"I don't know if it works or not," said Lepidopt. The Chaplin handprints felt as slick as the oiled glass had last night. "I haven't stepped out of my body yet."

"Well *step out,* man! We're captured!"

"I need to," began Lepidopt. Speaking words was like pushing broken teeth out of his mouth. "Think about it—a little more."

The van sped up, swinging the lightbulb overhead. "Then don't jump," said Malk hoarsely, "listen, scratch that altogether. Just hit the bomb." The van slowed, and again Lepidopt heard the turn signal. "Blow us up, Oren! We can't let these people get hold of Einstein's machine!"

"I'll jump!" shouted Lepidopt angrily. "Or I'll blow us up. But—not this *second*."

Sunlight gleamed on the white weather vane and the zigzag patterns of blue and yellow tiles on the pyramid roof of the tower.

Aryeh Mishal stepped out of the van that he had parked in the hospital lot, walked around to the other side and took Charlotte's elbow as she slid down from the seat to the pavement. Momentarily covered by Charlotte and the van, Mishal reached into his shirt pocket and switched on the transmitter.

"I guess the time machine didn't work?" she said. Her expression was blank, her eyes hidden behind her constant sunglasses.

"He's waiting in case I have a report about the thing in the tower," said Mishal with a smile. "In the meantime, we might as well walk through this exchange." He let go of her elbow. "Let's keep our hands spread and empty." They stepped out from behind the van.

But we shouldn't still be here! thought Mishal tensely as he and Charlotte began walking toward the tower with their hands open and held slightly away from their sides. God knows what I'd be doing right now if Lepidopt had delivered his message to Harel in 1967 and got the inscription from the Rephidim stone—but I wouldn't be doing *this*.

It didn't work, he thought as he stepped slowly across the painted white lines on the asphalt. Or this Vespers crowd caught them—no, I'd have heard the explosion in this quiet morning air, even a mile or two away.

Squinting ahead, he could see figures in the shade under a trellis by the entryway of the building below the tower—a bearded man in a wheelchair, and a white-haired man holding a little girl's limp body in his arms, and another man or two in the shadows behind them. They were about fifty feet away, with a curb and a couple of olive trees on a strip of lawn in between. None of them looked particularly out of place in this hospital setting; as he and Charlotte slowly walked closer, Mishal saw two white-clad nurses walk unconcerned right past the group.

Mishal smiled sideways at Charlotte so that his mouth was over the microphone in his shirt collar. "Jump," he said, "or run back to L.A."

She nodded. "You said it."

The man carrying the limp girl stepped forward out of the trellis shadow into the gathering daylight, and then paused.

Mishal and Charlotte stopped. "I think I go on from here alone," said Charlotte.

"I guess you do," Mishal said. "Uh—good luck."

"You too." She smiled bleakly at him, then turned toward the tower and resumed the careful pace.

Mishal heard several vehicles bouncing up the driveway into the lot a dozen yards behind him, and he slowly turned his head; and suddenly his chest was cold and empty, for the three compact cars turning into the lot were clearly escorting the familiar florist's van. Mishal could see Malk's stark face behind the windshield.

A man in a sport coat and jeans got out of one of the escorting cars and pointed to an empty parking space directly in line with the lot entrance; and Malk drove the van ahead, into that space.

Two of the escort cars pulled into the parking spaces on either side of the van, and a driver got out of each and simply stood by his car, watching the van. The third car carefully backed up to block the van from behind.

Mishal stood still, isolated on the pavement between the cars and the people at the clinic entry. His hands were still empty, but he was intensely aware of the gun under his jacket.

Though his left wrist was handcuffed to the spare-tire rack, Marrity could lean past the trembling, barefoot Lepidopt and see out through the front windshield, and the cigarette smoke caught in his throat at the sight of a white-haired man carrying Daphne's limp body across a sidewalk toward Charlotte, who was slowly walking to meet him. Marrity could only see Charlotte's back.

"I don't think I can move without getting shot from both sides," said Malk tensely from the front seat. "Oren, *will* you *jump?*"

Marrity stepped back, put his cigarette in his mouth, then knelt and thrust his right hand into the cat box. He got hold of the gun and lifted it out, shaking sand off it.

He pointed it squarely at the big glass cylinder, then spoke around the cigarette. "Hey."

Lepidopt turned his haggard face to him, and his eyebrows went up. "What are *you* going to do?" he asked.

"I'm going to wreck your time machine unless you uncuff me and let me go to Daphne."

"They'll just shoot you if you step out," said Malk. Marrity could see his narrowed eyes in the rearview mirror. "They *want* to shoot you, remember? But you're safe in here, they don't want to risk damaging the machine. Let Mishal get your girl. As long as you're in here, she's safe."

Marrity was shaking, and he forced his hand to hold the gun steady. "How's this trade supposed to work?" he demanded. "Look at them, there's nobody to carry Daphne back here! Obviously she can't *walk!*"

Smoke stung his eyes, but he didn't have a hand free to take the cigarette, and he didn't really dare spit it out in a confined space with a bomb.

"Mishal can—" began Malk.

"I'll shoot your damn machine, I swear. Uncuff me. They want the machine way more than they want Daphne. They won't start shooting till they're sure they can get it."

"Shit," burst out Malk, "uncuff him, let him get out of here, take his chances—you're going to *have* to hit the bomb, Oren. Or I will, even if they shoot me as I get up to do it. Marrity, you can leave by the passenger-side door." Marrity saw Malk's profile as he said out the driver's-side window, "We're letting our hostage go. He's a civilian, and that's his daughter over there, the little girl. If you kill him or take him out of our sight, we'll blow up the machine. Are we clear?" Marrity met his eyes in the rearview mirror, and Malk said to him, "Yes. Go. Get well clear of this van, if you can."

Marrity kept the gun trained on the glass cylinder as Lepidopt stepped barefoot away from the Chaplin slab and dug in his pocket for the keys; then he crouched and opened the cuff from around Marrity's left wrist.

"Thanks," said Marrity. He crushed his cigarette out in the ashtray on the counter, carefully avoiding touching the bomb mechanism, then hurried past the cylinder and the Chaplin slab to the front seats.

"Leave the gun, for God's sake!" whispered Malk. "And move slow!"

Marrity hesitated, then pulled up his pants leg with his left hand and tucked the gun partway down inside his sock. With both hands he tugged the elastic sock all the way up over the bulk and pulled his pants cuff down over it.

He grinned nervously up at Malk, who just shook his head.

"Nobody survives this, I guess," Malk said.

Marrity levered open the door and slowly stepped down. Immediately two of the men who had captured the van were beside him, gripping his upper arms tightly. They marched him a few steps away from the van and toward the tower, then halted, clearly not having any idea what to do with him. What had been predawn dimness was now long streaks of blue shadow across the parking lot. The air was chilly on Marrity's damp shirt.

Charlotte's straight back was still moving away, and the man carrying Daphne was still advancing toward her— Marrity could see that Daphne was struggling weakly in his arms—and now Charlotte called out, "We'll meet in the middle. You put her down there, and take me."

Marrity started forward, and was yanked back by the two men holding his arms.

"I'm getting my daughter," he told them, "since she can't walk. Come along if you want, but I'm going to her."

"You stay here," said the young man on his right, sounding nervous. "Somebody will fetch her."

Marrity just leaned forward with all his weight, and his captors took an involuntary step forward to catch their balance.

"I'm the one who'll fetch her," Marrity said.

"Let him go," said the man on Marrity's left, "they can all see him. We're supposed to be watching the van, anyway."

"Okay." The other man began patting Marrity's shirt and pants, but his companion said, "They'll have frisked him. Come on."

As they stepped away behind him, Marrity began cautiously walking toward where Charlotte and the man carrying Daphne were about to meet, and he hoped the bulge on his ankle wasn't conspicuous. His hands were raised.

Charlotte stopped when she was facing the white-haired man, and Marrity heard him say, "Good to see you again, sweetie!" as he crouched and carefully set Daphne down in a sitting position on the dew-dark asphalt; and Daphne braced herself with her hands to stay upright, and looked around, blinking.

"I've got her, Charlotte," Marrity called, stepping forward more briskly, his hands still up. He hoped to get Charlotte as well as Daphne out of this, though he had no idea how to accomplish it.

Charlotte looked back over her shoulder in evident alarm. "Frank!" she said. "How the—oh God—be very careful." The man who had been carrying Daphne took Charlotte's arm and led her off to the north, to Marrity's left.

"Daddy?" said Daphne, raising her knees as if to get to her feet.

Marrity was just shuffling toward her around one of the olive trees on the strip of grass when, ten yards behind Daphne and to the right of her, a figure stepped forward out of the shadow of the trellis. Marrity recognized the twisted face—it was the old man he had thought was his father, and who turned out to be his own shameful self. Then Marrity saw that the old man was raising a gun, and that it was pointed at Daphne.

Marrity's left hand was snatching up his cuff even as he yanked his knee up, and his right hand pulled the gun from his sock as the old man's first shot exploded a patch of asphalt a foot away from Daphne's hand and rang away to Marrity's left in ricochet.

And then Marrity had put the front sight of his little automatic on the old man's torso and he was pulling the trigger over and over again as the gun thudded against his abraded palm and the spent shells spun away to the side, and he was killing his own cowardice as much as he was protecting Daphne, and at last in the ringing silence he was just standing there in the chilly breeze tugging at the unyielding trigger. The slide was locked back, the gun emptied.

Abruptly a hard impact to his left shoulder spun Marrity around, and in the moment before four more rapid-fire shots punched into his chest and abdomen and flung him back against the olive tree, he saw the white-haired man who had carried Daphne squinting at him over the barrel of a revolver. Another rending shot to the abdomen doubled Marrity over and he pitched to the grass, rolling onto his back and then lying still.

Canino had violently pushed Charlotte ahead when he turned to face Marrity, and with no eyes looking at her, she stumbled and went to her knees on the asphalt as, through Canino's eyes, she watched Frank Marrity hammered to the ground beyond the jumping barrel of the .45 revolver.

Even before Canino had fired all six shots, she had reached around to the back of her waistband and snatched out her .38 and cocked it. And she was aiming it toward where Canino stood, so that when he turned his gaze toward her she only had to move the revolver slightly to see right down the barrel of it, and then she pulled the trigger.

Canino's halved viewpoint showed a fast spin of sky and parked cars and then was gone.

The parking lot echoed now with screams and running footsteps, and the only steady viewpoint Charlotte could fix on showed Daphne sobbing and still trying to get to her feet out in the middle of the pavement. Charlotte could see herself crouched beyond the girl, and so she stood up and sprinted forward.

"The two Frank Marritys are dead," came Rascasse's oddly high-pitched shout from up high—he must be in the tower, Charlotte thought as she ran. "Get hold of Daphne," the shrill voice went on loudly, "hold her, don't let her get hurt!"

Charlotte grabbed Daphne under the arms and yanked her upright, and she was sure now that the helpful gaze that was letting her see what she was doing was Mishal's—he had moved off to the south side of the parking lot, and nobody else had gone that way.

By Mishal's field of vision, she began dragging Daphne back toward the two Mossad vans, and she tried to hold Daphne to the other side as they neared the strip of grass where Frank Marrity's blood-splashed body lay—but now Mishal was seeing her and Daphne over the lined-up back and front sights of a pistol.

The stubby front sight edged down and to the right and centered on Daphne's chest.

Charlotte spun to block it, and the gun barrel wavered, and then Daphne's brown-haired head was visible by Charlotte's waist, and the barrel dove that way. Charlotte grabbed Daphne in a bear hug, turning so that Mishal could see only Charlotte's back. You'll have to shoot her right through me, Charlotte thought dizzily.

And he evidently decided to; the front and back sights lined up again, centered this time on the small of Charlotte's back, when several more shots concussed the dawn air—and Charlotte was still standing, unhurt—and through Mishal's eyes she saw the gun barrel disappear, replaced by a rapidly expanding view of damp pavement.

Twenty-eight

F rank Marrity's vision had narrowed as if he were looking down a tunnel at the distant morning world. He was aware of his right hand, and he made its fingers pry up the blood-soaked edge of his pants pocket and slide in.

His whole torso was a glass wrapped in a napkin and then stomped—the pieces were still loosely held together, but broken beyond hope of repair. Blood bubbled from his lips and he couldn't move anything in his shattered chest to get air in or out. Dimly he realized that he was drowning in his own blood, and he could feel arterial blood surging out through the rips in his belly.

His hand came back out of his pocket, clutching the crumpled Einstein envelope and the chip from the Chaplin slab. He managed to raise his forearm straight up, and then topple it the other way, toward his face; and he licked the Einstein envelope and clutched the chip of cement in his wet fist, and he stared up at bright spatters of his blood on the trunk of the olive tree.

I'm all the way up there, he thought dimly, four or five feet off the ground, and I'm way down here too.

The fact of dying made it easy for him to step out of his body.

And though the physical contacts with Einstein and Chaplin didn't summon those ghosts again, the contacts did tug Marrity's disembodied self in the direction of those specific moments in the past, and amplified the effects of the bloodstains in freeing it from strictly sequential time.

He could see the parking lot at some distance, as if below, though there was no up and down in this non-space. His body was the end-point in a line that trailed out of one of the vans. In their entries and exits the cars and vans made a static tangle of intersecting metal tubes in the lot, looking more like an air-conditioning system on the roof of a big building than anything else, but it was all receding as his focus expanded.

Arcs like jet contrails spanned the blank nothingness out here, and he knew they were lifelines. He could see his own, which ended in an exploded-looking rope-end very nearby, and he could see two others, at the distance of a few seconds in the direction of the past, which also ended in ragged bursts. Something native to this non-space was clinging—had always clung—to those ragged lifeline ends, and Marrity's attention was overlapping the thing. It was in some sense alive, and Marrity hoped that his own extended viewpoint was not a result of his sharing in the alien thing's consumption of the two recently ended lives.

Parallel with his viewpoint he could perceive Daphne's lifeline, and he found that his attention extended to it. And her attention extended to his—closer to her lifeline he could feel her awareness of him. In a point that had no location in space or time, they clung wordlessly to each other.

What Einstein had done with the lifeline of the suicide in the tower in 1932, Marrity was trying to do in reverse with Daphne. Einstein had pried the woman's lifeline up out of the four-dimensional fabric, and Marrity was now blocking Daphne's lifeline from moving in that extradimensional direction. In this timeless view he had always been here blocking it.

Their linked attentions amplified each other, occupied a wider focus—and Marrity was aware of a vast wall, or shear, or towering gap in the direction that was future. It was not just the ends of lifelines—it seemed to eclipse all lifelines, and whatever it was, it was no more than the distance of two minutes away.

Marrity hoped their attentions would widen in a perpendicular direction to get them "over the top" of it—and he tried to convey *Climb, climb!* to Daphne, and he projected the image of an airplane taking off on a short runway, desperately clawing the air to get altitude before it reached the boundary of trees.

Together, boosting each other, their attentions soared until even the woven lifelines were far away, and the world itself was just a far-ranging helix around the curving pillar of the sun, and then in spite of their tininess they even glimpsed the vast dazzling crown or blazing flower of galaxies moving apart through space that uncurled around them—

Their attentions fled, recoiled, narrowed sharply toward their little world again, like a rocket that comes back down only after the world has turned all the way around under it.

In the sunlit tower, the woman who was Rascasse projected her attention to the oiled glass that lay on the backseat of one of the cars in the lot below, and somehow for a moment it seemed to be a dinner jacket draped over a chair by a swimming pool at twilight. But she concentrated, and when she could feel the slick glass under her fingers as well as the tower's gritty cornice railing, and smell the car's upholstery as clearly as she smelled the morning breeze, she stepped back, out of her body, into the volume of space Einstein had been occupying in 1932.

And in the wall that was the tower extending in both directions through time, she could see the persistent ripple where Einstein had gathered up the vacuum energy, for God knew what purpose.

The hungry denizens of this state were present very close by, attached to the several newly chopped-off lifelines—this time Rascasse didn't need to kill anybody to pay her way onto the freeway. She let her attention overlap theirs.

On this bigger scale, she perceived the lifelines that stood out like comets in this non-sky, and Daphne's was there.

Rascasse's attention extended in the direction of Daphne's lifeline, but somehow Frank Marrity blocked her way, even though Marrity was dead. Both versions of Marrity were dead! Her father had somehow blocked Daphne's lifeline with his identity, so that focusing on her simply deflected Rascasse into the past direction, to where Marrity's lifeline hung truncated.

Rascasse became aware of something like a cliff, or static waterfall, in the future direction, and all perceptible lifelines disappeared from view where they met it. It was only seconds distant, and in panic she fell back into her four-dimensional body.

She was draped like a towel over the railing, and had to thrash and flail her limbs to get upright again.

M ishal's down," yelled Malk. He reached his right arm across and fired two shots out the open van window and then opened the door and leaped out. Lepidopt heard him yell, "Blow it up!" as he scrambled away.

From the back of the van, Lepidopt peered through the windshield and gritted his teeth. Charlotte was rapidly dragging the Daphne girl in this direction, though it was a wonder nobody had shot her yet, and beyond her he could see two sprawled bodies, Marrity's on the grass straight ahead and Mishal's on the pavement off to the right.

Do it, he told himself.

Lepidopt tore open his shirt and yanked off the tape that held his dried finger against his skin, and he threw the tape with the finger still clinging to it into the far corner.

We *did* win the Yom Kippur War, he thought, even without help from the future.

He turned to the ashtray and quickly picked up Marrity's recently crushed-out Dunhill filter, and he gripped it between the first two fingers of his left hand as he positioned his bare feet on the gold swastika, pressed his hands into the sweaty Chaplin handprints, and projected his consciousness out to the beacons on Mount Wilson and in Death Valley.

Two different breezes were whistling in his ears, and he smelled pine and weathered wood, and he felt a faint electric tingle in the soles of his bare feet—

For a moment it was the remembered out-of-body weightlessness, and he choked with vertigo—but then he was spinning down through darkness, and the cigarette filter between his fingers was vibrating as if he were dragging it fast along a finely corrugated wall, and he let himself step gratefully back into his body as a gust of energy whipped past him and rushed away downward.

He was still in the van, and in the first instant, he thought the bomb had gone off—a man holding a set of keys was knocked off his feet and the sand in the cat box in the corner was blown up against the van wall. The lightbulb overhead was swinging back and forth.

"What the hell was that?" snapped Malk from the driver's seat, his voice sounding strained to the breaking point. "The blasting cap?"

Lepidopt noted that Malk was still in the front seat. He had not yet got out of the van.

The man with the keys sat up on the van floor and blinked up at Lepidopt. Lepidopt stared down at him and dizzily recognized his own two-minutes-younger self.

A single infant wailed on the floor by the back doors, and both of them jumped and stared at it. As he instinctively started toward it, Lepidopt noted wispy dark hair, and little fists and feet waving—

I can't get it out of the field in time, he thought, and even as he reached for the baby—the infant duplicate of himself—it winked out of existence.

At some point Malk had turned around in the driver's seat, and now his eyes were wide at the sight of the two identical Oren Lepidopts.

In the still quiet dawn air Lepidopt heard Charlotte Sinclair, outside, say, "Frank! How the—oh God—be very careful."

While Malk and Lepidopt's own younger self gaped at him, Lepidopt twisted the dial on the kitchen timer beside the bomb. "One minute," he said. "We've got to get out of here."

The other Lepidopt scrambled up from the floor. "Because of Louis?" he asked.

"Because of everybody," Lepidopt told him.

Malk was trying to say something, but Lepidopt cut him off with a wave as he slid between the front seats and grabbed the passenger-side door handle. "Later. Fifty-six seconds."

At that moment the morning stillness was shaken by rapid-fire shooting, and the two Vespers men who had been watching the van whirled to look back toward the tower.

Frank Marrity was standing beside an olive tree and emptying his pistol into his older self.

Lepidopt flung himself out of the passenger-side door and, braced against the flanking car, aimed his .22 automatic across the parking lot at the head of the white-haired man who had stepped away to the left with Charlotte, and as the man shoved Charlotte away and drew his big revolver, Lepidopt shot him through the head.

The two Vespers men only a few yards away spun at the sound of the shot, and one of them managed to fire twice before they were punched backward by several fast shots from the driver's side of the van; one sat down hard and then tipped over, but the other fired once more before Lepidopt put a final bullet into his forehead.

Lepidopt was suddenly dizzy, and he thought he knew why. Here it ends, he thought. *Baruch Dayan Emet,* Blessed is the Righteous Judge.

Civilians were screaming and running, and Lepidopt hoped they were running away from this area, not into it. He shook his head to clear it and shifted his bare feet on the asphalt, making himself scan the scene over the barrel of his gun.

Marrity was crouched over Daphne out in the middle of the pavement, and Charlotte was hurrying toward them from the left; Mishal was running up to them too, from the right, and he was pointing a gun at them.

He can't let the Vespers have Daphne and her father both, Lepidopt realized. *He's got to kill Daphne.* Lepidopt remembered the Queen albums in the little girl's bedroom.

"Get hold of Daphne!" yelled an old woman from up in the tower belfry. "Don't let her get hurt!"

Mishal fired once, but he was running and the bullet struck beside Daphne's knee.

Charlotte paused, raised a revolver and yelled, "Mishal!" and when the old *katsa* glanced at her, she shot him in the face.

Lepidopt found that he was looking at Charlotte over the sights of his own gun, and even as his finger found the trigger, she had turned and pointed her own gun unerringly straight at him.

He lowered the barrel, perhaps simply too tired to shoot her—and then a shot from the portico beyond her clubbed him in the chest, and he rocked and knelt down, the gun spilling from his four-fingered right hand onto the pavement.

Louis, he thought—this disobedience has been for you.

Looking up from under his eyebrows, he saw Charlotte aim at the portico and fire several times at a wheelchair that jerked and jiggled under the impacts, and then she and Marrity were running this way, half-carrying and half-marching Daphne.

When they were still a couple of yards away, Charlotte jerked in evident surprise, then released Daphne's arm and reached over her to shove Marrity's head down, even as a bullet punched the pavement in front of him.

"Denis." Charlotte's breathless gasp was almost a sob.

She turned back toward the tower and aimed her revolver at the figure silhouetted up there in the western belfry arch.

For a moment neither she nor the figure in the tower moved.

Then they both fired at the same time, but though Charlotte remained standing while a ricochet spanged away next to her foot, the old woman flapped like a sail, then rolled over the cornice railing and drifted down through the slanted sunlight until she got tangled in the upper branches of one of the olive trees.

Lepidopt's sight was dimming, but he could see Malk crouching next to him. "Your other self caught it in that first exchange," Malk said. "I just pulled him inside the van. He's dying."

"I could tell," said Lepidopt. "So am I." He looked at his watch. "Fifteen seconds. Go."

"Right." Malk stood up.

Distantly he heard Charlotte call, "It wasn't me who shot you!"

Lepidopt managed a wave in acknowledgment before darkness took him.

M alk bellowed, "Bomb, everybody get back!" And then Marrity simply picked Daphne up in his arms and jogged after Charlotte and Malk to the florist's van, which was parked several spaces south of the van that was evidently about to explode.

He felt ready to vomit from tension and stark immediate memories, and he was anxious about Daphne, but every exertion was a physical pleasure; when Malk held the passenger door open, he bounded up into the van with Daphne still in his arms, and he stretched to step into the back of the van and lay her down on the carpet he and Charlotte had so recently lain on. His lungs pumped fresh air in and out, and his arms weren't fatigued from carrying Daphne, and he could still remember lying shattered and dying under the bloody olive tree, only moments ago.

Charlotte and Malk were in the front seats, and Malk had started the van and was backing out of the parking space.

"We went far up, didn't we, Dad?" said Daphne softly.

"Yes," he told her.

The van was gunning south through the parking lot, and Marrity put out a hand to brace himself on the floor.

"And we didn't come back down to exactly the same world, did we?"

The floor shivered under them as a jarring *boom* shook the air. The van kept speeding south through the lot.

"While we were up there," said Marrity, and he realized he was talking too loudly because of the ringing in his ears, "somebody changed the events under us," he finished more quietly.

They both jumped when something banged against the van roof, denting it, and a few moments later Malk made a left turn around a corner and braked to a halt.

"Out, all of you, *now*." His face was stiff in the rearview mirror, and his voice had the harshness of a man fighting back tears. "I've got to go back there before police get here."

Charlotte hopped out and took Daphne from Marrity.

"Go back why?" asked Marrity as he got out and closed the door.

Malk called, "To get your old body, mainly," and then the van sped off and made a left turn around the other side of the clinic building.

Charlotte and Daphne sat down on a curb, and after a dizzy moment Marrity let himself collapse beside Daphne. "We've got to get out of here," he said breathlessly.

He tried to focus his eyes on the sunlit palm trees and parked cars at this far south end of the parking lot.

"I—" he began, then cleared his throat. "I guess we walk to a gas station," he said. "Find a pay phone, call a taxi? Can't stay here." He looked at Daphne. "Can you walk, Daph? I can carry you. I could carry two girls your size."

"I can walk," said Daphne. "Slow."

The three of them got to their feet and began trudging across the asphalt. Where it ended they strode over a grassy hump to the sidewalk, and then slowly made their way east on Tacheva Way, in the opposite direction from Indian Canyon Drive. Marrity had to squint against the rising sun, but the breeze was still cool.

"Your old body," said Daphne.

"It's like the initials Moira and I carved in the Kaleidoscope Shed," Marrity told her. "I'll explain it when we, I don't know, get something to eat."

Sirens wailed from south to north behind them—lots of sirens, and under them the roar of big engines throttled wide open. None of the three looked back.

Then to Marrity's surprise his arms and legs were trembling, and he clenched his teeth to keep them from chattering. He sat down on the sidewalk and then just huddled there, hugging himself and breathing deeply. He realized that he still had the gun he'd taken from the cat box, jabbing him painfully now behind his belt buckle. "S-sorry," he said. "I'm okay, just—"

Daphne and Charlotte were both crouched beside him.

"It's only delayed reaction," said Charlotte.

Daphne pushed his sweaty hair back from his forehead. "You've had—terrible things, Dad," she said, and Marrity was belatedly appalled to realize that she must have shared his experiences of killing and being killed.

Daphne might have sensed his sudden guilt, for she draped one arm over her father's shoulders and the other over Charlotte's.

Charlotte took off her sunglasses, and Marrity saw her eyes meet Daphne's when Daphne looked at her. "So have you, kid," Charlotte said.

"I only had a couple of bad times," said Daphne. "And like you said, Dad, none of them tried to hurt me." Marrity felt her shudder. "But then everybody killed everybody."

"I think I'll be able to get up in a minute," said Marrity. I wonder if any bars are open yet, he thought. I could use a fast glass of scotch—and then he remembered the old man he had shot and shot and shot, actually less than five minutes ago. I guess a cigarette would do, he thought cautiously. We can get a pack when we find a gas station and a pay phone.

"I should call the college again," he said, just to break the silence, "there's no way I'll be teaching Twain to Modern today. Excuse me, Daph," he added, and he got shakily to his feet and brushed off the seat of his pants. "Three days now I won't get paid for."

"And our truck might be stolen," said Daphne, straightening up with Charlotte's help. "But there's still gold in Grammar's shed."

That's right, thought Marrity numbly, our truck. God knows if it's still on that street south of Highland where I left it yesterday morning.

"Well no, Daph," he said. "They took the gold. It was in that van back there, that blew up."

"Oh. So—we're just left with what we're left with?"

"That's it," said Charlotte. Marrity was looking at her, and so she put her sunglasses back on, but not before he had seen a glitter of tears in her eyes. To Marrity she said, "None of us got our new lives. The old you, Lepidopt, Paul Golze, me. 'Nor all your piety nor wit / Shall lure it back to cancel half a line, / Nor all your tears wash out a word of it.' " She ran her fingers through her dark hair. "There's an old letter I guess I'll want you to read for me sometime," she said. "From a, an old boyfriend I—did wrong to."

"Okay," said Marrity. He started forward down the sidewalk, and the other two followed. "At least *we* still *have* lives." He breathed in and out deeply, still savoring it.

"And tears," added Daphne, "even if they don't wash away anything."

Epilogue
Green Pastures

. . . to sigh
To th' winds, whose pity, sighing back
   again,
Did us but loving wrong.

—WILLIAM SHAKESPEARE, *THE TEMPEST*

Juniper and cypress trees, tall and shaggy with age, threw shadows on the flat stones set in rows across Lawn S. The faucets sticking up out of the grass all had signs on them that said *Don't Drink This Water,* and steel disks set flush with the grass were vases for flowers when lifted out and inverted.

Marrity had been surprised to learn that Grammar had joined the Episcopal church a few years before her death, but it was an Episcopal priest who was now speaking beside her casket at Mountain View Cemetery in Pasadena. A dozen elderly people Marrity didn't know sat under a wheeled green awning near the grave, on folding chairs made more dignified by green velour slipcovers. Marrity and Daphne and Charlotte stood off to the side, with Bennett and Moira.

Strips of livid green AstroTurf were laid around all four sides of the open grave, and Grammar's turquoise fiberglass casket rested on two aluminum bars above the "vault," a copper-painted cement box that the casket would fit into.

Marrity had noticed the domed lid of the vault lying on the grass a dozen feet away. The vault itself was suspended in the top of the open grave on steel saddle bars.

At the mortuary on California Street, the priest had given a generic sort of eulogy for Lisa Marrity—"our sister Lisa, loving wife, mother, and grandmother"—and had then played a tape of a woman singing "On Eagles' Wings" on a portable stereo. Now at the graveside he began, inevitably, to recite the Twenty-third Psalm.

Out among the older upright gravestones at the older southwest end of the cemetery, Marrity had seen a solitary walking man pause to look toward the funeral party, and Marrity had thought it might be Bert Malk, but the man had turned and begun trudging away. Marrity had glanced at Charlotte, who would of course have seen the man too, and she had shrugged.

It occurred to Marrity that Malk must have succeeded in taking the body of Marrity's older self away from the El Mirador Medical Plaza yesterday morning. If he had not, and the police had found a dead body with the fingerprints of Francis Thomas Marrity, they would probably have come around to tell the next of kin by now. Bennett and Moira had had plenty of questions this morning, but at least they had not asked why Marrity had been reported dead.

Though still shaky, Moira had recovered from her concussion of the day before, and in the mortuary parking lot she had told Marrity that Bennett had some money to divide with him. Bennett had gruffly said he didn't know how much it would be, after deductions for Sunday's air travel to Shasta, and the cost of the casket and the funeral, and the emergency-room charge. Marrity had just nodded, and gone on giving vague and reassuring answers to their questions about the last three days.

Marrity and Daphne and Charlotte had eaten a vast breakfast at a Denny's in Palm Springs yesterday morning, and then taken a 10:00 A.M. Trailways bus from Palm Springs to San Bernardino. They had walked from the bus station to the street on which Marrity had left his pickup truck, and the truck had still been parked there, and had started up at Marrity's first twist of the key in the ignition. He had been able to feel Daphne's profound, weary relief; he thought he had even caught actual words—*home soon.*

He knew now why he and Daphne had been experiencing their "psychic link" for the last couple of years, and why it had peaked and synchronized during these last several days, and why they would probably share it for a few more years before it faded away. And he knew why the 2006 version of himself had not had any such link with his version of Daphne.

It had been the moment, yesterday at dawn, when Marrity had projected his astral self out of his bullet-riddled body and then used himself to block Daphne's lifeline from Rascasse. Marrity's disembodied attention—his soul?—and Daphne's had clung together in that timeless non-space, and the connection they had established had extended in both directions, into the past as well as the future.

The old drunk Marrity had never done that, in either of his lifelines.

Daphne had not yet referred to the time line the two of them had climbed away from then—the time line in which Marrity had been killed. Lepidopt had saved Marrity by using the time machine to set the world back just a minute or so, but Marrity and Daphne had been "away" while he had done it, and so they had carried back down to the four-dimensional world the memories of the way it had been before Lepidopt's salvific jump.

Daphne had taken a long shower as soon as Marrity had driven the three of them back to the house, and she had used up all the hot water. But Charlotte, and then Marrity, had showered without caring what the water temperature was. Daphne was pleased to have towels and clean clothes.

Daphne had then slept until sundown, and at dusk Marrity had made a pot of Trader Joe's chili. He and Charlotte had been talking all afternoon, and after the chili the two adults sleepily sat through *Mary Poppins* as Daphne watched it again, since she had fallen asleep before it had ended on Sunday night. Marrity had felt free to doze during the movie, since Daphne was watching avidly and Charlotte could see it through her eyes if she wanted to.

Then they had all got twelve hours of sleep—Daphne in her own bed, Charlotte in Marrity's bed, and Marrity on the uphill living room couch.

In the morning Daphne wouldn't hear of their missing Grammar's funeral today.

Along with his keys, Marrity had put the crumpled Einstein envelope and the chip from the Chaplin slab into the pockets of his fresh slacks. He had had some idea of tucking them into the casket, but the casket had been closed at the mortuary. Marrity could come back sometime and shallowly bury the things under the grass.

As he touched them in his pocket now, he thought of the ghosts that should now all be put to rest. Lisa Marrity, or Lieserl Marity or Maric, who had come a long way to be buried in this California cemetery. Marrity's father, killed thirty-two years ago in New Jersey and unjustly hated since then. Oren Lepidopt, who had saved Marrity and Daphne by losing his own life. Einstein himself, who had watched helplessly as his discoveries, one after another, caused nothing but ruin.

Marrity was touching the still damp envelope in his pocket, and in his head the priest's words over Grammar's casket blended into Einstein's voice: *You will dwell in the house of the Lord forever. Thou art inclined to sleep. 'Tis a good dullness, and give it way. I know thou canst not choose.*

Marrity recognized the last three sentences; they were lines of Prospero's, addressing his daughter Miranda. For the last time, Marrity thought.

Good-bye, Grammar. Thank you for raising the two orphans my drunk, suicidal mother thrust into your hands. Thank you for trying to do the right thing, even when it was not the right thing—like not telling us the dangerous facts about our father, and not destroying the Kaleidoscope Shed when your father told you to.

The northern horizon was still gray with smoke over the

mountains, but Marrity sensed an absence there. The Einstein voice was fading, and its last words were, *This thing of darkness I acknowledge mine.* Then it was gone, and Marrity was sure Matt was gone too.

Daphne had taken his right hand now, and Charlotte his left. The priest had closed his Bible, and workmen were lifting the casket and pulling the aluminum bars out from under it and lowering it into the suspended concrete vault, and a muddy yellow backhoe was trundling across the lawn, puffing diesel fumes.

"It's over, Dad," whispered Daphne, tugging him away.

About the author

About the book

Insights,
Interviews
& More...

Read on

Meet Tim Powers

Serena Powers

TIM POWERS is the author of numerous novels including *Hide Me Among the Graves*, *Last Call*, *Declare*, *Three Days to Never*, and *On Stranger Tides*, which inspired the upcoming feature film *Pirates of the Caribbean: On Stranger Tides*, starring Johnny Depp and Penelope Cruz. Powers lives in San Bernardino, California. ↝

Questions for Discussion

1. Frank's present self and his future (older) self seem to disagree on the question of free will—whether or not a person can purposefully change his or her fate. What conclusion does the novel ultimately come to about fate? Do you believe in free will or destiny? Why?

2. Most of the characters have some moment in life they wish they could go back and change. The majority of these events (Lepidopt losing his finger, Charlotte losing her sight), however, are accidents that the characters could not truly foresee. Do you think they could have changed these events if they had tried? Is there anything you would go back and change in your own life? Any events in history?

3. This novel is a blend of fantasy and science fiction; what do you think "genre bending" adds to the story? What did you think of the use of real historical figures as key players in the creation and use of the time travel machine?

4. How does the use of Shakespeare and other well-known authors enhance the story? What connections do you see between *The Tempest* and *Three Days to Never*?

5. Before its use as a symbol of Nazi Germany, the swastika was a symbol of peace and luck/success. Much of the time travel in this novel seems to have negative rather than positive ▶

3

consequences. What do you think is the significance of the swastika as the bridge to time travel?

6. Daphne and Frank have a very close relationship, due not just to their psychic bond but also to their family structure. Why do you think that the older (future) Frank loses this sense of connection? Though he says he has come back to save Frank and Daphne, does he seem to empathize with either of them?

7. Why do you think that time travel causes the momentary appearance of "virtual babies," and why can they grow up and live normal lives if they are removed from the time travel site? What do you think about the questions of identity this raises? If a future self visits a present self, are they the same person? How does the novel deal with this dilemma?

8. Why does Lisa Marrity try to burn down the kaleidoscope shed? Do you think that if a time travel machine existed, it should be used? Who deserves the power to use it?

9. The family relationships in this story are fraught with betrayal: Bennett almost allows Frank and Daphne to be abducted, Frank's future self wants Daphne killed, and Frank believes his own father abandoned him as a child. How do these betrayals motivate the characters? Do you think they will recover from the ordeal they have been through?

10. Daphne is an interesting mix of traits in that she behaves like a child sometimes, and at others is more mature than most adults. On the one hand she is attached to her stuffed animals, but on the other she makes very insightful comments and is very emotionally advanced. What do you think has made her this way? What do you think this adds to the story? ⟡

More from Tim Powers

ON STRANGER TIDES

Aboard the *Vociferous* Carmichael puppeteer John Chandagnac is sailing toward Jamaica to claim his stolen birthright from an unscrupulous uncle when the vessel is captured . . . *by pirates!* Offered a choice by Captain Phil Davies to join their seafaring band or die, Chandagnac assumes the name John Shandy and a new life as a brigand. But more than swashbuckling sea battles and fabulous plunder await the novice buccaneer on the roiling Caribbean waters—for treachery and powerful *vodun* sorcery are coins of the realm in this dark new world. And for the love of beautiful, magically imperiled Beth Hurwood, Shandy will set sail on even stranger tides, following the savage, ghost-infested pirate king Blackbeard and a motley crew of the living and the dead to the cursed nightmare banks of the fabled Fountain of Youth.

"Powers writes action and adventure that Indiana Jones could only dream of."
—*Washington Post*

Read On for a Sneak Peek at *On Stranger Tides*

Prologue

Though the evening breeze had chilled his back on the way across, it hadn't yet begun its nightly job of sweeping out from among the island's clustered vines and palm boles the humid air that the day had left behind, and Benjamin Hurwood's face was gleaming with sweat before the black man had led him even a dozen yards into the jungle. Hurwood hefted the machete that he gripped in his left—and only—hand, and peered uneasily into the darkness that seemed to crowd up behind the torchlit vegetation around them and overhead, for the stories he'd heard of cannibals and giant snakes seemed entirely plausible now, and it was difficult, despite recent experiences, to rely for safety on the collection of ox-tails and cloth bags and little statues that dangled from the other man's belt. In this primeval rain forest it didn't help to think of them as *gardes* and *arrets* and *drogues* rather than fetishes, or of his companion as a *bocor* rather than a witch doctor or shaman.

The black man gestured with the torch and looked back at him. "Left now," he said carefully in English, and then added rapidly in one of the debased French dialects of Haiti, "and step carefully—little streams have undercut the path in many places."

"Walk more slowly, then, so I can see where you put your feet," replied Hurwood irritably in his fluent textbook French. He wondered how badly his hitherto perfect accent had suffered from the past month's exposure to so many odd variations of the language.

The path became steeper, and soon he had to sheathe his machete in order to have his hand free to grab branches and pull himself along, and for a while his heart ws pounding so alarmingly that he thought it would burst, despite the protective *drogue* the black man had given him—then they had got above the level of the surrounding jungle and the sea breeze found them and he called to his companion to stop so that he could catch his breath in the fresh air and enjoy the coolness of it in his sopping white hair and damp shirt.

The breeze clattered and rustled in the palm branches below, and through a gap in the sparser trunks around him he could see water— a moonlight-speckled segment of the Tongue of the Ocean, across which the two of them had sailed from New Providence Island that afternoon. He remembered noticing the prominence they now stood on, and wondering about it, as he'd struggled to keep the sheet trimmed to his bad-tempered guide's satisfaction.

Andros Island it was called on the maps, but the people he'd been associating with lately generally called it Isle de Loas Bossals, which, he'd gathered, meant Island of Untamed (or, perhaps more closely, Evil) Ghosts (or, it sometimes seemed, Gods). Privately he thought of it as Persephone's shore, where he hoped to find, at long last, at least a window into the house of Hades.

He heard a gurgling behind him and turned in time to see his guide recorking one of the bottles. Sharp on the fresh air he could smell the rum. "Damn it," Hurwood snapped, "that's for the ghosts."

The *bocor* shrugged. "Brought too much," he explained. "Too much, too many come."

The one-armed man didn't answer, but wished once again that he knew enough—instead of just *nearly* enough—to do this alone.

"Nigh there now," said the *bocor*, tucking the bottle back into the leather bag slung from his shoulder.

They resumed their steady pace along the damp earth path, but Hurwood sensed a difference now—attention was being paid to them.

The black man sensed it too, and grinned back over his shoulder, exposing gums nearly as white as his teeth. "They smell the rum," he said.

"Are you sure it's not just those poor Indians?"

The man in front answered without looking back. "They still sleep. That's the *loas* you feel watching us."

Though he knew there could be nothing out of the ordinary to see yet, the one-armed man glanced around, and it occurred to him for the first time that this really wasn't so incongruous a setting—these palm trees and this sea breeze probably didn't differ very much from what might be found in the Mediterranean, and this Caribbean island might be very like the island where, thousands of years ago, Odysseus performed almost exactly the same procedure they intended to perform tonight. ⌒

More from Tim Powers *(continued)*

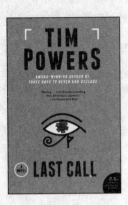

LAST CALL

Onetime professional gambler Scott Crane hasn't returned to Las Vegas, or held a hand of cards, in ten years. But troubling nightmares about a strange poker game he once attended on a houseboat on Lake Mead—a contest he believed he walked away from a big winner—are drawing him back to the magical city. Because the mythic game did not end that night in 1969. And the price of his winnings was his soul. And now a pot far more strange and perilous than he ever could imagine depends on the turning of a card.

"A thrilling tale of gambling, fate, and fantastic adventure."—*Los Angeles Daily News*

Read On for a Sneak Peek at *Last Call*

Leon had wanted an excuse to stop by the Flamingo Hotel, seven miles outside of town on 91, so he had taken Scott there for breakfast.

The Flamingo was a wide three-story hotel with a fourth-floor penthouse, incongruously green against the tan desert that surrounded it. Palm trees had been trucked in to stand around the building, and this morning the sun had been glaring down from a clear sky, giving the vivid green lawn a look of defiance.

Leon had let a valet park the car, and he and Scott had walked hand in hand along the strip of pavement to the front steps that led up to the casino door.

Below the steps on the left side, behind a bush, Leon had long ago punched a hole in the stucco and scratched some symbols around it; this morning he crouched at the foot of the steps to tie his shoe, and he took a package from his coat pocket and leaned forward and pitched it into the hole.

"Another thing that might hurt you, Daddy?" Scott asked in a whisper. The boy was peering over his shoulder at the crude rayed suns and stick figures that grooved the stucco and flaked the green paint.

Leon stood up. He stared down at his son, wondering why he had ever confided this to the boy. Not that it mattered now.

"Right, Scotto," he said. "And what is it?"

"Our secret."

"Right again. You hungry?"

"As a bedbug." This had somehow become one of their bits of standard dialogue.

"Let's go."

The desert sun had been shining in through the windows, glittering off the little copper skillets the fried eggs and kippered herrings were served in. The breakfast had been "on the house," even though they weren't guests, because Leon was known to have been a business associate of Ben Siegel, the founder. Already the waitresses felt free to refer openly to the man as "Bugsy" Siegel.

That had been the first thing that had made Leon uneasy, eating at the expense of that particular dead man.

Scotty had had a good time, though, sipping a cherry-topped Coca-Cola from an Old Fashioned glass and squinting around the room with a worldly air.

"This is your place now, huh, Dad." he'd said as they were leaving through the circular room that was the casino. Cards were turning over crisply, and dice were rolling with a muffled rattle across the green felt, but Leon didn't look at any of the random suits and numbers that were defining the moment.

None of the dealers or croupiers seemed to have heard the boy. "You don't—" Leon began.

"I know," Scotty had said in quick shame, "you don't talk about important stuff in front of the cards."

They left through the door that faced the 91, and had to wait for the car to be brought around from the other side—the side where the one window on the penthouse level made the building look like a one-eyed face gazing out across the desert.

The Emperor card, Leon thought now as he tugged Scotty along the rain-darkened Center Street sidewalk; why am I not seeing any signs from *it*? The old man in profile, sitting on a throne with his legs crossed because of some injury. That has been my card for a year now. I can prove it by Richard, my eldest son—and soon enough I'll be able to prove it by Scotty here.

Against his will he wondered what sort of person Scotty must have grown up to be if this weren't going to happen. The boy would be twenty-one in 1964; was there a little girl in the world somewhere now who would, otherwise, one day meet him and marry him? Would she now find somebody else? What sort of man would Scotty have grown up to be? Fat, thin, honest, crooked? Would he have inherited his father's talent for mathematics? ༄

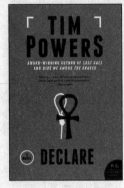

DECLARE

As a young double agent infiltrating the Soviet spy network in Nazi-occupied Paris, Andrew Hale finds himself caught up in a secret, even more ruthless war. Two decades later, in 1963, he will be forced to confront again the nightmare that has haunted his adult life: a lethal unfinished operation code-named Declare. From the corridors of Whitehall to the Arabian desert, from postwar Berlin to the streets of Cold War Moscow, Hale's desperate quest draws him into international politics and gritty espionage tradecraft—and inexorably drives Hale, the fiery and beautiful Communist agent Elena Teresa Ceniza-Bendiga, and Kim Philby, mysterious traitor to the British cause, to a deadly confrontation on the high glaciers of Mount Ararat, in the very shadow of the fabulous and perilous Ark.

"Dazzling . . . a tour de force, a brilliant blend of John le Carré spy fiction with the otherworldly."   —*Dean Koontz*

Read On for a Sneak Peek at *Declare*

Prologue

Mount Ararat, 1948

> *. . . from behind that craggy steep till then*
> *The horizon's bound, a huge peak, black and huge,*
> *As if with voluntary power instinct,*
> *Upreared its head. I struck and struck again,*
> *And growing still in stature the grim shape*
> *Towered up between me and the stars, and still,*
> *For so it seemed, with purpose of its own*
> *And measured motion like a living thing,*
> *Strode after me.*
>
> —William Wordsworth, *The Prelude*, 381–389

The young captain's hands were sticky with blood on the steering wheel as he cautiously backed the jeep in a tight turn off the rutted mud track onto a patch of level snow that shone in the intermittent moonlight on the edge of the gorge, and then his left hand seemed to freeze onto the gear-shift knob after he reached down to clank the lever up into first gear. He had been inching down the mountain path in reverse for an hour, peering over his shoulder at the dark trail, but the looming peak of Mount Ararat had not receded at all, still eclipsed half of the night sky above him, and more than anything else he needed to get away from it.

He flexed his cold-numbed fingers off the gear-shift knob and switched on the headlamps—only one came on, but the sudden blaze was dazzling, and he squinted through the shattered windscreen at the rock wall of the gorge and the tire tracks in the mud as he pulled the wheel around to drive straight down the narrow shepherds' path. He was still panting, his breath bursting out of his open mouth in plumes of steam. He was able to drive a little faster now, moving forward—the jeep was rocking on its abused springs and the four-cylinder engine roared in first gear, no longer in danger of lugging to a stall.

He was fairly sure that nine men had fled down the path an hour ago. Desperately he hoped that as many as four of them might be survivors of the SAS group he had led up the gorge, and that they might somehow still be sane.

But his face was stiff with dried tears, and he wasn't sure if he were ▶

still sane himself—and unlike his men, he had been somewhat prepared for what had awaited them; to his aching shame now, he had at least known how to evade it.

In the glow reflected back from the rock wall at his right, he could see bright, bare steel around the bullet holes in the jeep's bonnet; and he knew the doors and fenders were riddled with similar holes. The wobbling fuel gauge needle showed half a tank of petrol, so at least the tank had not been punctured.

Within a minute he saw three upright figures a hundred feet ahead of him on the path, and they didn't turn around into the glow of the single headlamp. At this distance he couldn't tell if they were British or Russian. He had lost his Sten gun somewhere on the high slopes, but he pulled the chunky .45 revolver out of his shoulder holster—even if these survivors were British, he might need it.

But he glanced fearfully back over his shoulder, at the looming mountain—the unsubdued power in the night was back there, up among the craggy high fastnesses of Mount Ararat.

He turned back to the frail beam of light that stretched down the slope ahead of him to light the three stumbling figures, and he increased the pressure of his foot on the accelerator, and he wished he dared to pray.

He didn't look again at the mountain. Though in years to come he would try to dismiss it from his mind, in that moment he was bleakly sure that he would one day see it again, would again climb this cold track. ◠

London, winter of 1862, Adelaide McKee, a former prostitute, arrives on the doorstep of veterinarian John Crawford, a man she met once seven years earlier. Their brief meeting produced a child who, until now, had been presumed dead.

McKee has learned that the girl lives—but that her life and soul are in mortal peril from a vampiric ghost—and the bloodthirsty wraith is none other than John Polidori, the onetime physician to the mad, bad, and dangerous Romantic poet Lord Byron. Both McKee and Crawford have mysterious histories with creatures like Polidori, and their child is a prize the malevolent spirit covets dearly.

Polidori is also the late uncle and supernatural muse to the poet Christina Rossetti and her brother, the painter Dante Gabriel Rossetti. As a child, Christina unwittingly brought Polidori's curse upon her family. When Polidori resurrects Dante's dead wife—turning her into a horrifying vampire—and threatens other family members, Christina and Dante agree that they must destroy their monstrous uncle.

Determined to save their daughter, McKee and Crawford join forces with the Rossettis, and soon these wildly mismatched allies are plunged into a supernatural London underworld whose existence goes beyond their wildest imaginings.

"[A] fine example of the work of a much-beloved author, and a spooky ride through Victorian London to boot. . . . Powers's work engages with something prerational that is buried deep, deep in our brains, and that won't be bullied into submission by mere reason."   —boingboing.com

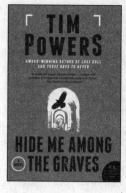

Read On for a Sneak Peek at *Hide Me Among the Graves*

Now, seven years later, Crawford again picked up his teacup, and his hand didn't shake.

"I—" he began hoarsely; then he cleared his throat and said, carefully, "I tried to find you, afterward." He realized that he was stroking his beard as if miming deep thought and stopped.

The bird in the little cage on the table whistled several notes. The woman nodded. "I believe you. But as I said, I gave you a false name that night. Griffin, wasn't it? That was the street I was—living on. And I never had a husband." She gulped some of the tea in her own cup, then abruptly set it down and whispered, "Of all the times I could ever have used a glass of whisky."

It was only an hour or two after dawn, but Crawford said, "Would you like some? I might join you."

"I gave it up." She exhaled and stared squarely at him. "I was a prostitute, in those days. 'Living upon the farm of my person,' as the law has it. I'm not any longer."

The little bird was darting glances from one of them to the other.

"Oh," said Crawford blankly. "Good. That you—stopped." Over the years he had wondered about that, a woman walking alone on Waterloo Bridge after midnight, but it was still a shock to hear it confirmed. "I enrolled myself in the Magdalen Penitentiary for Fallen Women, on Highgate Hill, and I spent two years there. Thanks to the sisters there, I was able to change my ways."

"Oh."

"And—before that"—she took a deep breath—"we had a daughter, you and I."

Crawford held up his hand to stop her, then stood up and crossed to the mantel and poured several inches of whisky into a glass, from, he realized, the same decanter he had poured from seven years earlier. He drained half of it and then clicked the glass down on the mantel, and for several seconds he kept his hand on the glass and squinted at it. Finally he let go of it and turned toward her.

"How can you be—if you were—"

"I used what they call prophylactic measures when I was on the job," she said flatly. "That night seven years ago was . . . spontaneous."

Crawford wished he had not drunk the scotch, for he was dizzy and nauseated now, and his heart was pounding.

She glanced toward the inner door, behind which he could hear Mrs. Middleditch ascending the steps from the below-stairs kitchen.

"Let's go for a walk," McKee said, picking up her gloves from the table.

But Crawford sat down again. "The last time you and I were together, we got into trouble."

She opened her mouth as if to say something, then apparently thought better of it.

"I mean *outdoors*," he added, feeling his face heat up. "Overlapping candle flames, you said. We were more visible, to"—he waved vaguely—"things."

"That was at night. They don't generally travel abroad during the day."

He shrugged and nodded. He recalled his parents telling him that. And Mrs. Middleditch was now audibly bustling around in the little dining room behind him.

He got to his feet again, reluctantly. "Very well. Let me get a hat and coat. And—" He stepped to the mantel and found the little bottle of ground garlic and slipped it into his waistcoat pocket.

She smiled. "In case we're out past sunset?"

He ignored that and waved distractedly at the little cage on the table. "I can put the bird somewhere the cats can't get to."

"He can come along with us." ∽